"I say it is mine. As [...] his sword with ruthless deliberation, he raised it, the tip pointed at the very center of her breast, although he did not allow it to quite rest there.

A feral smile slashed a white gash in the dark, unshaven face, but failed to warm that fierce gaze. "Might is right, lady. And as of this moment, with this sword in my hand, I hold the power here. You do not."

Rosamund froze on the spot, the implied threat too real to be discounted.

Suddenly, without warning, the point of the sword fell. Thank God! But Rosamund's relief was short-lived when the knight took a long stride forward to close the space between them. Before she could retreat, she found herself caught within his arm, tightly banding around her waist. Dragged hard against him almost off her feet, breast to breast, thigh against thigh.

If she had been speechless before, now she found herself unable to think, to marshal any thought at all. It was all sensation, all awareness of the power of his body, the heat of him, as she was held plastered against him. To see those cold gray eyes, gold-flecked, looking down into hers with what she could only interpret as hatred.

What could she hope for at the hands of this man? For the first time in her life Rosamund de Longspey feared for her safety and her honor.

* * *

Conquering Knight, Captive Lady
Harlequin® Historical #938—March 2009

Author Note

Rosamund, my heroine, escapes from her family to take refuge in Clifford Castle, which today is an atmospheric ruin on the bank of the River Wye in the Welsh Marches, not many miles from where I live. A tale is told of a lady who, in medieval times, was besieged there, taken prisoner by a local robber lord and forced to accept his hand in marriage. When the king came to hear of it he descended with an army, punished the lord for his despicable exploit and offered the bride her freedom and a purse of gold. Instead of snatching at the chance, the lady refused the king's justice and would not be parted from her impetuous husband.

And that, I thought when I read it, is the stuff of romance. I could not resist such a glamorous opportunity. It inspired me to explore the wilful passion between Rosamund and her own robber lord, Gervase Fitz Osbern. I have created for them a difficult path to travel before they can accept that one cannot live without the other, as I am certain the original lovers too experienced. Rosamund has to learn that sometimes a man needs to be seduced into a compromise, without his knowing it, when all the time he thinks that his is the controlling hand. Whilst Gervase, almost too late, realises that military force is not the way to his lover's heart.

I hope that you enjoy reading Rosamund and Gervase's journey of discovery as much as I did writing it.

As for Harlequin, I owe them so much—not least that they gave me my first opportunity to write historical romances for my own, and your, pleasure.

ANNE O'BRIEN

Conquering Knight, Captive Lady

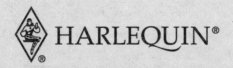

HARLEQUIN®

TORONTO • NEW YORK • LONDON
AMSTERDAM • PARIS • SYDNEY • HAMBURG
STOCKHOLM • ATHENS • TOKYO • MILAN • MADRID
PRAGUE • WARSAW • BUDAPEST • AUCKLAND

Recycling programs
for this product may
not exist in your area.

ISBN-13: 978-0-373-29538-8
ISBN-10:   0-373-29538-3

CONQUERING KNIGHT, CAPTIVE LADY

Copyright © 2008 by Anne O'Brien

First North American Publication 2009

www.eHarlequin.com

Printed in U.S.A.

For George, the hero of all my romances.

Prologue

January 1158—a cold, wet winter four years into the reign of King Henry II.
Clifford Castle—a remote border stronghold in the Welsh Marches.

'Stop! What in God's name are you doing?'

'As you see.' The unknown knight who commanded the formidable force of soldiers might have been surprised to see the lady, but with barely a flicker of an eye chose to spurn her. Even when she continued to shiver in the bitter wind at the top of the flight of steps leading up from the enclosed space of the bailey to the stone keep. Even though that lady was clearly seething in an enraged whirl of mantle and veil, another lady similarly muffled to the tip of her nose against the elements at her shoulder. The knight proceeded to give brisk, efficient instructions to his men for them to dismount and immediately secure the fortress.

The lady opened her mouth. Shut it, tight-lipped. Eyes of green, clear as glass in an ecclesiastical window and just as sharp, her eyebrows beautifully arched and dark, she surveyed the organized overrunning of her castle in horrified silence. Under her veil the rich red-brown of her hair, a fox's pelt with gold and russet depths, shining and glowing, as vibrant as the autumn fruit of the chestnut tree, was whipped into a messy tangle by the wind. She paid it no heed. For one of the few occasions in her life she could find no words to express the shock, the sheer fury, that held her motionless. But not for long.

'What are you doing here? Who are you? Who opened the gates to you?'

'I am Fitz Osbern.' He barely took the time to glance in her direction.

The lady narrowed her eyes at the device that fluttered and snapped on the profusion of pennons attached to the soldiers' lances. A mythical beast, dragon-like with a fierce snarl on its mask of a face, silver on black. Definitely not one she knew. Fitz Osbern—why was he here? As a marauding brigand? A robber lord? There were plenty of those in the March, wild and lawless men, answering to no man, not even to the King. He certainly looked the part. She scowled at the man who had by this time dismounted to stand, one hand fisted on his hip, in her bailey. Equally at the older knight, who had moved in silent support to his side, and the greyhound, as lean and rangy as its master, that loped and dodged with excitement between the horses' hooves. *Fitz Osbern…* She pitched her voice above the general racket that had descended on her home. 'I don't understand what you are doing here.'

'Which is a matter of supreme indifference to me, lady.' Fitz Osbern flung the reins of his dark bay stallion to his young squire. 'Bryn!' He snapped his fingers to the hound, bringing him immediately to heel, then made to walk toward the far stabling, still issuing orders to his men in a tone that brooked no disobedience.

But this spurred the lady into action. Who he was or was not was entirely irrelevant. 'I will not be defied in my own home!' She covered the distance down the steps and across the bailey in remarkable speed to grasp at a fold of his cloak with bold authority, grimacing at the slick coating of mud and rain that squelched beneath her fingers. 'You have no right to give orders here!'

'I have every right.'

He shook her off as if, she thought, she were a troublesome hound puppy, and then had the temerity to turn his back on her—again.

'This castle is my home—my property, my inheritance.' Disturbed by the note of dismay that had crept into her voice, the lady snatched at his cloak once more to hold him still. 'And yet you have the gall to ride in here and—'

The knight came to a halt, so suddenly that she had to step aside or tread on his heels. He rounded on her, dark brows drawn together into a heavy bar, so that she found herself taking a step in retreat, and he surveyed her, up and down, from her muddied shoes to the rich curls escaping the confines of the veil in the brisk wind. '*Your* inheritance, you say? Who *are* you?'

The lady's chin rose infinitesimally. 'I am Rosamund de Longspey.'

'Longspey?' The frown deepened, the eyes sharpened. 'The Longspey heiress? But she's a child.'

'She is not.' Rosamund made an inelegant noise not far short of a snort. '*I* am not.'

The knight eyed her, clearly weighing up the situation. Then lifted his shoulders in careless dismissal. 'So I see. But no matter.'

The lady squared her shoulders. 'It matters! This castle is mine.'

'No, lady. It is not.' Impatient now, he raised an arm in an expansive gesture to encompass his guards taking up position on the gatehouse, the palisade walk, his horseflesh being accommodated in the inadequate cramped stabling. 'As it has no doubt become apparent to you, this castle of Clifford is now mine.'

'Who says?' Confusion and indignation warred on her face, even a shadow of fear, as Rosamund de Longspey curled her fingers into the dense fur lining of her mantle where he would not see her panic building.

Fitz Osbern looked down his nose at the woman who reached hardly to his shoulder. And what a magnificent nose it was to look down, if the lady was aware of such inconsequential detail when cold grey eyes pinned her to the spot. High-bridged and predatory it was, with more than a touch of the autocratic.

'I say it is mine. As does this.' Drawing his sword with ruthless deliberation, he raised it, the tip pointed at the very centre of her breast, although he did not allow it to quite rest there. A feral smile slashed a white gash in the dark, unshaven face, but failed to warm that fierce gaze. 'Might is right, lady. As of this moment, with this sword in my hand, I hold the power here. You do not.'

Rosamund froze on the spot, her blood ice, the implied threat too real to be discounted.

Suddenly, without warning, the point of the sword fell. Thank God! But Rosamund's relief was short-lived when the knight took a long stride forward to close the space between them. Before she could retreat, she found herself caught within his arm, tightly banding around her waist. Dragged hard against him almost off her feet, breast to breast, thigh against thigh. If she had been speechless before, now she found herself unable to think, to marshal any thoughts at all. It was all sensation, all awareness of the power of his body, the heat of him as she was held, plastered against him. Never before had she known what it was to be under the physical control of a man. Barely able to catch a breath, her heart hammered in her breast. Furiously struggling against him did no good at all. She looked up into his face, as dismay transformed into fear to see those cold grey eyes, gold-flecked, looking down into hers with what she could only interpret as hatred.

What could she hope for at the hands of this man? For the first time in her life Rosamund de Longspey feared for her safety and her honour.

Chapter One

January 1158—two weeks earlier.

The troop of soldiers rode smartly north-west out of Gloucester, the promise of a warm homecoming at the Fitz Osbern castle in Monmouth luring them on to get in out of this thrice-damned persistent wind and rain. Unlimited ale and hot food. The soft stroke of a woman's hand. Even the proximity of hot water would not be sniffed at... They had been on the road for a long time in the worst of weather after a sharp campaign across the Channel to Anjou, where Gervase Fitz Osbern held a number of strategic castles.

Gervase Fitz Osbern set a fierce pace. The Channel crossing had been bad; he shuddered at the memory of being tossed and drenched and vilely ill for twenty-four hours—sea voyaging was not for him—but now they were on firm ground. He raised his head, much as his hound at his heels, scenting the air. Home was within easy distance as he caught the outline of the dark ridge of the Black Mountains through the ever-swirling mist.

But when a group of travellers approached along the road, bringing with them one item of news, it was enough to make Fitz Osbern change his plans.

'Rumours in the March. The Earl of Salisbury, William de Longspey, is dying.'

It was enough to shorten his breath, to drive a fist into his gut.

'Do we go on, my lord?' Watkins, his troop commander, all but nudged him into action as he sat in the rain in the middle of the road, brows drawn into a ferocious frown, his gaze focused on some distant place not altogether pleasant.

Fitz Osbern raised his head, refocused, gathered up his reins and signalled to his men to move off, the decision made. 'We stop overnight in Hereford.' The authority of their lord, coupled with the obvious lure of the fleshpots of Hereford, had the desired effect and put a halt to any murmurings of dissent. 'And in Hereford,' Gervase Fitz Osbern added, quietly, face settling into stern lines, 'I shall make it my business to discover William de Longspey's state of health.'

Meanwhile, some distance away in the prosperous town of Salisbury, Rosamund de Longspey was in a fractious mood. But then, who would not be? Approaching twenty-four years, with no husband on her horizon, no betrothed, and made fatherless for the second time in her life. No matter how good her blood, how attractive her face—and she could not deny that—her future looked less than secure.

So Rosamund, justifiably irritable, joined the family members of the household as they met together on the occasion of the death, from a malingering ague, of William de Longspey, Earl of Salisbury. He was no blood relation of hers, which might account for her lack of grief on this sorrowful occasion, merely a stepfather who had shown brief interest in and even less affection to her as she grew from child to a strikingly attractive young woman. A daughter of the Earl's wife, Countess Petronilla, from her first marriage to John de Bredwardine, Rosamund had taken her stepfather's name on her mother's remarriage, and now had a very personal interest in Earl William's will. In this room, within the hour, her entire future would be disposed of, with or without her consent.

There were no surprises when Father Benedict, the de Longspey chaplain, presented the terms of the late Earl's will. His family by his first wife had been well provided for. The de Longspey title and main inheritance in Salisbury, the bulk of the estates scattered throughout the country, passed to Gilbert, the heir, who looked smug. Walter and Elizabeth were not forgotten. The Dowager Countess Petronilla would retain the lands and income from her original dowry. If she chose, she could live in the castle in Salisbury as an honoured guest for the rest of her life. If not, the castle at Lower Broadheath was now hers, a pretty estate in gentle countryside. Earl William had been generous and even-handed.

'My lord thought that you would perhaps wed again.' Father Benedict smiled benignly on the widow who showed no hint of tears at her loss.

Lady Petronilla silently inclined her head, but Rosamund was not fooled. If Rosamund read it right, her mother had no intention of seeking another marriage, no matter how wealthy or superficially attractive the lord. She was now free to do as she chose. Two husbands in a lifetime and both of them unsatisfactory, Lady Petronilla had been heard to say in private moments, were quite enough for any woman.

I would just like the chance at one! Rosamund forced her fingers to unclench. For there was one matter here that had not been touched upon.

'Father Benedict.' Rosamund fixed her direct gaze on the cleric. 'What provision has been made for me? I shall at least need land suitable for a dowry.'

'Ah… Yes, Lady Rosamund…' Father Benedict cleared his throat. 'The Earl saw fit to grant three strongholds.' He nodded at Rosamund with an encouraging smile, entirely false, she decided. 'Three fortresses,' he repeated, 'and the income from the land and manors attached to them. For your own enjoyment and for your dower, Lady Rosamund.'

The fortunate lady raised her brows. 'And where are these three fortresses, Father Benedict?' Her voice was low, a little husky, usually with great charm, if not as on this occasion infused with deep suspicion.

'On the border, my lady.'

'The Welsh border? Be more exact, if you will, Father.'

The chaplain cleared his throat again with a quick glance toward the new Earl, who nodded in agreement. 'You have possession of the castles and lands of Clifford, Ewyas Harold and Wigmore in the Welsh Marches, my lady.'

'As you say—along the very border with Wales.' Rosamund looked down to where her hands had just re-clenched in her lap, face smoothly unreadable, but her mind clearly engaged. 'And will these three fortresses attract a husband for me?'

There was a loud guffaw from Earl Gilbert, hastily smothered. Walter did not even bother to hide his grin.

'There's no need to concern yourself, Rose,' Gilbert replied heartily. 'You'll not be left destitute and unwed.' She saw something like naked cunning in her stepbrother's broad face before he lumbered to his feet and walked across the room to her, to take and pat her hand consolingly. 'My father was remiss in this. Never fear. I am in the process of arranging all to your comfort, with three such *valuable* fortresses to attract attention from a suitable husband.' He chuckled unnervingly. 'No one will ever say that a de Longspey was left unprovided for.'

Behind Rosamund's grateful smile, anger simmered. By the time she was alone with her mother in the privacy of the solar, it had become a surge of pure passion.

'So I am now an heiress! With three castles to my name in the depths of the Welsh Marches, any one of them to be my home! It would be,' stated Rosamund, green eyes flashing, all attempts to govern her temper abandoned, 'like being buried alive. I have decided. Nothing will persuade me to go there.'

* * *

Rosamund's decision did not outlive the day. Barely had the mid-day meal been cleared than she was summoned to the new Earl's private chamber. She eyed him warily. Gilbert, in the magnificence of his father's accommodation, looked even more pleased with himself if that were possible, and addressed her with obnoxious good humour as soon as she appeared in the doorway.

'Rose. Some excellent news, as I promised you. This is a day for developments, it seems. Did I not tell you to leave everything in my care? The messenger has arrived.' He flapped a travel-worn document in her direction. 'Your marriage. I have in mind a knight who will take you for the castles you hold. It will be a most advantageous match.' Sure of his argument, he held her gaze at last. 'You've remained unwed far too long.'

Rosamund took a breath, a premonition heavy in her belly. So that was it. Set a trap to catch a prize on the Welsh border as she had suspected. And she was the bait in the trap. Now she knew the reason for Clifford and Ewyas Harold and Wigmore. She breathed out slowly.

'Who is it?'

'Ralph de Morgan of Builth. Quite a landowner in that area.'

'Ralph de Morgan?' He was a not infrequent visitor to the de Longspey household. The name instantly conjured up an image of the knight. Rosamund's palms grew damp against the skirts of her robe as that image became a weight on her heart. 'But he's older than Lord William was!' Possibly an exaggeration, she admitted, but not by much.

'He's an important man, Rosamund.' Gilbert leaned forward to make his point, preserving his smile. 'And newly widowed. He wants a bride who will increase his holdings within England. And for my benefit, he'll help to hold the March secure. I doubt you'll do better. He offers a substantial settlement.'

'I can imagine!' Who would not to wish to consolidate a connection with the powerful de Longspeys?

'You have no choice in the matter, dear sister,' stated the Earl as if he could read the rejection in her mind. 'It's arranged. Ralph has agreed and the terms are acceptable. He'll come next week to renew your acquaintance, as a suitor for a bride.'

Rosamund controlled her reply magnificently. 'Very well, Gilbert.'

Gilbert eyed the quiescent lady doubtfully. 'Hear me, Rosamund. You'll not antagonise him.'

'No, Gilbert. How could you think it?' She smiled serenely. *But I would not wager my new jewelled girdle on it!*

Escape to Clifford suddenly seemed an object of desire.

One meeting with Ralph de Morgan was enough to convince her of all her fears and to drive Rosamund into open rebellion. In a cloud of resentment she burst into the widowed Countess's bedchamber, where that lady was supervising her maid Edith in the packing of her possessions for the journey to Lower Broadheath.

'That's settled it. I can't do it.'

Lady Petronilla abandoned the silk mass of the rich green over-gown she was folding. She eyed her daughter with a painful mixture of sympathy and resignation. 'So I thought when *I* was presented with marriage, but sometimes, dear child, there's simply no choice.' The widow smoothed her dark skirts, her hands quick and restless, then stepped to the chest, which held cups and a flagon of ale. Not over-tall, her figure was well proportioned, her eyes grey-green and aware, her hair fair, un-touched by grey, worn in a neat plaited coronet. She moved with capable, energetic movements as she poured and returned to hand a cup to her daughter.

'No choice? How can there be no choice! Ralph de Morgan,' Rosamund announced, not mincing her words, 'is gross and balding. His clothes are rank with heaven only knows what! Did you see? He wiped the sauce from his fingers on his tunic. When his hands last came into contact with warm water I know not. And as for his breath when he kissed my cheek…' She whirled in a circle, her hair within its ribbon confines flying, and punched the bed hangings with her fist. 'He's disgusting!'

'Ralph is not a pleasant prospect, I agree—but your brothers are determined—'

'Brothers? They are no blood of mine! I've had enough of self-opinionated men telling me what to do and what not to do. What will be good for me and what I would be unwise to consider. I will not do it!'

'No. Ralph is not an attractive man. So…portly!'

'Portly? He is fat! I would rather wed the poor ragged creature, filthy and scabbed, who sits daily outside the Cathedral and begs for alms.'

'No, you wouldn't. And I don't think the beggar would actually want you!' The two ladies considered the dubious prospect for a short moment. 'But, dearest Rose, you need a husband,' Petronilla advised. 'You should have been married years ago.'

'I know. I agree that there could be advantages. But I want…' In her mind's eye Rosamund saw the man of her childhood dreams, lingered over the much-loved image. 'He must be young. Handsome, of course, fair haired. Gentle and courteous, who will treat me with honour and consideration. A knight who is civilised and cultured, can read and write, and will not harry me into actions I have no wish to take.' For a moment she lost herself in another improbable outcome. 'And he must at least have an affection for me,' she added finally. 'I do not ask for love, but I have no desire to simply be a hapless pawn in a power struggle.'

'Hmm. Now there's a list.' Lady Petronilla arched her brows, returning to the silk gown that slithered unmanageably under her hands. 'But does such a paragon exist? A man who would let you have entirely your own way…? Well, I don't know… And would you be happy if he did?'

Rosamund considered the matter. Marriage had not brought her mother much contentment. Why should her own experience

be any different? Of course, there had been that *one* man…
Now there was a memory to stir her to her very soul. Rosamund
turned away so that her mother should not read the sudden sharp
desire that closed like a hand around her throat.

Her Wild Hawk. Her Fierce Lord.

Gervase Fitz Osbern.

That *one* man… Some four years since now. The memory
of him came easily into Rosamund's mind, as if it had slid there
before, at regular intervals, along a well-worn path. The man
who had descended on Salisbury in the foulest of humours to
hold a dangerously fraught interview with the Earl. She had
never known exactly why. But a bucketful of bad blood had
existed between Fitz Osbern and Earl William from the very
beginning, obvious in the crackle in the air and the imminent
threat of drawn blades as they exchanged views. And the Earl
had planned to smooth the waters, to entice this enemy into an
alliance. So he had offered Rosamund to him, to lure him into
taking a Longspey wife.

She remembered as if it were yesterday being summoned so
that the lord might look her over.

But he had not looked her over. He had barely cast an eye
in her direction, after that first vicious stare when she had
entered the room. He had not even done her the courtesy to
appraise her merits as a bride. And after all her mother's efforts
to turn her out at her best, threading emerald ribbons through
her braided hair. What an arrogant appraisal it had been before
he turned his shoulder, one brief raking glance from head to foot
that had all but stripped the clothes from her body. Even now
at this distance she re-lived the moment that had brought a rush
of unflattering colour to her cheeks and an edge to her temper.
Not that *he* had noticed. The formidable knight was too busy
refusing Earl William's offer to consider her appearance or her
feelings at being so summarily rejected. She had been dismissed almost before she had set foot in the room.

You would buy me with a Longspey woman? You'll not

succeed. There's blood on your hands, my lord, that can't be washed away by the gift of a simpering Longspey virgin.

The hard-held fury, the harsh menace in his voice. The shame that she had felt as if his rejection of her had been due to some fault of her own. It remained with her still, as did a clear image of the man's face and stature. He might not have taken more than a passing acknowledgement of her but, no simpering maid at twenty years—and she doubted she had ever been known to simper!—Rosamund's fascinated stare had been as direct and all-encompassing as his had not.

The Wild Hawk he had become in her dreams, savage and untamed, never knowing the hood or jesses, the leash of the falconer. What a pleasure he had been to look at. Tall and lean with the well-muscled body of a soldier, a lord who would ride and fight, a master of weaponry, although on this occasion he was richly dressed, with embroidered bands at hem and sleeve of his tunic. He might wear a sword, but the leather belt was gilded and jewelled. He had obviously come to make an impression. If she concentrated, even now she could imagine his dark hair, grey eyes, gold-flecked. Eagle features, she remembered. A will of tempered steel. Now, what would it have been like to wed such a man as he?

Barely polite, he had been uncomfortably forthright. *I don't seek a marriage with one of yours.* One of his more discreet opinions. But then that one sweep of his hard grey eyes was an insult in itself. *All I demand from you, my lord, is the return of my father's property and recompense for the untimely death of my wife.* If she had wed the Wild Hawk, he would not have let her have her own way, that's for sure. He would *order* and *demand* and *insist* at every turn. Rosamund shivered at the prospect. That would be almost as bad as wedding Ralph de Morgan! Despite her own preoccupations, she found it in her heart to feel pity for the Wild Hawk's poor dead wife.

Her breath hitched a little. At the last he had, surely against his will, touched her once. As he marched to the door, furiously disappointed, he was forced to pass within an arm's length of her. He had stopped abruptly, thrust out his hand in command. She had placed hers there.

'My lady!'

And he had kissed her fingers. Fleetingly. Mouth and hand as cold as his ire was hot. Yet it had burned her, the heat of it slamming her senses. She still recalled it, as if the brand were still there. Imagined in her moments of despair what it would be like to feel the insistent pressure of those lips on hers, the slick knowledge of his tongue, those hands against her breast where her heart pounded for some desired outcome of which she had no experience…

Rosamund blinked away the scene. Well, the outcome of the clash between two such strong-willed men had put paid to any such possibility of the man taking her to his bed. The Wild Hawk hadn't got the land or the recompense he sought, Earl William had not got his alliance and she hadn't got a husband. Her unwilling lover had stiffened, his head bent, hair curling like black silk against her wrist. Then he had dropped her hand as if it had scorched him, leaving her without a backward glance. That was the last she heard of him.

And yet, Rosamund had found those strong features haunting her thoughts. Not a handsome man, his features too harsh for pure symmetry, but an arresting one. A powerful man with a dark glamour who would draw the eyes of any woman. A man who would let nothing stand in his way of seizing what he wanted. What *would* it have been like to have wed that Wild Hawk, to be his and his alone? To have given up her prized virginity to a man who prowled and smouldered and demanded. Four years on and she was still in possession of that prize, and no one valued it—except the despicable Ralph. She would probably take it to her grave. What value then?

'Rose…'

She blinked again, aware that her mother was beginning to fret under her own fierce and protracted stare. That was all long ago. Now her Hawk was probably as fat and unappetising as Ralph de Morgan, living in some cold secluded castle with a wife and children around his feet. Without doubt, he would have ridden roughshod over her just as much as the de Longspeys, which would not have been to her taste.

'Well, Rose, if Gilbert is set on it—' Petronilla's voice broke in to her uneasy recollections '—how can we stop it?'

A glint appeared in Rosamund's eye, which should have warned her mother. 'I know exactly how to do so. I am going to take up my inheritance.'

'In Clifford?'

'Yes. It's mine and I can live there if I wish. You can come with me or go to Lower Broadheath. Will you come?' A little smile touched her lips as she watched Petronilla consider, knowing the outcome. Of course her mother would come. She would admit that to change Rosamund's mind would be like trying to change the direction of the wind, and she might as well save her breath, but she was not so careless a parent as to allow her only child to journey into the wild terrain in the west unaccompanied.

'I will come with you,' Petronilla confirmed. 'Of course I will. Do you need to ask?' And then, with a sigh as reality struck, 'But Gilbert will stop you.'

'No, he won't. I have a plan.'

'But, Rose, it's so far.'

'Exactly! Far enough to get me out of the marriage with Ralph de Morgan. Once there, I'll be safe. I can live as I wish.' Rosamund's eyes gleamed with indomitable courage and sheer excitement at the planned adventure. 'If I flee to Clifford, rejecting all ties with Salisbury, Gilbert—and Ralph too—might just write me off as a lost cause. I doubt either of them will bother to send a force after us, to drag me back to Salisbury in chains or lock me in a dungeon until I am obedient. We shall both be free of the selfish demands of opinionated men. Which, I think, will suit both of us very well.'

Chapter Two

Fitz Osbern arrived in Hereford as the winter night closed in, rain still falling steadily. He settled his men as usual into the range of buildings that made up the Blue Boar, stayed only for a cup of ale, a platter of bread and tough meat of dubious origin, then replaced cloak and hood to begin a round of the ale houses and taverns.

Knowing the habits of his quarry, it did not take long. In the Red Lion he caught sight of just the man who would answer his needs. A thickset soldier with years of experience on his shoulders, he was in the act of raising a tankard to his lips, Fitz Osbern strode up behind him and clapped him on the back. He choked over the ale.

'God damn it!' The irate drinker wheeled round, tankard discarded so that it rolled wetly on the table. His hand flashed to the dagger at his waist, all the honed instincts of a hardened campaigner, until he grunted, grinned as he wiped his hand down over the front of his ale-spotted tunic. 'Ger! I might have known. But you might value your life…' Hugh de Mortimer swept the point of the short-bladed dagger in a menacing circle, before placing it on the table top and pushing forward a stool with one booted foot.

'As if you could stick me with that pretty toy, before I had you on the floor under my boot.' Gervase sat, cast off his cloak. 'Still frequenting stews such as this for your entertainment?' His lips curled at the rank smoke, the unpleasant mix of scents of rancid onions and sour ale, of damp and unwashed humanity. Hugh's weathered face softened into a smile of easy camaraderie of long standing, which Gervase returned as they finally clasped hands in greeting. Hugh continued to wear his years well. There were a good dozen years between them, but they had fought side by side over those years to keep the March at peace. Grizzled, stocky, the Marcher lord enforced his authority with steely blue eyes and a common touch that made him popular and easy to approach.

'For your information, Ger, I'm here for any news of interest,' the Marcher lord chided gently, yet with the authority of experience and the scattering of grey in his hair. From his power base in Hereford, Hugh de Mortimer had taken it upon himself to keep his finger on the tumultuous pulse of the March in the name of the King. 'I had a meeting with one of my informants here.' Hugh eyed Gervase, the growth of beard, the black, rain-matted hair. 'Thought you were in Anjou.'

'I was. Just returned.' Stretching out his right leg, a groan indicating a recent injury from a fall from his horse, one that still ached in cold wet weather, Gervase ran his hand over his rough chin and cheeks with distaste. 'Some hard travelling with little time for home comforts. As for the crossing…' His expression said it all. 'I was bound for Monmouth. And then I heard some interesting news on the road this side of Gloucester.'

A gleam lit the keen blue eyes. 'Salisbury?

'Salisbury. That's why I'm here. I thought you'd know more if there was anything to know. Your lines of communication are excellent. Tell me what's afoot.'

'Salisbury's dead,' Hugh confirmed, turning smartly to business. 'That's what you wanted to hear.'

'So it's true.'

'And you are thinking of the future of Clifford.'

'How would I not?'

'That this is your chance to get it back?'

'I don't know. I doubt it. The son and heir has as much an iron fist as his father. The lands will be held secure. I doubt the change in ownership will make much difference. And I'm too far stretched with the Anjou possessions to engage in a major conflict, however much I might desire the castle.'

Hugh's hand closed over the Fitz Osbern's wrist, pulled him closer. 'But listen, Ger. Rumour has it that the new Earl's primary interest will not be in the March after all. That he has not inherited Clifford, or the other two border castles. Nor has his brother Walter.'

Gervase paused, ale halfway between table and lips. Blood sang through his veins, a sudden bubble of warmth to lift his spirits.

'If not Gilbert, then who?'

'The Earl's daughter. A girl from his second marriage. He married Petronilla de Clare a dozen years ago. So this daughter must be young—a mere child, I think.'

'A child?' Gervase tapped his fingers against the cup at the new slant on affairs.

'That's what my sources tell me. It might be in your interest after all to spy out the land.' A sly smile on Hugh's face, at odds with the ingenuous open stare.

'It might. Well, now! Clifford in the hands of a child, a girl.'

Fitz Osbern sat and thought, staring down into his ale.

Clifford. The name had been engraved on his consciousness when a small child, written there in a forceful hand by his father. By rights the little border fortress was his, part of the Fitz Osbern estates. He knew it well, had once lived there for a short period when he was first wed to Matilda de Vaughan. Urgently, he pushed that unwelcome memory away to concentrate on what he recalled of the stronghold itself. For the most part a rough-and-ready, timber-and-earth construction, with only a token rebuilding in stone to provide basic living accommodation. But that was not important. What *was,* was that it held a strategic position on the River Wye, where the river could be forded, and was one of the original Fitz Osbern lands granted to his ancestor after the Conquest by the grateful Conqueror. It was undeniably part of his inheritance.

But then Clifford had been filched from his father, Henry, Lord Fitz Osbern, by the Earl of Salisbury when Lord Henry was campaigning in Anjou and he, Gervase, was holding court in his father's name in Monmouth. All was done and dusted by the time his father returned, or before he could raise his own force and march to Clifford from Monmouth. By that time Salisbury was smirking from behind the walls.

And so Clifford had become a constant thorn in the Fitz Osbern flesh, of loss and humiliation that had worn his father down. Not in the best of health, he had seen it as a disgrace, a stain on his honour. A suppurating sword wound had carried him off to his grave only twelve months after. Gervase's frown grew heavier. Any attempt by Gervase to recover the castles by force would have had Salisbury descending on him with the weight of a full battle force backed by all his Longspey wealth and influence, not to mention King Stephen's ear.

But now Stephen was dead, so was Salisbury. And Clifford was owned by a child…

'Does it mean so much to you?' Hugh had watched the play of emotions over what he could see of his friend's features. 'It's small, needs total refurbishment if you mean to keep a siege at bay. I doubt there's been much rebuilding or improvement since the first wooden tower and earth ramparts were put into place. Does it matter so much that you reclaim Clifford?'

'Oh, yes.' There was no mistaking the light in Gervase's eyes. The utter conviction in his voice. 'It means everything.'

'Because of your father.'

'Because of him. And family honour, I suppose.' A pause. 'And because of Matilda…'

'Ah, yes. I had forgotten…'

'I hadn't.' Gervase's hands clenched round the mug. 'I'll never forget. She died there, and I was not there to save her.'

The flat emotion in his face dissuaded Hugh from pursuing that line. He cleared his throat. 'So what will you do?'

'Tomorrow I ride for Clifford. I can hardly pass up so perfect an opportunity, now can I?'

'No. Want company?'

Gervase searched the Marcher lord's face. What better support could he ask for when planning a raid into hostile territory? A firm sword hand and a courageous spirit. A wealth of sound advice. Of recent years he had become used to acting on his own authority. Isolated, his mother said in moments of sharp honesty. Perhaps a friendly face at his shoulder would be welcome…

'Well?' Hugh prompted. 'Do you want me or not?'

Gervase noticeably relaxed, nodded. 'I do. If you have a mind to come and see me crow over my victory—then by all means.'

'Let's drink to it.'

With a combined force, on the following morning the two men took the road west out of Hereford toward Clifford. The day broke with a sharp wind and bright scudding cloud. The Black Mountains now came into sharp focus, rising out of the plain before them. Their objective, the small border fortress, stood on the south bank of the Wye to the north of the main ridge.

The company rode at ease in such familiar territory. Hugh stretched his limbs in the saddle, flexed his shoulders. He might appreciate town life—soft living, Gervase had called it— but it was good to ride in congenial company again. Conversation ranged wide, but gradually they circled to more personal matters. Hugh was quite prepared to take advantage of the long family association and touch on a sensitive nerve, the nerve he had neatly avoided the previous night. He knew Gervase would resist, but in the clear light of day broached the subject anyway.

'You, Ger, need a wife.'

'I know.' The reply was level enough. 'I could say the same for you.'

Ah! So that's the game! Feint and parry to distract the opponent. De Mortimer decided to play along. 'No, I do not. I was married for well over twenty years. I have two fine grown sons as heirs, now with young families of their own, to carry on my name and rule the Mortimer lands. I loved Joanna dearly. I do *not* want another wife at my time of life. I'm too set in my ways to start to conform to the demands and needs of another woman in my home. I like my own way too much.'

'Not even to warm your bed on a cold night?' Gervase slid a glance at the man who still carried himself with the vibrant energy of a younger man. The grey streaks, the fine lines beside eyes and mouth, were misleading.

'There are other ways, if that's what I choose. Such as a very personable merchant's widow in Hereford who would like nothing more than to be a permanent addition to my bed if I raised my hand and smiled in her direction. So, no, I don't see myself taking the oath again. But that's side-stepping the issue—as you well know.' His gaze sharpened and pinned Gervase, his advice becoming brutal. 'Imagine me in the role of your late lamented father! You have no heir and you need one. You could be killed by a stray arrow or a well-aimed sword-cut today…tomorrow. You cannot burn the flame at the fair Matilda de Vaughan's altar for ever. How long is it since she died? Five years now? Accept it, she's lost to you. So you must turn your thoughts elsewhere. What are you going to do about it?'

The level voice acquired a distinct edge. 'Find another, I suppose. Matilda, I should tell you, is not an issue. I doubt I'll ever burn a flame for any woman.' Gervase's lips twisted in a wry smile. 'Far too poetic for my liking. You sound like one of those damned troubadours, Hugh!'

Hugh barked a laugh. '*When* will you find another?'

'When I have time.'

'Any possibilities?' Hugh persisted. 'I suppose you have *some* preferences in the woman you will wed.'

'Yes, of course I do.' Gervase, obviously unwilling to spar with de Mortimer and determined to put an end to the discussion, rattled them off as if compiling a list of requirements for a battle campaign. 'What any man of sense would choose. Well born, passably attractive, of course. Biddable, obedient, well tutored in domestic affairs, an efficient chatelaine who can hold the reins of my households—you know the sort of thing.'

Hugh hid a smile. He did indeed. The milk-sop sort of wife who would present no difficulties or challenges for Gervase. Who would not question or comment or contradict, but behave with perfect compliance. Soft and malleable as a goose-down cushion. And just as smothering and dull.

'Had any offers lately?' he asked innocently.

'Not of late. Unless you count the de Longspey girl.'

'What's that?'

'Salisbury offered me one of his family, to tie and hobble me into a neat alliance.'

'Well, that surprises me.' Hugh cast about in his mind for knowledge of de Longspey females. 'Who was it?'

'I've forgotten,' Gervase admitted, annoyed at the tinge of heat in his face at this turn in the conversation. 'I don't think we were actually introduced. I was not interested and so refused.'

'So you were rude and brutal.'

'I was honest! What I *was,* as I recall, was grieving for my father's death, and not willing to be bought off.' He paused. Huffed a breath. 'If you want the truth—then, no, I was not temperate. I have regretted it since.'

'Was the lady not—ah, passably attractive, biddable, obedient, then?'

Gervase smiled, laughed with genuine humour. 'I've no idea.'

'I despair of you, Ger. But don't leave it too long,' was all de Mortimer could find to say.

'As soon as I have this matter of Clifford settled, I'll turn my mind to it.'

They worked their way around a particularly water-logged stretch of road, the horses' hooves squelching in the heavy mud. The sun vanished and the rain began again.

'What will you do if the child is already in residence at Clifford?' Hugh suddenly asked on a thought.

'I don't expect it.' Gervase's brows rose. It had not crossed his mind. 'Why would she? I would expect her to remain in Salisbury until she's old enough to be wed. Clifford is no fit place for a child—and a girl.'

'Probably not. But it might be so.'

'Then I shall pack her back into her travelling wagon with her nurse, her clothes and her toys and her kitten or whatever she has brought with her—and send her back to her de Longspey brothers in Salisbury. What did you expect that I would do? Consign her to a dungeon?'

'No, Gervase.' A hint of censure, even of warning, touched the Marcher lord's mouth for an instant. 'I would expect you to treat her with all honour and courtesy.'

'Don't doubt it. I shall do exactly that.'

With the seed inadvertently planted by Hugh in his mind, Gervase found his thoughts returning to that disastrous interview with Salisbury, remembering primarily being overwhelmed with an anger that threatened to slip beyond his control. It made uncomfortable remembering. In retrospect, with his father just dead, he should never have done it. It had always been an impossible goal, but in his grief Gervase had made an attempt to regain his rightful property by an appeal to justice. Which Earl William had refused, but had then tried to buy him off with a de Longspey bride. No, he had not been as temperate as he might have been. As if he would ever accept a woman from the murderous de Longspey stable. He recalled storming out of the luxurious rooms in the Salisbury town house with barely a thought for the unfortunate girl who had been tricked out for his inspection. No, not the best of moves. And, worst of all, it had left Clifford securely in the hands of Salisbury. But no Fitz Osbern worth his salt would commit himself to living in Salisbury's pocket as a dependent lord. It had pleased him mightily to fling the offer of a wife back in the Earl's self-righteous face without a moment's thought.

As for the girl… The lasting impression was one of—well, it was difficult to bring a complete picture to mind. He had barely registered her as other than a composed young woman with pale skin. A pallor that had warmed with bright colour along her cheekbones as he had bent his disdainful eye on her. Firm lips and a direct stare, more a challenge from an opposing knight than a soft glance from a well-born maiden. That was it. She had looked at him as if he did not come anywhere near to her high-vaunting standards as a husband. As if he was a marauding brigand just emerged from the Welsh mountains. Green eyes. Too direct, he recalled, too combative. Attractive, without doubt. But biddable, obedient? He would wager not. Nothing like Matilda. Not the sort of female he would ever want as a wife, whatever her breeding, whatever her connections.

As he left the audience chamber, failure rampaging through his blood, he had found himself standing close to her. She must have used lavender to wash her hair—the scent wound though his senses as she took a step back. And he had remembered, almost before it was too late, the courtesy with which he had been raised, and, digging deep through the fury, had enough nobility to make his farewell to her. He had kissed her hand. Why could he still experience that one moment with such amazing clarity? How the light texture of her fingers had for the briefest of moments cut through the anger in his head. Cool, smooth. Delicious skin like silk against his mouth. There had been that astonishing urge to kiss more.

Gervase deliberately pushed aside such unbidden thoughts with a grimace, clenching his jaw against the discomfort of his body's response. He did not want her then, nor did he now. The erection that strained for release was merely a symptom of lack of female company in recent months. Easily remedied.

Besides, the de Longspey incident was all in the past. He could not even recall the girl's name. Gervase shifted warily in the saddle. So why had he remembered her at all?

Chapter Three

Rosamund de Longspey had put her plan into immediate operation. A proposed visit to the fair in Salisbury, with a wagon to bring home any goods, two manservants, two armed guards and Edith, her mother's maidservant, had become a headlong flight to Clifford without Earl Gilbert being the wiser until it was too late. They spent the first night in their new home wrapped in their cloaks in one of the unfurnished chambers in the west tower. The lord's chamber would require much work to make it habitable. Nor would they trust any of the filthy quilts or covers to be had in the castle. So the night was a cold and sleepless one. The bread when she broke her fast was hard and unpalatable. Rosamund was thus in an ill-tempered mood when, on hearing a commotion in the bailey, she emerged to discover her gates open and an unknown knight with a force of soldiers in process of taking control of her castle from under her very nose.

'Stop! What in God's name are you doing…? You have no right…'

'Might is right, Lady.' The sword in the knight's determined grip caught the weak rays of the sun, glittering along its honed edge. The tip of it hovered over the very centre of her breast, although he did not allow it to quite rest there. His feral grin was as arresting as the lethal weapon. 'As of this moment, with this sword in my hand, I hold the power here. You do not.'

Rosamund froze on the spot. Suddenly, without warning, the point of the sword fell. Thank God! But Rosamund's relief was short lived when the knight took a stride forward to close the space between them. Before she could retreat, she found herself caught within his arm, tightly banding around her waist. For that one breathless moment she feared for her safety and her honour. Then, to her amazement, the fear disappeared. His arms might pinion her to the length of his body, but they held her safe, secure against unnamed dangers. Barely able to catch a breath, her heart leaping in her breast.

Then as reality struck home and she raised her fists against his chest. But, furiously struggling, she made no impact at all on that solid wall of muscle. Rosamund looked up into his face, fighting now against a tingle of fear, of desperation. To see those cold grey eyes looking down into hers with what she could only interpret as hatred.

Would he assault her? Dishonour her? Who had not heard tales of such fiendish attacks, where no woman from the lowliest of servants to the lady herself was safe from rape and brutal treatment? Is that what he intended, here in full view of every man and woman in the castle? The threat of such humiliation iced her blood.

'Let go of me,' she demanded, hammering at his impervious chest with her fists.

'I would be delighted to,' he snarled.

Except that his grip tightened further, lifting her off her feet. Forced to grasp his shoulders for balance, Rosamund cried out in fear.

'Don't squawk in my ear, woman.' Suddenly, with a tightening of the muscles in his back and thighs, he was lifting her higher to spin her aside. 'It would solve my problem immediately if you were run down by one of my out-of-control baggage wagons, of course. But your brother the Earl might take it amiss. I don't want him descending on me with an avenging army any time soon.'

Unnoticed in the mass of people and animals, one of the baggage wagons, clumsily manoeuvred, had creaked dangerously close, its burden of packages and barrels leaning precariously. As she glanced round, the wheel brushed against her skirts. If she had remained where she had been, she could well have been crushed under its weight.

The knight waited until the horses harnessed to the wagon had been led to safety, then, as soon as she was out of its range, he released her abruptly, letting her drop to her feet with a sardonic appreciation of her ruffled state. 'There, lady. You're safe to continue your objections if you so wish. Though I warn you, they'll do no good.'

Perhaps not, but Rosamund could not—would not!—simply accept this turn in her fortunes. 'But this is my inheritance, my dower.' She fought her way through her scrambled thoughts. 'Clifford is within the gift of the Earl of Salisbury—and now it is mine.'

'Only by default, lady.' The knight who had announced himself to be simply Fitz Osbern turned his attention to instructing his squire to supervise the unloading of the baggage wagons, bulging with supplies from Hereford. 'Clifford was given to my ancestor by the Conqueror for services rendered. It was stolen from my father by the late Earl William. By the letter of the law it belongs to the Fitz Osberns—and now Clifford at least has returned to its rightful owner.' He shouted an order to his sergeant-at-arms. 'All I have to do is reclaim Ewyas Harold and Wigmore. A small force has been sent to each.'

'Reclaim? But they are mine too.' Rosamund could feel panic building again, layer upon layer, straining to escape her control.

'Then it will not be a difficult task for me, will it? My men are in possession, as you can see, so there is nothing further to discuss. Now, if you would take yourself off to your chamber until I have time to deal with you…' He sheathed the sword, a harsh rasp, and cast an experienced eye over the disposition of his troops.

Rosamund simply stared at him in stark amazement, fury replacing her fear. He had simply dismissed her as of no account. *Take yourself off out of my way!* is what he clearly meant! She narrowed her eyes to assess him as he stood in her courtyard, ownership written all over his straight shoulders and raised chin, taking stock of her castle. And what she saw did not please her at all. A bloodthirsty ruffian, was her first impression. He was not a man used to argument or his will being questioned, that much was clear. His eyes were a cold grey, dark and stormy, reflecting the colour of the winter river that flowed past their gates. Crow black and untidy, his hair was ruffled into thick waves by the chill wind, sweat-matted from the close confines of the Phrygian cap that he had pulled off and tucked in his belt, and his cheeks shadowed by any number of days' growth of beard. His tunic and hose, his knee-length boots, were much as his cloak, wet and mud splattered. Filthy, she decided with distaste and a little sniff, refusing to take into account the state of the mired roads. But what did she expect? Cultured elegance? Fine courtly manners? Not from this man!

Rosamund frowned. As the knight moved, she noticed he favoured his right leg, a slight limp. Probably acquired in a tavern brawl or a drunken disagreement over dice. He was nothing but a mercenary, a robber baron, and not a moment ago she had been dragged into his arms, held hard against his chest. Disgust filled her, not least at her reaction to him. She could not find this man attractive! Her intense annoyance coloured her next words when she saw that he was quite prepared to dismiss her like a servant and leave her standing there in the mud of her own bailey.

'How dare you take what is mine! You're nothing but an uncivilised lout!'

Which got his attention well enough. Emotion flashed across his face. With shocked fascination she saw the slash of colour along the high cheekbones as he looked down at his tormentor, a particularly cold stare. For a long moment he contemplated her in silence, allowing Rosamund the opportunity to chide herself. What a time to make so unwise an attack. Then, when the weight in her chest had grown to major proportions, he grinned and sketched a mocking bow, strangely at odds with the mud and grime. The smile was not friendly. His eyes and his words froze the marrow of her bones.

'In the circumstances, lady, you should be praying that you are wrong in your estimation of my appearance and character. If I was an uncivilised lout, I would have designs on your person as well as your castle.' He took a stride forward. To her dismay Rosamund took one in retreat, but Fitz Osbern did not halt. Instead he stepped intimidatingly close. Rosamund, disconcerted, found herself lifting a hand to smack it firmly in self-protection against his chest. And drew in a sharp breath.

It burned. She could feel the heat of him, as she had before, as it crept from that inadvertent touch of her spread fingers to engulf her whole body. And not merely a physical warmth. Her heart seemed to swell with it, filling her breast so that her breathing shortened. Her belly shivered with nerves. Every inch of her skin seemed suddenly to be conscious of his looming presence. He might not be touching her, but she felt the hot slide of his glance over her flesh. Aghast, Rosamund swallowed against the dryness in her throat. She could feel the flame of it in her cheeks, and cursed her pale complexion that mirrored every thought. Could think of nothing to say, could only stare at him wide-eyed as his heart beat steadily beneath her palm.

Then, to her relief, the knight stepped back.

'I assure you, I have no designs on your person,' he growled. The grin widened to show even teeth. Wolfishly, she considered. 'As for yourself, lady, you are remarkably proud and haughty, considering that you are entirely at my mercy.'

Flushing again, vividly to the roots of her hair, Rosamund found her voice. 'At your mercy? I am no such thing!'

'No? I don't suggest that you challenge me on that point.' He looked her up and down as if about to say more, changed his mind. 'Enough of this. I have things to do here, lady. We'll discuss this…this little difficulty…over dinner at mid-day. If nothing else, we must arrange for your transportation elsewhere. So if you would be so good as to order the provision of hot food for my men with my steward, and for ourselves…'

Without a backward glance, Fitz Osbern strode off toward the stables, leaving her standing. *My steward!* Her clear brow furrowed into a scowl, her hands tightened into fists. She would have tapped her foot if her shoe had not been firmly anchored in the mud. *Order the food! As if I were a servant at his beck and call!* Stalking past her mother without a word, she climbed the stairs into the hall, head high, realising that she had no choice, that she would get nowhere with this situation until they faced each other again and hammered out the legalities. She refused to chase after him to demand his attention. So she would organise the meal. Present him with the documents of her legal ownership. And then force him to leave. Although how she would achieve such a conclusion she had no very clear idea. Whatever she had or had not learned about him in that short confrontation, he was not a man open to persuasion.

But that was not all she had learnt. And it was equally unacceptable. Rosamund found herself wiping her damp palm down her skirts. His touch still burned there.

Lady Petronilla remained standing at the foot of the staircase, a fascinated witness to the little scene, an avid spectator of a clash of wills that could not but fill her with anxieties for the future. She might have been unable to hear all the words spoken, except when Rosamund raised her voice beyond what was seemly to call the knight an uncivilised lout—perhaps not the best thing to do on first acquaintance—but the tone of the whole exchange had been abundantly clear. Sometimes Rose was too much her father's daughter for everyone's comfort. And now what? The Fitz Osbern men were quite incontrovertibly in control, occupying the gatehouse and the towers of the central court, their equipment stowed and their horses occupying the stables. Petronilla slid a glance over to where the elder of the two knights still stood where he had remained throughout, at his horse's head, hands clasped on his sword belt as he watched the proceedings with an undisguised appreciation. Now, sensing her interest, he looked across at her, his smile gaining a rueful quality. For some reason his quiet confidence, his tolerant smile and the gleam in his eye as it met hers across the width of the bailey brought a warmth to her face. She felt his sympathy, his quick understanding of the uncomfortable position that she had been thrown into, and it irritated her beyond bearing. She felt an urge to wipe the smile from his face. Before common sense could step in, she stalked across to his side.

'I don't know what you found to be so amusing in that little interlude,' she remarked with stern censure. Had she known it, the lift of her chin was very like that of her daughter. 'You should be ashamed of yourself!'

'What?' The smile duly vanished, the knight's rough brows snapped together. 'What did I do?'

'Nothing! That's the thing!'

Like her daughter, she turned on her heel and left him to mull over the enigmatic words as he wished, whilst Lady Petronilla wondered at her response to the knight and her temerity at castigating him for no reason at all.

Rosamund paced in the Great Hall—*her* Great Hall—her thoughts in confusion. As if her arrival at Clifford on the previous day had not been bad enough, with all its shocking revelation. As if the decisions she had been forced to make had not taken all her courage. And now this débâcle—this *monstrous* turn of events. From the moment when she had at set foot in the small settlement of some twenty timber-and-thatch houses on the bank of the Wye where the river could be forded with relative ease, everything seemed destined to go wrong. She had simply sat and looked in horrified awe at the central keep of Clifford, recently rebuilt in local stone, her inheritance and her chosen home. It was grey and entirely forbidding.

'It's not exactly welcoming, is it?' Lady Petronilla, lips pressed into a straight line to prevent an exclamation of sheer horror, sat in the bailey of Clifford Castle and viewed the near prospect from the safe advantage of her mare's back. Her hands clutched around the reins at what she saw.

'God's bones!' Less restrained, Rosamund's first impression of her new home was dire. Was *this*—this hellish outpost on the very edge of what she considered to be civilisation— to be her home?

'Don't blaspheme, Rosamund.' But the Countess's tone was mild. 'It's not as bad as all that.' A rat scurried across their path, larger than most cats. 'Or perhaps it is.'

Due to the striking de Longspey pennons in black and red, flaunted by their escort, the castle gates had been opened for them without question. The commander of the garrison, an elderly knight of lined and mournful visage named Thomas de Byton, stood elbows akimbo on the steps leading up to the entrance to the keep, sour and unaccommodating. He made no advance to acknowledge or receive the women who had turned up unwanted and uninvited on his threshold, but watched them with what Rosamund could only interpret as a jaundiced air. She could read his disapproval in his stance. Awaited his approach. When he made no move, she nudged her horse forward until she sat before him, her eyes on a level with his, as she had intended, and very direct.

'Thomas de Byton.' Her voice was clear, carried well. She had made it her business to discover the name of the man who held Clifford in her name, the protection of her property. 'I am Rosamund de Longspey.'

'Aye, my lady. I heard the Earl had given the castle to a *woman*.'

She ignored his words but, eyes widened, continued to hold

his. 'Perhaps you will make arrangements for the accommodation of my escort and for myself and the Dowager Countess.'

'And for how long would that be, my lady?'

She lifted her chin an inch, stared down her nose. 'For as long as I see fit. I intend to make my home here.'

'As you wish, my lady.' Sir Thomas turned, to stamp back up the steps, in no way discommoded by the interview.

'One moment, Sir Thomas. If you please.'

He halted, half-turned, but did not retrace his steps.

'If you would see to my horses and my baggage, I wish to inspect the private quarters.'

'As you wish, my lady.' With bad grace, he marched back down the steps and across the bailey to the thatch-and-timber constructions that housed the kitchens, resentment hovering round him like a swarm of flies in summer. She heard his muttered parting shot.

'Let me know when you decide you don't wish to stay, my lady.'

But she would stay. She must. The new Lady of Clifford braced for what was to come.

'Well, it could be worse. Some improvements have been made.' Petronilla surveyed the stone walls rising on every side to create an inner court.

'I fail to see them,' Rosamund lifted one soft leather boot to inspect the mud caked almost to the ankle. This inner courtyard enclosed within the defences of the stone keep was badly drained and awash with standing water. The walls were high, hemming them in, cutting off the light. The air was dank and chill and would be so, she suspected, even on the warmest of summer days. She shivered within her mantle. 'It's like being enclosed in a stone tomb.'

'At least you have the comfort of a stone hall. Timber lets in the draughts so,' Petronilla continued, trying to make the best of it. They looked around them at the five towers and the three-storied Hall, all connected by a strong defensive wall, a battlement walk around the top. 'And our safety here is guaranteed, even if the outer bailey falls to an attack.'

'Do you say?' Rosamund poked at some decaying mortar between the stonework. 'I think we should look at the rest before we go in.' She followed Sir Thomas's distant figure down into the bailey.

It did not take long. Rosamund's sense of disgust deepened with every step. Other than the gatehouse and the keep, both of stone and substantial enough, the rest of the fortification was still the original timber palisade with an outer earth bank and ditch. The buildings in the outer bailey were timber and thatch—stables, kitchens, store rooms, as well as shelters for the scattering of cows and sheep that roamed and mired up the surface. She stepped cautiously around the animals. Should they not be fenced in somewhere? Chickens sat broodily along one roof ridge. In the corner beside the keep, easily recognisable by the rank smell, a midden spread its foul contents underfoot. Her nose wrinkling, Rosamund quickly put distance between herself and the offending heap. Who could have allowed the midden to be positioned there, so close to the habitation?

'It could be worse,' the Dowager gulped, as if repeating the words would make them so. 'You've a secure water supply from the well.'

'So I have.' Rosamund suddenly smiled wryly at her mother, struck by the sheer awfulness of it all. 'Stop being so cheerful!' But this is where she must stay. 'Let's go in. You notice that our commander and my invisible steward—if I have one—are both keeping a low profile. I think it bodes ill.'

It did. The sight and the stench reduced the de Longspey women to a silence.

'Oh, dear!' Lady Petronilla managed at last.

The Hall showed evidence of hard and crowded living, being the nightly refuge of Sir Thomas's men-at-arms. Dark in the most sun-filled of days, rank with smoke from the open fire that did not find the intended outlets in the thickness of the wall and with the rancid reek of animal fat feeding the rush lights, it was a scene from a church wall-painting of Hell, to frighten the sinful into a better life on earth.

'These rushes have not been changed since last winter.' In awe of such filth, Rosamund tried not to disturb them too much as she walked in, flinching from the fleas and vermin that would infest them. Any sweet scent had long gone, replaced by the stench from putrid scraps of food and worse from the savaging hounds that drew back snarling as she approached. Over all, the whole place reeked of unwashed humanity.

The furniture was minimal, splattered and scarred. A few benches and stools stood by the hearth. The single standing table on the dais had seen better days. There were no tapestries to decorate the walls. Indeed, it would have been a shame to hang them where their beauty would have been spoiled. The stone-work ran with wet and soot from the fire.

'So what about the private chambers?' Rosamund started up the stairs to the next floor. 'For where shall we sleep tonight?'

'Not in here!' Lady Petronilla lifted the hem of her skirts from the outrage.

The solar, intended as a comfortable refuge for the women of the household, contained nothing but evidence of soldiers sleeping there—a discarded boot and assorted pieces of raiment, jugs of ale, remnants of ruined food. Equally, the ad-joining private chamber intended to heighten the authority of the lord and his lady had been taken over, Rosamund presumed, as the haunt of Thomas de Byton, and he had done nothing to remove his presence from it.

'By the Virgin!' Rosamund kicked over a pile of ques-tionable material beside what should have been an impressive oak bedstead, then retreated from platters of food with their layers of fuzzy mould. The smell that hit them at the door heralded the existence of the garderobe, built into the thickness of the wall to empty into the ditch below. It was altogether an appalling place.

Rosamund decided not to investigate further. 'I doubt this has ever been cleaned out since the stone keep was first constructed. It's hard to believe that Ralph de Morgan would want it.' She veiled her thoughts with dark lashes from her percipient mother, not liking their direction, unable to dispel the sharp bitterness that settled beneath her breast-bone. 'As a dower it does not recommend me highly to a husband, does it? And yet Ralph de Morgan would take me, to acquire *this*. Simply because it controls the crossing of the Wye. The cow byres in Salisbury are better kept than this! Yet it was thought to be a suitable dower for me.' She heard her voice rise, and strove without success to control the bleak vision of her future here. 'Perhaps at my advanced age Ralph is the best I can hope for. I clearly have no great value in de Longspey eyes, except to entice a border lord into their clutches.'

'Foolish girl! How could you think that you have no value! Believe me, Rose, this place will look far better after a good scrub!' Petronilla managed a semblance of a smile as Edith called on the Virgin to give them succour. Only too well aware of the probable live occupants of the mattress, they made a discreet exit from the chamber. The fleas and bugs might be invisible, but the mice and rats were not. Nor the enormous spiders that had spun cobwebs over every corner.

'I can think it well enough. Consider this. Earl William and Gilbert thought to attract a husband for me by using this…this *midden* as a dower. What value does that give me? What worth have I?' But Rosamund squared her shoulders against the hurt. She would not let it crush her spirits. She could at least pretend that the pain of humiliation in her chest did not exist. 'Perhaps the storerooms will give me hope.'

They did not. A cursory inspection suggested that Rosamund de Longspey owned nothing but a serious quantity of barrels of ale. A sad fact confirmed by the mid-day meal, served by an ill-washed kitchen boy in the squalor of the Great Hall. The array of dishes comprised, apart from the ale, nothing more than a thick mutton broth, a platter of boiled onions and coarse flat-bread, burnt at the sides.

They did their best with it in a horrified silence that at least gave Rosamund time to marshal her thoughts. She dipped her spoon into the fat that pooled glossily on the surface, pushing aside the gristle before pushing aside the bowl itself. She had three choices as she saw it. To accept defeat, retreat to Salis-bury and Ralph's noxious embrace. The shudder that ran over her flesh at the thought had nothing to do with the ferocious draught that had frozen her feet into splinters of ice. She could not do that. Why, oh, why had the Wild Hawk not agreed to take her? The shiver that rippled over her skin had even less to do with the cold, but a remembered awareness in her belly as his eyes had travelled over her body. It had lingered, a knot of heat, even when he had rejected her with nothing but the briefest of salutes to her fingers. Now to have his hands awaken her body…

Well, he hadn't wanted her. And as she could not possibly take Ralph, so she must turn her back on marriage.

The second possibility—she let her affectionate gaze rest on the Countess who was in the act of pushing the platter of onions toward Sir Thomas with a gracious and entirely false smile. She could take up residence at Lower Broadheath with her mother and grow old in extreme and graceful boredom.

Or…she inhaled slowly as her eyes travelled round the stained walls of her Great Hall…she could remain here and claim her inheritance as Lady of Clifford.

'If you wed Ralph de Morgan, you would not have to live here, Rose.' Petronilla's advice was tentative, but accurate.

'Would you give yourself into Ralph de Morgan's sweaty hands?'

'No.' The Countess sighed.

Rosamund had stiffened her shoulders. Despite the impos-sible horror of it all, she would remain here at Clifford, but there were changes to be made. Immediate and wide-ranging, and very much to her own liking. She would make this place her own. Was she not the undisputable Lady of Clifford? She remembered smiling serenely at the Countess and a suspicious Sir Thomas.

Now Rosamund scowled.

'Changes to my own liking?' she announced, coming to an abrupt halt in her pacing, her recollections overlaid by a bitter truth and a slick layer of dread. 'What could I have been thinking? Any authority I thought was mine has just been denied me at the point of a sword.'

Just when she had made her decision to stay, to make the best of it, what did she find? That *ruffian* taking possession of her castle, her dowry, her only protection to stand between herself and Ralph de Morgan. Just when she had come to terms with her new home with all its imperfections, had forced herself to challenge the sneers of Sir Thomas, had accepted the hard work it would take to make it her own, it was snatched out of her hands by this disreputable riff-raff. This oaf!

'Did you hear what he said? The audacity of that…that *plunderer*!' Rosamund rounded on her mother as soon as Petronilla entered the Great Hall.

'Yes. I could not help but hear it.' Lady Petronilla looked back over her shoulder, thoughtfully, to the distant figures, the sounds of activity.

'The castle is his and would I kindly see to the preparation of a meal!' Rosamund raised her hands, smacked her palms together so that the sound echoed sharply in the high roof-space. 'I have the documents, the seals of ownership. He can't do this to me.'

'I fear that he has.'

Rosamund gnawed at her bottom lip, frowned at her unperturbed parent. 'You seem very calm with all this.' Of late the Countess had a tendency to accept the vagaries of life with a lack of spirit, a worrying development, but now was not the time to discuss it. 'I will not eat with him.'

'We can't starve, Rose. Besides, hunger is bad for the temper. You need to be cool here, Rosamund, when you decide what you will do.' She looked at her daughter's flushed face. 'What *will* you do?'

The green eyes snapped. 'I have no idea.'

'Then let us set food before the two knights, as we should with all good manners toward our guests, and see what unfolds.'

Rosamund nodded at the wisdom of her mother's advice. Otherwise, would she not show herself to be as uncouth as the man who had just held the point of his sword to her breast? But she would not retreat, as he would soon learn. 'Very well. I will feed him. But mark this. I will not give my home up to some unprincipled Marcher ruffian—whoever he says he is—without a fight.'

'No, dear Rose. Of course you won't. But it might not be wise to antagonise him.'

If Gervase Fitz Osbern had any thoughts on his intimate encounter with the de Longspey heiress, he was not saying, although close acquaintants might have considered him more taciturn than usual. By mid-day the disposition of his troops was to his satisfaction. Not the strongest of fortresses, with only a wooden palisade, but he could not fault the recent constructions of the Earl of Salisbury. The stone structure of walls and towers on the natural rock-based mound forming a cliff above the river would hold all but the most determined army at bay. He frowned at Sir Thomas de Byton's busy figure in the distance. He did not like the de Longspey commander, but the man was capable and quick to carry out orders. Gervase's lips twisted. Preferred the authority of a man to that of a woman, no doubt. Perhaps he could be left to hold the castle in Fitz Osbern's name. So as the winter sun struggled to the meagre heights of mid-day, Gervase and his men-at-arms repaired to the Great Hall. The servant girls hastily commandeered from the village had been busy. Scents of roast meats and newly baked bread wafted across the bailey. Tables had been put up on trestles. His men crowded in to take their seats. Fitz Osbern, with Hugh accompanying him, walked forward to the dais where the two women waited.

Very pretty, Gervase acknowledged dispassionately, his second meeting of the day with Rosamund de Longspey confirming his first impressions in the bailey, and he was not a man immune to a pretty woman. There his quick assessment had taken in her vibrant colouring and glowing skin, the cold wind having brought a delicate tint to her face. The formidably straight nose, and the strikingly beautiful arch of her brows, spoke of nothing but trouble for himself. A woman, not a girl— the rumours had been wrong—who had far too much sense of her own importance. Came of growing up in the household of the Earl of Salisbury where her will would never have been thwarted, if he knew anything about it. But how she could be the child of the second marriage he could not guess. Nor did she follow the usual de Longspey colouring or feature… There was a little tug at his memory, but one that promptly eluded him. No matter. She was not to his taste. And the mystery of the de Longspey heiress aside, Rosamund de Longspey was here and claiming the castle as her own and, thus, she was a hindrance to his plans, which had otherwise worked to smooth perfection. Unexpectedly, uncomfortably, he was conscious of where her hand had pressed against his chest, of her slim figure held within the protection of his arms—even if she had felt the need to belabour him with her fists. Until she had fought against him, for just one heated moment, she had fitted perfectly against him so that he was conscious of every curve and flat plane of her flesh against his—he pushed the memory away. She would not be allowed to hinder him. His father's ruined inheritance and sullied pride had both been superbly avenged. The castle was his—as would be the other two Marcher fortresses before the week was out.

He caught the condemnation in the lady's eyes as she watched him approach from the high chair on the dais, read the contempt in the bold and supercilious stare. An uncivilised lout, was he? He quelled a sudden urge to laugh, well aware of his careworn and mud-splattered appearance. He must look exactly that—a border robber without finesse. She doubtless saw him as a penniless adventurer, boorish and illiterate, with nowhere to call his home but some squalid fortress of mud and timber. Now this lady was quite a different cauldron of eels, and had dressed for the occasion. And he'd wager she'd done it deliberately. A vixen, was the Lady Rosamund. The silk gown with its embroidered edgings to hem and sleeves, the veil secured by a matching embroidered filet were completely impractical for life in such a fortress on the far-flung edge of the kingdom. Yet the deep green enhanced the glowing translucence of her skin, the intense colour of her eyes, the rose-pink of her pretty mouth… Gervase Fitz Osbern breathed deeply and brought his wandering attention back into line.

She was simply a problem that he must solve, a vixen to be turned out of her lair. So she had dressed to put him at a disadvantage, had she? As she had, standing on the dais before him, the advantage of height over him. Well, he could change the latter if he could do nothing about the former. He came to the dais, stepped up, and halted before this unlooked for problem to be solved. And it struck him as he glared down into the beautiful face. Despite the flash of wrath in her eyes and the challenge to his authority in her very appearance, if he were not careful he might just feel a need to…well, to protect her, he supposed.

Rosamund de Longspey barely reached his shoulder.

His thick lashes hid a sudden gleam in his eye. The lady would get no protection from him, however decorative or vulnerable she might appear. His first priority, very simply, must be to get her out of his castle.

Rosamund had set the scene carefully. She had deliberately taken the lord's high-backed chair, the only such chair in the Hall, to stamp her authority on the proceedings. As it had given her great pleasure to oust Thomas de Byton from his habitual seat and force him to take a more lowly stool, now it would give her equal satisfaction to do the same to Fitz Osbern. She watched him approach, never once taking her eyes from his face. If he was aware of her cunning handling of the occasion, he gave no recognition of it. He turned his head to exchange some comment with the other knight who had arrived with him. So she took the time to re-appraise him. Well! He had not combed his hair, but had at least used his fingers to give it some semblance of order. He might have brushed his clothes free of the worst of the mud and had abandoned his cloak, although he still wore sword and dagger, but his boots needed more than a cursory clean. He still looked like a marauding brigand.

She rose slowly to her feet.

The knight halted before the dais, bowed with token good manners to the two women, then stepped up, almost planting his mired boots on the edge of Rosamund's silk gown. Intimidatingly close to her, a menacingly looming figure, Rosamund found that she had to fight not to step back. She held her ground, but the knight merely dragged forward a stool and sat without comment, without courtesy, even before she and her mother had taken their own seats.

'Ladies.' He swept the pair with an indifferent and preoccupied gaze. 'Let me make you known. I am Gervase Fitz Osbern. This is Hugh de Mortimer.'

Rosamund sat, inclined her head, very much the great lady. Her fears were justified. They were nothing more than border lords, both of them. No better than the leaderless rabble who preyed on the unwary. Nothing to compare with the sophistication of the noble de Longspeys and those who visited Salisbury from King Henry's royal court. Thus there was a touch of arrogance in her cool reply.

'I am Rosamund de Longspey. Let me make you known to my mother. Lady Petronilla de Longspey, Dowager Countess of Salisbury.'

'We welcome your hospitality, lady. Smell's good after a morning's work.' It was de Mortimer who responded, rubbing his hands together, his first words for Rosamund, but then his interest centred on the widow. 'I knew your husband a little, my lady. I last met him at the coronation of King Henry four years back. I heard of your loss. You must regret his untimely death.'

'Yes. Thank you. It was unexpected.' The Countess accepted the condolences with unruffled grace.

'I thought your daughter must have been younger. That you had not been married to Salisbury for so very long.' There was a decided twinkle in de Mortimer's eye. 'I did not think you old enough to have a daughter of marriageable age herself.'

To her astonishment, Rosamund watched her mother's face grow pink, her eyes hidden by a down-sweep of fine lashes. Rosamund did not think she had ever seen her mother react in such a charmingly self-conscious manner. But Petronilla's reply was quite composed as she saw fit to explain. 'Rosamund is not of Salisbury's blood, my lord, but my daughter of my first marriage to John de Bredwardine. I was married at a very young age, you see. It is simply that she took my lord of Salisbury's name on my marriage. Earl William…well, he insisted on it.'

'I see. You have my sympathies, lady.' De Mortimer's response was brusque in words, but gentle in tone. 'As I recall, the Earl was always a man to get his own way.'

Petronilla smiled hesitantly. 'Indeed, sir, I…'

Rosamund could wait no longer. She must stake her claim to her position in this castle immediately. With a stern glare at her mother, who promptly lapsed into a flushed silence, Rosamund gave a signal to her steward, Master Pennard, to begin the meal. Jugs of ale were brought in, the large platters of food. Master Pennard, with weighty ceremonial, carried in the lord's goblet, a poor pottery affair with a chipped edge. Rosamund watched with narrowed eyes. To whom would he present the goblet? The steward hesitated. His glance edged nervously from one to the other, then, with supreme tact, placed it with a little bow before her. Without expression, Rosamund inclined her head at the minor victory, then turned her attention to the man who sat beside her. He was already watching her with a sharp awareness in his eyes.

'We have much to discuss, sir.' She addressed herself directly to Fitz Osbern, who began to apply himself to the meal with enthusiasm after such an active morning. He was already tearing apart a circular loaf of bread, when he looked up.

'There's nothing to discuss, lady, as I see it. Except for your imminent departure from this place. I have ordered your horses and your travelling wagon to be made ready at first light tomorrow morning. It's too late now—it'll be dark within two hours. First light tomorrow will enable you to reach Hereford with comfort during the day. And then you can travel on to Salisbury at your leisure.'

Rosamund stared her amazement. So immediate. So damnably peremptory! So unfeeling of her plight. She leaned forward. 'I think you do not understand, sir. This is my inheritance from Earl William for my dower. I have all the legal documents to the land.'

'But as *I* explained, the castle was stolen by Salisbury from my father. So if we are talking legality here, the castle is mine.'

'And you would actually turn me out?'

Unable to sit calmly, Rosamund stood, forcing Fitz Osbern to look up. Their eyes met and held, fiery green locked with wintry grey, with no understanding between them. Fitz Osbern raised his shoulders and turned his attention back to a steaming platter of roast mutton, drawing his dagger from the sheath at his belt.

'Yes,' he stated. 'The accommodation is limited here. There's only one private chamber. It's not convenient to me for you to occupy it.'

'There are five towers around the court, all with chambers, all suitable! I know. I slept in one last night.' Her face paled and her heart thudded, but whether with anger at his presumption or the sudden fear that he had the power to do exactly as he threatened—to turn her out—she was unsure.

'This is no place for you, lady.'

'I will not go.'

He turned from the mutton with a deep sigh, giving her his full attention, making no attempt to curb his impatience as he clapped his dagger down on the board. 'I am giving you no choice. I will send an escort with you as far as Hereford, if that is what you wish, if you fear to travel. Although you got yourself here unaided without difficulty… From Hereford you can make your own way home. I expect you'll be well received at Salisbury.' He shrugged again as if it did not matter unduly to him.

'But I cannot go back there.' Her voice fell to almost a whisper as the uncertain future beckoned with all its horrors.

'Why not? Would your brother not receive you?'

'Yes. Of course he would. It's not that…'

Rosamund's ability to muster an argument vanished as the image of Ralph de Morgan came forcibly into her mind. If she returned to Gilbert's jurisdiction… For a painful moment she swallowed, closed her eyes against the corpulent figure of Ralph with his ageing and unwashed body, suppressed a shudder. Marriage to him would be a thing of unending horror, of disgust. Her only knowledge of marriage was from the sad experiences of her mother, always discreet, but her sufferings were clear enough. One husband, her own father, a disgracefully uncouth knight with no polish and less breeding, who had treated Petronilla little better than a servant in his Hall. The other had all the polish and style any woman could want, but had been as cold as a fish, without the ability to love. Petronilla had had a lifetime of unhappiness. Did Rosamund want that? A life of hidden tears, of carefully controlled emotions that no one might guess at? A loneliness that was bone deep? All this would be hers. And then, worse then all the rest, there was the loathsome rankness of the man she would be forced to marry. She could not tolerate that. But nor could she explain why it was impossible for her to leave Clifford. It would destroy her pride to have this man look at her with pity in his face. Rosamund shook her head.

'I won't go,' was all she could find to repeat. And, clenching her skirts, would have stalked from the dais except that Fitz Osbern, with the reflexes of a hunting hawk, put out a hand as she passed and grasped her wrist, firm as a vice. His voice was as harsh as his grip; once more his predatory eyes fixed on her face.

'Lady. Do not mistake my intent. You'll leave tomorrow if I have to lift you bodily into the wagon with all your possessions. Be ready at daybreak.'

Without success, Rosamund tried to yank her wrist free. The dread of the absent Ralph was immediately replaced by hatred of the terrifyingly present Fitz Osbern, and it drove her into speech, without thought or consideration for the outcome. With an impulsiveness that Lady Petronilla recognised all too well and made her heart sink, Rosamund uttered the first thought that came into her head.

'If you do that, my lord, if you use physical force against me, I shall camp outside these gates until you either let me in again or I die from exposure to the rain and cold.'

'Ha! A foolish idea! The empty threat of a thwarted child who wants her own way!' A bark of laughter shook him, full of sheer incredulity. 'How would you think of so outrageous an action? You won't persuade me, whatever empty threats you make. I warned you not to resist me, did I not?'

'Rosamund…' murmured Lady Petronilla, who saw Fitz Osbern's dark brows snap together and immediately dreaded the outcome.

'No, Mother.' Rosamund did not spare Petronilla even a glance. All her attention was centred on this man who would rob and ridicule her. 'I will not be disinherited by this man. I will not be sent away from what is my own.'

'Of course you will,' Fitz Osbern replied. 'When you have taken time to think of the advantages of your home, you'll see the wisdom of it. A border fortress is no place for a woman alone, so you'll be a sensible girl and take yourself back to Salisbury. In a month you'll thank me for showing you the error your pride might have forced you to make.' A condescending smile touched the firm lips. Which made matters even worse.

'Oh, no!' She braced her wrist against his powerful fingers, but he did not let go. 'I shall sit outside my gates for as long as it takes. And if I do indeed die of cold, my death will be on your head. Are you willing to risk it, my lord?' Her mouth curved with the challenge.

Which brought him up short. His fingers tightened. 'Don't question my authority, lady!'

'Don't *you* push *me* into defiance, my lord!' And, snatching her wrist from his hold, Rosamund de Longspey swept from the dais and up the stairs to the solar without a backward glance. They watched her depart, her head held high. Until her mother, after a moment of pregnant silence, stood to follow with an apologetic smile.

'I think I should warn you, sir.' Her calm eyes were austere as they rested on Fitz Osbern. 'It is unwise to underestimate my daughter. She tends to do exactly as she says.'

'She'll not defy me,' Fitz Osbern remarked.

'I'd not wager on it,' Lady Petronilla replied over her shoulder. 'She can't afford to allow you to win.'

And then the Marcher lords were alone.

'I think Lady Petronilla's right, Ger. The girl might just do it, you know. She's in the mood to.' Hugh watched the final departing twitch of silk skirts around the turn in the stairs with serious contemplation and the faintest smile of admiration. 'Are you, as the girl said, indeed willing to risk it?'

'Risk? Nonsense.' Gervase turned his attention back to the neglected food and used his dagger to slice into the mutton. '*I* wager it'll rain tomorrow. A thorough drenching will spur her on her way quicker than any words of mine. And thank God for it! I suspect she'd be more troublesome to me than all the vermin in this place.'

Hugh de Mortimer was of a mind to agree. In his experience, women could be very tricky, and, he suspected, the daughter trickier than most. As for the widow… After her initial attack in the bailey, when her opinion of him appeared to be lower than if he were the rat just now scurrying along the edge of the wall toward the door, her composure in the circumstances was admirable. But what he *would* care to discover—he poked at some unappetising and unrecognisable dish of stewed vegetables—was what had put the depth of sadness in the widow's eyes. He turned his attention back to the meat. But of course it was none of his affair.

It proved to be an uneasy night in varying degrees for all.

Hugh de Mortimer consigned his musings of the widow to a pleasant dream that could never be fulfilled, wrapped himself in his cloak in one of the vacant tower rooms and slept the sleep of the untroubled.

Fitz Osbern, with the experience of soldiering that enabled him to sleep anywhere, in any discomfort, was none the less kept awake by a range of insistent thoughts. No one ignored his wishes. No one! Not since he had come of age and taken over control of the Monmouth lands. Lady Maude, his forthright mother, had learnt that quickly enough when she had thought to order his affairs as she had done her husband's. But that damned girl had. Defiant to the last, despite the fragility of the bones of her wrist under his fingers. And then there had been that definite mark of fear imprinted on her face, in those marvellous green eyes, when he had ordered her return to Earl Gilbert's house, before the hot fury took over when she spat her defiance at him. He would not consider that.

Damnation. Worse than a nagging tooth! What could be so bad in her cushioned life that she could not recognise Salisbury as a haven of peace and comfort? Irritated with himself, Fitz Osbern pulled his cloak over his head and willed himself to sleep.

Petronilla, in her deliberate calm manner, well practised through years of marriage to men who had no consideration for her feelings, was equally irritated. Why in heaven's name had she felt the need to explain her situation to the de Mortimer lord? Yet she had read such consideration in his face that she was tempted to smile at him… How foolish to be so flattered that she should blush like a girl! Had she not had enough of men? She would enjoy being a widow with a jointure and a home of her own. Besides, after tomorrow she would be unlikely to set eyes on Hugh de Mortimer ever again.

On which comforting thought she still found it impossible to sleep.

Whilst at her side in the west-tower chamber—the lord's chamber still not clean enough to her liking—her daughter stirred and twitched and gave up on any possibility of sleep. Rosamund knew that she had wilfully stirred the flames into a blaze, and now she would just have to be prepared to face the consequences of making impulsive declarations. The hours before dawn could be usefully occupied in planning each careful step if, as she feared, she was ejected through her own gates. So she applied herself to her task, but not before she closed her hand around her wrist, and was once again aware of the heat, the power in the man's grasp, the fierce but controlled anger in his body.

She closed her eyes against the little brush of memory that roughened her skin and sent a shaft of heat to her belly.

No. Rosamund's eyes snapped open. She would not, *could* not allow him to defeat her. Nor could she allow him to step into her dreams. Because she knew exactly who Gervase Fitz Osbern was. He was her Wild Hawk, of course.

The man who four years ago had rejected her with no more than a second look. Beneath the grime of travel and the unshaven cheeks he was the same man whose striking face she hadn't quite been able to forget. Although on close encounter she thought her memory must have been at fault. Fitz Osbern was obviously not the eye-catching individual she remembered, whose alliance Earl William had considered to be of some importance. The Earl of Salisbury would never seek to associate with this ruffian. Perhaps Fitz Osbern had fallen on hard times and been reduced to thievery and living off his wits. She sighed her disappointment that it should be so, then remembered her present grievance.

Hardly surprising that, given his total uninterest in her, both at Salisbury and here at Clifford, he had not even recognised her.

Chapter Four

The de Longspey party was up betimes, all their possessions packed. Rosamund was not foolish enough to believe that Fitz Osbern would not be true to his word. Her plan was risky. A dangerous wager. Had her blood father not been fond of wagers? Until one had killed him when he had risked a raid on a neighbouring Marcher lord's prize cattle, and that lord retaliated with a storm of fatal arrows. But there were no arrows here to kill and maim. At worst a cold wind and heavy showers, but discomfort would be the only danger. The prize, if her plan worked, would be weightier than gold. Her freedom more precious than any jewel.

She would show Lord Fitz Osbern that she was not a woman to be underestimated.

'Wear your warmest clothes,' she advised. 'As many layers as you can. And leave the quilts unpacked to be placed on top of the wagon. And…' she fixed both the Dowager Countess and Edith the serving woman with an intimidating eye '…not a word of complaint.'

Fitz Osbern and de Mortimer watched from the gatehouse tower as the little cavalcade started out, four of their own men in attendance as promised to ensure safe passage to Hereford.

Deliberately the Lord of Monmouth had absented himself when the ladies had broken their fast, so there had been no final communication between them. There was nothing more to say. He had made his intentions clear enough. No need to bandy words again with the girl. He saw them move slowly from the gates beneath him with relief.

'That sees the end of my immediate problem.' He turned his back to walk down the stairs into the bailey, looking up to address de Mortimer over his shoulder. 'Will you leave, Hugh? I can't offer you comfortable hospitality yet, but you're welcome to what I have.' He gave a wry grimace in acknowledgement of their disreputable surroundings.

'Tomorrow, I think.' Still inclined to keep the little party in view, de Mortimer made to follow.

'I shall start some rebuilding here.' Fitz Osbern, oblivious to his friend's distraction, was surveying the flooded inner court. 'And then I shall—'

'My lord, my lord…' The voice echoed from a guard above their heads. 'I think you should come and look…'

They climbed once again to the gatehouse battlements. Looked over. Frowned. Within little more than two hundred yards of the gate, on the flat piece of flood plain between castle, river and village, the well-loaded wagon had come to a halt. Fitz Osbern's mounted escort dismounted. Quilts were being shaken out, some of the packages unloaded on to the grass. The soldiers, after some conversation with the more eye-catching of the distant figures who waved her arm in obvious dismissal, turned their horses to return to the castle.

'God's blood!'

'I did warn you,' Hugh remarked. 'The lady has a war-like look in her eye. She looks as if she intends to stay. She's pitched her camp, you could say…'

Ignoring the amusement in de Mortimer's voice, Fitz Osbern watched in startled disbelief as the figures spread the quilts on the ground, wrapped themselves securely in their cloaks, hoods pulled up, and sat down to await events.

'A whim,' Fitz Osbern muttered. 'She'll soon tire of it. By midmorning they'll be gone. I'd wager my sword on it.' He marched off.

'I wouldn't!' Hugh de Mortimer called after him, laughing.

The rain started, at first a light soaking mist. Then a heavier patter.

'This'll do it, Hugh.' The Marcher lords had been unable to resist returning to their vantage point to assess developments. The women were as they had been some hours ago, but now the quilts had been pulled over their heads, the three figures huddled beneath and together for warmth. It was possible to just make out the dark shape through the rain.

'You have to give her credit, though.'

'For what?' Fitz Osbern struck his fist against the stone coping, but a little thread of worry, even shame, had begun to slide along his skin. 'Obstinacy and hard-headedness? If she thinks she'll shame me into opening the gates and inviting her back, she's wrong!'

The intensity of the rain increased.

'What are we doing, Rosamund?' Petronilla cringed beneath the quilts, unnaturally but understandably petulant. 'We shall die here. I can feel an ague coming on. I can feel the damp settling into my bones. I don't want to die here in the mud.' Her voice hitched in misery. 'I would rather be at Lower Broadheath.'

'And so you shall be.' Rosamund put her arm round her mother's shoulders. 'Of course we will not die. No man of chivalry, not even Fitz Osbern, would allow that to happen. Just wait a little longer.' She patted the hand of Edith, who had begun to sob.

'Are you sure he's a man of honour?' Petronilla sniffed. 'I'm not. Lord de Mortimer perhaps, but not Fitz Osbern.'

'Perhaps he's not. But de Mortimer will persuade him, will not allow it even if it's only to save *you* from discomfort. I would say he's very taken with you.'

All Lady Petronilla could do was splutter into the damp neck of her cloak.

'I won't give in. Not yet. Be courageous, Mother. We have so much to gain. I promise I'll not allow you to come to any harm.'

Rosamund tucked another quilt around Petronilla, uneasily aware that she might indeed be putting her mother's health in danger, sitting in the cold grass as the rain swirled around them. And what guarantee that the man would back down? There was none. But now was no time for second thoughts—she could afford to retreat as little as he. He had rejected her once and could readily do so again. He did not even remember her! Pride spurred her on, just as the anger racing through her blood kept her warm.

The rain pattered heavily on the soaked quilts.

'Is she still out there?'

'Yes! God's Blood!'

'Ger—you must do something. It's neither seemly nor honourable.'

Gervase Fitz Osbern huffed a breath against the worry that had become a distinct unease. 'If only the daughter were as biddable as the mother. Very well. I can't leave them out there. I must try persuasion rather than brute force. I'll send de Byton out to fetch them in—until better travelling weather. But further than that I will not bend. They can't stay here.'

On hearing the approach of hooves, Rosamund lifted the quilt and peered out to see de Byton, surly, reining in his horse.

'Well?' She scented victory, but kept her face stern.

De Byton wiped his face on his sleeve. 'My lord says you're to come within, lady.'

'No. We will not. Tell your master—for it seems you have betrayed your de Longspey loyalties—' heavy irony despite water dripping from her hood '—tell him I need to hear it from his own lips that I shall be invited back. That I shall be allowed to stay for as long as I wish. That I shall not be bullied into departing against my will.' She thought for a moment. 'And that I shall have the solar and the private chamber for my own use. He must come here and tell me himself. Do you understand?'

A short grunt was the only reply. De Byton wheeled his horse and cantered back.

'She says what?'

De Byton repeated the conversation with relish and a rare disgust for all womenkind, at that moment fully appreciated by Fitz Osbern. 'She's intransigent, my lord. She'll hear it only from yourself, my lord.'

'Will she, now?' The icy flash of anger did not bode well. Fitz Osbern leaned on the battlement and fixed his attention on de Mortimer, an idea developing. He faced his friend, expression bland.

'A simple solution. *You* could fetch them in, Hugh. Your words would be kinder than mine. You have a gift when appealing to the soft heart of a woman…'

'No. I won't. You're going to have to grasp the dagger's edge, Ger. It's you she wants, your assurance. You have no choice.'

Nor did he, Gervase acknowledged, as he wiped the rain from his face. She had won her battle. But what would be the consequences for him? Uncomfortable with his line of thought, he shrugged his shoulders against the weight of his wet jerkin. What would it be like for him to have this woman as effective chatelaine of his castle? When it should have been Matilda, his young wife who had not lived long enough to make the place her own. He frowned at the unwanted memory. A soft, pretty, fair-haired girl, who would have been a good wife to him, carried his children, presented him with an heir to the Fitz Osbern lands; with tuition from him, she would have held the reins of power in his name. But Matilda was dead and in her place, if he weakened, he would have this de Longspey woman on his hands, who needed no lessons from him in exerting her will, and who would surely see his retreat as a victory over him, and take it as a precedent.

He did not want that. He definitely did not want that.

Yet Gervase looked out at the sad little party under their soaked coverings and exhaled loudly. No, he had no choice but to take them back. Even if it meant Rosamund de Longspey stepping on the hem of Matilda's increasingly shadowy gown.

'I dislike surrender,' Gervase snarled.

'No such thing,' De Mortimer replied cheerfully. 'See it as an organised retreat before superior forces.'

'God's bones!'

'Well, lady, I'm here, as you requested.'

'I did not think you would come.' Rosamund scrambled from under the covering despite the relentless downpour, face raised to him, noting the heavy scowl, but determined to hold firm. Regardless of the rain, regardless of her heavily thudding heart, she fixed her eyes on his, praying that he would not think the raindrops on her lashes were a sign of female weakness.

'What do you want from me?' Fitz Osbern demanded.

'To return. I'm sure de Byton informed you of my terms, my lord.'

Rosamund had almost given up. She would admit to it. She knew that her mother would stand with her to the bitter end, but how could she be so thoughtless of Lady Petronilla's welfare for much longer? She was on the very edge of ordering that they load up the wagon and find shelter in the village. Or even in Hereford itself before she took her mother on to Lower Broadheath, where she deserved to be in all comfort. Rosamund's conscience had been on the point of pushing her to abandon her defiance to make that decision. There was, after all, a limit to the power of pride when dealing with those she loved, so few as they were. But now against all hope the bane of her existence was here, sitting his horse before her with all the arrogance she had come to recognise, and so she would not weaken. She raised her chin against a probable rejection.

'Well, my lord?'

The stare was as cold as the rain that trickled down her spine. The voice as harsh as the wind that moulded her sodden skirts against her legs. But the words were the golden chime of victory.

'You have won, lady. I have come to tell you that I agree to your terms.'

Rain dripped from the end of her straight nose, spangled her lashes. Translucent as a pearl, her skin glowed through the moisture. Fitz Osbern found it difficult to look away as he dismounted and stood before her. She was probably soaked to the skin through every inch of her clothing, her face was pale, her eyes wide with tension. He could see her whole body was braced against the chill that would have made her teeth chatter if she had allowed it. But her courage was unbroken as her head was unbowed, as she was magnificent in her determination to achieve her goal. A pity it was at his expense. The muscles in his gut tightened in—well, in concern, he told himself as she shuddered with a sudden cold blast of wind. But his anger was stirred as well, a faint ripple of it beneath the admiration, that she had bested him.

'You will agree to them? All of them?' she asked.

'Yes.' He inhaled, praying for patience. 'I want you to return with me.'

'For as long as I wish?'

'Yes.'

'And you will not force me out again?'

'No.' A veritable growl. 'As I agreed. Not unless it is by your own choice.'

'And I can have the solar and the private chamber for my own use?'

'Have I not said as much?'

'On your oath, my lord.' He saw her eyes shine through the wet.

'Do you want blood as well? On my oath, lady.' He clapped his hand to his chest somewhere in the vicinity of his heart, a deliberately dramatic gesture.

The lady managed a brisk nod. 'Then we will return.'

'Amen to that. Let's all get under cover before we die of this infernal downpour.' He tore his eyes from her brilliant gaze and bent to help Edith to her feet, then Petronilla, who was neatly folding quilts around her. 'Leave those, my lady. I will see to it.'

'Thank you,' she whispered. 'I am grateful.' The clutch of her hand on his expressed her heartfelt gratitude, easing his acute sense of defeat at her daughter's hands.

'Thank de Mortimer for your rescue. I was tempted to leave you here all night.' But his eyes were warm, belying his hard words as he handed the lady over to the care of one of his men-at-arms.

As he had expected, he found no gratitude whatsoever in Rosamund's face, only the triumph of a victory snatched against all the odds. But he saw that she waited until her mother and the maid were cared for, lifted on to horseback, watching as they were carried back the short distance to the gatehouse, before she considered her own comfort. Then she looked across at him, dishevelled and muddy as she was, the challenge still there, but also the vestige of a plea that he knew she would never willingly voice. As well as a deep weariness—it seemed to him from more than merely making her stand against him in appalling conditions, but as if the battle she had just fought was a bloody conflict, vital to her. Any remaining anger toward her dissipated. All he felt was a desire to lift the burden—whatever it might be—from her shoulders.

He held out his hand, palm up.

'Come, lady, sheath your sword. You can fight the battle another day. I think you've done enough for now.'

She considered him, even now resisting. 'I'll walk back. It's a mere step. I don't need—'

Stubborn to the last! Why did that not surprise him? 'No!' He stopped her. 'You will accept my offer of help. And you'll not argue the point.' Fitz Osbern swung up on to his horse, leaned and reached down his hand, in invitation or demand, whichever way she chose to see it. He would brook no denial. And Rosamund, presumably reading the determination stamped on his firm mouth, his tense jaw, accepted, without comment, and in one lithe movement was lifted to the saddle before him where he settled her firmly in his arms and, with a click of his tongue, a shortening of the reins, urged his horse into a walk.

The girl sat rigid, precariously balanced, holding her body away from him as if she could not bear that he should touch her. If his stallion spooked, she would surely fall off.

'I won't bite,' he murmured against her wet hood, impatience returning. 'Or not yet at any rate. And I'd rather not have to stop and dismount to pick you up out of the mud.'

Although she made no reply, he knew that she had heard. She stiffened. Then, with a little sigh, she leaned back against his chest and the support of his arms.

So Gervase, with curling strands of his enemy's hair escaping her hood and brushing his chin, contemplated what might lie ahead considering the terms he had just agreed to. He was not optimistic for the outcome. For one thing, it could have no permanency. She could not stay at Clifford for ever, no matter what he had promised. Some suitable arrangement must be made for her. But the de Longspey heiress was too wilful by half, with no sense of what was reasonable behaviour. He simply could not see a clear path here.

The stallion side-stepped as Bryn loped beneath his hooves, causing Gervase to settle the woman more firmly against him. She did not resist. Indeed, he felt her fingers close on his arm and her body settle more closely against his, her spine relaxing. But then he recalled the previous day when some species of fear—or so he had thought—had robbed her face of all colour.

Perhaps he should take the time to discover the cause of such a reaction to his threat to turn her out. As for the moment, he was forced to acknowledge a pleasure in simply holding her close, the curve of her breast against his forearm.

Fitz Osbern dismounted in the bailey. He reached up to Rosamund and, his hands at her waist, helped her to slide down to her feet. Rosamund would have stood alone, calling on her dignity to hold her erect and still defiant, but the cold and damp had had their effect, stiffening her limbs. She staggered as her cold feet took her weight, so that momentarily she clung to his arms for balance, grateful when he held her.

His first words startled her.

'Did I do that?'

Looking down, she saw the faintest of shadows of a bruise on her wrist. And remembered that he had restrained her the previous night. 'Yes.'

'I will never hurt you again.' Soft-voiced, Fitz Osbern gently touched the mark with his fingertips, then astonished her further by bending his head to press his lips there.

'Don't…!'

'Don't what?'

'I don't want your attentions…' She snatched her hand away. Surely he would feel the tumultuous blood pulsing, racing through her veins, if he kissed her wrist again?

His eyes darkened, his mood changed immediately. 'If you mean by *my attentions* that you don't want my mouth against your skin—then don't put yourself in my way, lady. You have won your victory today. Make sure it's not at a price you are unwilling to pay.'

Rosamund could not believe her ears. Her lips parted in shock.

And Fitz Osbern promptly kissed them. Fast, but very thoroughly.

'Well, Rose? What have you to say now?'

She gasped. Could think of nothing sensible. 'That I have

not given you leave to use my name in that way,' she managed finally.

And before he could do or say anything further, tearing herself away from his relaxed hold, Rosamund fled to her chamber where, considerate beyond anything Rosamund could have believed, Fitz Osbern had already left instructions for water to be heated for the women, and the wooden tub to be carried there. The courtesy passed unnoticed. Fear gripped her, a depth of dread of which she had no experience. She had *feared* marriage with Ralph de Morgan. This emotion was entirely different. Her heart thundered, her cheeks coloured to the tint of a winter pippin. She was very much afraid of the Wild Hawk. Her reaction to him was quite inappropriate. Pressing her fingers to her mouth, she realised that she could still taste his kiss. And ran her tongue slowly over her lips to savour it.

This can't last, Rosamund, Fitz Osbern thought. It's like living in the middle of a thunderstorm.

It hung over them, a deep and lowering threat. The whole fortress waited uneasily, holding its breath for the approaching cataclysm. It could not be expected that Fitz Osbern and de Longspey would live amicably side by side for long. Disputed ownership would have to end some time, whatever promise had been forced from him when under pressure.

Before the storm could break, Hugh de Mortimer made his departure, his own concerns in Hereford needing his attention. He acknowledged to himself a reluctance to go. He would like to watch the outcome of this imminent clash of wills. He parted from Fitz Osbern when they broke their fast on a late dawn, the first lightening of the sky heralding a fine day.

'Farewell, Ger. You're well settled then, I think.'

'Yes. So it seems.' Fitz Osbern continued to plough his way through a plate of roast mutton.

De Mortimer thought for a moment, then drained his tankard

and pushed to his feet. 'Is this *impasse* between you and the lady to be long term?'

Fitz Osbern barely glanced up, as if his mind was elsewhere. 'No. I know not what's in her mind, but it can't be permanent.'

'But, as I recall, you promised—'

'That I would not get rid of her unless she agreed to ride out on her own decision. I know and I'll respect that.' He brushed crumbs from his fingers and rose to his feet. 'But there are ways and means to make life less than comfortable here. And if nothing else prevails to dislodge her, a good fall of snow will probably prompt her departure. To be snowed in for weeks at a time on siege rations will surely sap her stubborn will.' He angled his chin in thought. 'I think I can dislodge her without that.'

'So you intend persuasion.' They made their way to the door.

'Yes.' A distinctly wolfish smile touched the dark features. 'Nothing to bring harm to either one of them,' Fitz Osbern assured as de Mortimer's brows climbed. 'I can be boorish company, an uncivilised lout as Lady Rosamund put it, as well as the next man without putting either woman in any serious danger. If they decide they would rather live elsewhere—in pleasanter surroundings where chivalrous conversation is the order of the day…' his grin widened '…then so much the better.'

De Mortimer pursed his lips as he considered it. 'I suppose it'll work. You know your own mind, my boy. Good luck.'

'I don't need luck. By the time you return, the castle will be entirely mine.'

Thinking that it might not be as easy as that, de Mortimer took his leave of the women. Both smiled on him. Both wished him well and hoped to see him again in the future.

Did he imagine it, or did Lady Petronilla allow her fingers to rest in his longer than was entirely necessary when he took her hand in his rough palm and planted a kiss on her fingers? Did he read the shy invitation in her eyes correctly? But take care, he warned himself. She was a lady of birth and quality. This was not an area in which to consider anything more than a light-hearted dalliance. Certainly not a liaison of a deeper nature, nor the taking of mere physical pleasure. Petronilla de Longspey should be approached with respect and gentle handling. And he, on his own admission, had no thought of marriage. Nevertheless, she had a sharp wit and a quick astuteness he suspected, hidden under her careful composure. She attracted him. What's more, sensing some shadow of unhappiness lingering in her face, he felt an unexpected urge to protect her, from what he was not sure. She was small boned and delicate, and Hugh found himself considering the necessity of a man sheltering her from the storms of life. Foolish! But he would like to renew her acquaintance.

He caught Petronilla alone, not by chance for either party, halfway down the stairs from the solar.

'Will you indeed return?' she asked.

'I think I must.' An enigmatic reply, to cause the lady to arch her brows.

'And why is that, Lord Hugh?'

'To see you again, dear lady.' And, against all his previous good sense, and to the amazement of both of them, he leaned to drop a gentle kiss on her surprised lips, leaving to lope down the stairs with agile ease before he could commit himself further and before she could catch her breath.

When Rosamund commented on her mother's bright eyes and pink cheeks, she received an entirely unbelievable explanation that the Dowager Countess had run up the stairs too quickly. Which did not fool her keen-eyed daughter one bit as her mother hid her flustered movements in a thorough and unnecessary reorganisation of her embroidery silks.

'I take it Lord Hugh has finally gone.'

'Yes.' Uncharacteristically abrupt, Petronilla picked up a piece of embroidery, but did not sit or appear to be motivated to apply her needle.

'Are you sorry?'

'No. How should I be?'

Rosamund chose to make no further comment but cynically considered the matter to be of little moment. What had her mother said a mere matter of weeks ago? Two husbands are enough? Lady Petronilla was easily pleased if she could be flattered by the rough attentions of a grizzled border lord. Rosamund did not consider her mother to be easily pleased at all.

Casting that thought aside, Rosamund gave her attention to more pressing concerns. Her own apartments. She had never visited one of the royal palaces, but she had heard tell Queen Eleanor had magnificent style. A wealthy heiress in her own right, married to King Louis of France, she knew what it was to live in luxury and, since her second marriage some six years before to King Henry, she had brought her influence to bear.

'Tell me again of the Queen's bower at Woodstock,' she asked.

So Petronilla did, painting a beguiling picture of panelled rooms and tiled floors with glass in the windows. Silken hangings and oriental carpets cushioned the life of Eleanor and her ladies. Lit by sweet-scented oil, perfumed with incense, it was a far cry from the draughty, smoke-filled Great Hall at Clifford lit by flaring torches with their burden of soot, or guttering rush lights.

Rosamund listened as she stood in the bare solar, now hers. Closing her eyes, she could imagine what it could be like. A delight to the senses. Nothing as grand as the Queen's bower, of course. She grimaced, amused, at the thought of fine table linen such as Queen Eleanor used being mauled by grubby hands in her Great Hall here in Clifford. But Clifford was now her home and she would create a haven in her solar against the bleak borders outside her walls.

As she opened her eyes, her attention was caught by a quick movement by the bare hearth. A shadow slunk along the wall. A grey cat, little more than a kitten, one of the brood that inhabited the kitchens or stables. Thin and unnervingly sly, it ignored the de Longspey occupants, inspected the cold hearth with apparent disfavour, then leapt to curl into the corner of a settle. It stared at Rosamund with green eyes much like her own.

'Not a pretty animal,' Petronilla commented.

'No.' Rosamund laughed. 'But if nothing else, even if we can never replicate Eleanor's accommodations here, at least we shall be free of mice.'

Rosamund hugged the Countess with impulsive pleasure. There was nothing for her to fear after all; Fitz Osbern was keeping his distance from her. She would indeed make this castle her home. And Gervase Fitz Osbern could do nothing to prevent her.

Chapter Five

Hardly had de Mortimer ridden off than the baggage wagons belonging to Fitz Osbern eventually caught up with their lord to arrive at Clifford. They were unpacked and the contents, considerable in the number of chests and bundles, were carried into the west tower that had now become his personal domain. At least he has baggage! Rosamund thought. Although unspoken between them, it was quite natural that both de Longspey women expected to see some outer improvement in the new self-styled Lord of Clifford, something to reflect his new status as a lord of property, rather than a mercenary seeking an income from any man who would pay. No longer a soldier on the move, he would have no excuse but to improve on his unimpressive appearance. Rosamund secretly anticipated the result. Perhaps she would once again see the man who had come to face Earl William and throw his offer back in his face, rather than the robber who had stolen her castle from her.

But at supper over a dish of bland pottage, her heart plummeted. Spoon hovering in mid-air between dish and lips, she stared at his approach across the Hall.

'Well, lady?' He strode on to the dais. For a moment it seemed that he would bow to the Countess and herself. But she must have been mistaken. He turned abruptly, hooked up a stool, stretched out his legs and reached across the table to pull the flagon of ale closer. He filled a cup, clumsily splashing liquid over the sides, then lifting it to his lips, he fixed her with an uncompromising look, demanding a response.

'Not a thing, my lord.' She would not give him the satisfaction of knowing her disapproval, so pinned a smile to her lips. Unfortunately, despite the baggage, the uncivilised unkempt plunderer still remained. Hair, still untidy and untrimmed, fell lankly over his forehead. His cheeks remained rough with incipient beard. He had managed a change of clothes, to be sure, but looked no better clad than his men and far worse than some. A plain tunic, worn and threadbare in patches, was the short serviceable raiment of a soldier and his coarse hose still showed streaks of dried mud. From the state of his heavy boots, he had come straight to the table from the stables. No jewels, no decoration… He looked, Rosamund decided in that rapid survey, as if he had barely two gold coins in the world to chink together. Yet, to her disgust, the compelling stare from those grey eyes caused a curl of heat to centre in her belly where nerves fluttered restless wings. An image leapt into her mind of that stern mouth pressed against the soft skin of her wrist, even against her lips.

'What is it?' he persisted as she continued to appraise him.

She could hardly tell him that she felt an unsettling urge to raise her fingers to his cheek, to stroke them over the rough skin and unsmiling lips, so sought for an acceptable reason for her preoccupation, snatching at the obvious.

'I have noticed you are limping, my lord.'

'A healing wound. Nothing long-lasting,' Fitz Osbern pronounced, reaching out for the jug of ale again. 'My opponent on the occasion suffered worse injuries.'

'Oh…'

'I can be a man of vicious passions.' He sneered over his cup. 'I killed him. Is that all?'

And when she shook her head, appalled at the brutal

response, and dropped her gaze to her cup, it was not before she saw his lips curve disdainfully.

'He was a knight who discovered it was unwise to set himself up as my enemy. He's dead now.'

Rosamund found no reply.

From that point, Fitz Osbern gave all his attention to the meal and, since Hugh de Mortimer was no longer present, with barely a word for his companions. Instead he applied himself with enthusiasm to the platters of food and even more to the ale. There was no conversation broached by him. Any response to the attempts by Lady Petronilla to begin an exchange of views was monosyllabic at best, otherwise a mere grunt around a mouth of roast meat. Rosamund did not even try as her disgust grew. As soon as he had finished, with a curt inclination of his head as his only acknowledgement of his fair company, he pushed himself to his feet.

'Don't stay here.' His order was brusque, harsh. 'Unless you wish to join my men in drinking and coarse jokes. I don't advise it.'

Only stopping to drain his cup once again, he took himself off about his own concerns.

'Well?' Rosamund enquired of her mother as she tapped her ivory comb against the linen bed cover. It was late. The castle lapsed into silence around them, apart from the voices of the soldiers raised in raucous singing below them. Rosamund winced at a particularly loud roar of appreciation.

'What's that, dear Rose?' Lady Petronilla dozed comfortably by the fire.

'The self-styled Lord of Clifford. Courtesy and court manners have not yet reached the Marches, it seems. I was not impressed. I cannot imagine the content of his baggage wagons if that was the best he could do!' Rosamund had spent some considerable time in contemplation of the man who would own her castle and order her life.

'He was not attentive,' Petronilla admitted. 'Perhaps a Marcher lord sees no need to polish his manners. Your father could be just as boorish when preoccupied. Which was much of the time.'

'I don't know about that.' Not particularly interested in John de Bredwardine's lack of polish, Rosamund's dark brows knit into a frown as she considered her impressions of the meal. She removed her veil and began to loosen the bindings on her hair. 'All I can say is Fitz Osbern is no better than a savage. He took no care with his appearance, his conversation was no better than that of one of the grooms. As for his manners in polite company! It might be all very well when on campaign, but he wiped his mouth on his sleeve. He even admitted to bloody murder!'

Petronilla turned her head against the cushion, frowning a little. 'He had very little to say for himself, for sure. A little rough around the edges.'

'He dug into that platter of braised rabbit as if he hadn't eaten in a se'ennight!'

'True.'

'What's more, he drained the ale in his cup so frequently— how he was able to walk from the Hall I know not.'

Petronilla sighed. It was all true. 'But he is well intentioned, I think. We have him to thank for the improvements here.' She stretched her toes to the fire.

'Only because he wants the castle for himself, so it's in his interests to make improvements! Don't be deceived, Mother. He's not at all well intentioned toward us,' Rosamund remarked. She drew her comb through the length of her hair, feeling it prickle with the pressure and the warm air as she gathered the silky mass into her hands and considered the problem that she could not solve. It simply did not add up. Why would Earl William even consider an alliance with such an uncouth manner of man as Fitz Osbern? The eye-catching image of the Wild Hawk as she remembered him at Salisbury sprang into her mind. Remembering again now, recalling her unbidden reaction to him, the flutter returned to her belly. Just as when he had carried her on his horse back to the castle, when she had been lured into resting against him, against his strength and warmth. If she closed her eyes now, it was almost possible to feel the hard lines of chest and thigh against her body. To sense his breath warm against her cheek, to sense his arms enclosing her and holding her. And then he had had the temerity to kiss her. The muscles of her belly clenched at the heat of his mouth on her wrist, then on her lips in that one hard kiss. The dark heat, the seductive texture of his voice. *I will never hurt you again…*

Rosamund shook herself. How could she recall such disrespect with any level of pleasure? His apology—probably dragged from him—had turned to blatant threats within the space of a heartbeat. If she were not careful, it would make her forget her plan of revenge. And perhaps the change in him was easy enough to explain. Mercenaries were dependent on money earned for questionable services rendered. Clearly Fitz Osbern's fortunes had declined. He no longer had a lord to keep him in fine clothes to hide his coarse nature.

As for all that talk of Clifford being a part of the land granted to the Fitz Osberns by the Conqueror—a likely tale! A charade calculated to impress. No doubt she had been saved from a terrible fate when he had refused to wed her. What would life be like tied to this man? As bad, if not worse, as for her mother tied to boorish John of Bredwardine, she suspected.

Rosamund began to braid her hair for the night. Gervase. An attractive name, unlike its bearer. Still, she must deal carefully with Gervase Fitz Osbern. It could be dangerous to underestimate him. But if he thought he would frighten her into leaving, he was wrong. *She* would not be the one to go. Nor would she allow herself to be swayed from her self-imposed task. A little conspiratorial smile curved her mouth. And that task must begin immediately.

'Mark my words,' she finished her train of thought as she pulled the covers from the bed, 'despite his promise of fair treatment, I think we can expect nothing from Fitz Osbern but insensitivity and callous indifference. I think he will use any and every opportunity to get me out of this castle. But I won't go, whatever threats he makes against me.'

I dare not. For if I do, what is there for me in life? The uncomfortable thought slipped into her mind before she could push it away.

In the west tower, Gervase stretched and disrobed with smug satisfaction, in no sense displeased with Rosamund de Longspey's opinion of him. She saw him as the uncivilised lout she had accused him of being. Shrugging his shoulders against the coarse material of his campaigning gear as he stripped it off, Gervase Fitz Osbern laughed softly, causing the hound stretched before the fire to raise its head from its paws.

'What do you think, Bryn?' he asked. 'I think she suspects me of all sorts of evil intent, of any depth of uncouth behaviour. How I managed to pour so much ale into my cup and drink so little I'll never know. I think I even admitted to excessive violence toward my enemies.' He sat before the fire. 'It's exhausting being a robber lord. I must remember to swagger and glower more.'

The hound closed its eyes with a sigh.

'If you agree, then so much the better. I'm obviously so far below her in wealth, intellect and standing, she'll not be able to tolerate life under my control. She's as damnably proud and intolerant as any of the de Longspeys.' Gervase stirred the somnolent Bryn with the toe of his boot. 'Though I have to admit to the temptation to kiss her pretty manipulating fingers. Her lips were sweet enough.'

He yawned and for a brief moment stared down into the glow of the ash as if he would conjure up an image there. A fancy piece of work, Rosamund de Longspey, bred up in all the wealth and soft luxury of the de Longspey household. He might have sneered, then remembered that her true sire was John de

Bredwardine, a Marcher lord out of the same stable as himself. If he was her father, there must be a strain of toughness somewhere within her. But it had not been obvious as she sat at the board in a fine gown of Flemish cloth, covered over by a loose over-robe of distinctive style. Blue, he recalled, a deep vibrant colour. He hitched a shoulder. Cecilia, his vivacious sister, with her youthful mind stuffed with exploits of King Arthur's knights and fashionable attire, would have died for such a garment and called the colour *pers,* or perhaps even *pavonalilis,* a ridiculously fanciful name, but it was blue to his eyes. And very becoming, if not fit for life in a border castle.

The image of Rosamund gained in intensity. Nor were the jewels that winked on her fingers fit for anything but a Court appearance at Westminster, the gems in the brooch that fastened the neck of her gown, emeralds that rivalled the green of her eyes, or that glittered in the belt that cinched her slim waist. In fact, he discovered to his discomfort that he could imagine the gown hugging her figure to great advantage with no difficulty at all. As for her hair… Burnished gold bound with blue ribbons, it lay softly over her breasts, weighted at the ends with silver ornaments so that the length of it reached easily to her hips. Probably all false, he decided. Cecilia had just such an ambition if Lady Maude, her mother, did not stop her, to lengthen her own tresses to at least her waist with skeins of silk.

In fact, there were some uncomfortable similarities between his mischievous handful of a sister and Rosamund de Longspey. Both of them, he suspected, driven by an urge to thwart male authority. But Cecilia was still very young and hopefully biddable, a state of mind, he suspected, that could never be attributed to the Lady Rosamund.

The hard mouth softened under the memory. Women were capable of such subterfuge in the interests of their appearance. Without doubt, the de Longspey heiress was very decorative, which entirely failed to hide her strength of will. She'd been willing enough to camp out in the rain. He must beware of that stubborn strain of Marcher blood. Who would have thought that such a glamorous graceful creature would…?

With a grunt Gervase turned from the attractive picture in the remnants of the fire, pulled Bryn's ears to reduce the animal to a state of bliss, and poured a final cup of ale. Since when had he become a connoisseur of the female figure? And there was no doubt that she stirred his blood. The tightening of the muscles in his gut, the increasing pressure in his loins left him in no doubt of that at all. Not a reaction he would have sought in the circumstances, when his inclination was to strip the fine gown from her, discover every swell and curve of her with hands and mouth before taking her in ultimate possession.

God's blood!

Why not just get rid of her? Put her on her horse and escort her out whether she resisted or not?

Because he had given his word, he admitted. Not the wisest of moves, but he had given his oath, to allow her to stay on her own terms until she chose to go. As a man of principle, a man of honour, he could hardly change his mind. To break that promise even to a self-confessed enemy would go against the grain. She might consider him capable of any outage, but he was not so reprehensible as to break a freely-given oath.

Not that the de Longspey girl would know that. The curve of his mouth became wry. He must mask any honourable tendencies. Had he not almost apologised for putting that bruise on her wrist? Gervase frowned heavily. Such a thoughtless action when dealing with her had been unworthy of him, despicable. He shrugged against a wash of shame, that he had been so careless. He would make sure it did not happen again.

Well, he would give her a week here at Clifford. Two at the outside before the winds and rains drove her out. All in all, he was satisfied. She detested him and sneered at his lack of polish—all very well. Now the battle could begin. His sword was drawn. It was time to turn the blade and get the de Longspey women out of his castle.

* * *

On the following morning, unaware that he was being observed, in a lull in the persistent wet Gervase Fitz Osbern organised an impromptu mock-battle in the bailey between his soldiers, using sword and shield. Although there had been no call on their military proficiency since their return from Anjou, it would not do to allow their skills to rust through disuse. So Rosamund, attracted by the commotion, found herself kneeling on the window seat in the solar to look down into the bailey. She frowned at the swell of noise, and even more at the sight of Fitz Osbern himself in the midst of the *mêlée*. Rosamund would have denied that her mind was truly engaged in watching these manly pursuits, despite her blatant consideration of Fitz Osbern's splendid physique as he raised his sword in seemingly ferocious attack against his sergeant-at-arms. Her eyes widened, her lips pressed into a little *moue* of appreciation as he feinted, spun on his heel and drove the heavy weapon home against Watkins's shield with such force that the man was disarmed. Such incomparable grace, hard-muscled skill. She blinked as those muscles braced in shoulder and thigh, straining against a renewed attack from the sergeant. The flex of his lithe body as he grasped Watkins's arm to pull him to his feet, his face alight with a grin of conquest, held all her attention. Then a joke she could not hear. Laughter erupted from the group.

After which Fitz Osbern gave his attention to the young lad who was his squire. Owen, his name. Small of stature and still young enough to miss his own home, she suspected. Certainly still new to the use of arms. The sword and shield, hoisted in his thin arms, positively dwarfed him. She leaned forward to watch. With patient encouragement Fitz Osbern demonstrated how to hold the shield to prevent being skewered by a rapacious foe, how to feint and parry with the sword, then stood four-square before him, encouraging the lad to strike at him. Rosamund found herself laughing at Owen's attempts. There was never any chance that he would home in on his target.

Until Fitz Osbern dropped the blade of his own sword and allowed a fairly accurate lunge to strike against his shield over his heart. He staggered and groaned realistically before dropping to one knee.

'A hit! A kill!' Owen crowed out with triumph.

'Not any time soon!' she heard Fitz Osbern reply as he rose to his full height. 'But well enough, boy. Your eye's good enough.' He ruffled Owen's hair. 'Let's try again—and this time watch your left side. I could've stabbed you through the guts a dozen times. Then what would your mother have to say…'

Owen grinned and took up the heavy sword once more.

Rosamund was transfixed at the sheer good humour, the awareness of the boy's inexperience, yet with a care for his dignity. Fitz Osbern's physical dominance overawed her. He was magnificent, and for the briefest of moments she wished she could feel the slide of those sleek muscles under her hands.

Never!

So he had a good rapport with his men. Did that make him any less of a savage? For a lady who was not interested, she spent considerable time in enjoying the scene. Until, she persuaded herself, the racket of shouts and groans and metal striking metal became excruciating to the ears of a well-born lady. What possible interest could she find in a parcel of uncouth soldiery? Or their lord, who was just as infuriatingly masculine as they? In the end with a huff of a breath she turned her back, sinking deep in thought; thoughts that were, apparently, pleasing. Despite the groove between her brows, a smile hovered around her lips.

She had a plan. All it required was the courage to put it into action. And she needed an ally.

An hour later, Rosamund engaged in a lengthy conversation with Master Pennard, the perfect ally who resented Sir Thomas de Byton's crude authority, and was thus willing to side with his mistress against Fitz Osbern. Master Pennard's smile became slyer by the minute, his eyes hooded by drooping folds of parchment-like skin as they gleamed with appreciation of the chance to get one over on his adversary.

'I am entirely at your service, my lady.' He bowed low over her hand.

'I am grateful.' She tried not to snatch her hand away from the scrape of his dry fingers. Master Pennard was very much like the grey cat that had taken up permanent occupation in her solar, unprepossessing, unattractive, totally self-interested, but undoubtedly useful, she decided.

Master Pennard promised to do all he could.

'The Hall is where my men will eat and sleep and spend their spare time, lady. I don't expect them to be turned out because you are of a mind to renew the rushes, scrub the walls or any other such whim. Not even for one day in the present climate.' Gervase stood foursquare before her in the middle of the Great Hall, blunt and accusing. 'Watkins tells me you have barred them all until further notice.'

Rosamund had the vantage point of the dais, again, and looked down her straight nose at him. 'It is disgusting in here.' He watched the pretty nose wrinkle at the stench and had some sympathy, but now was not the time. 'This is my castle and I will tolerate it no longer.'

He raised his voice in deliberate aggression. 'Then take yourself off to your solar, lady. An easy solution.'

Whatever it took her to face him, and it took all her courage in the face of his simmering anger, the determined chin lifted. 'It would give me the greatest of pleasure not to enter this—this *cow byre*—but I will not endure the disgrace of this place any longer. It will take no more than a day, or two at most. Tell your men to stay in the stables. Or to make use of the east tower.'

'The east tower's as filthy as this. It's not fit.'

Ignoring his refusal, Rosamund turned to her steward, who waited for his orders. 'Master Pennard, I expect the servants to be in here with brushes and water within the half-hour. I want to see less soot on the walls by the end of the day. And I want these rushes cleared—all of them.'

Gervase advanced a step, hand on sword hilt. 'Did you not hear my refusal? You do not have my permission.'

'I heard. But I will have this midden cleaned, with or without your permission. Your men can find their comfort elsewhere.' Then, without another glance in his direction, Rosamund stalked past him, her skirts just about brushing against his boots.

As if he did not exist!

Gervase stood and stared after her. So she would defy him, would she? Not that he didn't agree with her about the state of the Hall. What man of any noble upbringing would not? But she would not ride roughshod over his demands or his men's needs. It was time she learnt that he was a power to be reckoned with. His fingers tapped against the hilt of his sword as he was forced to admit that his campaign was not without its difficulties and was not proceeding quite according to plan. Considering this immediate clash of wills, in which she had undoubtedly emerged the victor, he was about to have a major battle on his hands.

'God's blood! Is she always so uncompromising? She could at least wait until the rain stopped before turning us all out—'

'My lord?'

He spun on his heel, surprised to see the Dowager Countess, neat and trim, head tilted like a robin, watching him with interest—and not a little amusement. A gentler lady altogether, until he found mild grey-green eyes locked with his, with just as direct stare as the… as the *vixen*…who had just refused to do as he said. He thought the robin might just be about to snap up a tasty wireworm.

Gervase frowned. 'Your daughter, lady. Is she always so damned difficult?' he demanded, not mincing words. 'Intractable would not be too strong a word.'

'Yes…no.' The Countess's lips twitched. 'Well, sometimes…'

He gave a bark of laughter, his interest caught. 'That's clear enough, then!'

The Countess squared her shoulders, as courageous as her daughter. 'Perhaps I should make Rosamund's excuses, my lord. My daughter can be…forthright, when her emotions are engaged.'

'Then I must be sure not to engage them!'

'That would be difficult, my lord.'

'So I think.'

The Countess hesitated, then surprised him by placing a hand on his sleeve, her fingers curling softly into the cloth. 'You could try to give her the benefit of the doubt, my lord. Rosamund has had a very trying time of late.'

'So have I had a trying time.'

'But you have the upper hand here, you have the ultimate power, and my daughter does not. It will take her a little time to learn it. You might have…patience.'

Gervase became aware that all his frustrations had drained away, a dangerous situation, under the pressure of that one small hand. The Dowager Countess was of a managing disposition, it seemed, under her mild exterior. He would do well to bear it in mind. He covered her hand with his own. 'Lady Petronilla—you are the bringer of all good sense. Why can your daughter not be more like you?'

'She is her own person,' she replied calmly, 'and I love her for it.'

'You are an inestimable woman, I suspect, Lady Petronilla. I accept your advice.' At the last moment Gervase prevented himself from enfolded that small hand in his and kissing her fingers with rare grace. Saluting the lady's fingers in such a style was not in character for a marauding brigand who would rob a lady of her birthright. 'You have intelligence as well as beauty, lady,' he allowed himself to say. It crossed his mind that Hugh de Mortimer had better watch his step.

'So has my daughter!' replied the widow, blushing furiously at the unexpected compliment.

'If she had intelligence, she would have left Clifford long ago,' he snapped. 'Perhaps you should warn her to use her good sense and keep out of my way in future!'

Intent on baiting the thorn in his flesh, Gervase watched her cross the bailey, skirts held fastidiously high out of the mud, allowing him a glimpse of her neat ankles. His smile broadened. If she did realise she would immediately drop the skirts in the mud, regardless of the damage. Since she did not, he enjoyed her graceful figure as she disappeared into the ramshackle hut that called itself a kitchen. Gervase promptly followed her.

She was no longer to be found there, but the cook, engaged in stirring a pot on the fire, dimpling at the arrival of the lord in her little kingdom, nodded her chin toward the dairy. Snatching up a flat bread, he pursued his quarry. Still she was not to be found in the dank cool of the room. But he could hear voices in conversation, something about the rind on the cheese, from beyond the door that opened into a new makeshift enclosure for the animals. So he would wait for her. Taking a bite of the rough bread, he felt himself under the close scrutiny of the two dairy maids who, sleeves turned back, skirts tucked up, had been churning butter. They stopped, glanced nervously through their lashes, then curtsied. He smiled vaguely at them, his mind elsewhere. Then, hearing the return of the voices, of Rosamund's voice in particular, he seized the opportunity.

When Rosamund re-entered the dairy with Master Pennard in reluctant tow, thoroughly irritated by his lack of interest in the quality of the cheese, it was to find the bread discarded on the window ledge and Fitz Osbern with an arm around the waist of a hectically flushed dairy maid, engaged in whispering in her ear.

'Oh…!'

Rosamund halted. Master Pennard goggled. The girls giggled, in no way put out. Fitz Osbern did not let go, but planted a kiss on the nearest pink cheek.

'Fitz Osbern!' Rosamund sought desperately for words. How often had this man robbed her of sensible speech? And why this little scene had disturbed her so much she had no clear idea. 'Out!' was the best she could do, frowning as the two girls fled, giggling still. 'Master Pennard, I'll speak with you later.'

And then they were alone in the little whitewashed room. And he was positively smirking at her! Those predatory eyes looked her up and down, with a very knowing gleam, from the crown of her head to her muddied feet, until she felt herself as pink and heated as the maid who had fled the scene. She could feel the scorch of his arrogant stare even through the layers of her mantle and tunics. Her breathing shallow, she raised her chin.

'How dare you!'

'How dare I what?' He lounged insolently against the abandoned butter churn.

'How dare you look at me as if…?' She sank her teeth in her bottom lip to gain control of her temper.

'As if…?'

Was he laughing at her, mocking her? He was certainly enjoying her discomfiture. 'As if I were a cherry pie!'

A roar of laughter caused her blush to deepen.

'Cherry? Too tart for that, sweet Rose. Damson, perhaps.'

She gritted her teeth against the sheer foolishness of this conversation that she had allowed herself to start. It would have been far wiser to simply ignore the whole affair. But it was not in her nature to let it go. 'Perhaps, my lord…' with awful irony '…you could find better things to do with your time than inflict your presence on my maids. They deserve your respect, even if, apparently, I do not. I am informed that one section of the palisade is in imminent danger of collapse.' And she would have stalked past him, anything to put distance between them, but, quick as a snake, he side-stepped to bar her way.

'I don't think the maid objected. But I could kiss you instead, lady, if you would rather.' And snagged one of her braids to hold her still.

'Let go of me!'

'In fact, I think I would far rather kiss you. Let's try it.'

'You will not!' Before she could weigh the consequence of her actions, Rosamund lifted her hand to strike that imperious face, to force him to release her hair.

'Oh, no, you don't!' Gervase's reactions were faster than hers. He grasped her arm, but only to pull her hand to his mouth so that he might kiss the delicate skin of her inner wrist where her blood leapt and throbbed, at the same time preventing her from tightening her hand into a useful fist. 'Such thorns for so tender a flower! You will only strike me, gentle Rose, when I allow you to do so.'

Then as her lips parted to damn him for his temerity, he dragged her close, an arm around her waist to lift her to her toes, his hard mouth, suddenly unsmiling, a bare inch from hers.

Rosamund gasped.

Gervase held her tight, his breath warm on her face, so that all Rosamund's consciousness was wrapped up in the strong beat of his heart against hers. The awareness of his dominance, the sheer power of his body, swept through her veins to her very fingertips. Her own heart beat in unison. The heat of him against her rippled along her skin. She could feel the strength of his will, taste it. It was as if she were drowning in the gold-flecked depths of his eyes.

Then, without warning, he lowered his head to trace the outline of her bottom lip with his tongue. A little nip of teeth into the softness, followed by a soothing caress. Involuntarily, Rosamund's lips parted in invitation on a catch of breath. A hum of impossible pleasure. A hiss of shock. And before she could retreat, his mouth had captured hers. Hard and sure he took her breath.

'Oh!' He had released her at last, enabling her to drag an astonished gulp of air into her lungs, but still held her firm by her shoulders. 'I never thought…'

'Thought what?' he growled, his mouth enjoying the delicate skin beneath her earlobe.

Startled, confused, Rosamund uttered the first words to come into her mind. 'No one ever kissed me like that before.'

The predatory glint in Gervase's eyes sharpened. Angling his head, he stroked the pad of his thumb over her lower lip. 'So I am the first, am I? Perhaps I will kiss you again.' His fingers slid slowly along the edge of her jaw, slowly down the lovely line of her throat as he contemplated the possibility. Without pressure, his hand lingered there at the little hollow where her pulse beat strongly against his fingers, then on, over, the swell of her breast, again lingering, moulding. And Rosamund waited, tense as a bowstring, in an agony of anticipation for the descent of his mouth on hers.

'Perhaps not. Not sweet enough for me by far.' And Gervase dropped her back on her feet and stepped away, watching her reaction, a saturnine smile on his striking face.

Suddenly alone, ridiculously bereft, Rosamund was close to tears. All she knew was that she must escape from this room, from this man's disturbing presence. With a flurry of her skirts, attempting to preserve her dignity, she almost ran from the room.

Rosamund was furious. How dare he treat her like a tavern slut! How dare he kiss her in her own dairy! She prayed that he had not noticed how hard her blood beat beneath the skin when he had pressed his mouth to her wrist. Or how she had melted into his arms so that there was no space, no air between them. Her cheeks coloured at the thought of the intimate caress she had allowed. But then, after the longest moment of her life, when she had abandoned her pride to admit to him that no man had wished to kiss her before, he had dropped her as if he found her somehow distasteful. As if she had not been found worthy of his kisses.

He had been willing enough to kiss the dairy maid!

Why was I found so lacking, that he wouldn't want to kiss me again?

Well, that wasn't difficult to determine, was it? Her attempt to strike that ruthless face would not have endeared her. And as a little knot of disappointment hardened in her heart, Rosamund ran her tongue along her dry lips and found herself wishing, helplessly, that he had repeated the dreadful offence. Then stamped her foot in the mud at the impossible conflict between her responses to the man.

So, had she known it, did Gervase wish he had carried out his threat to kiss her again as he watched her storm across the bailey in a flutter of skirts and veiling and red-gold hair, yet berated himself for ever having been tempted in the first place. Those soft lips, red as cherries and parted in anger, had lured him into what would have undoubtedly been a mistake.

So no one had kissed her like that before? Of course they would not, unless an embrace from a secret admirer frowned on by her family, or a favoured suitor who had not materialised into a husband. She was no tavern wench to be kissed and tumbled into bed by any man whose eye she took. So he was the first man to claim her mouth, was he? She would be virgin, then. No man, other than he through the protective layers of her garments, had known the curve of her breast. No man had ever known the silken length of her limbs, naked, revealed. A tremor of desire caught in his gut. *He* could. If he were dishonourable, unworthy of the breeding of the Fitz Osberns.

Yet would she resist if he did? She had kissed him with such sweetness, her lips opening beneath his in soft invitation. It had taken him by surprise.

He smacked his hand against the wooden door jamb of the dairy where he still stood, appreciatively following her progress across the bailey. No, he couldn't do it. Besides, he didn't even like her.

But Gervase was not dissatisfied. He had unnerved her—and, by chance, made one discovery. Those splendid tresses were not false. Not false at all, but soft as the silk he thought they might be beneath his fingers. It was not difficult to imagine it unbound, shimmering down over her naked shoulders. He barked a laugh at the direction of his thoughts as he loped across the bailey to inspect the weak stretch of palisade. Her hair had been as vibrant and warm as a living thing in his hand. He had enjoyed it—both the silk of her hair and the kiss.

But that did not mean that he had to live with her.

'This has to stop, my lady!'

'What can you mean, my lord?' Rosamund's eyes widened in concern. 'Has something occurred to disturb you?'

'I am more than *disturbed,* as you put it.' Gervase Fitz Osbern glowered at her, fisted his hands on his hips. 'And you know very well what I mean.'

Rosamund stiffened her spine as she stiffened her courage. She had known that she must face this accusation at some time and must hold her own. He stood across from her, tall, forbidding, the table on the dais providing a welcome barrier. The air of the empty Hall around them positively hummed with expectation. The greyhound waited, tense and watchful, at his side. Still in his habitual soldier's garb, he was rough and unkempt and his temper was on a short leash. Rosamund braced herself to deal with the angry man facing her.

'I know of some recent problems, my lord, but I assure you—'

'*Problems?* As I see it, there's a deliberate attempt to cause mischief here.'

'No. That cannot be.' She shook her head, a picture of innocence. 'The household has too much respect for you. I don't think that Master Pennard or Sir Thomas would ever undermine your authority, my lord.'

'Nor do I. Not without provocation from another party.'

Their eyes held, his furious and glittering in the dim light, hers as mildly interested as she could manage. It was so hard not to look away.

'You appear sceptical,' he continued silkily. 'Shall I list the separate instances?'

'Well,' she admitted, 'I know that the pottages and dishes of boiled meat are often lukewarm when they reach our table. It is ever a difficulty—caused by the distance from the kitchens, my lord.'

'I know about the distance. The food is stone cold, not warm,' he snapped. 'And more often than not congealed in sauce. And the burnt roast meat yesterday? What's your excuse for that?'

'Unfortunate.' Her eyes widened in sympathy. 'I understand the kitchen lad tending the spit fell asleep, my lord.'

'Hmm.'

'I doubt it will happen again, my lord.'

'I wouldn't wager my inheritance on it. What's your explanation for the ale?' he demanded.

Rosamund tilted her head as if in serious contemplation. 'I have none. A poor brewing, I grant.'

'Nothing to do with the brewing. That cask had been tampered with.'

'An accident, I presume. Again, unfortunate, my lord.'

'Very, for those of my men suffering from a sore head and a severe bout of the flux. And then there is the condition of the fire in the Great Hall.'

She shook her head ingenuously. 'I know nothing of that. I had retired—'

'Ah! So you are at least aware of the problem. And I imagine, by some good fortune, that the fire in your solar was *not* built of green wood. I imagine it did *not* smoke and spit and fill the room with choking fumes.'

'No, my lord.' Irritated at showing any knowledge of the clouds of smoke that had engulfed the roistering soldiers, Rosamund adopted a doleful expression.

'Do I have to go on?'

'I cannot think that there are more...' Translucently innocent. 'I know you have remedied the state of the midden...'

'I have. What I have not yet remedied, lady, is the sudden

surge of vermin into my rooms in the west tower. A positive army of rats.'

'Then my advice, my lord,' Rosamund replied, gloriously amenable, 'is to get a cat from the stables.'

'So the vermin have not reached you.'

'*I* have a cat, my lord.' Rosamund did not resist a smug smile.

'Remarkable!' He hesitated. She watched him tilt his chin, the planes of his face flatten. Warning her… Then with hands planted on the scarred wood between them, he leaned forward until he was a mere breath away, to drive his words home, low voiced with studied menace. 'Thank you for your advice. And my advice to *you,* Lady Rosamund, is this. If the infestation of rats happens again, I shall be forced to take refuge from them. I shall move out of the west tower and into your solar and your private chamber. Are you willing to share your rooms with me?'

His looming presence overwhelmed. Rosamund felt the threat in his powerful shoulders, the fine muscles of his arms and chest as if he had actually set hands on her, as if he had taken her by the shoulders and shaken her. And she felt herself pale at the threat, knowing him quite capable of carrying it out. At the thought of him demanding admittance to her room, a shiver stalked through her. 'But you promised, my lord, that the solar should be mine…'

'So I did. But I have no intention of sharing my bed with a rat as big as Bryn. Quiet!' he roared at the hound that had barked at the sound of its name, startling Rosamund. 'I would rather share it with you, lady, vixen that you are! In fact, the thought of clean sheets with a pretty woman between them is enough to attract any man.'

'My lord!' The shiver intensified before she took herself in hand. She would not be intimidated! But the heat that had started in her belly and spread through every inch of flesh, to her toes and her fingertips, in liquid delight, had nothing to do with fear and everything to do with some strange longing. Silently cursing her flaming cheeks, she poured the blame for her discomfiture on to those impressive shoulders. The fault was all that of Gervase Fitz Osbern. He was a disgrace to the order of knighthood, with its tenets of courtesy and good manners. Preserving her outward calm as best she could, she expressed the words she had in mind from the beginning. 'If you are uncomfortable here at Clifford, my lord, you can always leave.'

He smiled, a feral glint of teeth. 'You won't win, you know.'

'I don't know what you mean, my lord.' Her cheeks grew even hotter.

'Don't lie to me, Rosamund.' He leaned so close that his lips, firm, masculine, were a mere breath away. She held herself perfectly still. He had kissed her in the dairy, there was no reason why he should not repeat his offence. Would he? She held her breath. No, he drew back, to his full height. 'And don't forget my warning. The door to your chamber is not sacrosanct.'

'It's not open to you. I'll bar my door against you.' Quick panic rippled.

'Will you, now?'

'Yes.' She saw him move toward her. 'Nor will you kiss me. I won't allow it.'

'No? And how will you stop me?' Two lithe strides and he had rounded the end of the table, stopping her before she could take flight, trapping her against the edge, one hand braced on either side of her. 'I warned you. If you don't like my attentions, keep out of my way and stop interfering.' His eyes lowered to her lips as if he would kiss her again. By the Virgin! Rosamund found herself wishing that he would. Humiliated, she turned her face away, aware of nothing but his breath hot on her cheek, his hard thighs holding her against the table's edge. His desire for her was readily apparent. She held her breath as the shivers speared down to her belly, toward her thighs. She hated him. She desired him. Risking a glance up, she found his eyes on hers and a slow smile that heated her blood until it scorched every inch of her skin.

Gervase's voice dropped even lower. 'Be warned, lady. If you don't stop meddling, *I* will be the one barring your door. With you on the inside. I'll lock you *in* your chamber, if I have to. For the safety of the whole castle.' The smile widened into what she could only interpret as a leer. 'Or I might even join you there behind your closed doors. I wager your bed would be more than comfortable for the two of us. The nights are long and dark. I could suggest any number of ways to pass the time.' His voice fell to the softest purr. A woman might find it seductive but Rosamund could not mistake the menace, and flinched. 'I would find that most…agreeable. Take care, Lady Rosamund!'

And he swaggered from her presence.

Of course she was to blame. Her eyes had shone with innocence, but she was knee deep in guilt. It was written all over her magnificently complacent responses to his complaints. And, in the privacy of his rooms, Gervase allowed himself the luxury of laughter. He had to give her credit for ingenuity. He must remember the stench from the midden if he ever needed to lay a siege again. It had been enough to drive any man into flight before the source was discovered. A consignment of putrid fish, he was given to understand, bought from a trader who was glad to get rid of his rotting load, and buried beneath the stable manure. How she had managed it… Probably with the assistance of Master Pennard. It stank to high heaven even in the coldest of weather, pervading every nook and cranny in the castle, eye-wateringly, until he had ordered a detail to dig into the noxious mound and burn the offending mass. A good plan, if of short duration.

He grinned at the threat to take over her solar. Blood had drained from her cheeks, but she had rallied fast enough. It would be almost tempting to do so, and with her in it. He recalled feeling a vicious pleasure when her cheeks paled. And now cursed himself. That was unworthy. The fact that she had done as much as she could to undermine his authority had to be admired. But he must not weaken, just as he must banish the alluring image of sharing Rosamund de Longspey's bed. As he had informed her, it could not go on, and he could retaliate far more effectively than she, as she would soon discover. A word or two with Master Pennard would effectively put the fear of God and Gervase Fitz Osbern into the steward.

'That man is impossible!'

As the wind direction changed, bringing gales from the north, biting temperatures, and a sprinkling of snowflakes, Lady Petronilla had ensconced herself in the solar with embroidery and a well-built fire, where she could follow her own thoughts without interruption. They led in one particular direction, in spite of all her attempts to turn them aside. A thick-set, stocky figure, not young but agile yet with well-defined muscle. Blue eyes that saw much, with attractive crinkles of weatherbeaten skin at their corners. A kind face, one that smiled easily. A good threading of grey through his brown hair that spoke of wisdom and experience...

'Impossible! Beyond tolerating!'

The solitude was over, her daughter entering like the blast of a storm. 'I asked to see the accounts of the estate,' Rosamund fumed to her mother. 'Master Pennard—who suddenly could not look me in the eye—sent the wardrober to me. *My* official, *my* estates, but he informed me that I might not inspect them, the accounts of my own property, except by Fitz Osbern's permission. I must apply to *his lordship* personally if I wished to see them.'

'So did you make the request?' the Countess enquired, guessing the answer.

'Request? I demanded it. And that...that *lout* had the audacity to ask if I could read and figure. I doubt that he can! I doubt he can do more than sign his name!'

'And you said?'

'That my education had been exemplary. So *he* said to my wardrober, very well. Show the lady the accounts.'

'So did you inspect them?'

'No. I told Fitz Osbern I had changed my mind. I will not be dependent on his good will. I will not accept my rights at his thieving hands, as and when he chooses to bestow them.'

'I think, my dear Rose,' the Countess observed as she set a row of tiny stitches, 'that you might have met your match.'

'Never! And then, would you believe, he roared at me and told me to get out of the Hall. His men were drinking—you know as men do. He said it was no place to be for a woman.'

'He was right.'

'But there was no need to *shout*. And he was drinking with them. As for the language…' She covered her ears at the memory. 'It was shameful! No doubt he was swearing as much as any of them.'

'Ah, well.' Petronilla hid her face over her stitchery. 'Perhaps it's best to leave men to their own uncouth devices.'

'An excellent reason for my remaining unwed!'

'Rosamund…' Petronilla placed her needlework in her lap and considered the wisdom of giving her daughter some advice. Well, she would. 'All I would say is beware. This is not a pretty kitten you are playing with. It's a full gown wildcat with teeth and claws.'

'I know that.' Rosamund's voice softened, Petronilla hearing almost a hint of a catch there. 'But if I do not fight him, he will win. And where shall I be? Back at Salisbury, with the prospect of Ralph de Morgan's ring on my finger. I can't afford to lose this battle, can I?'

Petronilla sighed. 'No, Rose. You can't.' Sadness touched her heart. She had always known it might be a lost cause, and feared for the outcome.

Chapter Six

At some point into his second week at Clifford, when the temperatures continued to hover around freezing, even at mid-day, Fitz Osbern found it necessary to take issue over the lack of a fire in the Great Hall—a minor matter, perhaps, but one of principle, he decided, with clenched jaw, as he viewed the pile of cold ash. Just one of the many minor matters where once again he detected the hand of Rosamund de Longspey!

'This fire will be kept burning at all times,' he thundered at Master Pennard. 'God's wounds! I want it well stacked and alight every morning. I'll not have this discomfort for my men. If you don't have enough servants to see to it, then I need to know about it. But it's your responsibility—'

He was in full formidable flow when he was hailed from the doorway. He turned with quick irritation. And then with relief. 'Thank God for some sane company!'

Hugh de Mortimer had returned.

'You look as if you need it.' Hugh advanced as servants now scurried round under their lord's jaundiced eye to re-lay the logs and coax them into flame.

'You have no idea.' Gervase took Hugh's arm to move him out of the path of the logs. 'So what brings you here?'

'I've business in Ludlow and so decided on a detour. It's the King. King Henry will be there within the week on one of his progresses through the country, and I've been summoned to discuss security in the March.' Hugh looked round, taking in the changes in sharp appreciation. 'You've been busy, I see.'

'I've had need to be.' Gervase continued to glower at his wily steward, despite his overall satisfaction. The rain no longer collected in stagnant puddles in the inner court. The rushes in the Great Hall were of recent collection, despite the winter weather, and relatively pleasant scattered with herbs. The layers of soot had been scoured from the walls.

De Mortimer stretched himself along a bench with a groan. 'I'm getting too old to be riding the March in this weather, but a cup of ale will put it right.' He cast a glance at his friend's fierce expression, then over to the steps leading to the upper floor. 'I presume she's still in residence.' He chuckled. 'And there's no real threat of snow on the horizon yet.'

'More's the pity.' Gervase joined him, but kept his attention fixed on Master Pennard whose loyalties were still open to question. He would have dismissed him out of hand if he had not been aware of the true culprit. 'Why she won't just accept defeat and leave. I can't take my eyes off her. She rejects my authority and wreaks havoc whenever her will is thwarted. If you stay, Hugh, I warn you.' His lips twisted. 'Talk about de Longspey cunning! We're having daily battles over household matters that should run smooth as milk from a cow, but have a way of being carefully undermined.'

'And you have not retaliated?'

'Of course not.' Quick colour flashed across his lean cheeks. 'The war is all on her part. I merely…well, let's say I don't make it easy for her.'

'If *I* might say—you look as if you've spent the morning in hard labour.' Hugh stretched out a hand to twitch the grimy sleeve. 'Fighting gear?'

Gervase grinned. 'I am the brigand of her nightmares.' He

ran his fingers through his untidy hair until it stood in spikes, then drew his nails over the dark shadow of unshaven chin.

'And you still can't get her out.'

The grin softened into a smile, but feral for all that. 'Not yet. She's courageous and determined. But I'll not give in.'

De Mortimer sought more attractive company, perhaps the cause of his going so far out of his way from the direct route between Hereford and Ludlow. He found it after much innocent searching—and some surprise—in the dairy, and bowed with pleasure.

'You're still here, dear lady.'

'Lord Hugh!' Petronilla pushed her veil back from her cheek with her wrist. 'As you see. We're trying to make cheese that's halfway edible. We've had some problems.'

'Perhaps you should tell me about them.' He could not imagine why the Dowager Countess should find a need to become engaged in so menial a task, but what a charming picture she made, her hair wound into a bright coronet to draw attention to her fine features. Whether her flushed cheeks were as a result of the exertion or his own sudden appearance into her domain he had no idea. He hoped it was the latter. It raised his hopes when she left the girls to their task, wiped her hands and actually took him by the sleeve.

'I doubt you would wish to hear of them.' She shook her head at his ingenuous smile. 'Come with me.' And led him outside into a sheltered corner where a half-hour of bright sunshine had made the temperature pleasant enough to sit for a short time. Mantle wrapped closely, she pulled him to sit beside her, folded her hands comfortably in her lap and faced him readily enough.

'Have you missed me, lady? Are you content here?'

'I'd rather be elsewhere. Ah! I think I should not have said that.'

Accepting that Petronilla had neatly side-stepped his first question, Hugh lifted her hands from her lap into his large clasp, pleased when she did not pull away. 'I won't tell. Where would you rather be?'

'In Salisbury,' Petronilla admitted. 'I enjoyed life in the town. I even think I would prefer my own jointure at Lower Broadheath. It's not as wild as this. I had enough of this country in my first marriage.'

'You should come to visit me in Hereford,' he responded promptly, seizing the opportunity, 'if towns are to your taste.'

She smiled wanly, but made no reply.

'Can you not persuade your daughter to retreat gracefully? Where is she, by the by?'

Petronilla sighed. 'Talking to the cook about some variety in our diet, I think. It's been boiled mutton every day this week. But, no. Rose will not go back. She'll do everything she can to stay out of Earl Gilbert's circle of influence. Even here, I'm not so sure that she's safe…' She frowned at him, as if daring him to repeat her careless words. 'I don't think I should have said that either.'

'Safe from what?'

'I don't think Rose would want me to talk about it.'

'But Earl Gilbert is not a bad man, surely.'

'No…not bad, exactly. There, now!' Her hands moved restlessly in his. 'I suppose since my tongue has been so careless, I must tell you the rest. Gilbert would force a marriage on Rose. Gilbert and my husband, Earl William, planned it before William died. It would be a…a strategic union, they said.'

'But would it be so bad?' Hugh asked. 'How old is she?'

'Twenty-four years. There were others, but nothing came of them.' The Dowager Countess folded her lips tight, clearly distressed.

So Hugh returned smoothly to the crucial matter. 'So who do they have in mind? It can't be so bad as to drive the girl into headlong flight, can it? Or bad enough to make her consider Clifford a desirable residence.'

Lady Petronilla raised her brows. 'It can. Ralph de Morgan.'

'Ah!' Hugh rubbed his face with a large hand. 'I know Ralph de Morgan.'

'Then you understand her reluctance.'

A wry twist of his lips was answer enough. 'He would not be my choice for a spirited young woman. Nor would life in Builth appeal. It's even more bleak than here.' And seeing the shadows in his companion's face, he regretted his words, tucked the information away until it could be effectively used, and took immediate steps to restore the lady to good humour. He pulled Petronilla to her feet. 'The day's too fine to allow us to linger on Ralph de Morgan, so let's agree to consign him to the devil. It's to my gain, lady, that you should still be here,' he remarked with a deceptively meek glance at odds with his weathered exterior. 'The sun shines and the day is set fair despite the cold. Come for a ride with me. We'll go along the Wye to the ridge. It's pretty country and I would not have you condemn it out of hand. Will you come with me, Petronilla?' If she registered the familiar use of her name, she made no objection. The shadows fled and her smile warmed, so that on a thought, 'No!' Hugh announced, startling her. Her smile promptly vanished again like the sun behind a cloud.

'No, what?'

'*Petronilla.* It's far too heavy a name for one so feminine and pretty. I shall call you Nell.'

Colour instantly suffused her face. 'No one has ever called me Nell.'

Unsure whether she was amused or affronted, but willing to wager on the former, Hugh did not retreat. 'I shall,' he informed her. 'So, Nell, will you ride with me?'

The Dowager Countess did not hesitate. 'Yes, Hugh. I think I will.'

Meanwhile, whilst Hugh was unwrapping the layers of Petronilla's reticence, Fitz Osbern had moved his attentions from the Great Hall to the stabling that looked as if a good gale would reduce it to a heap of sticks and straw. One end of the structure was already in a state of collapse and the whole of the thatch a sodden mass. He was considering the value of demolishing the lot and rebuilding from the ground up rather than patching the holes when Hugh joined him, already cloaked and pulling on his gloves.

'Where now? You've only just arrived.'

Hugh retrieved his own horse and ordered the saddling of the Countess's mare. 'Not far. Just a ride along the river with Nell—ah, that is, Lady Petronilla.'

'I see.' Gervase growled with some amusement. 'Nell, is it?'

Hugh merely smiled. 'I have solved your problem,' he announced.

'You've locked the daughter in the dungeon?'

'No. Perhaps I should have said I have discovered the answer to your riddle, Ger. I know why the Lady Rosamund will not leave, and has no intention of leaving. Why she's intent on remaining here until the day she dies.'

'Because she's spoilt and wilful and difficult—and can't bear to be thwarted.'

'No. The reason in very simple. Ralph de Morgan.'

Gervase bared his teeth in quick distaste, raised a brow. 'Well?'

'Earl Gilbert intends the girl to marry him.'

'So?'

Hugh grunted. 'Think about it, Ger.'

'Hmm.' Gervase did so as he tested the edge of a thatching knife against his thumb, deciding it was too blunt for any purpose. It was not a pretty picture, honesty forced him to admit.

'She'll do anything but return to Salisbury, where she might be forced into the match,' Hugh continued. 'She's here for ever.'

'God's blood!' Gervase's brows became a heavy black bar. 'Thank you for the warning, Hugh. Enjoy your ride!'

'I intend to. One piece of advice…'

'Do I want it?'

'No. But it's sage.' Hugh's expression remained bland, but

he was unable to disguise the gleam in his steady blue gaze. 'You could wed her yourself. That would solve the problem. She's twenty-four and would doubtless be glad of a husband.'

'And I would be more acceptable than Ralph de Morgan.'

'You might. It would settle the ownership of Clifford. She has the documents. You have the power. Combine the two…and it would make her grateful beyond words to be rescued from Ralph's clutches. Result? Domestic harmony.' Hugh worked hard to preserve his composure. 'You can both live here in marital bliss.'

'My thanks for mapping out my future, Hugh.' The studied dignity of the reply was belied by the fierce glint in Gervase's eyes. 'I can think of nothing worse. The lady does not fulfil my requirements.'

'Just thought I'd mention it.'

'Enjoy your ride with the Countess!'

Deciding that the water-logged mess of straw and reeds would not survive the rest of winter, Gervase continued to supervise the detail of soldiers in stripping the old thatch from the stabling. To all appearances, it took his complete attention. To his disgust, it occupied his thoughts very little. Hugh's words insisted on swimming through his mind, lurking at the bottom of every thought, a vicious pike in the depths of a deep pool.

It was ridiculous to suggest it. He would never—could never—ally himself with the de Longspeys. And Rosamund de Longspey was nothing like the woman he envisaged to replace Matilda. What was it he had said to Hugh when he had last suggested that he remarry? Conformable, biddable. A gracious chatelaine for his homes… Yet when, as he wielded the knife—now sharpened—to trim the bundles of reeds newly cut from the river bank, he tried to bring such a paragon of virtues into sharp focus, he failed dismally. It had even become increasingly difficult, if he were brutally honest, to recall Matilda, other than a young girl with a slight figure, an oval face with pale blue eyes and gentle features. All he could picture now, damn the woman, was the simmering heat and sharp responses of the de Longspey heiress. A flash of green fire in her eyes, of red-gold flame in her hair. A will strong enough to bend iron. Obviously the reason why she was not already married. No one was prepared to take her on, except for Ralph de Morgan with the three border castles as the irresistible bait.

With no husband, what would lie in store for her? A convent? That was beyond his imagining. More like a life dependent on the reluctant charity of her stepbrothers, a well-born companion for one of their wives to help with the upbringing of their children. Not an attractive picture for a woman of forceful character. He could almost pity her. No…! She was not a woman to stir his pity.

Marry her yourself.

The idea returned once more. Damn Hugh for planting it! Green eyes, clear as a stream in the hills to the west. Pale skin with the delicate scattering of freckles over the bridge of her nose. Not over tall, but a neatly proportioned figure. Hair he had never seen unbound, but that he could imagine drifting in a red-gold cloud over her naked shoulders, curling over the swell of her breasts…

His hand tightened on the thatching knife, swearing at the product of his imagination. It was like a physical blow to his gut. A tightening in his loins. Imagine if the rest of her was as pale and smooth as her cheek. Imagine what it would be like to smooth his fingers down over the delicate curve of her shoulder, to splay his hand on the rounded fullness of her hip. Gervase inhaled sharply as the tightening grew harder, more uncomfortable, to his annoyance, then grabbed a nearby pail of water, to dash most of the freezing contents over his face in an effort to regain control of his wayward body. It failed to have the desired effect. Gervase grimaced. The sooner Rosamund was gone, the better.

Where would she go? He would not allow his thoughts to travel down that path. He was not the one to rescue her from her predicament. She could not stay at Clifford, and where she would go was not his concern. Why not marry Ralph and have done with it…?

The thought appalled him.

By the Virgin! She had got under his skin.

Gervase abandoned overseeing the thatching to Watkins and decided to inspect the progress of the re-siting of the midden, as far from the living accommodations as possible. A foul task, unpleasant enough to concentrate the mind on the rank odours rather than the destiny of a bronze-haired, emerald-eyed woman, who had absolutely no claim on him, yet succeeded in disturbing both his conscience and his loins.

At daybreak Rosamund was awoken to the sound of her mother scrambling from her bed, to disappear through the door that led to the space in the thickness of the wall enclosing the garderobe. Distressing sounds of retching followed. Rosamund promptly leapt from the covers, followed to wipe Petronilla's forehead with a square of damp linen, to hold her shoulders as the retching continued. When the spasms were done, she led her back and helped her mother, concerned at her sudden frailty, to lie back against the pillows.

'What is it?' Hiding her anxieties, searching her mother's wrists and arms for any sign of a rash, Rosamund smoothed back the sweat-damp hair from Petronilla's clammy face. 'Do you have any pain?'

Eyes closed, Petronilla groaned and pushed her daughter's hand away. 'No, just…' She swallowed hastily. 'I'd be grateful for a basin. I felt uneasy last night after the boiled mutton.'

'I didn't eat it.'

'Very wise…' Petronilla made use of the basin with neat efficiency, then collapsed back in exhaustion, breathing shallowly, her skin grey and slick with sweat.

Despite the fear that gripped her throat and weighed as a heavy lump beneath her heart, Rosamund outwardly remained calm. Nothing would come of running in circles like a chicken decapitated for the pot. But she needed help. Her own knowledge of ailments and cures were insufficient to deal with this. After enquires from Edith, Rosamund sent for the services of a Mistress Kempe from the village, a stalwart widow who ran the ale-house, with the reputation for knowledge and a deft hand with healing.

Mistress Kempe arrived, large and impressively overbearing, to take over the chamber with a confidence that amazed Rosamund. With bracing efficiency, she delved into the bag she carried, searching out packets of aromatic content, and, after a moment's thought as she eyed her patient, the wise woman proceeded to administer a dose of vervain in ale together with a magic charm whispered in the afflicted lady's ear. As an afterthought she took a walnut and smashed it viciously into pieces on the hearth—*most impressive in guarding against the flux, my lady*—whereupon Petronilla fell into an uneasy sleep.

'Will she…will she soon recover?' Rosamund asked, dreading the reply.

'By tomorrow the lady will feel much more the thing. Continue to dose her. Merely a disorder of the belly,' Mistress Kempe announced with assurance. 'See, my lady. Here's the faintest colour already returned to the Lady Petronilla's cheeks.'

Which was true. Rosamund could feel some small sense of relief and was able to leave her mother's side, watched over by Edith with the basin to hand. So, after expressing her gratitude to Mistress Kempe with a purse of coin and a recommendation to take food and drink before she returned to the village, it was later than her habitual routine for the day by the time Rosamund was dressed and able to leave her chamber. Only to be summoned by Sir Thomas, barely had she stepped out of her door, to attend Lord Fitz Osbern. Concerned for her mother, without thought for the manner of the summoning that Sir Thomas plainly enjoyed, she took herself without complaint to the west tower.

He had had one of the rooms arranged to his comfort, she noticed, with a standing table, a high-backed chair and a number of stools, obviously the place where he intended to conduct business. A tapestry had been hung on the wall beside the fireplace. A travelling chest to house documents had been pushed against the wall and carried an array of weapons. Little personal touches. Rosamund's lips curled. Surprisingly comfortable for a brigand. And, from all appearances, he intended to stay. Not if she had her way. Once her mother was restored to health, of course, and she could concentrate again. She offered up a quick prayer that it would be so, holding to Mistress Kempe's jovial heartiness.

Fitz Osbern was sitting in the chair as she entered.

'At least you were quick in getting here,' he announced. He did not sound pleased that she had. He smacked the flat of his hand down on to the table. 'Is this…this recent *situation* of your doing?'

It was only than that she registered the tone of voice. The heavy line of his frown above eyes that glittered with hot rage. Nor did he show her the courtesy of rising to his feet, but left her standing before him in the middle of the room. It was almost, she realised, as if he sat in judgement on her.

'Which situation, my lord?' she asked cautiously.

'I can't believe that you could stand there in all innocence and deny it.'

'I don't—'

'At least half of my men are down with a flux,' he continued as if she had not spoken. 'Would you try poison my whole garrison to punish me for my possession of Clifford?'

'What? *Poison?*'

'I see that *you* are not suffering, lady. You look remarkably well.' His voice became a snarl. 'I can't imagine how *I* escaped. Perhaps you have something even worse in mind for me than flux and vomit.'

'Poison…' Rosamund repeated, her mind scrabbling for understanding amidst the accusations. 'You would accuse me of such a depth of malice…' Hurt and anger warred within her in equal measure. That he should suspect her of so outrageous an act…

But have you not brought it on yourself?

No! Never that! She had plotted a degree of discomfort for him and his soldiers, that was true. But poison! That was far beyond the line of what she would consider acceptable.

'I can think of no better explanation. How dare you resort to such immature and dangerous tactics, woman?' Suddenly Fitz Osbern was on his feet, striding around the end of the table to confront her. She had never been so threatened by anyone in her life. 'I should beat you for so foolhardy an act of wilful petulance.'

'But I have not.' Fear blossomed, knife-edged, overwhelming any personal concerns. Was it poison? Was her mother more seriously afflicted, in far greater danger, than she had thought? And if it was poison, whose hand had administered it? Horrified that tears should rise in her throat, to her eyes where they threatened to fall, Rosamund took a deep breath against them. 'Is it poison? If so, I have done nothing to warrant so great an insult.'

'And why should I believe you? When I can't trust you out of my sight?' Fitz Osbern sneered at her denial, utterly unbelieving, far too close, far too angry for comfort. How could he think so little of her, that she would put the lives of his men, of anyone, in deliberate danger? Had her character seemed so despicable to him? 'The ale was tampered with by your own admission.'

'But not *poisoned.* I do not lie. I admit to undermining your authority, but I do not lie. Besides, my own mother is ill.' She steeled herself, battling back her fears. 'I might make life uncomfortable for *you,* but I would never harm my mother. Whatever you think of me, you must believe that.'

An inauspicious grunt was the only response. He continued to glare at her.

'If your men are poisoned, then so is my mother…' At the

sudden return of the naked fear that her mother was at risk, she pressed her fingers against her mouth to hide the quiver.

'How is she?' Fitz Osbern demanded, eyes suddenly intent, searching, but voice no more sympathetic.

'Sick. Mistress Kempe has seen her and dosed her on vervain…'

'Did it have any effect?'

'I think she is easier. The vomiting has stopped…'

But she was aware that he was no longer listening. His thoughts were clearly elsewhere as he swung away from her to stare at the vibrant hunting scene in the tapestry, brow creased as if he considered something unpleasant.

'What is it?' she asked.

But he shook his head. 'If you are not the culprit,' he growled, 'there's only one answer. But if I find out that yours is the blame…'

And left her standing there, the threat shimmering in the cold air.

So if it was not poison, what had spread its sickness through the castle, harming some but skipping over others? With her mother's comment on the boiled mutton stew in mind, Rosamund began her own investigation, sending a reluctant Master Pennard on a distasteful task to question the suffering garrison as to what they had eaten at the previous meal. The result seemed to prove the case. She ran Fitz Osbern to ground as he strode out of the kitchens, driven by the frustration of failure. He would have walked round her without a word, but she stepped in his path.

'Did you eat the mutton stew last night, my lord?'

'No.'

He would have pushed past her, but Rosamund reined in a spurt of temper and raised her arm to prevent it. Her hand grasped his sleeve.

'Please, my lord,' when he would have shaken her hand

away. 'Neither did I eat the mutton. But my mother did. As did your men who are sick.'

He halted and focused on her. 'Ha!' Then spun on his heel and vanished back into the kitchen again.

From that point, Fitz Osbern took control. Operations were rapidly removed from the kitchens to the bailey, to the vicinity of the well. After a calming visit to her mother, who was sleeping and looking decidedly less frail, Rosamund watched the activity from the steps outside the Great Hall, accepting the value of keeping her distance. It entailed Fitz Osbern, Hugh de Mortimer, who had also escaped the blight, and a quartet of healthy soldiers. Also Owen and a length of rope. They all shivered in the biting wind.

A bucket was lowered into the well, hauled up, the contents inspected and then dumped on the floor. It was impossible for Rosamund to know the outcome.

'Let's see what's down there. Owen—you've drawn the short straw here. You're the only one of a size not to get stuck.' She heard Fitz Osbern's voice carry as they tied a rope around Owen's waist and shoulders and lowered him down into the mouth of the well, a bucket following.

Rosamund withdrew. In some sense it was a relief that he had taken over the investigation. It was her instinct to stay and watch, but sense dictated that it would do no good for her to hover. Her heart sank. He would seek her out, whatever the outcome.

'So that's it.' Hugh de Mortimer poked at the evidence with the toe of his boot as it lay in a wet decomposing heap of black fur and claws at his feet.

'So I think,' Gervase replied. Owen shuddered in his wet garments at his side. 'Well done, lad. Off into the kitchen now for dry clothes and a mug of ale. Tell the cook to feed you. Not mutton stew!'

Owen went at a run, with a grin, leaving Gervase to face

facts. Polluted water, as simple as that. Now, apart from the thorough cleansing of the well, he had another pressing obligation. He was the first to admit he had been wrong, and had accused the de Longspey witch of poisoning the garrison without evidence. Now, he supposed, he must make his apologies. A loutish brigand might not be so compelled, but he could carry that act only so far. His eyes glittered with distaste at the prospect. Without doubt she had brought it on herself with her foolishness, but she had not deserved his harsh words. So he must seek her out. He shrank from it, as he would not have shrunk from fishing a decomposing animal out of their source of water, but he would do it. He remembered her eyes wide, her face pale as he attacked her. He thought he had actually threatened to beat her. Never had he seen her so distressed. Angry, yes, but not so full of dread. Fear for her mother's safety, he thought in retrospect. And he had made it worse by shouting poison. Well! He would have to grasp the blade and put it right.

Leaving Hugh to supervise the cleaning of the well, he stomped into the Great Hall, where she wasn't, and up to her solar, where she admitted him without a word. He had to admire the manner in which she faced him, spine erect, eyes steadily on his. He could see control in every inch of her, from her neat leather shoes to the crown of her head. But he saw that she wiped her palms down the sides of her gown as she waited for his report. Her cheekbones were stark against her pale skin. She was not as composed as she would have him believe. Her first words were even stronger evidence.

'Well, my lord? Is it poison? If it is, I swear it's not of my doing.'

So he would put her at ease, with no more recriminations. Calmly, he decided, as he detected the shine of moisture in her eyes. He had no wish to reduce her to tears. How did a man cope with a woman in tears, even if she was the enemy?

'No. Not poison, but the water is foul. A cat fell in. I've seen it before, when dead bodies get into the water supply.' He decided not to mention that it was more often human bodies in the battle campaigns of his experience. 'The cat fell in the well and poisoned the water.'

'But no one drinks the water.'

'The mutton in the stew was heavily salted from last autumn, and so the cook soaked it in fresh water, as he thought, before cooking it. It poisoned the meat.'

'I see.' A silence fell between them. It unnerved him. What to say? Her eyes were bruised and tender, holding a heart full of grief and fear for Lady Petronilla. 'It should have no lasting effects on those who ate it.'

'No.'

'De Mortimer is putting it to rights.'

'Yes, of course.'

She wasn't making this easy for him, her eyes remaining un-blinking on his, deep pools of anxiety that touched his conscience. 'It's another consequence of poor housekeeping. The well must be covered. I've instructed Master Pennard. And now I must see to my men.'

'Mistress Kempe is still here. I'll send her to you.'

He took a breath. 'I have to apologise, lady. I was wrong.'

'Yes.'

'I hope you can accept it.' He remembered how her breath had caught and how he had attacked her without mercy, but could think of nothing more to say. Nor could he allow himself to offer his hand in comfort. Gervase knew his limitations. If he did, he might just be tempted to enfold her in his arms and kiss her until the sadness fled.

'I hope Lady Petronilla will recover soon.'

Left alone, Rosamund was forced to contemplate the day's events, and those of the previous weeks, with dismay.

How dare you resort to such immature and dangerous tactics, woman?…I should beat you for so foolhardy an act of wilful petulance.

She feared that he was right. What had she been driven to,

in her determination not to be cast into Ralph de Morgan's arms? And then even though Fitz Osbern had come to apologise for his mistake, he had abandoned her almost immediately, as if he could not bear to be in the same room, breathe the same air. He had looked at her as if he detested the very ground she walked on.

You can hardly blame him, can you?

The shame of her behaviour in the cold light of day and her mother's suffering weighed heavily. It was an uncomfortable experience, a self-condemnation that would not let her be.

Petronilla, still weak but able by evening of the following day to sit up and take note of her surroundings, did not help matters.

'You look out of sorts,' she informed her daughter. 'I shall be quite well by the morrow, you know. I just feel—*empty*—and light-headed. Not surprising in the circumstances. I hear it was a cat. I never did like cats.' She glared at the grey kitten that persisted in curling at the end of her bed, then peered suspiciously into the bowl of chicken broth that Rosamund had placed in her lap. 'I don't wish to drink this, but I suppose you'll sit and glare at me until I at least sample it.'

Rosamund smiled at the improvement and the return of her mother's wry humour, before stating bluntly, 'He accused me of poisoning his men.'

'I expect he did. What did you expect, Rose? I warned you you'd go too far. You tried to freeze him out, you served up burnt or cold food. What did you expect?'

It was as close to a maternal slap that her mother would make, and so effective. Rosamund lifted her shoulders uncomfortably under the fine wool of her over-gown.

Petronilla abandoned her spoon without making use of it with a sigh. 'Did Lord Hugh eat the mutton?'

'No.' Rosamund angled her a sly glance. 'Your mind can be at ease. He's as healthy as an ox. And asks after you with astonishing frequency. I've had to bar your door to him—or even now he'd be standing here to watch your recovery. I didn't think you'd want that.'

'No. But I'm glad he's as healthy as an ox.' Weary, Petronilla still managed a curve of her lips. 'Now go away, my dear girl. I shall sleep.'

So Rosamund was left to her own devices to worry over her conscience. Fitz Osbern had been civilised enough to apologise. It seemed that she too must be willing to make amends if she did not wish him to fix her with that cold stare. Although why it should matter to her, why it should rob her of sleep, she could not fathom.

Although it was late enough that the tables had been cleared in the Great Hall, supper long over for those of a mind to eat, Rosamund made her way once again to the room in the west tower. If she wished to sleep with a clear conscience, this could not wait. Nerves swam through her blood.

'I need to speak with you, my lord. It is important.' She would be scrupulously polite. Composed and dignified, whatever the provocation. She would mend matters between them so that they could exist on equable terms until…well, until she could devise another means of preserving her independence. It was unfortunate that Hugh de Mortimer was engaged with him over a parcel of documents and a pottery jug of wine.

Hugh rose to his feet. Gervase did too, slowly, and it was he who spoke.

'How is Lady Petronilla? Is she recovered?'

It unnerved her that he should think to ask, that he should care enough when matters between them were still so unresolved. How was it that he could so easily unsettle her? 'Much improved, my lord. She swears she'll never eat mutton again.'

It was Hugh de Mortimer who filled in the little silence. Walking softly to her, he took her hand, his usually laughing eyes solemn. 'Give the lady my regards. I shall hope to see her tomorrow.' He moved to the door. 'And now I'll leave you to your important business. Good night, Lady Rosamund…Ger.'

Hardly had the door closed behind him than Rosamund launched into her prepared speech. Simple, straightforward, unemotional. This was how it must be. 'I have come to ask your forgiveness, my lord. I admit I deserve your lack of trust. I have not been…thoughtful. Or…or trustworthy.'

Leisurely, as if contemplating how much value he could put in her words, which in itself hurt her, Gervase chose not to answer immediately, but walked to the chest, to pour a cup of wine and hold it out to her. 'So we have room for compromise between us?' he remarked at last.

What could she say to that? An apology could so easily lead to a promise to leave Clifford in his hands. And that she could not do. She sought carefully for appropriate words, for a promise that she could keep, as she took the cup. For whatever drove Rosamund de Longspey, she would keep her promises.

'Yes. A compromise, my lord, as you say. I will not make your life within Clifford uncomfortable again. I will not interfere with the smooth running of the household.'

For a long moment his eyes held hers. She could not look away, felt the power of them. He nodded, then broke the connection. 'Then let us drink to it.'

Well, he had not accepted her apology with any warmth, but at least he had not ordered her from the room. At his bland acceptance, hiding her amazement, she raised the cup and sipped as he too drank, but shook her head as he indicated that she should sit. Now that she had done the deed she would not stay. 'I should go…'

'We can't leave it like this.' She saw quick intolerance sweep his face as he came to stand between her and the door, felt her anxieties return fourfold. 'Look, lady. You must see the sense of my arguments,' he stated forcefully. 'This is no place for you. Can I not persuade you to leave? Your mother at least would be far more comfortable away from here, but she'll not desert you. And I can't believe that, after Salisbury, you enjoy it here either. A border fortress is no place for either of you. You can have no affection for it.'

It struck an immediate chord. 'I hate this place.' Only the strains of the day could have made her so unguarded as to admit to it, could have made her so conscious of his overbearing nearness. She found herself flushing at how foolishly immature she sounded.

He seemed not to notice. 'So leave. And Lady Petronilla will thank God for it.'

'I can't. I just can't.'

'I know why you think you can't go back to Earl Gilbert,' he stated bluntly. 'But still—'

Rosamund stiffened instantly. *'What?'*

'I know why you will not go back to Earl Gilbert,' he repeated, clearly unaware of her humiliation. 'He has promised you to Ralph de Morgan.'

Her blood trickled cold in her veins. 'How do you know about that?'

'Your mother. She told Hugh.'

Rosamund prayed now for tolerance. 'I might have guessed.'

'You have my sympathy.'

'I don't want your sympathy,' she retaliated, denying his concern. That would be too much. Why had her mother found it necessary to speak of her deplorable marriage? She felt the shame of it, as if the deficiencies of her bridegroom were of her own doing, as if she were incapable of attracting a more appealing offer. Rejection was a sharp wound to bear and pity was the last thing she wanted from this man. All she wanted was to escape from his room, his dominant presence. Putting down the cup, turning her face away because it was becoming increasingly difficult to hide her distress, she would have brushed past him. 'My marriage is not your affair, my lord.'

He moved smartly, seizing her hands. 'No, it is not,' he admitted, his calm words at odds with the sudden clasp to hold her still. 'But why are you not married already? Well bred, presentable, well connected as you are. Why do you need to consider Ralph de Morgan? Surely there are better offers.'

'Easy enough to explain, my lord.' By some miracle she kept her face still, emotionless, although she felt the skin tight across her cheekbones. Nor did she pull her hands away. If she refused pity from him, she would never, *never,* allow herself to be accused of self-pity. 'I have not been without offers. One died with a knife in the gut in a drunken brawl in Salisbury. One was killed in a chance skirmish over a strip of woodland on the edge of his estate. One just died—rumour said of the pox. A fortunate escape for me, many would say. And there were others.' She listed them as if they were a tally of household supplies.

'Unfortunate,' he observed laconically.

'Yes. As you say. Now if you will release me, my lord…' Against her intentions, she braced herself against his hold. When it failed to move him, she risked a glance, and wished she had not. There was an expression in his face that she could not interpret, but it had the effect of heating the cold in her blood to molten fire.

'I thought it might be that you were unwed,' he murmured, drawing her closer, inexorably, almost as if he had no choice but to do so, 'because no man could tolerate your temper. When you scowl at me like that, I could well believe it.'

Rosamund's careful control evaporated, quick as a candle snuffed at dawn. 'My unmarried state is no concern of yours!'

'Well, you're not comfortable for a man to live with. As you have proved all too effectively.'

Temper built. 'I apologised for my unwise actions. Is that not enough?'

'Yes, you did. But I'm still not sure I can trust you.'

'Well, I don't trust *you,*' she heard herself retaliating when she had meant to deal with him with all dignity. 'Showing me kind sympathy and soft words, to persuade me to leave for my mother's health… You'll never persuade me that you're any better than the robber I first thought you to be.'

'Soft words?' There was a hint of anger now. It should have sown fear in her but instead the fire leapt into flame. 'I'll show you no soft words, lady!'

If she had expected him to release her, for her to go her own way, she had misjudged him entirely. It was her undoing. Taking advantage as she relaxed her guard, he pounced, tightening his hold, so that she must lose her balance. Rosamund discovered that she could only regain it as his arms closed around her, pulling her firmly against him. As her hands found purchase on his shoulders, she looked up at him in shock to see his eyes narrow as they raked her face, the cold grey of them glittering in the light from the candles. Then all sight was blotted out at he bent his head and took her mouth with his.

The speed of it took her breath away. Suddenly for her there was no past and no future, only that firm insistent pressure of mouth and tongue that forced her lips to part against his. The hot force of his body against hers, the ridge of his erection against her belly. Then as fast as he had swooped, he lifted his head.

'Speechless at last?' She found herself dragged even closer. With one hand he captured her chin and tilted her face up. 'You are really very beautiful, my delectable Rose, especially when you are angry.'

She stared at him in amazement, in utter disbelief that he should treat her in such a manner when she had thought his primary emotion to be one of dislike.

'Perhaps my kisses are more acceptable than my soft words.'

'They're despicable. To force them on an unprotected woman…'

'It seems to me that you can quite well protect yourself, Lady Rosamund. Let's see.'

He promptly forced another, and not, she discovered, to her displeasure. As the other was brief and hard, this was a kiss to overwhelm her utterly, to claim her breath. A fierce kiss, as much anger, she thought in her total inexperience, as any emotion of a softer nature as his lips scorched hers, until it segued into something far hotter of which she had no experience whatsoever.

For a long moment her thoughts scattered, leaving her aware

only of the strength of his arms that encircled her, the hard power of muscle in his chest and loins against which she was held firm and unable to move. And his mouth. Hot, searching, possessive, discovering responses within her that rippled across her skin. His mouth methodically took her lips, then the edge of her jaw to the tender place beneath her ear, then traced a scalding path down her neck to where her blood beat at the base of her throat where he finally lingered, his lips soft at last.

She could not fight. Had no desire to fight. Her blood raged as a bracken fire on the hills in high summer, yet with unutterable delight sparkling through it as rain would glitter in long grass. Her whole body quivered so that she had to hold on to him. And wish for more. Breathless, Rosamund felt herself to be stranded in unknown territory. Never having been kissed in this manner before, she had no point of comparison. Was this what it was like to desire a man? She had no idea, but the effect was beyond all her dreams. Such intense pleasure, that she could neither control it as it rioted through her blood, nor fight it. It robbed her of all sense, left only a need to stay within the heat and fire. A need to respond and return his kisses.

'Rose…'

When he murmured her name against her lips, instead of pushing him away she tightened her fingers in the sleeves of his tunic, shivered as he pressed the lightest of kisses to the softness at her temple. She could never have believed the depth of longing a man's touch could bring. She angled her head when he drew his fingers down the length of her throat in one rippling caress. His name came to her lips a whispered caress in itself.

'Gervase.'

The falling of a log in the fireplace and the resulting shower of sparks brought her back to her senses, her surroundings, the implacable cunning of the man who held her, now so gently. Warnings began to trickle through her brain.

No, don't give in. He is my enemy. He has taken what is mine. He would drive me out without compunction.

Of course this was his plan. He knew exactly what he was doing, following his own dictates. She must not allow herself to be intimidated, as much by his skilful kisses as by a show of force. Rosamund struggled to be free, and, after an initial resistance, he allowed it. When she searched his face it was to find that his eyes were no longer filled with the glitter of basalt fire, but were as flat and grey as newly hewn slate. There was no softness there. Had this assault on her merely been a punishment? To stir her into desire and then to abandon her? She could believe anything of a robber lord. How could she have allowed herself to let down her guard before him? And yet at the end his lips had been so tender. She could still imagine the soft whisper of them against her hair, on her eyelids, spreading spangles of light through her blood, like rain drops on a spider's web…

The magnificent pleasure burst, to fall and shatter at her feet.

Rosamund felt the hot flush rise in her cheeks, the moisture of tears long held back. She must escape, with pride intact, before he could do more damage.

'If you will allow me to go…'

It seemed that he might not. Trepidation fluttered as wings of a caged bird. Then Gervase's hands fell from her arms and he moved away. He walked to the door and opened it for her with a curt inclination of his head.

'My lady.'

Without another word, without looking at him, Rosamund stepped past him. Head held high, she made her way, slowly, gracefully down the stairs, but conscious that he watched her all the way.

In her heart she fled from him.

Chapter Seven

Petronilla rose from her bed feeling fragile, but restored to something like good health as long as she did not think about food. But her spirits were low. For some reason the past weighed heavily on her today. Probably to do with increasing years, she decided. How could a lady feel optimistic when approaching her fortieth year? Fresh air would do the thing, she decided. And she needed to air her concerns—some of them at least—with someone who would give her counsel.

Whilst Edith braided her hair into its habitual coronet with solicitous murmurings, she looked in the polished silver disk given to her by Earl William on the occasion of their marriage, and wished she had not. Her mood descended to the region of her soft leather shoes until she took herself to task. The hint of lines beside her eyes could not be denied—surely there were more than yesterday? Nor could the slight roughening of her skin from winter winds. At least her hair was so fair that any sprinkling of grey was indecipherable—yet. But she was so pale, as if that appalling mutton had finished her off and she were indeed a corpse!

This would not do! It resulted in Edith being sent to rummage for a precious jar of cosmetics. Applied to lips and cheeks, it made a vast improvement. She looked far less like a death's head, she decided with a pout of her newly reddened lips. Earl William would not have approved, but then he did not have to. She had no one to please but herself.

So she did. She found Hugh de Mortimer just finishing breaking his fast in the Great Hall. Keeping her eyes from the remains of the meal with a shudder, she took a stool at his side.

'Dear lady.' He immediately put down his knife and gave her his whole attention. 'I think you are on the road to recovery.'

'And I shall be better yet as long as you don't eat that roast venison in front of me.' He pushed it aside with an apologetic grimace. 'I need some information, my lord. I think you can provide it. What happened between my daughter and Fitz Osbern?'

'Never mind Fitz Osbern!'

She was quite taken aback. 'But…'

He took her hands, holding them palm to palm within his own. Momentarily she blinked at them, thinking that she had never felt so safe, so cared for. Then as she lifted her eyes to Hugh's, seeing there the sympathy, the calm wisdom, she wished, not for the first time in her life, for a complexion that did not herald her every emotion.

Meanwhile the Marcher lord who had forsworn any thought of marriage found the beat of his heart to be not as steady as he would want it. Petronilla looked a little worn, not surprising in the circumstances. The hands held fast within his were cold. There was a subdued quality about her, a dullness in the sharp morning light that was more than the effect of her days without nourishment. Hugh could readily imagine her face alight with laughter, her soft grey eyes shining, more green than grey when she smiled, but laughter seemed far away from her today. She was sad.

'What is it?' he asked gently, not really expecting an answer. She was a very private woman who kept her own counsel. Yet he felt a need to offer comfort. 'It's not just the ongoing feud between Rosamund and Fitz Osbern, is it?'

'No. But it's nothing of importance.' She dredged up a smile. 'Forgive me. I'm poor company.'

'I can't believe you're ever poor company.' He would try a little light dalliance to woo her in to a lightness of spirit, and to pass the time.

But the lady looked askance. 'My experience would suggest otherwise.'

His gut twisted at the stark admission, at the flat misery in her eyes. He persisted. '*My* experience suggests you need someone to entertain you. Perhaps you will choose to wed again and go to London, to Henry's court.'

'No.'

Well, that was definite enough. He wondered why. 'If you will allow me so intimate an observation, Nell, you are very…' He hesitated as her eyes snapped to his, almost in a warning. 'Attractive,' he finished. 'I wager you will be much sought after as a wife by the men of Worcester when you eventually return to Lower Broadheath…'

'I will not accept.'

'Why not? You don't seem to have a high opinion of men, my lady.'

'No. I don't, do I?' Distressed, she stood as if she would walk away, having forgotten her reason for seeking him out in the first place. But Hugh found himself wishing the absent Earl of Salisbury and John de Bredwardine to the fires of hell, and considering the possibility of teaching the lady that some men were worthy of her regard. With a hand to her sleeve, he pulled her back to her stool.

'You called me Hugh before you were stricken. Perhaps you could do so again.' His eyes twinkling, he shrugged when she simply stared at him. 'You wanted to know about our little domestic conflict. Well, they both apologised—and that's the end to it as far as I know. I understand the Lady Rosamund has promised to mend her ways.'

'I don't know about that…'

'You don't believe her?' He rubbed his finger along the length of his nose. 'I've noticed nothing. Fitz Osbern has been…brooding, shall I say, but he's rarely loquacious.' Hugh chuckled. 'Enough of that.' He pushed himself to his feet and held out his hand. 'No point in worrying over what might not happen. Since you're restored, would a stroll along the palisade walk aid your recovery further?'

Petronilla smiled. 'I have my mantle to hand for just such an occasion. If you will accompany me, my lord…' She put her hand in his without hesitation.

'Hugh!' And he raised her hand to his lips, perfectly satisfied with the outcome of his little campaign to make her smile again.

'Yes, Hugh.'

'Let me, Nell.' Petronilla allowed Lord Hugh to wrap the mantle around her shoulders and fix the fur-lined collar with her brooch. How deft and capable his hands were for so large a man. She must remember to call him Hugh. A little warmth spread beneath her skin that had nothing to do with the winter sunshine. How pleasant it was to speak with a man who was so much in tune with her thoughts and concerns. Of having him kiss her fingers because he wished to, not as a matter of formal respect. And spending time with a man who noticed how she looked and considered what would give her pleasure.

Whilst Hugh de Mortimer, in his forthright way, admitted his own attraction and set himself to wear down Petronilla de Longspey's understandable reluctance, life in the castle at Clifford settled into an easy routine. To take her mind off recent events, Rosamund took it upon herself to set about the refurbishment of the east tower, so far ignored. Master Pennard kept pace with her in reluctant agreement. The stonework was sound enough. For the most part empty of even the most basic furniture, all it needed was a good clean. Some vigorous sweeping and scouring would make it habitable. Returning to the Hall, issuing instructions as she went, she lifted her head at the eruption of noise from across the bailey. She had heard the gates open, but this tumult was unexpected.

'And what is that?'

'Quarried stone, my lady. To replace the palisade. Lord Fitz Osbern has a mind to rebuild.' Master Pennard left, list in hand, before Rosamund could add to it.

Why did men have to make so much noise and commotion about all that they did? Emerging to stand on the outer stairs to look down, a scroll of provisions in her hand, it was to see that a delivery of stone had arrived in a convoy of wagons, to strengthen the outer wall. Men of the garrison were engaged in the final unloading, manhandling the huge blocks, a dangerous business with ropes and pulleys and wooden staves. She would have retreated, leaving them to their shouted orders, the roars of laughter, their oaths and ribald joking as stones slipped to crush feet and fingers. She was not unaware of the tendency of men in a group to resort to coarse behaviour as she remembered her de Longspey step-brothers with little affection. This was no place for a woman unless she wished her ears and sensibilities to be assaulted.

But she stayed, lured by the busy scene and the bright sunshine, despite the cold wind that continued to blow snow flurries from the north. The task was complete, the wagons leaving, making the most of the hard-frozen roads. Jugs of ale were being brought out from the buttery. Now the men were drawing water from the well, stripping off dusty tunics to drench themselves in buckets of bone-chillingly cold water to swill away the dust and grime of the newly cut stone, with bellows of shock as water splashed and drenched indiscriminately. Rosamund shivered at the thought. Where was discipline here? And ridiculous on so cold a day to soak themselves to the skin…

Rosamund took a step forward with an eagle eye. Not only the men of the garrison were so engaged. She should have known it. It seemed that wherever she looked, he was there. Not content with issuing orders as any lord should in his castle, he had put his own hand to the ropes and levers, and was even now raising his arms to pull his tunic over his head in one fluid movement. There was Gervase Fitz Osbern, standing in his own bailey, stripped down to his hose and boots.

Go inside, her common sense ordered.

Not until I have looked my fill!

What if he sees you watching?

I don't care. I shall have seen him. Is he not worth looking at?

Splendid was the word that came to mind. Well, she knew that must be so, even under the heavy woollen tunics he habitually wore. Now she need no longer use her imagination as she had when he had engaged in combat with young Owen. The smooth muscles of back and shoulder flexed and stretched like water under the skin. Bronzed skin from campaigning and outdoor work glittered with drops of water that clung and ran in rivulets to soak into his hose. She allowed her eyes to play over his figure, so well displayed. Slim waist sleekly flowing into lean hips. Long powerful thighs... Her mouth dried. Palms were damp against the unfortunate scroll. What woman would not like to run those palms over the firm muscles of his chest, to see them quiver at her touch, to savour the soft spattering of dark hair that arrowed toward his groin? She would like very well to wipe the sparkles of water from his chest and flat belly, to put her hand *there* where she knew his heart beat, to feel the perfect match of it within her own body. She would like to... It took all Rosamund's will power to repress the need to run her tongue along her lips. She would like to do any number of things, if only she knew how. If only she dare.

A jolt of memory took her, refusing to be smothered. Two to be exact. Being plastered against that chest on their first meeting. The heat of it even in the cold, even fully clothed. And then, in the west tower, being pulled into his arms and kissed ruthlessly, relentlessly, until all thought of resistance had been obliterated. The sheer raw, male energy of the man.

How I would enjoy that male energy being focused on me again.

Gervase lifted his head, tunnelling his fingers through his

dark hair to scatter a sparkle of drops in the sunshine. Then looked up as if suddenly conscious of her gaze. Of the direction of her thoughts. Even at this distance from him, she flushed at the possibility that he might read what was in her mind. At the very moment that she decided that retreat was in order, he turned his head, his hands raising a cup of ale to his lips, his whole attention becoming centred on her before she could step back into the shadows. Brazenly he took her gaze and held it. Lowered the cup and bowed. A solemn, formal little movement, at odds with his disarray.

Rosamund froze with a sharp stab of embarrassment at being discovered so flagrantly spying on Fitz Osbern. But not for long. So he would mock her, would he? Stamping on her discomfiture she swept her dusty, cobwebbed skirts in a magnificent and equally formal curtsy. And not once did she allow her eyes to escape the unspoken demand in his.

Look at me. I am Lord of Clifford. I have held you captive in my arms and tasted your lips. I would do so again.

And Rosamund was aghast at the honesty in her own thoughts. Furious as much with herself as with the specimen of masculine beauty before her eyes.

I know you. I know who you are. I cannot forget your kisses. I dream of them.

'What's taking your attention, Rose? Visitors?' Seeing her acknowledgement of someone or something, the Countess had emerged, with Edith, to stand at her side. 'Ah…not visitors!' Following her daughter's stare, she laughed softly. 'He would take my attention too, if I were twenty years younger. Even ten.' Wistfulness overlaid by playful good humour.

'He's taking the attention of every maid in the castle, for sure.' As giggling chatter sounded from outside the kitchen, Rose turned her glare on Edith, daring her to be drawn in. 'And I am no better than they are.'

'But he's worth looking at, Rose.'

It did not help that her mother's admission should repeat her own awareness of him. With a huff of breath, Rosamund escaped into the Great Hall, a flag of colour high on each cheek. She could not pretend to be unmoved by him.

'What use in denying it,' she announced to the empty Hall. 'My blood is all on fire.'

Now what was she doing? Gervase, standing on the battlements, studying a plan of the new barbican he envisaged to make this castle one of the strongest down the length of the March and so stop the Welsh raiding parties from crossing the Wye, could hear raised voices over by the smart new timber-and-thatch stabling. One of them was instantly recognisable, attractively husky, and entirely displeased. The other gruff, polite enough, but uncompromising. He strolled closer intrigued to hear what ruffled her pretty feathers this time.

'I wish to ride, Sir Thomas. If you will saddle my mare…'

'Lord Fitz Osbern's orders are that you are not to go beyond the gates without an escort, my lady.'

Gervase could see neither speaker, but did not need to, to hear the lady's strength of purpose. Or her growing annoyance. He grinned at the exchange.

'But *I* order—'

'Escort or nothing, my lady, he says. Too dangerous without.'

'Danger from what?'

'Lord de Mortimer reports that the local Welsh tribes are restless. There've been attacks…'

Gervase could almost hear the heavy sigh, the irritation. 'Then I have no choice.'

'No, my lady.'

Continuing to smile grimly, Gervase sought out his squire Owen, then, after a brief instruction, returned to the rough sketches before him as Rosamund's mare was saddled and a small escort of four soldiers accompanied her as she urged her horse into a sprightly walk through the gate and along the river banks. Owen spurred his own mount to catch up. For reasons he could not have put a name to, Gervase found it necessary to climb to the guard's lookout on the gatehouse to watch her progress.

Fleetingly—or not so fleetingly—he wished he had accompanied her himself. Bright cold had brought colour to her face. Her braids were whipped in the breeze, living flames of gold, as she kicked her mount into a canter, glowing like an autumn beech against the blue sky. It was the first day of sunshine with no hint of rain in days. Who would not wish to ride purely for the pleasure of the exercise, the lightening of spirits after days of gloom? He watched her go. She rode well, showing good control and a graceful seat on the lively mare. What man would not enjoy riding at her side? He would like to see her laugh, her eyes sparkle with sheer exhilaration. Who would not wish to feel the light brush of her fingers? Or even the warmth of her palm against his skin? Or the softness of her mouth that held such unexpected sweetness?

'Thought you might join her,' remarked Hugh, leaning comfortably at his side and equally enjoying the view.

Gervase grunted. 'She'd have damned me to hell and back if I'd suggested it. She didn't relish any escort, much less my presence.'

'A handsome woman.'

'She's beautiful,' he murmured, unaware of his choice of words. Unaware of Hugh's speculative glance. And she was, creating a vibrant picture, like an image in stained glass. The rich blue mantle. Neat bay mare. All full of life and sheer vivacity, full of intoxicating laughter and animation. As he had seen her the previous day. He frowned as if it might not be the pleasantest of memories that insisted on playing through his mind.

It was a chance view of her that had ambushed him, in the unkempt area to the east of the keep that had been fenced off to provide a kitchen garden, one that had become seriously overgrown and neglected over the years. Now in the depths of winter it looked at its worst with dead stems and mounds of rotting leaves. Presumably as an excuse to get out of doors,

Rosamund had decided to beat it into shape, and it had provided him with one of those uncomfortable jolts from the past. One, with its layer of guilt, that he had not enjoyed.

Matilda had worked in that garden in the brief early days of their life together. He seemed to recall her tucking up her skirts, clipping herbs into a basket, pulling onions and other such feminine, domestic tasks. Delighted with her first home, her new position as Lady of Clifford. She had told him with such naïve enthusiasm that she enjoyed growing plants in her own garden, making her own choices without her mother's interference. She had laughed as the boughs from an old pear tree tangled in her veil, pulling it from her fair hair. How young she had been, how hopeful of their life together, whilst he had been gently indulgent. Long ago now, but it was one of those tender memories that had stayed with him.

And suddenly there was Rosamund, imposing her own arresting presence on the bleak space, scattering his fond memories so that he knew not what he felt. She was supposed to be clearing out the rank foliage, cutting back, raking the debris, wielding a sickle with impressive skill. A charming scene, he supposed, until distracted by the laughter of the younger servants from the kitchen who were intent on driving chickens back into their run. Bryn too had abandoned his master to join the hunt. Gasping for breath as the hens showed a cunning aptitude for escape, laughing at the clumsy attempts of one of the kitchen lads, Rosamund grabbed the hound and held him back as they were herded into their coup. Any lingering tender thoughts of Matilda had been swept away by the blaze of desire that swept through Gervase's body. He wanted her, a need that could not be banished. In that moment Rosamund filled his vision, his imagination. He knew the softness of those curves. Would like to know them even better.

What was it his father had once said, after a third cup of ale when he felt moved to give his young son some plain advice based on experience? Gervase remembered it perfectly. Wed a young girl. Train her up to your ways to please you, like a young horse or a hound puppy. Wed an older woman and all you have is trouble for life. Independence gives a woman ideas, opinions. A liking for her own way. Wed a young girl and your household and family will be managed to your liking. Well, he had wed Matilda with his father's advice in mind, had he not? He had not loved her, he realised with hindsight, but had an affection for her. He supposed they would have been comfortable together and raised a brood of children to carry on the Fitz Osbern inheritance.

Gervase blinked at the image that he could not quite bring into focus. Truth to tell, he could no longer imagine growing old with Matilda, despite the uncomfortable prick of guilt. Now Rosamund de Longspey… She had every unfortunate trait of character his father had warned him of. And more. A damned uncomfortable wife she would make. Yet he could imagine returning home to her. Looking for her on the battlements at Monmouth. Riding with her. Of her welcoming him with a smile in her glorious eyes and an infant in her arms with eyes green as new beech leaves…

Gervase scowled at the retreating figures. She should not be here. It should be Matilda. The guilt was uncomfortable to live with, that his mind, his physical responses, should forsake Matilda's memory so readily, to be replaced by this unpredictable creature who had got under his skin. And not just his! Against his will Gervase laughed aloud as he saw, in the distance, loping along beside the mare, that Bryn had again forsaken him for the lady. So much for loyalty. The hound was won over by a soft hand to scratch his ears and feed him scraps when she thought she was unobserved.

He wished she were so forgiving toward him. He wished he did not feel the shame that Matilda should pale into insignificance beside Rosamund de Longspey. He had not realised he was so fickle. Gervase shook his head as if to dislodge such disloyalty. Nothing to be gained from dwelling on it. Matilda was in the past and his future did not contain Rosamund de Longspey.

'They should be safe enough.' He pushed himself away from the wall with a shrug and a friendly punch to Hugh's shoulder. 'Enough of the scenery. Come and tell me what you think of the plans to—'

Distant shouts.

Gervase whipped round, black hair swirling in the wind. Blood turned to ice. Sharp memories stained with blood.

It can't happen. Not again!

A compact band of men, moving fast on small ponies from the north. Flash of sun on metal. Gervase and Hugh stared narrow-eyed, the better to assess the danger. They could not make the raiders out with any definition, but could imagine the bows they carried, primed with wicked arrows

'Ger…! An attack…and so close? Surely not.'

But Gervase was gone, leaping down the steps, shouting orders as he went to raise a force. Outraged that the Welsh should feel strong enough to attack so near to home. Did they think they could do so with impunity? But the outrage was forcefully obliterated by an overwhelming deluge of fear. It gripped him, cold and deadly, enough to paralyse him if he allowed it to take hold.

It was Matilda, all over again. He had not seen her death, only her body, bloodied and torn. Her face cold, smeared with dust and blood. Had it been in this exact place? Could fate strike twice in so devastating a fashion? Could lightning strike the same blasted oak twice?

Would Rosamund too be lost to him?

Gervase dared not stop to think.

The little party was hopelessly outnumbered. God grant that Owen had enough sense to take shelter. And surging through his heart, white hot as a bolt of lightning, was the self-recrimination that he had allowed her to ride out of the castle at all. His men were already grabbing weapons, saddling horses. The gates were opening. His mind circled in a never-ending loop. Pray God the escort and his squire had their wits about them. He should never have let her go. Then they were out of the gate, riding hard. It wouldn't take long to reach the distant *mêlée*. But would they be in time?

Conscious of his men riding with him, there was only one thought in Gervase's mind. To get to her before the Welsh arrows did. Gervase used his spurs without compunction to ride like the wind.

Then all was noise. Confusion. Shouts of warning from the Welsh as the heavily armed soldiers swept down on them. They would run, of course, escape into the woods and hills. He had no doubt of that. That was the warfare they were good at. But he couldn't see her. Could not see the flutter of her veil, the deep colour of her mantle, so she must be unhorsed. Her mare was down. As the knowledge was driven home, a flight of Welsh arrows heralded death.

It was all his fault.

'Drive them off! Use all force!' His voice cracked on the order.

All around him was red with the clash and fury of battle and his mind focused, cold and deadly. A short, sharp clash, as he expected. With a final flight of arrows, the Welsh ponies headed for the woods. Gervase directed his men to follow—but only enough to put the fear of God into them. No point in pursuing a lost cause.

He dismounted, wiping his bloody sword, sheathing it, Bryn leaping around his knees, barking furiously. Owen was at his side, breathless, excited, flushed with the fear and victory of the battle. Grinning foolishly, his young face shining with relief from sheer terror.

'Came down on us from nowhere, my lord. Hidden in that copse,' he gasped. 'One man winged, one horse down apart from the mare. The raiders were too lightweight to do much damage.' He gabbled as the fear ebbed. 'The lady's safe, my lord. Not a war party, a chance raiding party only that caught us napping…'

But Gervase was pushing past him. A rapid eye cast over his men and their mounts told him that there was no serious injury. The injured horse had a flesh wound to its shoulder from an arrow and would recover. Leaving Hugh to order the return to the castle, he gave his full attention to Rosamund.

Relief dripped through his veins. His belly felt hollow with it, his throat dry. Owen had had the sense to pull her into the shelter of a rocky outcrop, pushing her to the floor. It might just have saved her life. Now seeing her scramble unharmed to her feet, his outrageous relief recreated itself in an unnerving instant into a shattering anger. Gervase addressed her, harsh voiced, gripping her shoulders to pull her upright, making no attempt to harness his fury even when she winced under his grasp. Her survival was a matter of pure chance. If he had not seen the attack, she might even now be lying in the grass with an arrow between her shoulder blades.

His accusations, fired one after the other, were brutal. 'See what you have done! What your wilfulness almost achieved, insisting on riding out. You put in the balance the lives of my men, not to mention your own. You have no thought for anyone but yourself.' He could not let go, hands clenched on her shoulders as if he needed to feel her flesh and bones, vibrant and living, beneath his hand. And the old remorse blasted through him. Matilda had died without him to rescue her. Died in the arms of some nameless man, a Fitz Osbern soldier who had been there to comfort her. He had not been there to stop it. And he had almost allowed it to happen again. The words tumbled from his lips. 'I am as much to blame as you. I knew of the dangers. I should not have let you go.'

'I—' Rosamund blinked at him, apparently without understanding, which made him even more angry.

'You'll not disobey orders. As long as you remain at Clifford, you'll do as I say.' And Gervase, as if viewing the scene from a distance, was honourable enough to acknowledge within the blazing heart of his fury, that it was directed as much at himself as at her.

Still Rosamund barely seemed to hear him. A glassy look of shock was in her eyes, her skin clammy, pale as wax. Seeing it, his blaze of anger reduced to a steady simmer. Then, as her gaze slid from his to some distant object, and became fixed there in horror, he finally understood. And as he did, Rosamund pulled away from his slackened grip, stumbling across the grass, to fall to her knees beside the stricken mare, regardless of the mud and blood that smeared on her skirts and mantle. She stroked her hand down the silken neck, still warm, still impossibly alive. Tightened her fingers in the rough mane. Dry eyed, she murmured softly, until the mare's stillness caused her to fall silent.

'She's dead, isn't she?' she said as Gervase moved behind her, to crouch on his heels at her side. 'They killed her.'

Gervase sighed. 'Yes. See, the arrows…'

'I did not think we would be in any danger.' Still her hand smoothed the cooling shoulder.

'Who's to know?' All anger gone, Gervase lifted her, gently now, with a hand under her arm, turning her away from the stricken animal. 'We must go back.'

'But…' She looked down at the mare.

'I'll see to the mare.'

'I'm sorry I put your men in danger.' Her cheeks were dry, but her eyes were bright as she wiped them with her sleeve, leaving a smear of mud. 'You were right to take me to task. It was ill done of me.'

'But no harm in the outcome.'

'No.' Her voice shook, but she controlled it. 'No harm. I am so sorry…'

Gervase led her to his horse, swung into the saddle, and beckoned for Owen to come and lift her to his saddlebow, to tuck her skirts neatly. Small practical movements to fill her mind so that she might keep her dignity. He felt that she would want that. As little as he knew her, he realised that she would not want to give way to grief under scrutiny. Settling her against him, he felt a shiver run through her. Her tears were not too far away.

'It seems I must carry you home again.' He clicked his tongue at the stallion to encourage it into a calm pace. 'We must try not to make a habit of this.' A hopeless attempt to distract her. Again she shuddered, then hid her face against his shoulder and wept.

'I'm sorry,' she whispered.

'It doesn't matter. No one sees.'

He held her close with one arm, guiding the horse with the other as they walked steadily back, his men returning around them, empty handed from their chase. Gervase raised his hand in acknowledgement, but at that moment he did not care. All that mattered was that she was safe in his arms. She had lost her veil in the skirmish, so that it was so easy to turn his cheek to rest against her hair. If he turned his head to press his lips there, she wasn't aware. All he knew was that she was warm and alive, her heart beating strongly against him. He could do nothing to assuage her grief, but he could give her the comfort of his arms.

'She was my own,' she murmured at last as they turned into the castle gates.

'I will give you another, Rose. One of my own from Monmouth.'

She nodded and clung to him. He did not think she understood, but the storm of her grief was past. Back in the bailey, he dismounted, lifted her down and stood her carefully on her feet, standing between her and his men to hide her ravaged cheeks. Until she winced as his arm caught her shoulder.

'Are you hurt?'

She shook her head. 'A bruise only, I think. It is just sore…'

When he pushed back the mired mantle, she gasped from pain. Without further thought, he waved the anxious servants aside and lifted her as gently as he could and carried her into the keep. Even there he would not relinquish her, but strode up the staircase as if she were no weight at all, shouldering his way into the solar where he placed her on the settle before the fire.

'Candles!' he ordered the hovering Edith, not taking his eyes from Rosamund's face, which seemed even paler. Was her shoulder broken? Her collarbone? When he had done nothing but haul her to her feet, without thought for any injury when the mare fell. No wonder she had flinched from him. 'Fetch the Countess.' Stripping away the mantle, he applied himself to the side-laces of her over-tunic. Without great success.

'Ah…!' Rosamund winced and set her teeth into her bottom lip.

'God's wounds!' Without another word he took his knife from its sheath at his belt and used it to more effect with an agile turn of his wrist. First the over-tunic and then the laces of her gown, sweeping the point of the knife through them from neck to waist and below. Finally even against the cloth of her close fitting shift, careless of the damage or her half-hearted attempts to push him away.

'You're not gutting a rabbit!' she objected as the laces fell at her feet.

'Don't argue!' Aware only that she was shocked and tearful and in pain. Baring her shoulder at last, the heavy discolouring and chafed skin was already clear across her shoulder blade and arm.

'I think I fell on it.' She choked back a sob, squinting to see over her shoulder like a small child. 'When my mare fell, when she was…'

'Yes. When she went down. You were lucky she didn't roll on you.'

'I suppose so… It hurts.' She groaned. 'Especially when you press it like that!'

'Don't complain! I thought you were made of sterner stuff.'

'I am!'

Gervase gentled his touch, probing the wounded area with light fingers as fear drained from him. Rosamund sniffed and scrubbed at her face, apparently unmoved that he should be inspecting her naked shoulder. As he smoothed his palm over her skin, relieved that there were no broken bones and no lasting damage, a touch of hard-edged humour surprised him. She would be mortified when she remembered.

'It will be painful, but will soon mend,' he assured her.

'You are very kind.'

Unable to resist, Gervase continued to stroke his hand down over her shoulder, the curve of her throat, as he might an injured mare to soothe and reassure. Conscious all the time of the stark contrast of his weathered hands, calloused and work-worn, against the pale silk of her skin. Relieved when he felt the tension leave her so that she rested her head against his supporting arm. Then with a little murmur, she sat up, their eyes met, locked, Gervase wallowing in the depths of pain and anguish in her trusting gaze. Until without premeditation Gervase lowered his head to press the gentlest of kisses to her brow.

'I don't deserve such consideration,' she whispered.

'Yes, you do. You are hurt and sad and I would comfort you.' And since she did not draw away, he allowed himself another kiss, equally gentle, to her lips.

And then, when she simply looked at him wide-eyed, as if she could not contemplate such gentleness from him, the Countess was there. And Edith, who clucked and fussed. With an unsettling sense of loss, Gervase found himself pushed firmly into the background as they took over. He smiled sardonically. He had just been swept aside as if he had no place here, no role in women's affairs.

'Shall I send for Mistress—I forget her name—the witch from the village?'

'Mistress Kempe,' Petronilla admonished, her whole attention elsewhere. 'Yes—and she is no witch! If you would, my lord.'

And he was dismissed again.

It was true, that he had no place in Rosamund's life. He ran down the steps, shouting the order to fetch Mistress Kempe, thinking only of the softness of her skin beneath his touch. The vicious bruising. Thank God she was safe. His part was now complete. Except for… Never one to ignore his debts, Gervase sought out Owen. He found him under Watkins's care in the stable where the wounded horse was being tended. Owen was white-faced and shaken now that the danger was over, never having faced such immediate violence in his twelve years, and the sergeant-at-arms had decided to blur the edges of the boy's fear with a mug of ale. Gervase nodded his approval and sat on the straw bale next to the boy.

'You did well, lad.'

Owen gulped. 'The lady is safe, my lord?'

'Yes. Safe.'

'I didn't see them, my lord. They were on us before—'

'You did as much as any man.' He put a warm hand on the boy's shoulder, squeezed. Then ruffled his already untidy hair. 'You probably saved her life.'

It mattered more than he would have thought possible. But now he must put it out of his mind.

Rosamund sighed as Mistress Kempe bustled in. It promised more pain.

'If it's not one thing, it's another. First foul water, and now this. Let me look at you, my lady…' She swept Petronilla and Edith out of the way, poking with fingers far less gentle than Gervase's. 'Bruising. Discolouring of the skin.' She prodded and poked again. 'No bones broken. No permanent damage, lady. Mind you, I can't say it won't be sore for a few days.'

'Ow!' Cross, Rosamund made no attempt to hide her discomfort.

'A cup of wine,' Mistress Kempe demanded, then burrowed in a leather pouch at her waist and extracted a small pottery vessel. 'I brought this on the off chance.' Removing the stopper, she shook a quantity of dark powder into the wine and stirred. 'Drink this.' She grunted as Rosamund grimaced. 'It'll not poison you. There! Good! Common knapweed.' She gave Edith the pot. 'Put the rest in warm water and apply it to the lady's shoulder frequently. It will take away the stiffness.'

Rosamund allowed the events to flow on around her. It seemed to have nothing to do with her. Now that she was warm, the pain retreating a little, a strange lassitude took over, so that even the loss of her mare, although a constant beat of sorrow, seemed to be at a distance.

'Excellent!' Mistress Kempe peered at her. 'I'll send some more knapweed up with my daughter. And the bark of the white willow—steep it in wine and drink it to ease the pain. Send for me if she does not get her full movement back in her shoulder. I warrant she will.' Her little eyes, almost hidden in wrinkles, twinkled. 'My lord seemed distraught.'

'He was concerned for my daughter,' Petronilla remarked.

'Concerned, is it? Seemed more than that to me.' The witch peered at Rosamund again. 'He's a potent lord, and no gain-saying. I'd give you a love potion to attract the man if I thought you needed one.'

'A love potion? That's the last thing I want.' Startled, Rosamund flinched as Edith began to lace her into a loose gown.

'No, you don't. He already has eyes for you.' Mistress Kempe chuckled at Rosamund's misunderstanding. Then she slid a sly, mischief-making glance at Petronilla. 'Or perhaps you could make use of it, lady. For my Lord de Mortimer. A pinch of lavender, pinch of valerian root, mixed on a Friday evening when the moon is waxing. That'd do the trick, my lady. He'll look at no one but you.'

Petronilla smiled calmly with firmly pressed lips and superb dignity under the circumstances. 'Thank you, but no.' She pressed a coin into Mistress Kempe's gnarled hand.

'As you wish. I'll leave it here anyway!'

Whether from the effects of the knapweed or her own exhaustion, Rose slept soundly, but struggled from her bed on the following day stiff and aching, her shoulder and arm a mass of blue and purple bruising. Lifting her arm hurt more than she would ever have believed and she was not reluctant to drink the bitter willow. Left to her own devices, reluctant to move far, she let her mind pick apart the memories that came back.

It was not a comforting operation. He had accused her of being thoughtless, selfish, which was true. She must be more aware of the dangers in living in the lawless Marches. She could have caused the death of more than just her mare. She had to blink back sudden tears as the loss rolled over her again. But that was not her main preoccupation. Gervase had rescued her, driven off the raiders, cared for her, brought her home. Handled her gently when he had finished shouting at her. Seen to her comfort. He had kissed her as if she were the most precious possession he owned. Such small, particular kindnesses—but she must have a care. They would break her, weaken her resolve. Even now she was aware of the faintest hairline cracks appearing in her hard shell of resistance to him.

Gervase Fitz Osbern held a dangerous attraction for her. Tears leapt again, to be quickly wiped away.

She could not remember whether she had thanked him. It all seemed blurred and distant. Although she did remember him taking his knife to her laces. She did not know whether to be shocked at such intimacy or admiring of his initiative. How she would face him she did not know, but she must thank him.

And tried to do so, when she came down, awkwardly but without complaint, to the mid-day meal. She had practised her words, practised a calm demeanour. To her dismay, he was not there. It would have been so easy to abandon her self-imposed penance, but she could not. So, directed by Sir Thomas, she traced him to the stable, where he was inspecting one of the hooves of his stallion.

Except that he brushed her stammered apology aside. Gave no thought to it or to her once he had assured himself, with the briefest of glances from under his black brows, that she was some way to being recovered.

'The ambush…' she tried. It was a concern that had settled in her mind on waking. 'It was not Owen's fault. I would not have you blame him, my lord.'

Another sharp appraisal. 'I'll deal with Owen as I see fit.'

'Of course.'

'I presume you are suffering no ill effects.'

'No.'

'Good.'

On which bleak, curt response, he had immediately returned his attention to the problem hoof, summoning Watkins to give his opinion of the heat in the leg.

Rosamund retreated. He had not shouted at her, neither had he seemed angry. Instead, he had treated her apology as an irrelevance. So he must still blame her after all. She must have imagined the tenderness in his face when he carried her to her solar, or the concern when he had promised to deal with the mare for her. His preoccupation was clearly elsewhere, so Rosamund could do nothing but let the matter rest. She had after all wept all over him. Perhaps it was enough to turn any man from her in disgust. Shame settled heavily.

Well, if Fitz Osbern would not talk to her, at least she could express her personal gratitude to Owen.

'Owen…'

Owen, fair, untidy head bent, engaged in the unpleasant task of scouring the rust from Fitz Osbern's weapons, looked up, flushed, and leapt to his feet, a dagger in his hand.

'I did all I could, Lady…' His colour deepened. Did he fear her retribution? She must put him at his ease, even if Fitz Osbern would not.

'You saved my life. You pulled me into shelter when my mare fell.'

Owen swallowed visibly, eyes wide. 'I did what I thought was best.'

'I hope you have not been punished.'

'Punished?' His brow immediately furrowed. 'No, my lady. My lord says I will make a good knight. That my father will be proud of me.'

'Did he?' She could not hide her surprise.

'He did. And he gave me this.' Owen turned and delved into the pile of swords. Extracted one and held it out. 'Lord Fitz Osbern gave me this. For my own.'

Rosamund could not but smile. The chased grip was far too large for his small hand, but he would grow into it.

'It is one of my lord's own swords.'

'Then you must be very proud.'

So Gervase Fitz Osbern had both praised him and rewarded his squire. Rosamund left Owen to his task, her thoughts of Lord Fitz Osbern once more in total confusion.

Rosamund paced her chamber, the short distance between bed and window, considering the predicament she had unwittingly tossed herself into. It seemed to her that she was torn in two directions, and did not like either. She owed Fitz Osbern her life, thus creating a debt of honour on her side. She had promised Fitz Osbern that she would do nothing to undermine the smooth running of the Clifford household and garrison, and she was, as she acknowledged in response to a tweak of conscience, not a woman to break her promises. But this stalemate between them could not last. His kisses, his careful handling of her, had changed everything for her. Attempting to close her mind to the memory of his mouth on hers and her own inexplicable desire both for more kisses and to return them, she failed entirely as hot colour flushed her cheeks, as heat prickled along her skin.

Stop thinking about the man, Rosamund! she lectured herself. His embrace means nothing. It would mean less than nothing to him. He probably kissed women frequently. Dozens of them. Her own reaction was merely a symptom of the surprise of the event, overlaid by simple gratitude that he had ridden to her rescue. The sooner she pushed aside and forgot the two disastrous episodes, one of diamond-bright lust, the other of heart-wrenching gentleness, the better. For if nothing else, her mind's preoccupation with the Marcher lord had proved that she could no longer live side by side with this man. He might give the impression of a moneyless mercenary who would prey on the weak to his own ends, but she could not deny her attraction to him or that he had so dangerous an influence over her.

On the other hand, and here was the crux of the matter, retreating to Salisbury could never be a choice for her. Ralph de Morgan would be waiting for her at the end of that road. Nausea shook her, fear gripped her, a queasy weight in her belly. A knot, hard as granite, lodged in her throat so that her head ached with it. Because in spite of everything, in spite of all his promises, it had been made more than plain to her that Fitz Osbern was planning to remove her from Clifford.

Why had she ever trusted him, believed him to be a man of honour? She had known what he was from the very beginning. He had done nothing to hide his base instincts. How could she have allowed herself to be swayed by that bright shard of attraction that persisted in lodging in her heart, no matter what he did? Of course he was not a man of honour, as he had, that very morning, proved to her.

Rosamund had spied him in deep conversation with the leader of one of his frequent patrols just returned. It was a serious discussion. Deep furrows scored his brow as she approached to discover what was afoot.

'What is it?' she demanded as the patrol disbanded for ale and food.

'Nothing. Or there again it might be… Rumours of a large raiding party.' Gervase had stared at the mud at his feet, rubbed a hand over his jaw, his thoughts obviously elsewhere. 'Not your concern, lady.'

'Yes, it is,' Rosamund had responded sharply. 'If it threatens my castle, it *is* my affair. What are you planning?'

Which got his attention. Fitz Osbern scowled at her. 'It's no threat to your pretty skin, my lady. Only to my own home in Monmouth. Perhaps to my mother… That's not your concern— nor your interest. My plans are nothing to you.'

Rosamund had flushed vividly with shame that she should have immediately thought of her own safety rather than that of Fitz Osbern's family, then with anger that he should judge her so harshly. She listened as he gave orders to Watkins to look to the equipment and horses of a fast troop of soldiers.

'Are you leaving?' she demanded.

'I might.'

'When?'

'When it's necessary.' At last he looked at her directly. The curve of his mouth, the gleam in his eye was not pleasant as he grasped his sword belt with fisted hands and appraised her from her veil to her hem. 'Now I see you're interested. That's what you would want, isn't it? For me to leave, taking my troops with me?' He positively leered. 'Don't raise your hopes, lady. If I go, I won't leave *you* here in charge. You might not be quick to let me back in.' He stepped close, a little too close so that his sleeve brushed hers, threateningly. She could feel the heat of him. 'If I go, I'll take you with me.'

'No. I won't go.' Hurt brushed her skin. Why did he always think the worst of her?

'No choice, lady. I'll deliver you to Hereford myself on my way south. I'll leave de Byton in charge here.' He made to walk away, face stern.

'You said you would let me stay.' Outrage gave her voice an edge.

'But not in my absence, lady. Now take yourself off about your own affairs, out of my way. I'll inform you when you need to be ready to ride.'

So summarily dismissed. He thought her selfish and un-trustworthy. And he had the power to carry out his threat. Ralph de Morgan instantly beckoned with his gross belly and greasy fingers. In sheer fright, when Gervase would have turned away, Rosamund fisted her hand and punched his arm.

It was a glancing blow, ridiculously light against this hard

muscles. It shamed her anew. It startled him. He recovered first
with a harsh laugh.

'Lady Rosamund! Is that how a de Longspey behaves?'

'Yes.' She swallowed at the expression of disdain in his face.
'When she is tried beyond patience by a man who is as insen-
sitive as he is dishonourable.'

'Ha! Well, let me show you how a Fitz Osbern reacts, when
he is goaded beyond endurance by a bad-tempered woman.'

He swooped, plunged, fast as a hunting sparrowhawk. His
embrace, the hard banding of his arms, simply robbed her of
her breath. Mouth capturing, tongue possessing, hand owning
in one long sweep of hard caress down her side, she could not
struggle. Too shocked, too stunned by his power and her own
needy response as her heart leapt. Until he released her, with a
quizzical expression.

'Don't goad me, lady,' was all he said.

His arms fell away. His face rough-hewn, lacking all expression. His mouth twisted, thin-lipped, almost cruel. Which had
left her breathless, terror ripe that she would have to obey his
commands if he chose to go. The demons of fear that had
gradually loosed their hold since the day of Gervase's ride to
save her life, of his extraordinarily compassionate treatment of
her, raced back, sharp-spurred, to dominate her every thought.

So now, in her chamber, faced with the stark reality that her
future might be determined by events beyond her control,
Rosamund cast about for an answer, and it was not difficult to
find. To remain safe at Clifford, as was her right, she must use
honest, legal means. Nothing underhand, nothing unseemly, but
clear recourse to the law of the land. And who better to trust,
if she could not trust Fitz Osbern, as clearly she could not, than
the King of England? King Henry who was in that very moment
not twenty miles away at Ludlow.

So that night whilst her mother slept, she sent for a quill, ink
and a sheet of parchment. And, she determined as she wrote,
she would not speak of this little matter to Lady Petronilla, who

could not, for some unfathomable reason, keep a secret where Hugh de Mortimer was concerned.

The voice of her conscience whispered in the silence of her bedchamber. *Does this not have the smack of dishonourable dealing, Rosamund? A stab in the back? Is this not cold treachery against Fitz Osbern, who saved your life?*

'Not if it's legal and right,' she replied to the sly cat. 'How can that be dishonest? If I wish to stay out of Ralph's clutches, I must use the means I have. What choice do I have? I can't trust Fitz Osbern to keep his word. Has he not made his future plans plain?'

The cat yawned silently and returned to grooming its fur.

So, satisfied with the result—as far as she ever would be—Rosamund accosted Thomas de Byton next morning.

'Sir Thomas—I need a courier to deliver a letter for me—to my brother the Earl of Salisbury,' she improvised. No need to tell him the truth of it since he would carry the knowledge straight to Fitz Osbern.

'That's as may be, my lady.' Sir Thomas appeared to deliberate. 'I must ask his lordship's permission first.'

'You are *my* commander, Sir Thomas, not Lord Fitz Osbern's.'

'A moot point, my lady. I take my orders direct from Lord Fitz Osbern.'

Although this exchange had been entirely expected, it made a furious Rosamund even more determined to pursue her goal. There were other means. A word with Master Pennard to arrange a lad with a horse, a handful of coin, and she saw her letter set off at a canter down the track in the direction of Ludlow.

Not toward Salisbury.

There was no need to feel guilty at all, she assured herself as the horse and rider dwindled into the distance. No need at all. What would the loss of Clifford really mean to Fitz Osbern? She twitched her shoulders as if to rid them of an unwanted weight. Why he was so determined to hold on to a small border fortress she had no idea.

Chapter Eight

'**B**y the Virgin! The woman is impossible.'

Fitz Osbern muttered the oath, not for the first time using those same words, to a passing pair of unresponsive ravens. She had no business to still be at Clifford. He'd be glad to see the back of her, never to set eyes on her again. He scowled at the glossy birds wheeling in the brisk breeze. Except that he would like nothing better than the opportunity to kiss her again. More than that, he acknowledged. To strip the clothes from her—he bared his teeth at the memory of doing almost that, with his dagger, without finesse—and take her to his bed.

'Devil take the woman!'

Shrugging off so illogical a reaction to a woman who did nothing but defy and irritate him at every step, Gervase gave all his physical efforts with his men into the strengthening of one section of the palisade. Until he could arrange the transport of stone for the rebuilding of the entire wall, he must make do with a renewal of timber in the weaker sections. Necessary with the rumours of large raiding parties. Satisfying work, but it did not take his mind off Rosamund de Longspey. Nothing took his mind off her! She had kept out of his way since her brush with death in the ambush, but his mind remained disconcertingly with her.

He couldn't explain why he had kissed her in the first place after the cat in the well incident. Or when she had refused categorically to accompany him if he found the need to take a force to Monmouth. He had acted on sheer impulse on both occasions, of course, not a reasoned step. In anger, he admitted, when she had challenged him. There she had stood, all fire and bright defiance, accusing him of God knew what. Her soft lips parted, those astonishing green eyes brilliant. One short hard kiss was all he had intended, just to savour those lips. After all, she was far too high born to consider a tumble between the sheets with a lover who was not lawfully wedded to her. Whilst he, he admitted, had far too much honour to even consider it, however attractive her face and figure might be to any red-blooded man. Besides, she was definitely not his choice of woman at all. Nothing like Matilda.

He stopped, his hands still on the stave of wood he held. Hugh had said he should marry her. Ha! He wanted a quiet life, not a daily crossing of swords with the woman he would chose as his wife.

And yet…why not? Would it not solve the problem overnight, as Hugh pointed out? If she became his wife, Clifford would return to his dominion. The lady was capable and could run the place for him, could live here if that was her wish. His teeth glinted in an appreciative grin. Once she had abandoned the idea of driving him out by an evil-smelling midden, she had proved herself to be a most efficient chatelaine. She could read and write and figure, a distinct advantage, if unusual in a woman. Of a determined cast of mind, she could hold the reins strongly, and he imagined she could collect the rents owed with a firm hand against any man who would try to take advantage of a woman's softness.

The grin faded. Was there any softness in Rosamund de Longspey?

But of course there was. He deliberately directed his mind into more comfortable channels. As his wife, she would enjoy the authority at Clifford, in his name or her own. He could leave her here and return to Monmouth. All in all, it seemed that he had heard worse advice than marriage to the woman.

Taken with the idea, Gervase moved out of the way of two of his men who were manhandling a newly felled tree trunk between them. The only problem as far as he could see—would she do it? Would she see the advantage of such an alliance, even if it was clear to him? It would remove the threat of Ralph de Morgan hanging over her. She was of age and so could make her own decision, without the consent of Earl Gilbert. If her inclination was toward independence, he would leave her at Clifford and she could have it.

A perfect arrangement, convenient for all. He did not have to like her or even see her very often.

And yet… Infuriatingly, the banished images sprang to life again. He remembered her mouth, the softness of it against the hardness of his. How her body had fit with his within his arms. He had kissed her—well, as a warning not to meddle in his affairs, a punishment of a kind. That was the first time. Unwittingly he had been drawn against his will to repeat the experience. Such sweetness as he had discovered beneath her proud defiance when she had come to him in the west tower after the incident of the damned cat. When she no longer resisted him, she melted in honeyed sweetness so that he drowned, senses swamped with its heaviness. He recalled the throb of her heart, beating furiously beneath his mouth in that soft hollow at the base of her throat. It had caused his own blood to riot and surge in response, his body to strain with the power of his arousal. He could not remember a woman who had had such an effect on him. And her hands had clung to him…

But then she had changed, in the blink of an eye, all ice and dignity, and he had let her go.

It could not be denied, however much he might wish to cast her into the character of a vixen. The softness, the consideration for others, was definitely there. When her mother had been struck down. When her mare had been killed. Then she had been inconsolable and had turned into him and wept. How difficult he had found it to face her pain or the chance that she had died under a Welsh arrow. So that when she had come to make amends he had deliberately shut her out. Stated coldly, brusquely, that she appeared to suffer no repercussions, when it was clear to any man that she was rigid from pain. He had had to work hard not to snatch her up into his arms to assure himself of her safety. By God, what had she thought of him! He had focused on his stallion's perfectly healthy hoof as if he had never seen one in his life before. Watkins must have thought he was all about in his wits. No, he was not proud of that. But the fear that she could have met the same unhappy fate as Matilda had driven him to mask his emotions. Despicable indeed that he should have added to her unhappiness. Yet even then she had shown her concern for Owen's welfare.

How difficult women were to read.

Gervase squinted his eyes against the low ray of winter sun as new wooden staves were driven into the earth, the sound echoing round him. Since then she had barely exchanged a word with him. It was his own fault, he acknowledged. Had he not lived up to his self-imposed role with exceptional skill? As the villain of the piece—who had all but stripped her robe from her body, using his knife—she probably thought he had rape and pillage in mind. She had no idea how close he had come to abandoning his façade and showering her with tenderness. It had been a mistake to kiss her as he had.

But had it? When he had held her and kissed her in his room, there had been a response beyond the pure innocence. She had not found him objectionable. She had clung to him, offered her mouth. Her hands had held him close rather than pushing him away. And when she had been hurt and sorrowful she had been able to accept comfort from him and weep into his shoulder.

So why not just take her? You have the bed and the woman,

*make the most of the opportunity fate has cast in your way. If
you desire her, then have her, and assuage the need. Ease your
desire to your own satisfaction. Easy enough to do. She accused
you of rape and pillage. Prove it. Once you've had her, you'll
probably obliterate the need.*

Gervase growled in disgust. That was not the path to take.
He could not, would never dishonour a woman that way, no
matter what she thought of him. Would not defile his own
honour. Certainly he would never deal out such foul treatment
to Rosamund de Longspey. He could not think of her in the light
of a casual liaison. In fact, he was in the greatest danger of…

No! Love was not a word he would consider.

But if he offered her marriage, on his own terms, she might
just be open to persuasion.

Never one to back away from a problem, Gervase decided
to meet that problem head on. At present it was standing on the
palisade walk, looking out over the rough track toward Ludlow.
She had been there all morning. Now was as good a time as any.
He loped up the open staircase and made his way toward her,
beating the wood shavings from his tunic, raking them with his
fingers from his hair.

'Lady…'

He had taken her by surprise. She turned, lips parted, eyes
wide, almost he might have said with apprehension. 'I did not
hear you, my lord.'

'I saw you watching the road. Waiting for Ralph? For your
brothers to come and rescue you from my clutches?'

She flushed and looked away, unsettled, so that he wished
he had not made the remark.

'No, my lord.'

Without further thought, he leapt into the quagmire. 'I have
a proposition, lady.' As she turned her direct gaze on him, her
brows rose haughtily, beautifully. To ruffle her a little, and
because he decided it would please him, he lifted her hand from
where it lay clenched against the edge of the parapet and raised

it to his lips, which made her fair skin tint even more becomingly. When she would have snatched her hand away, he held on, acutely aware of her slender fingers enclosed within his own. 'Do you realise that we could solve the whole problem of this impasse between us without difficulty?'

The flush deepened to the heat of a fire, and for an instant she dropped her eyes. Then, 'how would we do that, my lord, other than by you leaving Clifford?'

'We could marry.' Bald, unadorned. Had he truly intended to make it so brutal? Silence greeted his announcement. He was conscious of her whole body stiffening beside him, her fingers becoming rigid. 'You need a husband to rescue you from the threat of Ralph,' he continued bluntly. 'I have no wife and have need of a chatelaine. It would solve the ownership of Clifford perfectly.'

It was astonishment he presumed that banished the colour from her cheeks so that she was as pale as her veil that lifted sluggishly in the breeze. A shadow flitted across her face. Something troubled her. Perhaps she simply did not believe him. And in that moment it mattered to him that she did. Turning her hand within his, he pressed his mouth to the soft palm, and then to her wrist, marvelling at the fragile femininity there at odds with her vibrant spirit. As he lifted his head, the fragile femininity vanished. Her fingers curled into a fist.

'Will you wed me, Rosamund de Longspey?' he asked again, ignoring the danger signs.

'Wed you?' she repeated through stiff lips.

'A neat arrangement to settle the ownership.'

'No.'

He had expected a more gracious reply. 'Perhaps you would think about the advantages before you reject the offer out of hand.'

'No!'

Her lips parted, as if she was about to say more. So focused were they that they had missed the distant beat of hooves. Until they were attracted by a call from the guard on the gatehouse.

'Armed force. From the north.'

Small, compact, shining horseflesh, the glitter of weapons, a well-drilled escort approached. And pennons, their device gleaming in red and gold. Gervase slid his eyes from the defiant lady before him to that glittering evidence. If he was not mistaken… He glanced back at his companion. She was quite still, her attention as caught as his, but her eyes gleamed. Now why…? The smart troop pulled to a halt. Their leader stood up in his stirrups and hailed the gatehouse.

'In the name of the King, I command you to open the gates!'

Breathing deep against the tightening of an unpleasant anticipation in his gut, Gervase raised an arm that Sir Thomas should comply. 'We'll continue this discussion later, lady,' he remarked somewhat grimly as he strode down to meet the visitors, Hugh emerging from the keep to take up an interested stance at his shoulder.

'An unexpected visit,' Hugh observed thoughtfully, as the force clattered into the bailey. 'And Sir Jasper Griffiths in all his pompous glory, I see. If you want my advice, Ger—keep your temper!'

'Difficult. But I'll make the effort,' he responded drily. 'I wonder…' Gervase became aware that Rosamund too had come to join the welcoming party. He set his jaw, clamped his hands around his sword belt and steeled himself to receive some sort of royal pronouncement he suspected he would not enjoy.

'My Lord Fitz Osbern!' The royal official drew his glossy mount to a standstill before him, gave a curt inclination of his head. 'His Majesty the King bids me give this to you.' He held a document with the royal seal in his hand.

'Welcome, Sir Jasper. What is it?'

It seemed to Gervase that Griffiths, an arrogant individual even without the weight of royal authority, smirked as his bright eyes travelled from one to the other of those who awaited him. 'It has come to His Grace's attention that there is some dispute here. His Grace has given some thought to his judgement in the matter. His ruling is that the castle is properly in the ownership of the Lady of de Longspey as her dower from Earl William of Salisbury. Earl Gilbert confirms it. Your claim, my lord, is still unclear to the King. Therefore His Grace orders that you must take your troops and leave this place forthwith until the matter is settled. You must ride with me immediately to Ludlow to appear before the King, where he will make his final decision.' He bowed gracefully. He definitely smirked. 'I have here a writ from his Grace to confirm it.'

'*What?*'

It was like the clap of a sword's face against his ribcage, a vicious blow. That the King would hesitate in supporting the rightness of the Fitz Osbern claim was beyond belief. And yet here Henry had all but pronounced royal judgement against him, taking no account of the unprincipled thieving habits of the dead Lord William. Would the King order him out like a common robber, without a hearing? And he a Marcher lord who held the borders safe for a king with vast dominions to oversee. Gervase Fitz Osbern, a man of high reputation and service to Henry Plantagenet's family. Had he not fought for the Plantagenet claim in the recent wars? Had he not supported Henry in his claim to the English crown?

Your claim is uncertain.

Was it, by God! He did not think so! Yet here was Henry dismissing his own claim to his family's inheritance as if he were no better than a peasant. Which made it clear as spring water that the Earls of Salisbury had far more clout than a Marcher lord when it came to bending the King's ear!

Fury built within him. That he would be twice robbed of his own property, Clifford Castle, and this time by the decision of a king who had barely held his throne much beyond four years. That his own father's name should again be slighted with the loss of Clifford. And the gnawing suspicions of how this disaster might have come to pass lit a flame in his belly.

'It's in the document, my lord.' Sir Jasper still held it out with insufferable self-importance and not a little impatience. 'You can read it for yourself. You are to hand over this place immediately and ride with me.'

As he saw the man smile, as he saw out of the corner of his eye Rosamund give a faint nod of acceptance, the flame blazed into a conflagration. His temper snapped. Before anyone could read his intention and react to prevent it, he had leapt forward, grasped Sir Jasper's mantle to pull him, together with the offending document, from his horse. He shook the man once, as a terrier would shake a rat, before depositing him heavily on his feet in the mud.

'How dare you set hands on the King's representative…!' King Henry's messenger spluttered with markedly less confidence than on his arrival.

'I dare do more than you can imagine! Give up my birthright? By the order of an absent king who will not come himself to face me?' Reaching forward again, the irate Fitz Osbern hefted the man by his furred collar so that they were eye to eye. 'I've a mind to make you eat the writ. And the seals with it.'

'My lord…!' he croaked.

Gervase snatched the writ from the man's hand, cracking the seal, running his eye rapidly down the legal order. 'Does the King think no better of me than to order me out by a few words scrawled on a piece of parchment? No, by God. A woman can't hold this place securely against the Welsh raiders, but I can. You can tell your royal master—'

'No, my lord.'

A hand closed on his forearm. A cool voice speared through the hot mist in his mind. The fingers increased their pressure against the taut muscles when he did not at first respond. And as he looked down into those green eyes, he was sure. She knew. Of course, she knew. She had probably been waiting on the battlements for this royal reply. How could she be capable of such deceit when she had promised her compliance? He had been right not to trust her. Yet she had such beautiful eyes…even when they contained a flash of warning, as they did now.

'No, my lord,' she repeated. 'Release the courier. It will do no good. Let me answer this.'

Brought back to his surroundings, he released the official, who staggered to regain his balance, attempting to straighten his clothes. Hugh, an awestruck observer through all this, thoughtfully retrieved his jewelled hat from where it had fallen in the mud. If Gervase had never been quite so angry as he was at this royal intervention, Hugh decided that he had never been quite so entertained. He worked to keep his face in solemn lines. It might just do his autocratic friend some good to be undermined by this clever woman. Not that Gervase would see it in that light. Not yet, at any rate. The blaze in his eyes was awesome. Hugh attempted to wipe the worst of the mud from the foolishly stylish cap, handed it back to Sir Jasper, as Rosamund stepped forward.

'Thank his Grace, King Henry, for his ruling, sir.' Still with a grasp of Fitz Osbern's sleeve, Rosamund drew herself to her full height and addressed the man as if there had been no altercation. 'Say that Lady Rosamund de Longspey is grateful.'

'*You* are grateful…!' Fitz Osbern snarled, shrugging off her hand.

'Tell his Grace that his wishes will be acted upon. And that he will always be welcome here in my home.'

Gervase could listen no more. 'Tell King Henry from me that this castle will be held by a Fitz Osbern as long as the name lives! I have no intention of meeting him in Ludlow to allow him to decide against me. Tell him…' He stalked away toward the keep, trying to hold together the shredded remains of his temper. It was, as he was usually the first to admit—but not on this occasion—a blight on a man. He had learnt to control it over the years, but in the face of such back-stabbing, it had almost slipped beyond his control. He was not proud of it, but it seemed to him that the provocation had been overwhelming.

It was all the de Longspey hellcat's fault.

* * *

Sir Jasper departed back to Ludlow, somewhat soothed by the lady's gracious acceptance, leaving Rosamund to pick up the crumpled writ with its broken seal from the mud of the bailey. She had got what she wanted, hadn't she? So why did she feel so uncomfortable? As if, in a cowardly attack, she had personally buried the point of a dagger between Fitz Osbern's shoulder blades.

What she had done had been prompted by sheer common sense. Who better to back her claim against Fitz Osbern than the King himself, a young man with a reputation for law and order and a heavy hand against any lord who was foolhardy enough to resist him? Was he not in Ludlow even now? It had been the simplest of solutions. There was no need to feel guilty at petitioning the King on her own behalf. None at all. Fitz Osbern deserved all he got if he were summarily driven from her door.

She recalled the letter she had dispatched, dramatic and to the point. All she had done was state her case.

To his Grace, King Henry II
Sire,
I throw myself at your feet in my quest for justice. The border fortress of Clifford is mine, my dower by right of inheritance. I have the documents and seals of Earl William of Salisbury as proof. My authority has been stolen from me by the Lord Fitz Osbern, who now occupies the castle. I beg your ruling in this matter. I am living at Clifford with my mother, the Dowager Countess of Salisbury, under the control of Fitz Osbern who has no sense of the rightness of the case.

I beg that you will give your ruling in my favour with all speed.
From your loyal and most obedient subject,
Rosamund de Longspey

The result of her demand for justice could not have been bettered, and within the week. She smoothed the document with her hand. It seemed from Sir Jasper's words that the King would decide in her favour. So why should she now experience a sense of foreboding, a heavy weight that squeezed her heart and robbed her of her victory?

Fitz Osbern had offered her marriage!

That was the problem, she supposed. It was so far from what she had ever expected from him. How could she have anticipated such an eventuality? Rosamund recalled her moment of sheer delight when his mouth had burned a brand on her palm. When her heart had leapt to her throat to steal her breath. Before common sense took over, of course. Before she remembered that she detested him because he had once rejected her, because he had snatched her inheritance, and—with a slick of guilt—that she had invited the King's authority to step in and defeat him where she could not.

Marriage with him was out of the question. Even though she had once more been forced into some re-evaluation of this man who presented himself as nothing more than an uneducated soldier. Whatever he had pretended, he could read perfectly well, as he proved when he ran his eye down the document. He had understood its content all right. Sir Jasper had only just escaped from a particularly unappetising meal.

Rosamund squared her shoulders. Now she had some explaining to do to an impossibly irate Marcher lord.

'You appealed to the King against me. You stabbed me in the back.'

Gervase prowled along the edge of the dais in the Great Hall waiting for her. His accusations mirrored the very doubts that had shaken her own confidence. When she entered the vast room, he came to a halt. Legs braced, hands fisted at his side, head thrown back and a harsh sneer on his face, he watched her approach down the length of the room. Rosamund forced herself to walk calmly forward, to stop and look up, into his hawk-like stare, where she saw the imminent storm. It descended on her immediately, a thunderclap, as harsh and damning as anything she could have anticipated.

'You betrayed me!'

'I did not!' she flung back. 'You were going to make me leave with you when you went to Monmouth.'

'*When—if* I went to Monmouth! Only if the threat materialised.'

'You said you would leave and take me with you. Send me back to Salisbury. Escort me to Hereford…'

'I asked you to *marry* me.' His voice dropped to a disbelieving murmur, all the more intimidating.

'But you talked of leaving. You said you would not leave me here alone. I must leave with you.'

'I said…I said… Have you no sense, woman? What could possibly drive you to bring Henry's law down on our heads? And now you expect me to pack up my baggage wagons and get out.'

'At the King's orders, yes, I do. At least until he has made his decision.'

He spread his arms wide in disgust. 'And what is so wrong with your going back to Salisbury? I know about de Morgan, but surely your family will treat your objections with sympathy.'

Rosamund shuddered at the onslaught. 'No, they won't. I dare not go, dare not risk it. So, yes. If it was a betrayal, then I am guilty. I could see no other way. I had no one to stand for me. Do you not see?' Silently she begged for understanding. It suddenly mattered so much that he should not think of her as treacherous. 'I had to go to Henry. He was the only one who would uphold my claim.'

She forced herself to meet and hold his eyes. She had expected the blazing fire she had seen in them only minutes before when he had hauled Sir Jasper to his toes. Instead they were the deep grey of a winter river, flat and dangerous. It was like dealing with a caged wolf. He had regained control, his anger icily cold, but he was as taut as a bowstring, ready to loose lethal arrows at any moment. There was no understanding.

'Then you must be rejoicing in your victory, my lady. I was right not to trust you.'

'There was no other way,' Rosamund repeated, breathing in his anger in despair. She could even taste it, flat and metallic as blood. 'You would not move and I could not face Ralph de Morgan. You gave no consideration to my position…'

'No consideration? I offered you *marriage*. Is that not consideration enough?' He took a step forward to the very edge of the dais, forcing her to look up. 'I would have rescued you from a situation you found distasteful. Your claim on Clifford would have been assured, your authority without question. You refused me, knowing the course of events that your deceit had put in motion. You refused me and all the time you were waiting for King Henry to come knocking at the gate with an army to force my compliance. You would rather bring the King's judgement down on my head then consider a more acceptable and permanent compromise between us.'

Rosamund listened to the hard voice and the harder words. The accusations were driven home and they hurt. She had rebuffed and tricked him, yes, but only because…, She took a breath because she dare not retreat, then found herself uttering the words she had never intended.

'Yes, I rejected you. Are you surprised? *You* once rejected *me*, without a second look. You did not even recognise me when we met again here! Because you refused to give me the courtesy of actually looking at me before you refused the offer of me as a bride.' It still burned, still shamed her after all these years. She had not meant to say it, but the words tumbled out before she could stop them.

'*I* rejected *you?* What's this?'

It helped to stoke the flames. 'You see? That proves my point. When Earl William offered you a de Longspey connection. You refused my hand in marriage.'

'I refused your late stepfather's unsubtle attempts to bind me into the chains of an alliance I did not want.' The reply came back, swift as an arrow. 'Was it you he paraded before me? I don't remember. No. I admit it. I wasn't interested—a Fitz Osbern to take a de Longspey bride? My father would have turned in his shroud to see me so shackled. I wanted the land back that was stolen from me, not to be saddled with a wife who would demand my obedience to her father.'

'So you rejected me out of hand.'

'Yes.'

She raised her chin. 'Perhaps you thought you could look higher than a de Longspey?'

'Certainly I have no taste for de Longspey arrogance. I could find a more *amenable* bride in any family in the land.'

'And you a robber lord?' She could not resist it as she drove the blade even deeper.

'Do you think?' His mouth twisted as if she had finally pierced his armour. 'At least *my* word—as you say, the word of a robber lord—stands for honesty and right. Your father was a man without scruple who would break his word, rob and plunder, if it suited him.'

'William de Longspey was not my father!' But near enough. She bit down on her lip. Fitz Osbern had given an uncomfortably accurate reading of the Earl.

'Father by marriage. There's little difference. I see that living under his protection, the *finer* points of the de Longspey character have been imprinted on you. You broke your promise to me.'

'I did not. I never promised to accept your ownership.'

'A matter of words.' Now he strode down, was on her level, swooping to catch her forearms before she could step back. And he shook her 'A lucky escape for me, I think, that you refused my offer.'

'And for me. All you wanted was a chatelaine for Clifford, someone to hold the fortress whilst you go back to your mercenary lifestyle! And why, in Heaven's name, do you want Clifford anyway? How can it possibly be so important to you?'

'That's not your concern.' A slash of high colour slanted along his cheekbones. 'As for a chatelaine—I'll make do without. I don't want a treacherous wife.'

'And *I* do not want an uncouth lout for a husband.'

'How fortunate that we agree.'

'It's the only thing we agree on.'

'I threatened to beat you once and lock you in your room. I should have done so. I hope you don't regret your decision to invite Henry's long fingers into the pot.'

'I shall not regret it.'

'You are too confident, lady.'

'I am. I will see your defeat, Fitz Osbern.'

The air sparked between them as Gervase once more clawed back on his self-control. Regretting his ungoverned words, he was astonished at his body's reaction to her. She had rejected him with terrible finality, there was so much turbulent emotion between them from the past, but still he wanted her. A rampaging desire to hold her, kiss her into complete submission, held him mercilessly. Had she been the de Longspey bride? In truth, he had no recollection. The identity of the woman had not been an issue, merely the insensitivity of Earl William in attempting to solve the dispute by dangling a bribe before him.

Yes, he had rejected her without a second look. She had the truth of it. And, knowing that, he realised how it must have hurt her. Nor was he going to tell her that it was his wife, Matilda, who should have been chatelaine at Clifford rather than she. That would hurt her even more and add to his own guilt in allowing Rosamund to steal into his heart, his emotions.

But her jibe about leaving her at Clifford had hit home. That is exactly what he had intended. There she stood before him, courage stamped on every inch of her, jewel-bright defiance sparkling in her eyes. He could not but admire her. To take such a step, and be willing to face him.

Desire to possess that brilliance, to feel its heat, surged through his blood. As he held her, her mouth was so close. And, as if she read his intent, she still defied him.

'Would you really kiss me when I am in no position to stop you? When you have just finished telling me how much you despise me?'

He bent his head and did what she dared him to do.

So much soft promise, so much sweetness, such delicacy. It overwhelmed him. So he allowed his mouth to take and take again, holding her pressed hard against him, aware of every breath she took. Aware of nothing except that her initial struggle in refusal of his power over her simply melted away. Aware that her hands had moved to lock behind his neck, her fingers to tangle in his hair. Soft and pliant, she was his for that moment, responding to every demand he made on her.

For an instant he drew back to look down at her face. To see her eyes open reluctantly, blind with—what? Astonished desire? A denial of passion? Not outrage, he was sure. Repressing a groan for the uselessness of it all, he kissed her again, because it was what he wanted more than anything in the world.

But it had to end. And Gervase refused to give way to the pleasure it stirred in his heart, through his body. 'You could have had me,' he spoke, low and harsh. 'Me and all my lands. See what you have turned down.'

Pale, shaken, still she could defy him. 'A robber lord? I think I have not turned down so very much.'

Brave words, yet he thought there was a shine in her eyes that brought him up short. His blood cooled and he stepped back. Allowed his hands to fall.

'We have said all that can be said, lady.'

'No. Not all. What will you do when the King arrives? Refuse him entry?'

She had him there.

Nor did she wait for a reply. She made him a formal curtsy and walked away.

* * *

'Well?'

Rosamund found Petronilla waiting for her when she took refuge in the solar. There was a glint in the maternal eye that did not bode well. If her mother had not caught the end of the conflict, Hugh would have ensured that she know the whole of it, if not the final outcome in the Great Hall. She looked uncommonly stern. If Rosamund had hoped for a sympathetic ear from her mother, she was unsure that she would get it. A price she would have to pay for keeping her mother in the dark over the letter to the King, she supposed. Rosamund sank on to a settle before the fire and rubbed her cold hands over her face.

What had she done? Unleashed a wolf that had pounced and awoken such feelings within her, that had awoken feelings toward Gervase Fitz Osbern that she had suspected but must now acknowledge. She could hardly explain that to her mother.

'He was so angry,' she admitted.

'Gervase? Well, of course he was. What did you expect? To bring the King's justice down on his head, as you did. Now, if you had asked my advice…'

Rosamund sighed. 'I didn't. Too late to repine now.'

'It was ill considered, Rose.' Petronilla came to sit beside her, but left a little space between them. A tiny detail that Rosamund was sensitive enough to notice. Her mother would offer no comfort. 'And now you must both face the consequences,' she continued, an edge in her usually even tones. 'Earl William always used to say—and one of his few sensible pronouncements—that life was simpler and more comfortable if you could keep the King at arm's length. Henry has a tendency to interfere and manage to his own ends. If we find him at our gates, it will be your fault. You'll be lucky if he does not seize the castle for himself and set himself to find you a husband even less acceptable than Ralph de Morgan.'

'Is that possible?' The weight in Rosamund's chest grew heavier yet. When her mother and Fitz Osbern were in agreement against her, her certainties wavered. Wilful pride had led her to this.

And she had thrown Gervase's offer back in his face.

'What else could I do?'

'Truly, I don't know,' Petronilla had the grace to admit.

'I don't see why he was so angry with me…'

'I do. You shamed him, Rose. Hurt his pride, going behind his back as you did to a superior authority. If the King had come himself, it might have been better, but to send a self-important, self-satisfied courier with a permanent sneer—' Hugh had definitely spoken to her '—to issue orders to a man of Fitz Osbern's temperament… A man has his pride, as you should know by now. Clifford has been in his family's hand for almost a hundred years. And you were surprised that he was angry!'

Rosamund could find no words of denial. She pressed her hand to where her lips still burned from his furious kisses. And then to her heart, which still throbbed with a need to repeat the experience, but shocked that she had allowed him, encouraged him, in such intimacies. When his tongue had traced her lower lip, she had been lost. When the pressure of his mouth had forced her lips to part… She shivered in shame at her willing response to her enemy.

'He offered me marriage.' A bald statement that told nothing of her utter surrender under the slide of his hands.

'He did? When?'

'This morning. Just as Henry's writ arrived.'

'Excellent timing!' Rosamund winced at the heavy irony. 'And?'

'All he wanted was a solution to the problem and a chatelaine for Clifford. He did not deny it when I accused him. So I refused.'

'There! I might have known.' Petronilla raised her hands in despair. 'You are both as headstrong as each other.'

No sympathy there! Although she was beginning to suspect she deserved none. 'Are you suggesting that I should have accepted him? In spite of everything?' A burst of hot tears took her by surprise.

'In spite of what? Rose...' At last her mother shuffled close, enfolded her, stroked her hair. 'You will go your own way, whatever I say.'

'I don't deserve your comfort.'

'I know. You are impossible.' She caught a little laugh, un-wittingly echoing the furious lord. 'But you are my daughter and I love you. Don't weep now for things that are past. That's my advice, for what it's worth.' The laugh disappeared from Petronilla's face, from her voice, then she shook her head and pressed a kiss to her daughter's temple. 'You are too alike to live comfortably together, that's the problem. A pity...'

'What is?' Rosamund blotted her tears with her sleeve.

'No matter. We must just wait and see what transpires.'

King Henry has an annoying habit of interfering, her mother had warned. So it was no surprise to Rosamund that, hard on the heels of Sir Jasper Griffith's disgruntled retreat, the King himself made a sortie to descend on Clifford. Accompanied by Queen Eleanor in a magnificent fur-lined mantle and gold filet to anchor her veil, he erupted hot-foot into the bailey in a flurry of escort, banners, a hearty blast on the trumpets and a heavy frown. As the Countess had also seen fit to remark, *If we find him at our gates it will be your fault.* With a sinking heart Rosamund felt the truth of it. She might want justice, but the King's presence was all too formidable. And, since he was evi-dently not pleased, the outcome uncertain.

She hoped the royal displeasure would be directed at Fitz Osbern.

Rosamund wrapped her mantle around her and, Countess Petronilla struggling to keep up with her, strode to the bailey to make her saviour welcome. Unfortunately, Gervase Fitz Osbern and Hugh de Mortimer were already there. King Henry was already swinging down from his stallion. She halted beside Gervase, thoroughly irritated that she could not have been the first to make a good impression on the King as the Lady of Clifford.

'I suppose you arranged this as well.' Fitz Osbern's face was as cold and bleak as his voice. She could feel anger almost vibrate within him and shivered at its intensity, relieved that she did not have to face it alone as she had done the previous day.

'No.' She forced herself to meet his hostile stare with a confident smile. 'I simply asked the King for help.'

'Then if your luck holds, I'll be out of your beautiful hair by the end of this day.'

'Pray God that it's so.'

But if that was what she wanted, why did it make her feel so low? She shrugged inside the warmth of the heavy cloth. Perhaps it was just the dank cold of the morning that made her feel so out of sorts. Nothing to do with the furious man at her side who would soon be ordered to leave her be, to manage her own affairs. An outcome that should fill her with joy. And if Fitz Osbern chose to turn his back on her and advance toward the King to welcome him, well, that did not matter. She concentrated on listening in on the sharp conversation that must surely ensue between the King and his recalcitrant Marcher lord.

Henry, King of England, all fiery red hair and beard, blue eyes snapping with energy, prowled in the bailey and surveyed it as if he owned it. His russet tunic with its gold embroidery might clash outrageously with his hair, but there was no doubting his presence. Little older than Rosamund herself, solid yet impressively athletic, he already had a reputation, and gave off an aura of unquestionable and confident power, as he bent his keen gaze on the man whose stubbornness had brought him here out of his way. He came to stand before the two men.

'Fitz Osbern,' he acknowledged bluntly. 'And Hugh de Mortimer, I see.'

'Your Grace.' Fitz Osbern's face was still set in mulish lines that did not bode well for the forthcoming exchange as he and Hugh bowed respectfully before the King.

Henry, unceremonious as ever, ignored the respect. 'You did not come to Ludlow, as I ordered.' The red brows rose in hauteur.

'No, your Grace.' The black ones settled into a bar above the hawkish nose. 'I did not.'

'We have a clash of wills here, it seems.' Mild enough, Rosamund considered in the circumstances.

'We have no justice here, sire.'

'No justice?' Henry delivered a straight-armed blow to Fitz Osbern's shoulder with a large fist, that the Marcher lord bore with stoicism. That there seemed to be no love lost between them raised Rosamund's hopes. 'I sent you royal justice. I would consider you and your claim in Ludlow. You refused to obey my commands, Fitz Osbern.'

'Commands delivered by a pompous fool, sire.' A risky response, Rosamund considered. She held her breath. Surely the King would take issue with this.

'Ha!' Henry gave a crack of laughter. 'I wondered what you would think of Sir Jasper.'

'Very little, sire.'

'He has his uses.' Henry's broad freckled face broke into a grin, then settled once more into stern lines. 'But my written word and my seals should speak for themselves.'

Gervase's lips acquired a saturnine curl. 'I have to admit to a hasty temper, sire.'

'Then you haven't changed.'

'I think the years in the March have brought me some good sense, sire.'

'Good sense? I remember you once taking on a good half-dozen men in Anjou, all armed to the teeth, to save my life. That was no good sense. It was a miracle I was there to give you a helping hand.'

'A miracle indeed. As I said, sire, maturity brings better counsel. And to you too, I hope, since you were foolish enough to lay yourself open to such dangers of attack from a parcel of thieves in the first place.'

Henry laughed aloud, repeated the punch, then grasped Fitz Osbern's hand in his, a warm clasp. 'Well said. I was always too headstrong for my own good. I enjoyed our campaigning together. I value both your courage in battle and your good counsel, Ger. And your loyalty.'

'My loyalty to you is without question, sire.'

At which Rosamund, to her astonishment trying to follow the subtle change in this conversation, saw Fitz Osbern's face break into a smile. It warmed his eyes, smoothed the lines that bracketed his mouth, softened his harsh features so that she could not look away. It made him look positively approachable, causing her heart to pick up its beat. Until the direction of the exchange was driven home to her. This was not as she had expected, the King taking his disobedient subject to task. Henry had addressed him by his given name. They knew each other. They had a past history of camaraderie and fighting together. The King owed his life to Fitz Osbern at some time in the past. Was that good or bad for her situation? The answer was writ clearly. Reminded of his friendship and debt to Ger, would Henry be swayed in his direction?

Meanwhile, the King took Fitz Osbern's arm in a friendly gesture. 'What are you about, Ger?' Henry asked. 'The lady's case is plain enough.'

The approachable smile vanished. 'It's based on thievery and malpractice.'

'Hmm. And the lady? Can you make no headway with her? Persuade her?'

'Ah…no.'

'What's wrong with her, then? Is she as ugly as sin? Old enough to be your grandmother? There must be some reason you can't charm her. De Longspey, I think she said. I know Earl Gilbert, but I couldn't place Lady Rosamund… If she's as whey-faced and stubborn as Earl William's daughter who married into the Bohun family, I can understand your reluctance to get close to her. Bad tempered and…'

Fitz Osbern cleared his throat uncomfortably. Henry's words died on his lips as his eyes slid uncomfortably on an angle. They came to a halt on the two female figures. Rosamund leapt smartly into the simmering silence, to her own defence.

'I am Rosamund de Longspey. I am here, sire, as you see.' Sinking into a deep curtsy, Rosamund enjoyed the look of horror that froze his lively face. Enjoyed the hastily hidden grin as Hugh raised his hand to his face. Fitz Osbern remained infuriatingly unmoved. Then Henry was bowing before her, taking her hand in his huge clasp, and she was swept along by the sheer vitality of his personality. He smiled, eyes sparkling with admiration and humour.

'My lady. I ask your pardon a thousand times, even if I don't deserve it. I see that my remarks were far from the truth. I deserve to be whipped for my impertinence.'

'I am Earl William's adopted daughter, sire,' she explained gracefully, fully conscious that his smile could charm the birds from the trees. 'This is my mother, Countess Petronilla.' Henry bowed again. The ladies smiled. It was impossible not to. 'I value your decision to come here, sire, to listen to my petition for justice.'

'My pleasure, my lady. Now, if you would feed me, I will hold my own court and enforce my decision in person.'

'Hold a court?' Gervase's eyes sharpened.

'Why not? It will settle the matter once and for all.'

'When?'

'This afternoon. I want to be in Hereford before tomorrow. I've no time to spend on petty disputes.'

'Thank you, my lord.' Smugly, Rosamund dared not look across at her adversary. Knew those fierce eyes were fixed on her. But any relief that it might soon be over was short lived.

'Good. That's settled.' Henry rubbed his hands together. 'Come, then.' He slid his hand companionably through Fitz

Osbern's arm, beckoned to Hugh. 'Meanwhile I'll sample your ale. What do your spies tell you about the west country, Hugh? And you can tell me about Anjou, Ger. I think you were there recently. I expect to sail next month, but would value your thoughts on the state of the peace…' Off they went, all three of them, in a typical masculine discussion of fighting and castle-building, leaving Rosamund to follow them with despairing gaze. What hope that the King would judge in her favour, when he was arm in arm like a common drinking companion with her enemy? And how was it that the marauding brigand who had stolen her castle was on such intimate terms with the King of England?

'Just look at that!' she muttered as a loud shout of laughter united the three in unholy collusion.

'I see it.' Lady Petronilla looked equally stunned, not entirely pleased. 'Hugh de Mortimer too. Perhaps, Rose, we have underestimated our border lords.'

'I think we have.'

'Don't worry.' A soft voice spoke in Rosamund's ear, making her jump. Sitting quietly on her mount throughout the initial greetings, watching the discussion with as much attention as Rosamund, Queen Eleanor had unobtrusively dismounted and moved unobserved to stand beside her. Rosamund hastily turned to face her, uncomfortably aware of her ill manners before this remarkable woman of whom she had heard so much. She curtsied with less than her usual grace, then looked up to see a smile of sheer delight on the proud face and was instantly captivated.

Although Rosamund had never met the Queen, the tales of her beauty and her scandalous past were legendary. And here she was at Clifford, reaching out to take Rosamund's hand. Tall, statuesque in figure, supremely graceful, breathtakingly beautiful, Eleanor carried herself with all the regal dignity apparently lacking in her energetic husband. She also carried her years well. No one would believe she was well past her thirtieth year.

'Henry will give you justice, you know.' Eleanor's voice was softly persuasive, well-modulated, intimate.

'I doubt it, your Grace,' Rosamund found herself snapping back, encouraged by the knowing smile. 'I didn't know they were such close friends!'

'Not so close, but it's true they have a long association. Shared battles bring men together. But, I assure you, despite the friendship of soldiers in arms, my lord will not be swayed.'

'Fitz Osbern can be persuasive.'

'But he has not persuaded you, I see.' Queen Eleanor's perfect teeth glinted. 'Are you quite sure you wish to drive him out?'

'I must if I wish to live here myself.'

The Queen tilted her elegant chin. 'An attractive man. And unwed, I think.'

'Yes. He has offered me marriage.'

'And?'

'I refused him.'

'Truly?'

The amused interest in the Queen's face brought colour to Rosamund's cheeks, but she held her own. 'Truly. I could not wed a man with a hasty temper and a bad case of arrogance.'

The perfect lips twitched. 'Nor I. But come, Rose… May I call you Rose? Excellent!' Without waiting for permission, she turned her steps in the direction of the keep. 'Have you somewhere comfortable out of this wind? You can tell me all before my lord sits in judgement. You should know that I am a connoisseur of forceful men. They can be very difficult to handle, but not impossible for a clever woman, as I take you to be. Tell me what can have possessed you to reject a man of Fitz Osbern's presence.'

So Rosamund found herself accompanying the Queen to her solar, much pleased and at one with the lady over the subject of dominant and difficult men.

'That man is uncultured and uncivilised. He dresses and behaves no better than one of his soldiers, drinking and carousing with them long into the night. He goes to his bed drunk on ale every night, for all I know.' Not that she knew the truth of this but it sounded damning enough. 'The infernal din of their raucous singing deafens me in my own chamber. As does the racket of rebuilding that goes on hour after hour. The dust and the filth, the hammering every hour of daylight continues until my head aches.' It would not do to admit that the rebuilding and improvements would eventually be to her benefit in strengthening the castle. 'My commander—in de Longspey employ, would you believe—will answer only to Fitz Osbern and *he* will not take the man to task over it. And you ask why I refuse his offer of marriage? He's aggressive, he swaggers around the place as if he owns it, threatens and disturbs me with his shouted orders. He abandoned me and my mother to sit in the rain for a whole day, cold enough to give us both the ague. And Hugh de Mortimer is no better…'

Eleanor had been settled comfortably in the solar, eased by soft cushions, apologising for her unusual lack of energy. She was well into a pregnancy, as the ladies could now see from the pronounced swell of her belly beneath her loose robes, carrying her fifth child to Henry, but rejected any admiration that she should choose to accompany her husband on his progress. Her constitution was excellent. She had never had a day's illness in her life. Now she made an appreciative noise as she sipped a cup of Bordeaux. And Rosamund proceeded to make the most of having a sympathetic female ear other than her mother's, who was not always guaranteed to see her complaints from her point of view.

'A ruffian, in truth,' the Queen agreed.

'He is. He has threatened to beat me and lock me in my room,' Rosamund added with relish and fire in her eye.

'Rose…' Petronilla broke in. 'You make him sound like a monster.'

'I swear he is. He ignores me at meals…'

'He sounds remarkably like Henry when he is distracted,' Eleanor agreed. 'Is that all?'

'Probably not. I'm sure I can think of more.'

'Has he no good points?'

'None.'

'Rosamund…' Her mother sighed.

'Very well.' Rosamund's pretty lips showed a tendency to pout. 'I have to give some credit. We had a problem with the water supply that he put to rights.'

'And the Welsh raid?' Petronilla suggested mildly, enjoying the moment. 'I think we can put that to his credit.'

Rosamund flushed. 'Well, yes. He saved me from an attack by a Welsh raiding party when my mare was killed and I was almost captured,' Rose informed a startled Eleanor. 'There have been no attacks since. I know he sends soldiers out daily to patrol the river.'

'That's worth something, of course.' Eleanor nodded and traced the pattern on her cup with a slender finger. 'Does he treat you with respect?'

'No. He ignores my wishes.'

'Hmm. Can you defend this place without him? It's a matter to consider.'

'Well…' Rose gave it a passing thought, afraid she would not like the answer if she dwelt on it.

'Your brother said you were to wed Ralph de Morgan.' Eleanor raised her brows.

Rosamund sighed. The Queen was remarkably well informed. 'Earl Gilbert says I must. But I won't.'

'Very sensible. Do you want my advice? Wed Gervase Fitz Osbern and you won't have to consider Ralph.' She held up her hand as Rosamund's lips parted to deny any such possibility. 'He has much to recommend him. I know you consider him to be little better than a rough mercenary, but I would rather a man of action, high tempered and virile, than any other.' She paused, head tilted, then merely added, 'I think Fitz Osbern could surprise you. Henry certainly surprised me.' She laughed softly, as if at a tender memory. 'Many consider Henry to be too blunt, too restless, too foul-tempered. He can be all of those. But all I would say is that appearances can be deceptive.'

Rosamund studied the beautiful smiling face, the determined set of the Queen's jaw. Here was a woman who had been wed to the King of France, rejected by him, forced through a scandalous divorce, and then had allowed her eye to fall on Henry Plantagenet, when he was merely Duke of Normandy. A woman who might be ten years Henry's senior, but could win his heart and his hand in marriage to make her Queen of England. Would her advice not be worth heeding?

As if reading Rosamund's mind, Eleanor lifted her jewelled hands, palms spread. 'I would be happy to give you some advice, if you wish it. Based on my own extensive experiences, naturally.'

Extensive experiences? Rosamund, astonished, flattered that the Queen would consider it, and well aware of the rumours surrounding the Queen's reputation, could do no more than nod her head.

'Sometimes it is necessary for a well-born lady to cast aside maidenly modesty and all the tenets of her upbringing if she is to seize happiness.' The Queen smiled deprecatingly at Petronilla, who had worked tirelessly, if not always successfully, to instil those tenets of modesty and good manners in her daughter. 'If she does not, if she fears the gossip and condemnation of society, it may be that the lady is destined to live a lonely and loveless life, until death creeps up and robs her of all her dreams.'

Struck by the impropriety of this forthright advice, Rosamund was also conscious of the tightening of her mother's hands in her lap. Of course, this would speak to her heart too. Eleanor continued, hands smoothing over her belly, eyes glinting in memory. 'My first husband, King Louis of France, was capable of giving no woman happiness. In bed or out. I soon discovered, even as a young girl, that I had married a monk, not a man. And a monk not open to feminine wiles.' She lifted one shoulder in disgust. 'He would rather pray than pleasure me. Our marriage was annulled, at his wish and my absolute delight, because he could get nothing on me but two daughters. He needed a son, of course, an heir. He proved to be incapable with me. His excuse was that we were third cousins.' She brushed his needs away with a sweep of an elegant hand, took a sip of wine, lost in the past. '*I* could tell him the reason for his impotence. How he bored me!'

'And did you? Tell him, that is?' The detail of Eleanor's adventurous life fascinated Petronilla as much as it did Rosamund, both unable to imagine such intimate discussions with the King of France. Eleanor had no compunction.

'I did. We did not part on the best of terms. But enough of him. What of me?' Her graceful arrogance was stunning. 'I was a great heiress. Twenty-nine years old and ripe for a potent husband. And also ripe for abduction by any European lord who thought he could get his hands on me! There were some who tried, but I evaded them all.'

'So did you return to your home? To your father's dominion?' Petronilla understood how painful that could prove.

'My father was dead. There was no compulsion on me from that quarter!' Eleanor's face softened as if she knew of Petronilla's misfortunes. 'I knew what I wanted. Or should I say *who*. I wanted Henry Plantagenet. Duke of Normandy he was then. He was very young, of course. A mere eighteen years, but not inexperienced in the needs of a woman. He had already taken my eye when I first met him in Paris. How tall and handsome he was. How vigorous and energetic, and so excitingly masculine. Quite as handsome and vigorous as his father, Count Geoffrey of Anjou.' The complacent gleam in her eye shocked Rosamund, even more Petronilla, who decided not to ask how this supremely confident woman knew about father Geoffrey's vigour.

'So, what did you do? Did you…?' How to put it. How difficult it was to ask the Queen if she loved Henry, enough to make her risk her reputation, to make herself the talk of European court circles.

'Did I love Henry?' Eleanor helped. 'Oh, I did. The moment I saw him. And I knew I wanted him. I put myself in Henry's way and made sure that he was mine, even before my annulment was made. After the annulment, there were eight weeks of legal wrangling and a papal dispensation. Those eight weeks seemed endless to me.'

'It seems very short to me!' Petronilla announced at this flouting of convention.

'So my counsellors warned,' Eleanor continue smoothly. 'But I wanted him and I wed him. I took him to my bed even before the bishop had pronounced his blessing. I was not disappointed. Living with Louis had made of me a nun.'

Rosamund regarded the Queen, so stately and regal, with new admiration. Flouting convention indeed, she had manipulated her life to suit her own needs. Of course she was rich and powerful, but she had allowed no one to stand in her way. 'Did you ever regret it? Your marriage to Henry?' Rosamund flushed at what was a most intimate question, but she needed to know, and did not think that this outspoken woman would rebuff her.

Eleanor wrinkled her straight nose. 'Regret? Sometimes he infuriates me, I admit. I cannot *manage* him as I thought I would. He is too decisive. But then I could not love a man who was a milk-sop. I need a man and a lover with power.' She tilted her chin in contemplation. 'Henry has given me sons. He is potent. This is my fifth child within the six years of our marriage and he kicks within me as if he will be like his father.' Again she stroked her hand on the curve of her belly beneath the fine cloth. 'Henry listens to me, asks my advice, even if he does not always take it.' Then she laughed. 'No. I have no regrets. Who could resist a man such as Henry? There is a fire between us that cannot be denied. I cannot resist him, or he me. I knew it the moment I met him. What a woman can find in bed with a man is all important in life.'

Rosamund found herself leaning forward to take in every word. 'So…what is your advice, your Grace?'

'Simple. A woman should use her head and her body to entrap the man she wants. Even so determined a man as Henry Plantagenet. Or even Gervase Fitz Osbern,' she added slyly. Her laughter filled the room with warmth.

'But I don't know that I want him.' Rose scowled down at her linked fingers.

'You do, Rose. I know it.'

Rosamund's thoughts scrabbled to make sense of the Queen's magnificent revelations, as the lady, admitting to weariness at last, retired to rest briefly before the onset of the court. Breathtaking revelations, they were. But it was all very well for the Duchess of Aquitaine to cast off one king and lure another to her bed. What had such advice to say to her? Even if she did want to entrap Gervase Fitz Osbern. Which she didn't, of course. Was she not doing all in her power to get rid of him?

'I think a mother's response should be to order you not to listen to any of that!' Petronilla stated, still in awe of their regal visitor.

'And you didn't, of course.'

'Well…'

At the solar window embrasure, the two ladies turned as one to watch the three men make their leisurely way across the courtyard, engaged in some deep conversation.

'I take it, then, that you're not going to use your feminine wiles on Lord Hugh?'

'Certainly not.'

Rosamund let her gaze rest on the broad shoulders and fiery hair of King Henry. 'She said he was so excitingly masculine.' But Rosamund's appraisal of the King was fleeting, quickly moving on to the taller, darker man at the King's side, with the familiar flutter of awareness. She could well imagine that Gervase would be equally so.

'Do you feel nothing for Gervase Fitz Osbern? No attraction? No affection?' Eleanor had asked her.

Affection? That was far too mild a word for what she felt for him, if she were honest. But did she want to bare her heart to the Queen, when she wasn't at all certain of its state herself? *There is a fire between us that cannot be denied. I cannot resist him, or he me. I knew it the moment I met him.* All Rosamund could think of, could bring into her mind in that moment, was the force of that first meeting when he had dragged her close, imprisoned fast against him to shield her from danger. And the subsequent occasions when the air between them had shimmered with heat and tension.

'Not affection,' she had said at last. 'But…'

'Does Fitz Osbern like you?'

'I think he despises me.' That was easy to answer.

'I doubt it.' Eleanor had placed her hand on Rosamund's arm as she had escorted the Queen to a chamber to take her rest. 'Some more advice then, from a woman with more experience than you. Let him have his own way in the ordering of things. And when he doesn't, make it seem as if he did. A clever woman can manage a man with a smile and lowered lashes to cover a will of iron hidden beneath. I think my lord Henry will decide for *you* in this case, which will put you at a disadvantage with Fitz Osbern. If you want Fitz Osbern, and I think you do, you must make sure you give *him* the choice. Let him think he is the victor. It's always a risk, of course, because he could reject you. But a clever woman can make it very difficult, well-nigh impossible, for a man to do so.'

And later as they made their way down the stairs into the Great Hall where Henry would hold his court, first halting at the top where Rosamund found herself being nudged by the Queen in a most undignified manner, Eleanor nodded toward the group of men who awaited them, a gurgle of laughter in her throat.

'I see that my Lord of Monmouth has used the past hour

most skilfully. Now, I wouldn't turn a man like that from my bed, would you, Rose?'

Rosamund had no breath to answer. For the man she saw below her, and so unexpectedly titled, was far from the unkempt common soldier with manners to match who had inflicted himself upon her in recent days. He had fooled her. Deliberately. Outrageously. And she had been entirely taken in!

Chapter Nine

Lord of Monmouth?

The thick black hair, worn so casually, had been washed and trimmed, tamed into a semblance of neatness that curled into his collar, to frame the stern face with its straight dark brows and autocratic nose, all lean planes and stark cheekbones. The fledgling beard had gone too, to reveal a square chin even more forceful than she had suspected. The worn campaigning clothes had been rejected, replaced now by fine hose, soft boots of high-quality leather with side lacings and a heavy knee-length tunic in a deep russet that threw highlights into his dark hair. Hem, sleeve and neck were impressively decorated with thick bands of embroidered silk, shining against the fine linen of his under-tunic. Dispensing with the heavy-duty sword belt, the formal girdle was eye-catching with its trim of metal gilding and a jewelled clasp. An emerald ring glittered balefully on one long-fingered hand. Even beside the impressive stature of King Henry, Gervase made an imposing hard-muscled figure to draw the eye. Against all her instincts, Rosamund could do nothing but stare. Her heart bounded within her ribcage.

The transformation from robber baron to elegant courtier was startling.

'Lord of Monmouth? Is he, indeed!'

'Did you not know?' Eleanor murmured on a chuckle.

'There are any number of things I did not know!' she admitted, soft but biting. 'Perhaps you should tell me more, your Grace. I think my Lord of Monmouth has been laughing up his scruffy sleeve at my expense. I think he's been playing with me, a cat with a mouse that he thinks he can lure into his claws. And I'm fairly sure I know why.'

But anger at the subterfuge was not the only emotion to stir her blood. By the Virgin! He was strikingly attractive. No doubt a deliberate ploy, to impress the King. If she had known he would do something so underhand, she would have changed her own gown for something more becoming than her work-a-day woollen gown, lacking any decoration. But the irritation dispersed. To be replaced by another emotion that definitely had nothing to do with *affection*. Rosamund could do nothing but stare at the miracle below her, ignoring the choke of laughter from her mother. Ignoring the implacable stare as Gervase, hearing the footsteps on the stairs, turned to look up at her.

There is a fire between us that cannot be denied.

Queen Eleanor's words.

Now that fire flashed between Gervase and Rosamund. Almost against her will, but driven by a passion that drove her on, Rosamund found herself marching down the stairs toward him. Gervase immediately turned to her, inclined his head. What his thoughts were she had no idea.

'Lady Rosamund.'

She raised her hand, a swift movement of deprecation. Addressed him in a low whisper, not to draw attention. 'You lied to me, Fitz Osbern!'

'No, lady, I did not.'

Infuriating! 'You let me think you were a brigand. One of the common riff-raff that frequents the March.'

'As I recall, you were more than ready to damn me as such without any encouragement from me,' he replied drily. 'You announced your opinion at our first meeting.'

'You treated me without respect.'

'And as I also recall, you were not unwilling to be kissed, if that is what you would term disrespect. On occasion I found you most accommodating.'

Rosamund tried to ignore the heat that flowed from her breast to her temples. She could hardly deny it, could she? Yet she would make this audacious man admit his faults. 'I have discovered much about you from the Queen. You are no rapacious pillager. Nor are you a mercenary dependent on a lord for his bread. The Fitz Osberns came with the Conqueror...'

The dark brows lifted a fraction. 'I told you they did. How can it be my fault if you did not believe me?'

'You behaved as if you had never met the notion of courtesy or good manners! As if hot water and grooming were completely beyond your cognisance. All lies, as I now know from the Queen. Your family was rewarded with lands, vast possessions in Anjou. You are Lord of Monmouth and obviously—*obnoxiously*—hand in glove with the King. Your mother Lady Maude is hale and hearty and administers your estates in Monmouth in your absence. You fought for King Henry in the civil wars when Stephen had usurped the throne, earning a high reputation as a soldier. You have a flighty younger sister whom you care for mightily...' Rosamund took a breath. 'You played a cruel game with me!'

'Yes. I did.'

His blatant, unashamed admission robbed her of a further tally of his sins.

'It was the only way I could see to get you to leave of your own free will. If you thought your honour was in danger.'

'And would you have dishonoured me?'

There was the tiniest pause. 'No, Rosamund. I would not. How could you believe that I would? You might have betrayed me, but I hold you in a far greater esteem.'

Now as pale as she had once been flushed, Rosamund sought for what to say. A bitter wound. But the glow in his eyes warmed her heart. She would have replied but Henry, impatient, called his impromptu court to attention, forcing Rosamund to order her thoughts back into line and move toward the seat indicated for her. She dragged her eyes away from his face. Appearances meant nothing. Words meant nothing.

She followed the Queen to take her seat at the table on the dais, refusing to give the Lord of Monmouth the satisfaction of another glance in his direction, keeping her focus entirely on the King, and hoping Gervase noticed. Henry had taken his place in the centre of the board, Eleanor moving automatically to sit at his right hand. Rosamund watched them together. Despite his restless impatience, he had a care for her. He stood as she approached, handed her to her seat. When he looked at her, he smiled, his eyes softening, the lines around his mouth smoothing. Yes. There was more than affection there. Something far deeper, more intense. Rosamund found herself wishing that she might see such a gentling in Gervase's eyes when he looked at her, rather than the habitual annoyance, the fervent wish that she was anywhere but under his feet.

Rosamund took a stool at one end of the table, Petronilla beside her. Lord Hugh ranged himself with the Lord of Monmouth, who sat at the far end, as distant from her as possible. Like two antagonists, she considered dispassionately, about to become engaged in combat. And all hanging on the whim of the man who imposed his presence on the court between them.

Henry lost no time in taking control.

'I think I know the bare bones of this case.' He already had the documents of Rosamund's inheritance and dowry spread before him. Leaning forward, elbows on the table, he perused them rapidly and addressed Rosamund. 'The castle of Clifford is part of your dowry from Earl William, with Wigmore and Ewyas Harold, all in the March. This was the only settlement made on you for your future comfort and to attract a husband. And you wish to live here.'

'Yes, sire.' Rosamund was impressed. He had it in a nutshell.

'No problem with that.' Henry angled a glance at the far end of the table. 'What's your dispute with it, Fitz Osbern?'

Fitz Osbern's reply was clipped, immediate. And, as Rosamund was forced to acknowledge, impressive. 'Quite simply, the three fortresses were not de Longspey's property to dispense. They were filched when my father was fighting in Anjou. On your behalf, sire, I might remind you. All three are part of the original Fitz Osbern endowment by William the Norman after the Conquest. De Longspey had no claim, and, further, Clifford was dear to my father's heart. I myself have lived here for a short time. By all due process of law the fortresses are mine. Theft is no basis for good legal cause. I want Clifford back. Besides that…' He frowned. His mouth snapped shut on the thought.

'Yes, my lord?' Henry waited.

'Nothing of consequence, sire. My case stands.'

'Hmm.' The King placed Rosamund's documents neatly in a pile, tapping them together, a groove deepening between his brows. What was he thinking now? She still had no idea which direction he would take.

He leaned on an elbow, faced Gervase again. 'I have a memory of this, I think. The year before I took the crown. Am I right in recalling, Fitz Osbern, that your young wife was killed in the skirmish when the castle was taken?'

'That is so.'

What was this? Rosamund turned to stare at the man who acknowledged the bitter deed with the curtest of replies. She had not known. Yes, Gervase had been wed, and his wife was now dead. But brought to her death here? In some tragedy connected with Clifford? How had she not known that?

'You lived here together?' Henry was continuing.

'We did, for the few short months after our marriage.'

'Who was responsible for her death?'

And as Rosamund continued to stare, she saw all emotion

drain from Fitz Osbern's face, all trace of feeling, leaving it
brutally cold and bleak, as the blood drained away to leave him
pale as the wax of the candles that lit the proceedings.

'It is not relevant to my claim, your Grace.'

'Perhaps not. But humour me, if you will.'

The Lord of Monmouth inhaled deeply as if to set himself
to a task he detested. 'Very well, sire. Matilda, my wife, was
trying to escape the attack on Clifford. There was news that they
were about to be besieged, so she was riding to join my mother
in Monmouth.'

'And who ordered this attack?'

'The Earl of Salisbury.'

'Did he know she was here alone?'

Gervase pressed his lips together. 'He must have done. Nor
need she have died. Matilda was ambushed by de Longspey
soldiers. Her escort was insufficient to save her. They were all
summarily dispatched by Earl William's men, to prevent the
need for taking prisoners. So was my wife.'

Dispatched!

So brief, so cold a recounting of a young girl's tragedy.
Rosamund shivered at the bleak finality of it, now understanding, where before she had questioned. He had lived here at
Clifford with Matilda. Had he loved her and mourned her all
these years? Was that why he had not wed again? And she had
been needlessly killed by de Longspey men. Hardly surprising,
then, that he had no wish to see a de Longspey woman lording
it over this castle, in the place of his lost wife. What had he
thought when he had watched her, Rosamund, take on the tasks
that his wife had once held dominion over? Simple things.
Cleaning out and renewing the rushes. Pruning the herbs.
Ordering the digging of the kitchen garden, the care of the
livestock. Discussing the daily needs of the household with
Master Pennard. All the daily demands on the time of the lady
of the castle. What had he thought when he saw her usurping
the tasks his wife had once done? When her father-by-marriage,

whose name she bore, had been responsible for the terrible deed? She could read nothing in his face, his eyes hooded by heavy lids. There was nothing there but firm control, a well-constructed façade.

She wished she had known of this. Death came frequently and easily, through accident or design, but this waste of a young life was hard to accept. She felt the weight of sorrow on her heart for him and the unknown girl.

'I am sorry.' Henry broke the silence that had fallen on the room.

'Yes. She was very young. She did not deserve to die in such a manner. She was no threat to de Longspey or to his plans. He could have ransomed her to me without difficulty. He had no pity.'

'No. She was no threat.' Henry went back to frowning over the parchment.

And how would Henry judge now, in the circumstances? Gervase had a strong case. So would the King go for strength, to hold the castle against Welsh marauders? For soldierly cama-raderie? In the name of Gervase's dead wife who had lived and loved here? Rosamund feared he would be so influenced, and could not entirely blame him in her new bleak knowledge. She looked down at her clasped fingers, white with tension, and awaited her fate. And was grateful when the Countess rested light fingers on her arm.

Queen Eleanor leaned to whisper in the King's ear. Henry nodded. Then brought the flat of his hand down on the table, drawing all eyes. The bright blue gaze appraised Rosamund, then Fitz Osbern.

'Here is my judgement. It would please me to have these border castles in strong hands. It's a dangerous area for insur-rection, and there's no doubt Fitz Osbern's claim is strong.' Rosamund's heart sank. 'But conquest has its own strengths, as I know. Earl William took it fairly in battle—that can't be argued against. Therefore it was his to dispose of in his will. As he did to the Lady Rosamund.' Henry inclined his head toward her.

'Fairly in battle?' Fitz Osbern all but exploded, would have surged to his feet if Hugh had not clamped a hand on his sleeve. 'Nothing was fair about it. Just the usual de Longspey deceit and cunning. He waited until my father was out of the country in Anjou—'

Henry held up his hand. 'Your late father should have seen to the castle's defence. As for these present circumstances, you took the castle by force, Fitz Osbern, putting the lady under considerable distress when she had no one to come to her aid. Enough distress that she felt she must turn to me.' The King's face set into condemnatory lines. 'You were at fault, Fitz Osbern. You conducted your attack on the lady in a brutal manner…'

No! Rosamund, it would seem perversely, clenched her hands against the edge of the table.

'You acted without chivalry. You stole her lands, rode roughshod over her rights and treated her with a disrespect, not worthy of a knight of gentle birth. You denied her authority written in law. You have shown yourself to have no compassion for her situation and have treated her despicably, without restraint…'

What was this? Distress? Disrespect? Lack of compassion? A tally of sins that Rosamund barely recognised when painted by the King.

'No! Not so!'

Nothing could prevent Rosamund from leaping to her feet. She shook off the Countess's hand that had changed in the blink of an eye from comfort to restraint. She heard the King's accusations with mounting horror. She might not condone what Gervase had done, but he was not the…the *monster,* to use her mother's words, of the King's accusation. Furthermore, she now had an understanding. She saw his anger and determination in another light, in a desire to restore family pride and avenge his wife's name. And, of course! The ambush when he had ridden to her rescue. So angry he had been. Had he feared that she would meet the same fate as his wife? She had blamed him for his temper, for his unwillingness to accept her apologies. If only she had known. But she did now and it was not right that the King should heap the blame on his head so totally. Had she not played her own part in the conflict between them?

She would not—would never—condone such an unjust blackening of his character!

So without further thought, Rosamund found herself on her feet. She did not even wait to be invited to speak. She would defend him whether he wished it or not.

'No, sire. That's not so.' Rosamund halted the brutal accusations. 'I must speak for my Lord of Monmouth. There was no distress. I was not harmed, nor was I treated harshly.' She swallowed as she was forced to admit the truth. Dare not look at him as she made this amazing *volte face.* 'Although my lord would not agree to leave my castle, he allowed me to remain and to order the running of the household to my own wishes.' Refused to look in his direction as she made that admission. 'I have always been treated with respect.'

'I thought you felt yourself to be beleaguered?' Henry stated with querulous astonishment. 'Held under an unacceptable power? If not, what was your need to write a petition for justice at *my* hands? What am I doing here when my time is precious? If relations are so smooth between the two of you, it seems to me that you do not need my help, lady.'

Rosamund flushed rosily at the flicker of royal anger, but she would not be deterred from making her plea. Her innate honesty demanded it. 'Lord Fitz Osbern has always dealt well with me. He took the castle, true, but he treated me with care and respect and concern for my comfort. It would not be justice for me to claim otherwise.' She felt the force of his concentration. A little laugh of sheer nerves surged in her throat. Fitz Osbern was quite as astonished as the King at her sudden defence, but no matter. 'I can never claim that I was ill treated. Perhaps I have been intemperate. I did not know the full facts of my Lord of Monmouth's previous connection with Clifford. All I would ask from you, sire, is an acknowledgement of my rights.'

'Hmm.' He did not appear to be convinced. Again the Queen found a need to murmur in Henry's ear. Upon which he frowned at Fitz Osbern from under heavy brows 'So be it. I note the lady's defence of my Lord of Monmouth. Nevertheless, I can't condone such an attack on a defenceless female. It was a bad move. Nor do I like the repercussions. If I take the land from the lady, it leaves her dowerless. That would not be a chival-rous action on my part. I will not be accused of dishonouring defenceless women. Therefore, Fitz Osbern, my judgement goes against you. My decision is that you have occupied this castle without just cause or right. You will pay the lady a sub-stantial fine in coin for the injustice done to her. You will take your men and leave Clifford tomorrow morning at first light. On pain of my severe displeasure.' His frown deepened. 'Do I make this judgement clear?'

Gervase bowed to the inevitable. 'You have made your wishes more than clear, sire. Perhaps I too must admit that I dealt with the lady less than fairly.'

'Thank you, sire.' Stunned by Gervase's admission, the relief that washed through Rosamund like a summer shower after a drought was heartfelt, but still failed to wash away her regrets for all that she had learnt.

'Excellent! A good day's work. A cup of wine, if you please, lady, then I must be on my way.' Henry beamed down the table in enormous satisfaction toward Lord Hugh, ignoring the flat stare from Fitz Osbern. 'Will you ride with me to Hereford, Hugh? It will save time. We can talk over security matters in the March.'

If Hugh regretted the invitation that could not be refused, he gave no indication. 'I will, sire.'

Henry stood. 'Then my work here is done.'

But it was not done for Rosamund and Gervase.

It was as if a barrier between them had been demolished, a curtain stripped away. The air between them stretched thin. Whilst those around them stood and moved away from the dais, the King and Queen intent on rapid departure, the two remained as they were, the length of the table apart. Their eyes met, could not look away, shimmering green, gold-flecked grey. An unspoken acknowledgement between them, a connection they could no longer ignore. A recognition of the undertow that had been pulling them toward each other, despite all their efforts to deny and resist, dragging them together as vicious and unrelenting as a river in spate. Inexorably, since that first meeting when Gervase had pulled her into his arms from the path of the wagon. Rosamund knew that she had misjudged the force that drove him, ignorant of his grief. Gervase saw only that she had leapt eloquently to his defence against what she saw as an injustice at the King's hands, even at the very instant that victory was tossed into her lap. A long moment held them, in which the swords of the past were sheathed. To be replaced by what, still undetermined when the King demanded Gervase's presence and Rosamund felt her mother's hand on her shoulder.

Both might give their attention elsewhere, but both knew that it could not be left like that.

He had a debt of honour to repay for her support.

She had a need to make an apology for her ignorance.

Neither was the King's work at Clifford, of an astonishingly devious nature, quite done. Not to his surprise, Fitz Osbern found himself manoeuvred into a quiet corner as the royal escort assembled.

'Do you want my advice, Ger?' Henry demanded companionably, as if he had not just pronounced his fierce judgement against him.

Fitz Osbern's face remained set in sardonic lines, instantly suspicious, wondering just what the King had in his cunning mind. 'I don't think I do. It might be too expensive. You've just robbed me of three of my castles, sire.'

'Ha! A trivial matter to a man of your wealth and standing. You'll not notice the loss. Justice must be seen to be done. And it has. It would not do for the King to appear less than chivalrous, now would it? My wife would have some stern words to say if I decided against Lady Rosamund.'

'So, to please your wife, you blackened my character instead!'

The King's face shone with the joy of plotting. 'I knew you'd understand, Ger. Eleanor would have her way and it would be an unwise man to stand against her. But all is not lost. Now, my friend, this is what *I* would do.'

'What?' Flatly uncompromising.

Undeterred Henry laid out his plan. 'Take your leave tomorrow so the law is satisfied. Then before Lady Rosamund can set up any kind of defence, come back and lay a siege. She'll not withstand you for long. Open negotiations if you have to, and threaten starvation. That should get her out. Or bribe the commander to open the gates—he looks to be your man rather than hers.' Henry scowled at Sir Thomas, who was engaged in the difficulty of organising the escort in the small space, looking less than pleased with the final outcome. 'Take both the castle and the girl in one fast attack. Get the priest from the village up here, and wed her. Tie her to the church door if you have to. Then you've got both—castle and wife. She's not unattractive. I might have considered luring her into my own bed before…' His eyes cut toward Eleanor who was waiting, not too patiently, for him. 'You could do a lot worse and you need an heir for your lands.'

Gervase found himself staring at the King, uncomprehending of so outrageous a suggestion.

'Well?' Henry demanded. 'Is it not a good plan?'

Gervase considered the unorthodox approach. 'I can't besiege her in her own castle! And she'll not agree to marriage,' he stated simply. 'I've already asked her.'

'I didn't say to *ask* her to *agree*. Just do it. Once the knot is tied, the problem is over. I wager she'll not find you beyond tolerance.' Henry guffawed. 'She leapt to your defence fast enough!'

'It sounds easy. Somehow I don't think it is. It's certainly not chivalrous!'

Henry shrugged, happy now to abandon chivalry. 'Threaten to send her to Ralph de Morgan if she refuses.'

'The last time I threatened her, she camped outside my gate and refused to move!'

Henry grinned. 'Then good fortune to you! I wish I could stay to watch the outcome.'

Gervase turned a full stare on the King. 'And if I follow your advice, do you return with an army, sire, to crush me for my presumption in retaking Clifford?'

But Henry was already pulling on his gauntlets. 'All I've told you is what *I'd* do. Action, Ger, that's the answer. How do you think I won Eleanor when she was set free from Louis's clutches? I was the least of her suitors in power and prestige. But I wanted her. I swept her off her feet. Don't let anyone stand in your way and don't give the lady time to think or she'll start to find reasons why she should refuse. Besides, I'd rather have your hands on the reins in this central March. So I'll turn a blind eye, Ger, as long as you keep the peace, I promise you.'

Gervase considered the devious complications. 'What if I disobey your orders? What if I simply leave her in possession of Clifford, because that is what she wants?'

Cold fire in Henry's eyes that left Gervase in no doubt of his King's opinion on that outcome. 'And leave a border castle in the hands of a woman? That's *not* what I wish. I might order you out of Clifford now, for the sake of chivalry and the Queen's smiles.' He took up his bridle before making his parting shot 'But let me put it like this, Fitz Osbern. I shall be more than displeased if the castle is *not* back in your hands when I return! I don't take kindly to disobedience, so unless you want a taste of my justice in a royal dungeon…'

Henry clapped Gervase on his shoulder.

'You don't seem to be suffused with happiness and victory,' Eleanor observed.

'I am, of course,' Rosamund stated, entirely uncertain.

'You know my advice, Rose. You must be mad to let him go.'

Rosamund thought about it. 'The King has ordered him to go. I can't now beg him to stay, can I? Even if I wished it.'

'I would!'

I can't! 'After tomorrow, I doubt I'll ever see him again.'

Eleanor leaned conspiratorially. 'He'll haunt your dreams, Rose. And I wager you'll see him again before too long. I notice Henry has been dispensing advice. Always a dangerous situation.'

Rosamund looked startled. 'You think he will return?'

'All is not finished between you.' And Eleanor smiled and turned away.

Leaving Rosamund to acknowledge the truth of it. All was not finished between herself and the Lord of Monmouth.

'So you are leaving, Lord Hugh. To go with the King.'

Petronilla had dreaded this moment, but being a lady of supreme common sense had forced herself to make her farewells to this man who for some unfathomable reason had wormed his way into her heart. Silently she denied her disappointment that within the hour he would be gone, leaving behind the hollow space in her chest where she presumed that heart might be. So much she wished to say to him, so much she could not find the words to express.

I have no experience of this!

Best keep it calm and matter of fact.

'Yes, my lady.' Hugh replied gently as if he saw the conflict within her. 'He requested it. It is not in my power to refuse.'

'You must be flattered to have the ear of the King.' Petronilla kept her chin high. It was more difficult to keep her lips curved in what might pass as a smile. 'I shall be sorry to see you go, of course.'

'And I to leave.'

'You'll be pleased to return to your home. I doubt that I shall see you again,' Petronilla found herself saying when she had determined not to.

Hugh enclosed her hands in his calloused fingers, then raised them, first one and then the other, to his lips. There was no smile on his rugged features, only a solemn acceptance of what must be. 'God keep you, Nell.'

'And you. Goodbye, Hugh. Safe journey.'

As Hugh took his bridle and swung into the saddle, the bottom promptly fell out of Petronilla's world. Why could they find nothing to say to each other now, when it mattered so much? When riding beside the Wye or walking the palisade walk, they had found no such difficulty. Why should it hurt so much to watch his broad shoulders move away from her across the bailey? The loneliness that enveloped her was excruciating—but would pass in time, she assured herself. The sudden dampness on her cheeks was merely the effect of the cold wind. She scrubbed surreptitiously with her fingers to remove the evidence. The Dowager Countess of Salisbury must preserve a dignified exterior.

She would soon forget.

He had a debt of honour to repay. She had a need to make an apology. So he came to her that night. She knew he would. And if he had not, then she would have been driven to make her way to the bleak west tower and seek him out. There had been too much left unsaid, entirely incomplete, between them. Too much to be broached in a public domain. Rosamund was not even sure that anything could be said to put matters right, or to explain that extraordinary charge of power that danced in the air between them.

What was it that had united them, eye to eye, mind to mind, after Henry's decision? She did not know, could not put a name to it from anything in her own limited experience, but it could no longer be stepped around. It had been there, a flashing blade between them, even from the very beginning, when those piercingly direct eyes had challenged her right to her property, when those strong arms had caught her up to protect her, and she for that one moment had felt inexplicably safe even as she struggled against him. But it was more than safety, more than physical attraction between her and her Wild Hawk. Had it really taken Eleanor's prompting for her to realise it? Perhaps it had, for she had no knowledge of love. All she knew was the inner turmoil that robbed her of her appetite and her ability to sleep. That tingled through her blood like so many shards of ice in a frozen puddle smashed underfoot.

Surely he must feel the same. Surely Gervase must be aware every time they came into each other's company, that rooms were too small to contain the both of them? Could he not sense the shimmering vibration that hummed between them? But perhaps he could not. Maybe she was the only one to be so afflicted.

Which misguided troubadour at Earl William's board in Salisbury had sung in honeyed accents that love was sweet, and so had left her yearning for just such a gentle emotion as a young girl? The soft sentiments echoed in her mind.

Love is soft and love is sweet, and speaks with accents fair
Love is utmost ecstasy, and love is keen to dare

Ha! Not for her it wasn't! A further couple of lines in the troubadour's song sprang to life.

Love is mighty agony and love is mighty care.
Love is wretched misery: to live with its despair

That was more like it! If Gervase Fitz Osbern was indeed the object of her love. It was all impossibly distressing, impossibly disconcerting.

But now he was leaving her. Had she not wanted this, worked to achieve it? Why should she now be cast into the wretched misery of the ballad? And what could possibly pass between them before he left? Rosamund shivered at her inabil-

ity to see the future. Only knowing what was in her heart and
what she wished for. If she had the courage to grasp it.

And then he was there, come to her as she knew he would,
still magnificently clad, the jewelled chain glinting in the light.
Still the impressive Lord of Monmouth, uncomfortably forbidding. Rosamund found herself standing slowly to face him, eyes
wide and questioning, no words at all coming to her mind as the
same connection arced with fire between them as it had in the
Great Hall, surrounded by a mass of people, royal and common,
all completely unaware of it. But here they were alone.

Gervase held out his hand, she placed hers there as if under
some spell from the compelling lustre of his eyes, and his
fingers closed around hers. His voice, softer, gentler than she
expected, stroked over the nerves that fluttered as a trapped bird
in her belly.

'I leave tomorrow at Henry's orders.'

When he made no attempt to kiss her fingers in formal
farewell, but remained tall and straight before her, she turned
her hand so that she might grasp his.

'Gervase. I didn't know…your wife…'

'No.' His voice took on an edge, but nothing to distress her.
'Don't speak of that now.'

It seemed that words and explanations were beyond both of
them. With a little movement, he pulled her a step closer, then
stretched out his hand to touch her face, she thought because
he could do no other, as she too was unable to resist. They were
close enough that he might run a finger along the edge of her
jaw, trace the delicate outline of her lips with the pad of his
thumb. And Rosamund held her breath, shivered as awareness
slithered down the length of her spine.

Sensing it, feeling her tremble, he dropped his hand. 'Are
you afraid of me?'

She swallowed the quick bloom of panic. 'No.' Wishing her
reply was not so husky.

'There is no need. I don't know what is between us, but it

drives me to do this.' And he bent his head to kiss her. Gently at first, almost tenderly so that the troubadour's sweetness, like honey, filled her veins. Then he deepened it, changing the angle, demanding that her lips part beneath his, yet still careful of her. The honey was transformed into bright flames. 'I wish it had been different.' It seemed to her that his words, whispered against her mouth, were wrenched from him, his eyes dark with emotion.

And he kissed her again, sliding his hands over her shoulders, smoothly down the length of her arms, circling around her waist, finally pulling her close until she was moulded against him, nothing to separate them. Then suddenly, when she sighed a little and would have rested her forehead against his shoulder, she was free. He stepped back. Rosamund found herself standing alone in a little space, quite bereft. Was this how it would be for her for the rest of her life? Was this it then, the end? Her Wild Hawk to walk out of her life again for ever? Before she could consider either her pride or her dignity, the prospect of loneliness spurred her on. Taking one fateful step, she reached out and tightened her hands into fists on his sleeves so that his brows rose in a question.

'Don't go. Don't leave me this way.' She heard her plea, was in some way appalled that she should make it. Then held her breath for his reply.

'Rose…'

'I know the consequences.'

'I don't think you do.'

'I am inexperienced, but not naïve, Gervase. I know what happens between a man and a woman.'

His eyes caught the flame from the candle, so they glittered as if lit from within. 'This is no path for an honourable man with a woman he respects. No path for us.'

'And if the woman wants it? If I want it?' She shook her head when it seemed that he would speak in refusal. 'Stay, Gervase. Let us prove what lies between us, or deny its very existence. I don't think I can deny it.'

'Nor can I.' Now he did kiss her hands, holding them enclosed in his, touching his mouth to her palms, leaving Rosamund to study his bent head and wish more than anything to push her fingers through the dark waves of raven-black hair. But before she could allow herself the luxury, she tugged on his clasp to lead him into her bedchamber, where he closed the door, soft as a whisper and stood before it, hand still on the latch.

'There's time to change your mind. I will respect that and leave you, however hard it might be.'

'I will not.' A little tilt of her chin.

His smile was gentle, without irony. 'Then I suppose I have to deal with these laces again.'

'Ah, Gervase… No need for your knife. I'll help you.'

And she did, their fingers brushing, making her breath shorten, catch in her throat, until the gown, then the under-gown, slipped over her hips to the floor to lie at her feet, until Rosamund stood in her shift and finally quaked at the reality of the consequence of her outspokenness.

Gervase closed the distance between them, to kiss her forehead. 'Do you want the candle?' he asked.

'No.' Apprehension trickling through her.

So Gervase quenched it before lifting her to set her against the pillows, leaving only the glow from the fire to soften the outlines of her bed and the man who would come to her. But enough for her to see, all burnished in red-gold, the shine of muscled arms and chest, the lean power of thighs as he stripped off tunic and hose and cast them carelessly on to the chest. Enough for her to see the spatter of dark hair on his chest that arrowed over his flat belly to his groin. Enough for her to acknowledge the evidence of his aroused masculinity.

Her breathing was shallow. What had she done? Now was no time for retreat and regrets. Summoning all her courage she held out her hands, her arms open wide in invitation in the dim light. Without hesitation he responded, then for a moment Gervase sat beside her, outlined in gold, the width of his shoul-

ders a dark spread of wings, as the hawk she called him, to block
out the fire so that shadows hid her flushed cheeks. 'I think this
was meant to be, from the beginning,' he murmured, then leaned
to press his lips between her breasts, against the soft linen, where
her heart beat wildly. 'Your heart beats as strongly as mine. I'll
not hurt you, not willingly. Will you trust me, Rosamund?'

'Yes,' she managed, her mouth dry with what she had set in
play. 'If you will forgive my lack of knowledge.'

'It's of no consequence, lady. I have the knowledge for us
both.'

In any other man she would have considered it empty
boasting. But not with Gervase Fitz Osbern. And she thanked
the Virgin for it, as he began his campaign with his mouth
against the soft skin above her shift, whilst his fingers loosed
the ribbon fastening.

'This is not a surrender!' she found herself stating. An impulsive, entirely necessary statement, in case he should
consider her weak.

'Of course not.' The soft kisses continued to drift along her
collarbone, halting for a moment where the bruising had faded
to a mere shadow. 'I never assumed it was. Rosamund de
Longspey would never surrender.' A little laugh whispered
against her breast. 'Nor is this a conquest on my part.'

'No. I know it.' It sent a glow of warmth to her belly.

Then there were no more words. Rosamund was swept along
so that it was impossible for her to consider either surrender or
retreat, or even conquest, for she had no control over her
response to him. For that shadowed hour she belonged to him
and would glory in it. It was all sensation for her as he lured,
enticed, aroused with clever hands. Without doubt he was experienced, knowing instinctively how to make her heart
thunder, her skin heat until she was on fire and slick beneath
his caresses. How could she have guessed that those fingers,
so calloused from sword and rein, could caress her with such
skill, such finesse, seeking out every sensitive place? It shocked

her, that she could abandon any shyness, any embarrassment of lying naked in his arms, and shiver without inhibition as his tongue sought and roused her nipples. Sent uncontrollable tremors along her skin.

And yet such gentleness. The rough marauder had vanished for ever. Every inch of her blossomed under the slide of his hands, the press of his body. And if he gave her pleasure, how much delight it gave her when he shuddered, hissing in a breath under her own touch. Increasingly confident, she reciprocated the caresses with her own fingertips, experiencing the contour of muscle and lean hard flesh for herself.

Still the natural fear of their coming together remained hovering over her pleasure, firmly lodged in her mind. When he moved his body above hers, his thighs pinning hers, when she felt the power and hardness of his desire surge against her, her courage finally ebbed.

'Gervase. I am afraid…'

'Hush. You said you would trust me.'

And despite her inexperience, she knew he made it easy for her, taking his weight on his arms so that he might not crush her. Muscles taut with control, even though they strained for release, he was careful to keep his own desire in check. She knew what would happen between them, but that did not make it easier for her to bear. He helped there too when he felt her stiffen with nerves, nails digging ferociously into his shoulder blades in apprehension. His hands continued to stroke her, as he might reassure a frightened mare, as his arousal pressed hard against her for entry. Kissing her, his tongue explored, touching hers, soothing the soft inner skin of her lips until she gasped.

'Now!' He entered her slowly, holding back so that she might become accustomed to his weight and size when she froze. 'Don't resist. Lie still a little.' Sensing her need to struggle against the intrusion, he held her face between his hands, held her gaze captive as he forced his body to move slowly. 'Gently,' he murmured, his eyes as dark as night, his whole body smooth and strong and powerful. 'Don't fight me.'

She could see the stark lines on his face as he forced himself to thrust slowly, inexorably to ultimate possession. Until he could hold back no longer and drove on to his own fulfilment. Taking her mouth with his when she cried out. Kissing her throat and neck, her closed eyes, with lingering passion as the tension drained from him.

Rosamund held on, arms locked tight around him. It was all she could do.

He has filled me. He has made me his. He has given me a satisfaction that I could only have dreamed of. I have been waiting for this my whole life.

Gervase buried his head in the pillows beside her as his breathing settled. Then, keeping her securely within his arms, rolled, tucking her against his side, pressing his mouth against her hair as a delectable warmth and contentment spread over her, soft as a fur mantle.

'You are a beautiful woman, Rose, the most beautiful I have ever seen. And eminently desirable. Next time it will be better.'

'There will be no next time,' she murmured, her cheek resting against his chest, accepting the inevitable. Sorrow, regret, intense loss might find their way into her heart, but she kept her voice level. There must be no blame between them. Willingly she had given him her virginity and he had, in his thoughtfulness, his exquisite, unselfish concern, prized its value. Gervase had given her all that she could have imagined.

He made no reply. Instead, with a final lingering kiss to scald her lips, he released her and slid from her side, folding the coverings neatly around her shoulders against the chill of the room. She would have held on to him, but knew she must not. Instead she allowed him to dress without comment, closing her eyes against the sight of him preparing to walk out of her life even as she yearned to watch and savour every movement. Until he leaned over the bed. One more kiss on her mouth, firm, a possessive brush of tongue against hers, yet enclosing a breath of sadness.

'I must go. God keep you, Rose.'

Then he was gone.

Rosamund lay sleepless, watching the faintest flicker of shadows as the fire fell into ash on the hearth and died, considering whether she had made the most dangerous mistake of her life. She had invited the intimacy. Of her own free will Gervase had introduced her to a realm of pleasure, led her along paths of delight that she could never have believed possible from all her readings of the tales of chivalry, or her knowledge of the songs of romance. Her whole body tingled at the memory of his taking her.

It will be better next time.

But now he was gone, and so he had rejected her at the last. They were further apart than they had ever been. That was their destiny.

Except that now she knew what love was. An intense longing that flowed over her, through her, flooding her so that there was no space within her for anyone or anything but Gervase Fitz Osbern. A yearning pain, that was almost physical, to be with him, to experience again his caresses, his ultimate owning of her. To sleep in his arms, to awake to a tender repetition of all she had learnt. And instead he had left her. He had to, of course. The King had left him no choice in the matter. But it was not *that* that shredded her heart with sharp claws. He had left her with no idea of his feelings toward her beyond that sharp physical awareness that had refused to release them from the moment he first set foot in her castle. No words of love had been exchanged. Well, she scolded. He hardly deserved her recriminations for that. Was she not as guilty as he? Where were all her fine intentions of asking his forgiveness? She had been unable to find the words, or to tell him of her love.

And perhaps it was as well that she had not. Rosamund

frowned down at where her fingers picked at the loose threads in the linen sheet. She had no wish for her love to be a burden on him. Perhaps he had simply pitied her unwed state, or been driven by sheer male lust to take for himself the woman who had been put beyond his reach by royal decree.

Although her heart sank even lower, in the core of that heart Rosamund did not believe that of Gervase. Surely there must be more, as there was in her own heart? But it did not soften the pain of rejection to any degree. And she sighed heavily. She must force herself to be positive, she had her castle, she could be free of Ralph de Morgan. But beyond that there was no love, no marriage, no hope. Only the memory of his burning kisses, and what they had found in each other's arms.

Would that be enough for a lifetime?

Gervase packed his belongings into his campaigning chests, his heart wrenched apart. Owen could have done the task, but at least it gave his hands something to do. He found it impossible to distract his mind. Even at the mere thought of Rosamund de Longspey his blood surged hot and powerful.

By the Virgin! It was enough to make a strong man tremble.

Of course he had known what would happen when he went to her rooms. So had she. Somehow his intention to simply acknowledge her miraculous support for him and then leave her had been burnt up in the aftermath of that leaping flame that had drawn them together. His lips curled in a sardonic twist. He was not entirely sure who was the moth and who the flame. For sure his wings had been singed. It had made for a strange interlude between a strong-minded man and a determined woman. I know the consequences, she had said. And her eyes had told him that she wanted to know what it was like to have a level of physical intimacy between them. *Let us prove what lies between us, or deny its very existence.* How could he have denied her? It was as much his wish as hers. Just as he could not deny the strong links of the chain that inexplicably bound them

But now… It solved nothing. He would leave her as Henry commanded, and cursed himself viciously for his lack of control. What a fool he had been! He should not have given in to the temptation to sample those soft lips, but he had found it to be beyond his will power when she had held on to him so strongly. Opened her arms to him, even as she shivered with unnamed fears. It had been his undoing. There was no thought of retreat when desire had flared through his body and he knew he must have her.

And how could he regret it now? He would remember the gift she had given him until the day of his death. How her skin had glowed, pale beneath his sunburned hands. The seductive curves and dips that beckoned irresistibly to hands and mouth, all sleek and supple, strong as finest silk, soft as cobwebs. Her body had answered his every demand, she had put her utmost trust in him, allowing him that ultimate knowledge of her that she had given to no man.

His hands stilled on the mantle as he folded it on top of the chest for the following day. She had admitted to no mild fondness, no gentle affection toward him, certainly had spoken no words of love. And how could he have told her that he loved her, a sentiment that was anything but mild and gentle, when it was still his intent to rob her of the castle she now thought was indisputably hers? To return with an army because Henry demanded it of him.

His smile was crooked. *It will be better next time.* Thoughtless words. What was he thinking to speak something so crass? *There will be no next time.*

If his were foolish, hers were some of the saddest words he had ever heard. By God! There would be a next time if he had anything to say to it. But she was a proud woman. Was there a way to her heart?

Chapter Ten

Everyone was astir before the late grey dawn crept above the ramparts. The rain fell steadily. Not a day for journeying, but the King had issued his decree. Fitz Osbern must leave. The jingle of horse harness, the creak of saddle leather. The stamping of hooves, and the feet of the soldiers as the cold nipped. The occasional oath from sleepy men struggling with ties and bindings with wet fingers. They broke their fast hurriedly. Their lord was unnaturally preoccupied and short in his orders. They hastened to load the baggage wagons before they caught the sharp edge of Fitz Osbern's tongue. His expression, not surprisingly, was as bleak as the weather.

Sir Thomas de Byton, intent to be surly over the change in ownership of Clifford, found himself facing an uncompromising lord.

'You're a good commander here, de Byton.'

'Yes, my lord.'

'You've been efficient in carrying out my orders.'

'Indeed, my lord.'

Fitz Osbern appeared to be considering his words. 'In my…ah, absence…the lady is in command.'

De Byton sniffed his disgust.

'Hear this, man.' Fitz Osbern leaned close, harsh, deliberately intimidating. 'You'll obey the lady's orders to the letter, quickly and with good grace. You'll do all in your power to ensure her safety. If I hear ought to the contrary—and I shall assuredly hear if it occurs—you'll answer to me. Is that clear?'

De Byton visibly swallowed, a painful movement in his throat. 'Yes, my lord.'

'You'll take care of her. I'll hold you to account for her life.'

De Byton bowed, sensibly keeping his features devoid of expression. Gervase studied him for a long moment to make his point, then nodded and strode out to where his restless stallion waited with Owen hanging on to its head. There was nothing more for him to do here. He had done all he could to ensure her safe keeping. Briefly he looked round for the women of the castle, perhaps on the staircase to the living quarters if they had a mind to witness his departure, but in vain. Then the gates were opening with a creak of rope and timber. He could make no more excuses to stay. Casting a final eye over his arrangements, Fitz Osbern rode through and out over the bridge, his men falling into formation behind him. Once on the road, he turned his mount south in the direction of Monmouth.

As if in sympathy with his mood, the rain pattered heavily on his cap and shoulders. The sense of loss twisted in his gut. Taking a deep breath to ease it, and failing, he took himself to task as he had throughout a long sleepless night.

You must be relieved she did not come to you this morning. What could you possibly have to say to her after last night? You took her virginity and then left her with no word but farewell. How could she possibly see that as anything but rejection? What a fool you were to leave her as you did. What an unmitigated fool!

Gervase's brows snapped together. What could he have done but leave her with all that was between them left uncertain? What choice had he? The King had left him *no* choice but to get out of Clifford. So here he was, the rain soaking him to the skin, obeying royal orders. As for Henry's advice…it did not appeal. Henry might consider forcing a woman into marriage, but it was not to *his* taste. Sweep her off her feet, Henry had said, give her no time to think. Not a good idea. If he tried it with Rosamund, he might just risk a fist to the jaw, even if she had given him her virginity with such grace. He ran a hand over his chin wryly. She had refused his offer of marriage once. He could have asked her again last night... But somehow it had seemed all wrong. No doubt she would have refused him again!

A seed of an idea slid into his mind beneath the bitter layers of his self-condemnation. There might, after all, just be something in Henry's atrociously devious scheme to achieve what he wanted. Was he, a Fitz Osbern, not a man of experience in planning campaigns? Why not a campaign to capture Rosamund de Longspey's love?

Was that what he wanted?

Oh, yes. There was no doubt in his mind. To batter down her defences was not an option. If he could persuade her to open the gates, to open her arms to him as he had last seen her with firelight glimmering along the silken skin of her shoulders and arms. If she would welcome him again into her bed with words of love rather than recrimination. His groin tightened inconsiderately at the bright memory of Rosamund's arms holding him close, of her lips soft and responsive beneath his.

The stallion shied and sidled at the clap of pigeon wings over his head, destroying the persuasive image, and he firmed his grip on the rain-slicked leather. Now there were things to do, to keep his mind occupied. Home to Monmouth first, where, if he was to execute his plan with any hope of success, there were certain items he needed to acquire. He knew exactly what he needed—at least the restless hours of the night had proved fruitful. And then? And then he would set in motion the events to ensure his ultimate victory. No Fitz Osbern would be bested by a red-haired woman who barely reached to his shoulder!

Rosamund kept to her chamber. Until she heard the final beat of hooves echoing over the drawbridge, she refused to set foot outside, only then allowed herself a sigh. Only then did she climb to the battlements, the high colour in her cheeks owing nothing to the sharp wind. She could not face him. Did not know what to say to him after her outrageous behaviour. What must he think of her? So for once, furious with herself, she took the path of cowardice and waited until he was gone and there was no need for them to speak.

Hands white-knuckled on the stone coping, she stood in silence, straining forward to watch the troop grow smaller, disappearing in the swirling mist of rain clouds, her veil clammy against her cheek and neck. Her discomfort meant nothing to her. Never had she felt so bereft. Even when her mother came to join her, she made no response beyond the slightest turn of her head, an unhappy twist to her lips. She could not explain what she felt. Had never felt so miserable in her life.

Are you afraid of me? he had asked, before his mouth had taken hers.

Yes, she should have answered. Afraid of your possession of my heart.

For without doubt he had ensnared it with masterful caresses, incomparable grace, a shattering competence in the face of her own lack of skill. Her behaviour might have lacked dignity, but he had treated her with a consideration that was beyond belief. And Rosamund shivered, almost as if she still felt the intoxicating trail of his fingers between her breasts, across her belly.

A little movement at her side brought her mind back to the present and she turned her head. Petronilla, with her mantle clutched to her chin, was equally doleful. With a sharp glance Rosamund saw that her cheeks were pink and perhaps even her lashes suspiciously damp, and was immediately full of remorse at her own preoccupation with her own sorrows. She was not the only one to suffer loss.

'What is it that makes you unhappy?'

'Nothing.' Petronilla pulled her fur collar up to the tip of her nose so that she need not attempt a smile. 'Standing in this damp, I expect. It's always damp.' She stared straight ahead. But Rosamund knew. She put her arm around her mother's shoulders and hugged her tightly.

'Perhaps you should go to Lower Broadheath after all—with a short stay in Hereford first?' Rosamund summoned a smile.

It did no good. 'No. I shall remain here with you, Rose. It is my duty.'

'What about your duty to your own happiness, your own wishes, after all these years?'

'There is no happiness to be found with Lord Hugh,' Petronilla stated bluntly. 'He'll not wed again. Life is too comfortable for him without—without *responsibilities.*'

'Has he said as much to you?' Rosamund was surprised.

'No. He did not have to. He is perfectly content as he is. He could not wait to return to Hereford with the King. And who can blame him? He has grandchildren to entertain him.'

'Ah…I'm sorry.' Rosamund felt the sting of it, sharp as a slap in the face. Not only had she been unable to acquire a husband, she had failed to give her mother grandchildren to spoil and love.

'Rose—I did not mean that.' Her mother must have read her thoughts. 'That was not what I intended, at all. I was just melancholic. Take no notice of me…'

'Perhaps it was not what you intended. But it's true enough.' Rosamund admitted. 'Are you not attracted to Lord Hugh? Do you have an affection for him? I was sure you did.'

'Yes,' Petronilla muttered into the fur.

'Do you…do you love him?' Rose asked tentatively.

Petronilla burrowed deeper, shrugged. 'I know nothing of love.'

'Nor I.' Rosamund laughed softly. 'What a pair we make.' They fell silent.

'I might love him,' her mother finally considered. 'But since our paths are unlikely to cross again it's not a matter to give any thought to, is it?'

'No. No thought at all.'

On which bleak acceptance, there seemed no more to say, for either of them.

The escort was moving into the distance now at a fair clip. Soon they would be swallowed up by a sturdy stand of trees. Rosamund strained to see through the wet that had eased to a thin drizzle. To see that one of the party had stopped in the road and wheeled his horse to look back. She knew who it was. Could recognise that dark bay stallion, the hound at his heels. On impulse Rosamund lifted her hand in recognition, unsure whether he would see her. But he did. Or even if he didn't, he gave his own sign of farewell. Even at that distance she saw the glint of light along metal. He had drawn his sword and raised it in some formal salute. Before wheeling and cantering after his men.

'He has gone,' Petronilla observed.

'Yes. What could I have done, other than what I did?'

'Nothing. It is not in your nature.'

Rosamund stepped close and rubbed her cheek against her mother's shoulder. Spoke from the heart. 'If I had the time again, from the beginning, I would do it differently.'

The castle settled silently, chillingly around the undisputed Lady of Clifford, but she was not content. As if to mirror Rosamund's mood, gales blew in from the west, carrying a burden of rain. The courtyard showed a tendency to flood again. Sir Thomas proved to be astonishingly amenable to carrying out her commands. It almost made her think that Fitz Osbern had… But no. He had no more to do with Clifford. It would be best if she did not allow her thoughts to stray in that direction.

But they refused to be drawn into line. Her Wild Hawk simply would not be banished. She missed him inordinately, a raw wound of misery that would not heal. And she was lonely. How was it possible that she should miss him so? A man who had deliberately misled her into believing him capable of any rough sin, any coarse behaviour, so that she would abandon her property and retreat to safety in Salisbury. A man who had taken her in his arms, stripped her, kissed her, and reduced her to a pleasure she could never have imagined. Tears came easily in the night when she was alone.

Sometimes, frequently, she was moved to take the one tangible reminder she had of him from the bodice of her robe. To smooth the creased and well-blotted parchment. He had left it for her, for her to find in the west tower. Black angular writing to express so brief a farewell.

Rose,
There was no dishonour between us. Your gift moved me beyond
words. I will treasure the memory for ever.
    It is not my wish to leave you but the King's word is the law.
Your servant, Gervase Fitz Osbern

Furious with herself, Rosamund wept again, smearing the ink into illegible blots.

Sometimes Rosamund found within the routine of the day that it was necessary for her to go to the rooms of the west tower that he had occupied. She opened the door and stood in the silent stillness. It brought her no comfort. The rooms had been swept clean, restored to their unused state. Only the furniture that had been moved in remained as evidence that anyone had lived there within the last ten years.

It was almost as if he had never been there at all.

Chapter Eleven

A thundering on the door of the solar woke Rosamund in her bedchamber. Dragged from sleep, she sat up, reaching to grab her robe as she heard Edith shuffle, yawning, to demand from the owner of the fist if the castle was burning down around their ears. It was barely dawn, the dark hardly touched with shades of grey. Rosamund shivered at the prospect of another damp day. Edith arrived at her door as she pushed her feet into clammy shoes.

'What is it?' She laced her over-gown clumsily, loosely.

'Sir Thomas, my lady. He says you need to come and look.'

'At what?'

Edith shrugged at the habitual rude demands of the commander. 'He says it's urgent. It must be, to get us from our beds when not even the cockerel's crowing…' She went off muttering to build up the fire in the solar.

Not waiting to hear more, Rosamund wrapped a mantle around her and pulled the hood over her disordered hair. If Sir Thomas thought she needed to be there, then she must. No one was more acutely aware than she of the meagre number of her garrison if the Welsh should mount a determined attack on Clifford. Of course they would keep a poorly equipped raiding party at bay, but nevertheless… Sir Thomas had already gone.

She shivered as she crossed the Great Hall, the fact that its usual snoring occupants had already left their beds intensifying her fears, and picked her way across the bailey, around icy puddles, toward the gatehouse where she could see activity and the light of torches. Then up the steps to the battlements, where the wind caught her in a blast and made her shiver more. But nothing like the shudder that shook her from head to foot as she looked out to the expanse of flat ground between her gates and the road.

'By the Virgin!'

'Its Fitz Osbern, my lady.' Sir Thomas loomed to inform her, a morbid satisfaction in his voice.

'So I see,' she snapped. There in the greying light floated the familiar dragon-like creature, silver on black, on banner and pennon. Emotions surged in her breast, almost choking her. He had come back. She would see him again… But not like this! The heat of fury momentarily burned away the liquid spurt of desire. She leaned forward, concentrating on what she could see below as hard-edged lines gradually emerged from the soft grey.

A tidy little force was camped before her castle. Tents were already pitched. Horse lines stretched out of sight, the sound of the animals stamping and snorting reaching her on the still air. She knew, she just *knew* there would be troops on the other side of the castle as well, between her walls and the river. A hammering began over to her right. If she were not mistaken, her *guests* were constructing a siege tower. Yes, there they were. Men were already dragging lengths of timber. Piles of hides lay on the ground to clothe it in damp leather in case she was of a mind to destroy it with fire-arrows. Meanwhile, campfires were being stirred into life. The smell of boiling mutton smote her senses unpleasantly. Voices intensified and carried easily. Banners lifted and snapped in the wind. And somewhere—somewhere!—in the midst of that atrociously busy scene was Gervase Fitz Osbern!

Her lover. Her heart's desire. The man who had come once again to rob her of what was hers!

'The King told him his claim had no validity. Henry told him to leave!' Rosamund did not know which emotion was uppermost as they all clamoured for her attention. Fury that he should disobey the King. A leaping, uncontrollable joy that he was there, almost within her touch. Admiration at his deplorably cunning tactics, to obey the letter of the law, then as soon as the King's back was turned, to come back and snatch what he considered his. She could imagine him, even now, grinning if he could read her thoughts. Fury won. 'Henry told him to go!'

'Well, he did,' Sir Thomas observed with a grim smile. 'No faulting that. And now he's come back.'

'He's laid a siege.' Leaving her garrison on full alert, Rosamund detoured to her mother's chamber on her way to take stock of the store rooms.

'He's done what?' Petronilla blinked, disbelieving. She still sat against her bank of pillows, sipping a cup of ale—until the news arrived and she halted, her lips barely on the cup, whilst Edith brushed out her gown for the day.

'Fitz Osbern. Siege.' Rosamund paced the width of the chamber, kicking her skirts from her path as she turned at the wall and paced back to stand by the bed. Her eyes glittered in the light of the candles. Her hands were clenched at her sides. 'We're surrounded. We've got water, but there'll be no more supplies getting in. He means to starve us out. Or launch an attack. Would you believe? The man's building a siege tower!'

Petronilla's eyes widened. 'I don't believe it.'

'Then go and look for yourself. And if I'm not mistaken, I see de Mortimer's standard keeping company with Fitz Osbern's. As brigands they're as bad as each other.' Rosamund made another circuit of the room.

'Really?' The Countess sipped the ale slowly to hide a little smile. 'How ridiculous!'

'You seem remarkably untroubled about this!'

'I can't believe for one moment that Gervase would harm you.'

'Gervase, is it? I see where your sympathies lie! He wants my castle!'

'My sympathies, as you put it, are all with you, dear Rose. Gervase might want your castle, but not at the cost of your life. I can't believe he'll carry out a bloody attack on us.'

'So why the siege tower? And you might not be so sanguine after any number of weeks on short rations, when you're eating the stable rats for want of anything else.'

'Ugh. I won't.'

'Do you think the heroic Lord Hugh will come to your rescue, a chivalrous knight for his lady?'

'Well, I hope so…' She coloured rosily under her daughter's eagle eye, but laughed as she pushed back the bed covers. 'You know that I think no such thing. Are you sure you won't give in and come to terms?'

'I will not! What are you smiling about?'

'I was just wondering. Does he want the castle? Or does he want you?'

She stared at her mother. 'The castle, of course. No doubts on that score.' And as her mother dissolved into laughter, Rosamund stalked to the door. 'When you have recovered from your inexplicable amusement, perhaps you would talk to Master Pennard about siege rations. I shall be in the store rooms!'

Rosamund was furious as she tallied the barrels and stores that would keep them through a siege. How dare he! How dare he obey the King, meek as a milkmaid in one breath, then camp on her castle foregate, as bold as you like, to force her obedience. And this time, when—if—he was successful, the last thing he would accept was Rosamund de Longspey as a permanent occupant.

She frowned at the dried joints of mutton hanging from the row of hooks in the cellar, conscious of the beginnings of a headache. As soon as he got his hands on Clifford, he would pack her and her possessions into her baggage wagons and see her on the road to Salisbury. Well, she would not make it easy for him. They were well supplied now. She would hold out for ever and show him that she was not a woman to be trifled with. Her blood rippled and raced through her body, with a sparkle that had been entirely lacking in recent days. She would not think of the heat of his hands around her waist. The way his fingers discovered sensitive spots she had never known. The delicious sensation of his mouth on her throat to make her shiver with longing. Never! If he wished to parley she would listen to what he had to say, she would consider his offers. And then refuse outright. It would give her the greatest of pleasure.

She came to a halt in her counting, dropping the tally sticks on to the top of a barrel of ale as she lifted her wrist to her face to remove the cobwebs. A tremor of regret. She had a fair idea of what amused her mother. Petronilla thought Fitz Osbern had a care for her, and perhaps he did. Certainly she did not fear death at his hands. But she feared his feelings for her went no deeper then a mild attraction. For he had never mentioned love, had he?

Satisfied with the disposition of his troops, Gervase rubbed the crumbs of bread and meat from his fingers and emptied the ale cup. Around him his men were doing the same, preparing for a day of planned inactivity. All he had to do now was wait. He knew the state of the supplies in the store rooms of Clifford. Had he not overseen their improvement, the storing of flour and hams, of ale? He also knew the weakness in the castle, the wooden palisade being the primary target for any man intent on capture. He could reduce it to capitulation within a matter of weeks.

But there was the crux of the problem. He eyed the partially built walls, the rough wood of the new palisade. Whatever robust advice the King might have given, it went against the grain with him to force the woman he loved into ignominious surrender. He could not. It did not sit well in his gut. How could he force so spirited a lady as Rosamund de Longspey into starvation—for he had no doubt that she would resist him—and then in the next breath tell her that he loved her beyond sense and wanted her hand in marriage? Not for the convenience of her value as a chatelaine for his numerous castles, but because he had discovered to his intense discomfort that life without her lacked an edge. Lacked seasoning, like meat without salt. He loved every inch of her and could not imagine life without her at his side. Yet here they were, separated by the walls of Clifford Castle and a degree of stubbornness on both sides.

Gervase stared at the obstacle as if sheer will power would make it disappear. Well, he might be throwing down the gauntlet to Rosamund de Longspey, as Henry had advised, but the siege would be conducted on his, Gervase Fitz Osbern's, terms, not the King's.

'Now what?' Hugh pulled up a stool beside him and stretched for a leather bottle of ale. 'You're not really going to starve her out, are you?' unconsciously echoing Gervase's thoughts.

'Not unless I have to. I take it you're not keen.' Gervase glanced up. The Mortimer lord had an edge of frustration about him this morning.

'Not very,' Hugh confirmed bleakly. 'It's not siege weather.'

'I was surprised you offered your support. Not that I'm not grateful… I suspect you have an ulterior motive.' Gervase abandoned any attempt to disguise his humour as flags of colours flashed across the grizzled features. 'If you had not already discovered for yourself, which I am sure you have, the widow is of a managing nature beneath those beguiling blue eyes. She'll have you in her bed, Hugh, if you don't watch out. Even shackle you into matrimony.'

'That's the point. I don't think she wants any man in her bed!'

Morosely, lapsing into brooding silence, Hugh contemplated the lady's reluctance. Time had dragged heavily on his hands of late. In the bustle and chatter of Hereford, in the comfort of his home, with servants to answer his every need and friends and family to visit, Hugh had discovered that his habitual haunts and work did not fill his time. Or they filled his time well enough, but left his mind free to wander. If his family found him poor company, they had put it down to the eccentricities of increasing years.

Unconsciously Hugh bared his teeth as he recalled their concerns. Perhaps he should not tax himself so heavily with the King's work, should think twice before riding the length of the March on royal business. Until, drawing himself to his full height, and with a sharper tone than his family usually heard, Hugh had informed his opinionated son that age was not an issue and to keep his advice to himself. Furthermore, Lord Hugh would be more than grateful if his elder son would keep his officious nose out of his father's affairs! After which, leaving the Mortimer heir open mouthed and lost for words, Hugh had stomped off, realising that for the first time in his life he was lonely.

Now he ran his fingers through his damp hair and turned his attention back to the immediate. 'I suppose you couldn't just admit defeat and go home, Ger.'

'No.'

'Henry will be on your trail, breathing fire, when he hears.'

'Ha! Henry was destined for Anjou, leaving Eleanor in London. We'll not be seeing the King in the Marches for some time.' Gervase cut a glance to his friend. 'After threatening me with severe retribution, Henry suggested I overrun the fortress and force her into marriage!'

'It's in character, I suppose. Act first and repent later. Not that it's in Henry's nature to repent at all.' Hugh pursed his lips distastefully. 'It would not be my advice. And will you do it?'

'Force her? No.'

'Well, then?'

In reply, with a sardonic curl to his mouth, Gervase summoned Owen, who was hovering with his horse, already saddled and bridled, beside Fitz Osbern's tent. He looked the lad over more critically than might have been expected in the middle of a siege. The squire's livery was impeccably turned out, the dragon shining, as if he expected to be sent on an important mission.

'Well, you're smart enough to do the trick, Owen,' Fitz Osbern observed. 'You know what you have to do? What you must say?'

'Yes, my lord.'

'Then take this.' He handed over a flat packet.

'She won't imprison me, will she, my lord?'

'If she does, I promise to rescue you.'

'Or worse…' Owen ran his tongue over dry lips.

'If it's worse, I'll tell your mother you died bravely in my service.' Gervase chuckled as Owen's face drained of blood. 'No, lad. She'll not harm you in my name. She might take a dagger to *me* when my back is turned, but *you* need have no fears. Off you go, now.' He gave a helping hand to lift the young squire on to his horse and watched as he cantered toward the castle, the pennons of his little escort fluttering bravely to announce their visit to the unsuspecting lady.

'I still don't understand.' Hugh frowned, impatient.

'A little subterfuge that might just work. Although I wouldn't wager my inheritance on it. Still…' Gervase watched as he saw a familiar figure appear on the battlements, to lean over to look down. There was no mistaking her energetic actions, the proud tilt of her head, even at this distance. He could even imagine the red-gold of her hair glowing in the grey light, the shine of her eyes as curiosity brought her to investigate. A chancy escapade, of course. If she was not amenable, he might be driven to Henry's advice after all. Yet surely there would be no need. When Gervase recalled the heady beat of her blood beneath his mouth, it sent one message to him.

Her heart was there for him to win.

Rosamund leaned over the battlements. So he would parley, would he?

'Well?' She frowned down at the three riders and the hound. Not Fitz Osbern!

'A message from my Lord of Monmouth. For the Lady of Clifford.' A youthful voice, with a tremble.

'Owen? Why does he not come himself?'

'I am to deliver the message and take back your reply, my lady.'

It seemed innocuous enough. Fitz Osbern's squire, two soldiers as escort to give him an importance as a messenger, and the ever-inquisitive Bryn. And all very smart, Owen's livery remarkably clean. She signalled to open the gates and went down to meet him.

'Well, Owen?' she repeated. 'What does Fitz Osbern have to say about this unlawful attack on my property? Don't look so nervous. I shall not eat you. Not yet at any rate, it's too early in the day.'

Owen grinned sheepishly as he dismounted and bowed low. Bryn trotted over to sniff her skirts and receive a pat of welcome, her fingers sliding over the smooth coat. She might despair of his master, but that did not mean she should take her irritation out on the hound.

'I am to deliver this message, my lady.' He drew a breath as he remembered the memorised words. 'It is not my lord's intent to storm the castle by force, but take it he will. He would rather do so without conflict. In recognition of all that is between you, he offers his dedication and service to you, lady, if you would have it so, and requests your hand in marriage. In recognition of this he bids me to give you this…'

He sank to one knee in exquisite deference, thrust his hand in his tunic, and held out the wrapped package as if it were a snake.

Rosamund found herself glaring at the innocent gift. Or was it innocent? This was not the first time he had raised the subject of marriage between them. But before, when they had stood on the ramparts, she waiting for the King's reply, it had been placed before her as a pragmatic solution to an otherwise insoluble problem. This was different. Was this not a stark choice she was being offered? Marriage or forceful eviction from her home? Or was Fitz Osbern offering something other…? She stripped the wrapping from the flat parcel, allowing it to fall to the ground.

'The Lord of Monmouth is indeed a cunning man.'

In her hands rested a pair of exquisite gloves, carefully, deliberately offered to her by Owen in a gesture of homage. A clever sign that Gervase recognised his debt to her, that she had come to his defence before Henry. A pretty conceit of chivalry, in which he was clearly well versed. Oh, he had tricked her well, had he not?

'And this will win my hand and my castle?' Owen shuffled uncomfortably as she turned her magnificent glare on him. 'I should lock you in my dungeon for your impertinence.' She saw him gulp and was sorry for her brisk words. 'Except that it's not your fault, is it?'

'No, my lady.'

Delighted in spite of everything, Rosamund gave her attention back to the gift, examining it carefully. She had seen such craftsmanship before in the merchants' houses in Salisbury. High-quality Cordovan leather, she suspected, and much prized, beautifully stitched, the gauntlets skilfully embroidered in gold silk thread. Any woman would be enchanted with such a love-gift. She could imagine their close, silken fit on her fingers…

Stern faced, hardening her heart, she commanded Owen, 'Tell your lord that I refuse his magnanimous offer. The castle and my hand are worth more than a pair of gloves.' Stooping to recover the wrapping, she re-wrapped them, carefully, because they were a beautiful thing and she coveted them. And held them out.

'My lady.' Owen bowed again, remounted and retreated, obviously in some relief.

'Did the lady refuse?'

'She did, my lord,' Owen reported. 'Lady Rosamund said that you were a cunning man—and that her castle and hand in marriage was worth more.'

'I thought she might.'

Gervase took back the package and stowed it carefully in the travelling chest in his tent, struggling against his natural impatience. Yet not entirely displeased or unhopeful. Had he expected Rosamund de Longspey to throw herself at his feet quite so readily? She would not be the woman he loved if she had. But early days yet, after all.

Is this the right path to Rosamund's heart?

God's wounds! He sincerely hoped so. How had it come to this, when as Lord of Monmouth he could have his pick of any number of well-born girls from influential families as his bride? And he had to become besotted with a red-haired vixen! Attempting to woo a hostile lady when engaged in a siege against her was the devil's own task. What if she would never open the gates? He grimaced. He would not consider that unpalatable possibility.

'What are they doing now?' Petronilla asked as she joined her daughter at the gatehouse.

'Nothing.'

It was infuriating. Rosamund folded her arms, narrowed her eyes to discover any sign of activity in the camp, then tapped her fingers restlessly against the wall. How could she be expected to talk with him, come to some arrangement to both their satisfaction—she swallowed against the sudden heat that flowered in her belly and sent shivers over her skin at the prospect—when he was camped out there and she was walled up inside? Not that she wished to, of course! When they had lived cheek by jowl, compromise had proved to be an impossibility. How could affairs between them be any different now? She sighed a little. She would just have to get used to Fitz Osbern doing *nothing* on her forecourt. This could be a long siege. But if he thought she would weaken, he was wrong!

'Good morning, Owen.' Rosamund smiled.

'A message from my lord. And this, my lady…' Owen handed over a little leather-covered box. 'My lord says that he will not give up his chance of winning your consent. He hopes you will reconsider.'

The sun, mild enough to promise the approach of spring, set a fire in the heart of the jewel in the box. It was old. A family piece, she suspected, as she tilted the case to allow the light to glimmer over the clever setting, momentarily astonished that he would give her so important a gift if it had belonged to some long-dead Fitz Osbern lady. A brooch from the days of the Conquest, set with pearls, ornamented with enamels, created by clever fingers to hold a mantle firmly in place. Its heavy gold was made more delicate with a fine filigree edging. In the centre was a dark blue stone, a sapphire by the fire in its heart.

'My lord says the sapphire will compliment you colouring, lady.' Hand formally on heart, Owen faithfully repeated the words as instructed.

Rosamund looked up with a keen glance. 'Owen…what did your lord say when you returned the gloves?'

'That he expected no less, lady.' Then flushed as he realised the uncomplimentary nature of his honesty.

But Rosamund raised her hand to brush it aside. 'Tell your lord that, no, I will not reconsider.'

Regretfully she handed back the ring brooch, perversely charmed by this unorthodox wooing, if that was indeed what it was. Owen's nervousness had also become a thing of the past and, although he took the brooch, to her amusement he persisted.

'My lord asks that you will consider the advantages to ending this impasse,' Owen announced.

'This impasse will only be ended when your lord takes his soldiers and returns to Monmouth,' replied Rosamund.

Rosamund did not even stay to watch Owen return to camp. She walked thoughtfully back toward the keep with Petronilla, who had been equally thoughtfully and silently present throughout the exchange, considering the advantages of intervening, keeping her company. The silence became too much.

'Say it, Mother.' Rosamund came to an abrupt halt. 'I know what you're thinking.'

'I doubt it, dear Rose. Only that I wish Lord Hugh would send me such a gift. It was exquisite,' Petronilla replied mildly, abandoning any thought of giving her opinion since her daughter was clearly of an edgy turn of mind. Nor did she feel a need to mention the letter discreetly passed to her by one of the escort, now hidden beneath her mantle, a much-desired letter that she would read privately later. She found the days just as long and wearing on the nerves as did her daughter. When Lord Hugh was so near, but too far for any communication, it was almost tempting to ride out of the gates to meet him… But enough of that. First she must sort out her daughter's prolonged courtship. For that is surely what it was, even if Rose insisted on seeing it as an attempt to buy her off.

'It's just a ruse to get his own way!' Her daughter, if nothing else, was predictable.

'Yes. I expect it is.' The Countess laughed softly, which drew a fulminating glance from Rose. Who would have thought the Lord of Monmouth would have a turn for the romantic? Perhaps this would not be the best time to point it out to the furious lady whose heart was clearly being rent in two. Which she would also deny.

'The squire's here again, my lady,' Sir Thomas informed her, before stomping off, muttering about the strange ways of some of the nobility.

Her heart struck a heavy beat. Abandoning any pretence at being busy elsewhere, Rosamund covered the distance across the bailey with undignified speed, untucking her sleeves and over-skirts, not even staying to catch up a mantle.

'What is it today?' Was it so perverse of her to enjoy these moments? To appreciate what Gervase might send—and then refuse it? Always wondering what would happen when he abandoned this careful campaign of persuasion. 'Is it some exotic trifle from the east?' Her eyes sparkled as she looked up at Owen where he sat, still mounted, just within the gate. 'Another jewel or a length of silk? Or perhaps even a popinjay?'

'No, lady. None of those. This gift was brought especially for you from my lord's own lands in Monmouth.'

Solemnly, Owen dismounted, approached, and with a bow presented the bridle to her.

'Oh!'

At the end of the bridle stepped a perfect little mare. Dark bay, with a polished coat and a soft eye. She tossed her head and snorted, side-stepped in a flirtatious manner as if perfectly aware of her own importance and exquisite beauty.

'Oh, no!' How could she possibly reject such a gift as this?

'There is no message, my lady. My lord says the mare speaks for herself.'

Drawn forward against all her good intentions, Rose stroked her hand down the silken neck, patted the sleekly rounded shoulder. And instantly fell in love.

'I can't keep you,' she whispered, resting her forehead against the warm coat, her hair mingling with the rough mane. 'Damn him for sending a gift I would find almost impossible to refuse! I love you already, but I cannot...'

The mare rubbed her nose into Rosamund's shoulder as if she would persuade her to reconsider. It would have taken very little. He had remembered her loss, and chosen to give her such a particular gift. Gervase Fitz Osbern knew exactly the way to her heart. Even if the mare were not so very pretty, it would take a harder heart than hers to fling the gesture back in his face. Yet she must not weaken, despite his magnificent consideration. Tears pricked behind Rosamund's eyelids.

'You are so beautiful, so perfect...'

And then before she could shame herself in the eyes of the interested garrison, she picked up her skirts and fled to the empty solar, tears streaming down her face. Leaving Petronilla, who was not too disturbed by all this, to send Owen back, with kind words, and the little mare.

The gift of the mare proved to be Rosamund's undoing, forcing her to face a difficult reality. Until that moment she had managed against all the odds to keep her heart stony in its rejection of Fitz Osbern, dwelling on his male intransigence. His craftiness. The sheer calculating dishonour with which he had disobeyed the King and besieged her. His underhand scheming in presenting her with such tempting inducements to hand herself and her home over into his control. But now she wept as she had not since her own mare fell prey to Welsh arrows. He must have remembered her grief, her sharp loss. He had sent her one of his own. How could she remain unmoved in the face of such thoughtfulness? And yet she had still sent the beautiful animal back. Was her pride so misplaced? Should she not simply abandon her defiance and open the gates? Was she not being foolishly wilful in resisting all this time? She clenched her damp fingers into fists of frustration. What was stopping her from grasping at what her heart told her was the thing she most wanted in all the world?

But the reply that sprang into her mind was stark.

How do you know that he will not inveigle you into opening the gates, thank you with supreme arrogance for returning his property in one breath, then callously rid himself of you in the next? There is no guarantee. Not after you have been so difficult and obdurate since the day you first met. You dare not risk it. How can you even trust his offer of marriage?

How do you know that his heart is as completely engaged as your own? He never spoke of love, did he? You might have lost your heart to him, but how do you know that Gervase even has a heart to lose?

Rosamund fought against the well of tears at the bleak picture.

You know because he cared enough to give you a little silken-mouthed mare!

The tears welled and flooded down her cheeks again.

'This can't go on, dearest Rose.' After dispatching the mare with a final reluctant pat, Petronilla had run her daughter to ground and now took her hands in hers for comfort. 'It's making you too unhappy.'

'I know.' She turned her face away, conscious of her ravaged looks.

'So what are you going to do?'

'I can't just give in to the gifts, the offer of marriage…'

'Why not? It seems to me that it would not be such a disaster.'

Rose set her teeth at the gentle humour in her mother's voice, knowing that there was no point in evading the issue. The Countess could be decidedly determined for a lady of so gentle a mien. So she might as well face the truth.

'I can't because he has never said he loved me.'

'Oh. I suppose it matters.'

'How can you ask it? You know what it is to be trapped in a loveless marriage.'

'So I do. Do *you* love *him?*'

Rose sniffed, again considering evading the issue, then under her mother's keen scrutiny, gave up. 'Yes!'

'Well, Gervase never will tell you one way or the other unless you give him the chance. He'll hardly announce the state of his emotions by herald from outside the walls, now will he?'

'No. And even face to face, he's more likely to offer me an alliance, publicly in the Great Hall, all signed and sealed with witnesses, like a peace treaty. Unless he changes his mind and sends us on our way, of course.'

Petronilla clicked her tongue against her teeth at what she clearly saw as defeatism. 'Then arrange it so that he can't.'

'Can't what? Offer an alliance or send us packing?'

'Both! Either! Have I brought up a daughter of mine to be so lacking in spirit? We can't keep on with this, Rose. We could be here, receiving and returning gifts, until we are old and grey, especially *me.*'

Which, as intended, made Rose smile. 'I'm sorry. Forgive my selfishness. Do you want me to arrange free passage for you? I know he would allow it. You could be comfortable settled at Lower Broadheath within the week.'

'No, that's not what I want. I want your happiness, Rose.'

'I want love, not gifts,' Rosamund said regretfully. 'I want his heart, because, without doubt, he has mine.'

'Then tell him!'

'How can I? Do I open the gates and cast myself at his feet? I have my own pride too.'

'And too much of it, I think.'

As her mother departed with barbed comments about daughters who did not know what was good for them, Rosamund was left to wonder, even if she could open her heart to him, how would he ever forgive her for all she had done? Her intransigence. Her humiliation of him by inviting the King's interference. So he had kissed her, possessed her, but lust was not love. Then, when tears threatened again, to her shame that she should be so weak, Queen Eleanor's advice hovered at the edge of her mind, nudging her memory.

You must be mad to let a man like that go.

I don't want to let him go. That's the whole problem!

A man has his pride. Let a man think the desired outcome is of his own devising. A woman should use her head and her body to entrap the man she wants. Even so determined a man as Gervase Fitz Osbern.

As the echo of Eleanor's confident laughter filled the room with warmth, Rosamund's tears dried with astonishing rapidity. The advice from the Queen kept her thoughts occupied for some considerable time.

If only she dared put the advice into practice.

'She's not taking the bait, Ger.' Hugh gave the mare an affectionate smack on the flank as she was led away. 'I thought the mare would do it.'

'I know. So did I.' Gervase considered the travelling chest containing a pair of gloves and the brooch. His horse lines now must provide stabling for a homebred blood mare.

'How many more gifts do we have to sit through? If it's many more, I've a mind to leave you to it and take myself back to my home that I have not seen nearly enough of, of late.'

'None. I'll persuade no more. Let's get it over with.'

'At last! The north corner is the weakest. Are you considering mining beneath? Or fire would be quicker…'

'Both too long and unnecessary. We'll set up a diversion in one place and attack on the opposite side. She hasn't enough garrison to hold us off if we run a diversionary tactic. We'll be over the wall before she blinks.'

'I see you've planned it.'

Yes, he had. Not entirely surprised by the outcome, although he had hoped the mare would tip the balance. Disappointed, if the truth be known. But then Rosamund would not be the lady she was if she could be bought by costly bribes.

'And if any get injured?'

'She flung down the gauntlet.' He took in the narrowed stare, the curl of distaste on Hugh de Mortimer's mouth and clapped him on the arm. 'Don't worry, Hugh. We'll spare the women.'

'I have to say I don't like it.'

Neither did he. What if, despite all his care that this should be a bloodless conquest, either Rosamund or Petronilla were injured in the attack? He would never forgive himself. It was not beyond a possibility. Nor was it in his nature to unnecessarily risk the lives of his men.

Why could the woman not do the sensible thing and give in?

But he had already been over that ground. Throughout a sleepless night, when his body ached for her and his mind cursed itself and the dilemma that had entrapped him, Gervase frowned into the darkness. Damn the King and his callous advice! He did not like it one little bit.

In the end he could not do it. With set features, he gave

orders to strike camp. The siege would be abandoned. Rosamund de Longspey had won. And if he had to face Henry's wrath, then so be it.

Petronilla smoothed the parchment as far as she could. The curled edges looked as if it had been torn from a larger document, the smears and stains as if it had travelled many miles. It wasn't very long.

To Petronilla, Countess of Salisbury,
Nell,
We are kept apart by unforeseen circumstances. I find that I regret it. It was my intention to abjure any further romantic attachments, being unseemly, as I thought, for a man of my years. My own marriage to Joanna was fulfilling and I did not seek for more. I tell you this because you may have thought me lacking in sentiment.

Petronilla's eyes widened in surprise. Well, that was plain enough. Nevertheless, she was charmed by it.

I would say that I have noted your absence. I enjoy your company and our exchange of views. I miss our rides along the Wye. You make me laugh. I enjoy looking at you. Every day I have spent away from you seems too long.
You might consider me old and set in my ways. I must accept that. But if you might allow me to tempt you out of your comfortable widowed state, it would give me great pleasure. Forgive me if this is too forthright. I am too old to beat about the bush.

Petronilla chuckled. How clearly she could see him writing this, frowning over the words. No, they were not flowery or poetic, but they came from the heart. And to her astonishment, they made her own heart beat that much faster.

I hope that when we meet again we can have a frank exchange of views on this. I would ask you to wed me. I can provide you with a home and every comfort to make life pleasurable for you. I will never ignore you or refuse to consider your wishes. You can be assured that you will never be invisible to me. I would like to see you every morning when I wake, every night across from me at my board. Every day when you might accompany me when I ride about my business.

With my utmost regard,

Hugh de Mortimer

At first glance a plain letter from a plain Marcher lord. Or a friend who would spend time with her within marriage. But she was not sure. It had a straightforwardness that held an appeal beneath the word. A crafty appeal to her needs, she decided. And although he had not written the word *love*, Petronilla felt the sense of it in every line. Did Hugh de Mortimer actually love her?

Yes, he did. Was he not willing to abjure his comfortable, uncluttered existence to take on another wife? Definitely he loved her.

A warm glow of delight spread through her veins, wrapped her around, heated her chilly blood. Was it possible? Why should she forswear love simply because she had no experience of it? Until now, that is, when the plain Marcher lord took up far too much space in her thoughts. Perhaps now was the time to take that step…if Hugh was of the same mind by the time this abominable siege was at an end!

The word began to spread within the castle, at first a flicker, then as a fire over summer heathland. By evening there was a quiet rejoicing. Some of the Fitz Osbern troops were on the move. Looked as if they were preparing to go. Was not the siege tower being dismantled? Money was wagered that soon after dawn they would all be gone. The siege would be at an end.

Rosamund heard the rumours, saw for herself. It was true. What had happened to change his mind?

But Rosamund neither knew nor cared. If she did not act soon, he would be gone, and lost to her for ever. No longer a case of *dare* she follow Eleanor's advice. It was imperative, unless she wished to accept life without him and sink into helpless misery.

Chapter Twelve

In the dark hours when Gervase's troops slept before their departure, his decision was thrown into rapid reverse. He was dragged from sleep by Watkins and two of the guards outside his tent.

'My lord.' They kept a tight hold of a wiry struggling figure between them. 'We've got a prisoner. Thought he'd escape us, cut through the lines. Thought we'd all be asleep.' They jerked him upright when he squirmed.

Gervase tunnelled his fingers through his hair, rubbed his hands over his face and beckoned them into the light of a torch, his mind racing with possibilities at this unlooked for turn of the coin.

'Where did you find him?'

'Sneaking through the lines. He came over the palisade.' The guard gestured toward the river. 'Disturbed the horses or we might not have seen him. He's small and nippy.'

Gervase took the arm of his captive and turned him to the light. Small, indeed. Not one of the garrison, sent to get help, but a young lad. Pale faced in the torch light with a shock of dark hair. He thought he might remember him.

'Kitchens?'

'Aye, m'lord.'

'I don't remember your name.'

'Tom, m'lord.' He wiped his nose on his sleeve. He did not appear unduly afraid.

'Escaping?'

'Aye, m'lord. To the village. My mother lives there.' He grinned. 'Had enough of starvation rations.'

'So you risked being shot down by my soldiers.'

'Didn't think you would, m'lord. You let me play with your hound.'

Gervase grunted at the naïvety of youth. 'Where did you get over?'

'Over there.' He pointed helpfully. 'The far corner where the palisade's weak. Then I dropped down into the gulley that leads to the river. Used a rope.'

Gervase grinned. Even the kitchen lad could see the weaknesses in Clifford. Something he must remedy. 'Hmm. Where's your rope now?'

'Still hanging on the palisade, m'lord. Until someone finds it tomorrow. Will you let me go?'

'No. Could you get us in that way?'

'I'm not going back!'

Coin glinted in Gervase's fingers. 'Think about it. You'd not be empty handed when you got home if you did.'

The eyes gleamed as bright as the coins. 'I could, m'lord.'

'Very sensible.' Gervase gestured to Watkins. 'Raise the troops. And quietly. Now, lad, come and tell me about the state of the guards within the castle. Where and how many at this hour?'

Tom squinted, an eye to the main chance. 'I'm hungry.'

'So I'll feed you as well. Come on.'

It was as easy as that. At the crack of dawn when a man could just see his hand in front of his face but no further, a stealthy approach was made by a handful of men and Tom the kitchen lad, via the gulley, one man after the other. A quick climb up the palisade via the rope took the little party within. A short skirmish with no real damage done other than a bloody nose and a cracked skull or two, and the gate was opened to admit Fitz Osbern and his army. The de Longspey ladies slept unaware, dreamlessly.

Clifford was once more the property of Gervase Fitz Osbern.

What followed was a brisk, efficient disposition of troops, animals and baggage. It did not take long. Had it all not been done before, not many weeks previously? If the occupants of kitchen and Hall, dairy and stables, viewed the new regime with cynicism at least there was no disquiet. Better Fitz Osbern, known to be a fair man, than many a lord of unsavoury reputation. Within the morning Fitz Osbern soldiers had moved into their quarters, horses into the stables. The cook was roasting venison to feed a much extended household. Sir Thomas hovered to receive orders from his preferred source of authority, whilst Tom, with a reminder to his new lord, received the promised coins, and went off with a grin and a light cuff on the head for his cheek.

At last Gervase sent Master Pennard to the solar to escort the de Longspey women to attend him in the Great Hall, hardly able to contain his astonishment that they—that *Rosamund*— had not already been there to challenge him since the moment he had ordered the opening of the gates to his men. He shrugged. She would do as she pleased. It was clearly her choice, in the face of defeat, to remain out of his way.

He had considered accosting her in the solar, but rejected that as unseemly. The solar was her preserve and he would not encroach. It would drive his victory home with too heavy a hand. So it must be the Great Hall. He made sure that it was empty of soldiers and servants, having no intention of heaping even more humiliation on the lady than having his soldiers on the battlements, his hand on the reins. Her defeat would wound her, he knew, without any further help from him. He would simply tell her of his plans for her, and put them into operation. Even so, he was conscious of a tightening of tension as he waited. Why was she not already here, berating him for his actions? Accusing him of every crime short of murder.

He cast himself in the high-backed chair, Hugh prowling at his back, and waited. Contemplated sending for wine. Decided not. This would not be a celebration. And waited, fingers tapping against the crudely carved arm. What was she doing? Deliberately keeping him waiting? Intentionally stoking his temper? His request had been polite enough.

He had reached the point where he could sit no longer, was about to go and find her for himself, when there came the sound of soft shoes against stonework and Master Pennard's appearance at the top of the stairs. Hugh nudged him. Both of them, the Countess and Rosamund, descended the steps, both of them magnificently turned out, as if for a court banquet. For an instant, humour rippled through him, replacing his impatience with blatant admiration. It *had* been quite deliberate, he was certain. To make an impressive gesture. To make him once again conscious of his less-than-well-scrubbed appearance after a week outside the castle gates.

Well, he would not be impressed. Not when she had thrown back in his face every offer of compromise he had placed before her.

But then Rosamund was standing before him on the dais, on a level with him. He could not take his eyes from her. She filled his whole vision. As she had intended. Not of a poetic mind, having had little time for it in his turbulent youth and adolescence when a sword came more readily to hand than a book of French poetry, yet he could not be unaware of her striking beauty, or how she had chosen her garments to enhance it. The rich blue of her gown was the exact colour of bluebells in spring sunshine. The soft fabric skimmed over her neat figure, breast and waist and hips, leaving him in no doubt of her feminine curves. A linked belt cinched the narrowness of her waist, whilst rich embroidery banded her sleeves to draw attention to her fine-boned hands. If he had ever forgotten, she had chosen to remind him. She was Rosamund de Longspey, adopted daughter of the powerful Earl of Salisbury. Not some unimportant girl from some minor landowning family, but a young woman of taste and education. The long transparent veil was held in place by a jewelled filet that could do nothing but draw his attention to the gleaming ribbon-bound hair that reached down to her waist.

He wished her face was not so pale. That he was not aware of the faintest of violet smudges beneath her eyes on her delicate skin. Did he not know how soft and delicate it was? Her eyes might be clear and direct, but guarded, as if she did not wish him to read her thoughts. Soft and alluring, her mouth was carefully controlled as if her lips might give too much away.

'My lord. You have my castle.' He had forgotten how intoxicating her voice could be, how arousing with its husky overtones. Mentally he shook his head to dislodge such treacherous thoughts.

'As you see, lady.' He might as well get it over with. As soon as she was out of his sight he could be comfortable again. He kept his voice low, dispassionate. This was not the occasion to be overheard. He kept his face set in stern lines as if addressing a recalcitrant sergeant-at-arms.

'This is the end of our acquaintance, lady. You refused my tokens of friendship. You rejected my offers of marriage and questioned my honour, my integrity, my sincerity.' He set his jaw. He would *not* ask her again, as if he were a beggar petitioning for crumbs from a lady's table. 'You will leave tomorrow. I shall personally send you with an escort to Salisbury to ensure your safety. *And don't even think of defying me! I shall personally carry you to a travelling litter, tie you to it and deliver you to Earl Gilbert's door!* That is my decision. You have time to organise your possessions. If you need help, I will provide it.'

'Yes, my lord. I shall be ready to go at dawn.'

Gervase felt his muscles stiffen. What? No arguments? It seemed to him that her face had grown even more pale, her lips even more tightly pressed together. Her hands were clasped one on the other before her, her fingers white-knuckled.

'I know that I am beaten,' she continued, soft voiced. 'I will not stand in your way, my lord.'

By the Virgin! He controlled a sharp inhalation. To his utter amazement Rosamund's eyes, green as new spring grass, glimmered and tears began to slide down her cheeks. Her breath caught as she buried her teeth in her bottom lip.

'Forgive me, my lord.' The words hesitated with heart-breaking grief.

And Gervase found himself stretching out his hand toward her.

'Ah, no, lady… It was never my intent to—'

But Rosamund ignored his hand, on a little sob dashed the tears away with her fingers.

'I shall be ready to leave at dawn.'

And before more tears could fall, she turned and fled from him, up the stairs, vanishing through the archway at the top with a swirl of blue skirts.

Astonished, pierced by sharp guilt, all Gervase could do was stand and stare after her. This was not the Rosamund he had come to know. Had he reduced her to this?

'What?' Startled, he looked to the Countess for enlightenment.

She was not as lost for words as her daughter. With terrible formality she addressed him. 'What did you expect? You have treated her abominably, my Lord of Monmouth. You should be ashamed to reduce so spirited a lady to the depths of emotion by your words and actions.' The Countess, without even a glance in Hugh's direction, curtsied with impeccable grace and heavy irony. Then, with a hand on Fitz Osbern's arm, leaned close, her voice low. 'If you're half the clever man I think you are, Gervase, you'll watch your step in this contest and keep your wits about you. I'll petition the Virgin for the outcome. One word of warning. If you take my daughter as your wife, you'll deserve everything you get.'

On which, with a compassionate pat on his arm, she stalked away. The enigmatic advice was not lost on the Lord of Monmouth. Conscious of heat in his lean cheeks, all he could do was stand speechless, looking after them, thoroughly unnerved.

Until Hugh guffawed with laughter. 'This should be a victory. It does not feel like one.'

'It should and it doesn't,' he admitted. 'And instead I feel as if I have just been found guilty and condemned for drowning a bag of unwanted kittens!'

He could only remember the hurt on Rosamund's face.

Throughout the day whilst Gervase nursed his grievance at unpredictable women and inspected his defences, Rosamund, it would appear from her deliberate absence, kept to her chamber. He might listen for her vigorous step, her bright laughter, look for her slight figure, the brilliance of her hair, the splash of colour of her gown against the grey stone. Not a sound, not a glimpse. Perhaps as well, he decided, trying to shuffle off the heavy weight beneath his breastbone. By tomorrow it would all be over and life would settle back into its habitual routine. Fighting off an attack from Welsh tribes would be far more acceptable than dealing with Rosamund de Longspey. At least he would have a fair idea that he would win the contest.

He had won! He set his teeth against the constant tingle of disquiet, hot down his spine, as irritating as the itch of a flea after a hard campaign.

If he could only get her tear-drenched eyes out of his mind. If only he could banish her from his heart. But she was there, in every breath he took, every decision he made. She haunted him, shadowed him down every corridor. Were these the much-lauded delights of love? They had brought him nothing but pain, worse than the gut-wrenching agony of a sword wound.

Noisy, intent on celebration, the Fitz Osbern garrison took their seats in the Great Hall for supper. The serving girls thumped leather flagons of ale on each board. Master Pennard approached the high table. Bowed low.

'Does it please you that I serve the food, my lord?'

'We will await the lady,' Gervase replied, a line beginning to dig between his brows. The Countess had taken her seat with cool graciousness, as if her sharp words had not been delivered with the assurance of a dagger blow earlier in the day, and was now engaged in some trivial matter of conversation with Hugh. Gervase frowned at the stairs. He had not looked forward to this final confrontation, but surely they could eat together calmly, if not amicably. They would apply an acceptable standard of good manners to sup and converse and then tomorrow she would be gone.

Gervase glowered again at the empty staircase. Nothing. God's wounds, where was she?

The voices of hungry men rose around them.

He could hang on to tolerance no longer. 'Master Pennard. If you would be so good as to tell your mistress that I expect her to…' He swallowed the words. Perhaps not the best approach. 'If you would invite the lady to attend the meal, I would welcome her presence.' He thought a moment. 'Make it a request, Master Pennard. It is not an order.'

'Yes, my lord. No, my lord.' The steward departed.

To return promptly, alone. Agitated.

'Well?'

'My lady says…'

'Says what?' Gervase leaned forward, his tone like the threatening growl of a hungry wolf.

'She says…she says she'll not eat with a thief in her own Hall.'

'Does she now?' Soft, dangerously so.

Then softness vanished, patience dissipating as smoke in a gale. Had he not given her every chance? Had he not shown her more understanding then he would ever have thought possible? Most men would have clapped her in a dungeon and had done with it if she had played the tricks she had used against him. Had her tears, her soft trembling mouth, not disturbed his equilibrium all day? And now she would issue her challenge as if he did not hold her captive in her own castle. As if he could not demand her obedience. She would insult him with her blatant refusal, would she? Without a word, he surged to his feet. Strode across the dais and mounted the stairs. His fluid movements might still contain the dignity expected of the Lord of Monmouth, but his eyes were ablaze.

'Oh, dear,' Petronilla remarked mildly, inconsequentially, quite at odds with the explosion of temper.

Hugh slid a wary glance. 'What did you know about this, lady?'

'I? How should I know anything? My daughter is her own mistress.'

'I thought you were smiling.'

'Not I.' But she was.

'So what now, Nell?' Hugh considered the hungry men, heard the rising voices.

'I think, Master Pennard,' the Countess addressed the waiting steward, 'that you should serve supper immediately. Lord Hugh will preside in the absence of the lord and lady.' And then to Hugh. 'A bout of tears followed by a touch of defiance should do the trick, I think.'

Hugh chuckled, his eyes widening in admiration. 'Like that, is it?'

Petronilla sighed. 'I hope so. I really do. I don't think I can stand the strain any longer!'

Chapter Thirteen

Gervase allowed himself one peremptory knock, determined to preserve that much control of the situation at least. But he did not wait for a reply, flinging back the door so that it squealed on its hinges, and took two strides into the room. An ultimate feminine preserve now, it struck him, far different from its filthy state as he had first seen it under Sir Thomas de Byton's occupation. Alluringly comfortable. A cushioned settle beckoned. A chair with carved back and arms. Tapestried walls to soften and warm, to hide the ravages of damp. A fire settled gently in the hearth where a grey cat raised its head and watched him with a glint of suspicious eyes. Shutters were closed against the early dark. It was seductively welcoming with the scent of spiced wine.

Then he no longer noticed his surroundings. His quick appreciation was suddenly scattered. Gervase swallowed hard.

What had he expected? Tears, perhaps. Defiance, certainly. Temper and a downright refusal to see sense. He could work through all of these, take her in hand and demand her presence at the meal. For her to preserve at least the outward signs of civility and gracious acceptance of defeat.

But nothing had prepared him for this.

'Welcome, my lord.'

'Lady…!'

'I have been waiting for you.'

He remained frozen to the spot, his breath backed up in his lungs as if, expecting a cold acquiescence at best, a heated parley at worst, he had just been challenged to mortal combat. By a challenger who now moved purposefully around him to close the door at his back. Graceful, as feminine as her surroundings, Rosamund circled him to approach the cups and flagon on the coffer with smooth competence, to pour wine with deft elegant hands.

Rosamund de Longspey lay in wait for him.

He set his jaw. In all the days he had known her, he had never seen her like this. In the plain skirts and over-tunic of a woman engaged in household tasks, frequently he had seen her. Drenched to the skin from sitting in the rain. Muddy and dishevelled, blood-smeared from her tumble from a horse. Elegantly groomed to entertain Henry and his Queen or to challenge his own deliberate lack of style. Blazingly angry, infuriatingly defiant, supremely arrogant, tearfully grief-stricken—all of those and in any combination. Never like this…

His mind sought for a reason. Ambush! The only one to come to mind. Was this a deliberate ploy? How should he react to this strategic entrapment? Then he abandoned the task of making a decision, for it suddenly did not seem to matter. His heart thudded, his blood throbbed in his veins. His body responded uncomfortably with arousal at the gleam in her eye, the curve of her mouth.

Rosamund stood before him, holding the cup with delicate ease. Her gown, a magnificent silk *bliaut,* light as a whisper, cascading to the floor whilst its myriad little pleats managed to hug and smooth over her figure, both hinting at and defining what lay below. But that was not it, even though he was conscious of, intimately acquainted with, every one of those dips and curves. It was her face that captured his attention; he stared, as if he were some inexperienced naïve youth to be entranced and seduced. Pale, surprisingly serene, flawlessly oval with straight nose, softly moulded lips, she was a picture of enchantment. And when that pretty mouth smiled at him… Green eyes, jewel bright, lifted to his, to reflect the light from the candles. And as he looked, because he could do no other, he saw a faint hint of rose that touched her slender throat, her cheeks.

And then her hair. Unbound, unbraided, uncovered. Gold and red, and every colour of russet and bronze in between that he could imagine. It lay loose, to fall with the softest curl over breast and shoulder, to her waist and beyond, rivalling the richness of the silk *bliaut.*

What is she doing?

But that was not important either.

Can I let her go? Can I let this splendid woman walk out of my life into the arms of Ralph de Morgan?

No. And no. He needed no time to contemplate the answer. He wanted to keep her, to wed her, to keep her by him, so that she might continue to smile at him as she was doing at this moment. Even though he *knew* this was a deliberate seduction by a clever woman, it did not matter. He loved her. In spite of all they had been through, even though it might still be a ruse to get the damned castle from him. Sitting outside her castle walls, he had realised that to be estranged from her brought him nothing but pain. She had battled her way into his heart so that he was her prisoner as much as she was now his.

What's more, seeing the colour deepen in her lovely face at his silent appraisal, he did not think she was indifferent to him. Indeed, he would wager…

With a graceful gesture she offered him the cup.

'Will you drink with me, my lord? Will you toast your victory over me?'

He swallowed, dry mouthed. Why a man of his experience should be so foolishly inept—he was no better than Owen, who had developed a bad case of admiration for the lady. He forced his face into a frown. So she thought she could seduce him, did she? He would prove her wrong. He would not allow her to get the better of him without some show of backbone. Yet he could not resist taking the cup she held out to him. And as his fingers grazed hers for an instant, desire sprang to life to flood through him. But he did not drink, forced himself to remain, at least on the surface, cold and aloof.

'You said you would not eat with a thief in your own Hall, lady.'

Rosamund's lips curved enchantingly.

'But I did not say that I would not share a cup of wine with that thief in my solar, my lord.'

Beneath the gracious exterior, composed and smoothly hospitable as she had intended, Rosamund's heart thudded hard in her chest as if it would break through the fragile silk. Like a rat trapped in a cage, she thought, as nerves raked a fingernail down her spine. This was the culmination of what she had worked for. Gaining a willing accomplice in Tom, who would follow instructions for the excitement of the plot, and the promise of payment, probably from both sides, she had ordered only a token defence when the Fitz Osbern troops had climbed over the palisade. No point in shedding blood unnecessarily. They were her people and must not be put in danger for her whims. Then all she had had to do was face the Lord of Monmouth. What a scene that had been. Since she had discovered her talent for acting was as keen as his, it had not been difficult to conjure a descent into feminine tears to melt the heart of the devil himself.

But had it melted him, the battle-hardened Lord of Monmouth? All hung now in the balance. A man had his pride, demanded that he be in control, Eleanor had stated, and she should know. That was exactly what Rosamund had plotted. Gervase had captured the castle, it seemed by his own cunning, not accepted it as a gift on a gold platter at the instigation of its lady. And now? Now, if she had her way, she would lose neither the castle nor her robber lord. As long as the plot could be worked out to her own desired ends.

She had never before laid an ambush. Timing was essential, as well as keeping her nerve beneath his eagle stare. But now she would have to be prepared for honesty. For laying her heart bare. For if she did not, there was no value in the victory. And by telling him what was in her heart, she must expose herself to possible rejection and heartbreak.

The thoughts sped through her mind, chilling her blood with the threat of failure. Yet she knew it must be done. She must tell him of the love that would not let her rest. And *if* he loved *her,* he must tell her so. Ah! There was the worm in the apple. Would she still wed him without his love? No… The chill became an icy cold. But as she looked at him filling her solar with his intensely masculine presence, felt her reactions to him move from simmer to burn, she was no longer sure. She was, she admitted, as much ambushed as he.

Throat so dry she could barely speak, how could she have forgotten in these few short days, which had seemed so long, just how magnificent he was? Particularly as he had deliberately played the courtier in glorious dark silk with fur at hem and sleeve to honour her at the meal she had refused. Dark hair strong and straight, glossy as the mare he had given her. Grey eyes, keen, assured, assessing, with those remarkable hints of gold, and at present not a little indignation. The predatory nose that dominated his face. Lips firm, even though she knew the softness of them against her throat. All heat, all raw male energy beneath the fine tunic, all hard-toned muscle. She had seen him in action, at leisure, in playful sport. Riding, hawking. Magnificently naked and sweat-streaked. Always impressive, always imposing. What more could a woman want in a mate?

Even when those eyes looked at her as if he were a hawk contemplating a particularly tasty mouse.

Rosamund roused herself before her courage failed her and offered him wine. When his fingers brushed hers, her skin burned. To live with him, touch him, see him every day, to share his bed, bear his children—would that not be enough? Once again she was forced to fight down the panic at the compromise she might be forced to make, if he did not love her. Perhaps it would be enough to live with him without his love, if the alternative was to never set eyes on him again. For that would be beyond pain, an anguish she could not tolerate.

'You said you would not eat with a thief in your own Hall,' he stated, his voice harsh with emotion that shimmered just below the courtly surface.

So her barbed message had stung, as she had hoped. To bring him hot-foot to her room. Rosamund's lips curved. Now, the ultimate victory *must* be hers. She summoned all her courage, all the strength of her heart and her love.

'But I did not say that I would not share a cup of wine with that thief in my solar, my lord.'

His brows twitched, the faintest uncertainty. 'No. You did not.'

'Nor did I say that I would not share my bed.'

Marvelling at her courage, she awaited his reply as the loom of impending humiliation spiked her skin with ice. Blatantly she had cast aside all her pride and offered herself to him, a gift, a festive dish served up on a golden platter, a peacock in the glory of its iridescent feathers. And all Gervase Fitz Osbern could do was stand there, without words, and look at her. So stern, so controlled, so impossible to read! Rosamund resisted the urge to glare at him. She had gambled everything on this, throwing the glove down at his feet, and must play out the challenge to the end. Would he turn and walk from her room, now that the castle was his? Had she demeaned herself to no purpose? No, she chided herself. There was nothing demeaning here. She loved him.

But if she had misread him, if the Queen had been wrong in her reading of men… In that case, she had lost everything. Her castle, her pride, her dignity. In the end, her confidence draining away, she veiled her eyes with her lashes so that she might not see the condemnation in his brilliant gaze as he finally decided to reject her offer and leave her.

So she felt Gervase move rather than saw him, so that when she lifted her lashes he was standing close. So close that she had to look up. She might have stepped back with a little spurt of surprise, but one hand closed on her wrist, gently enough, and held her steady.

'You offered to drink with me.'

'Yes.'

'Then let us do so. Let us drink to…' Gervase hesitated, a hint of a smile.

'To what?' Her voice husky with misgiving.

'To a successful culmination of the siege, of course.'

That was not what she wanted! 'Very well. To success.'

And raised her cup, drank, as did he.

'Then since we are of the same mind…' Gervase took the cup from her hand and placed them both down on the coffer. Rested his hands on her shoulders, drawing her a step closer. Rosamund's breath tangled in her lungs, but she kept her eyes locked on his.

'Well, lady?'

'Nothing, my lord.'

'I have been waiting to touch you again for some time.' He lowered his head and kissed her mouth so softly. 'That's it.' He kissed her again. 'I have wanted to do *that*.'

Rosamund breathed out, tensions uncurling, against the fluttering in her belly that no longer feared rejection. 'Yes.'

'Events came between us.' Gervase pressed his lips at the soft place where her brows met.

'Yes,' she whispered again, finding words impossible at the last.

'Is this what you want?'

'Yes!' Impatience now. Since she was making no effort to repel him, was she not plain enough? Would he make her beg? Well, she would! 'Kiss me again, Gervase. I have been waiting an age.'

His brow arched, his face lit by his swift and devastating smile, so that the flutter erupted into a beat of strong wings. 'It's something I have loved about you. Your courage in setting your will against mine. On this occasion, my lovely Rose, I am more than willing to obey your orders.'

And did so. His mouth, his body against hers, was just as unyielding, just as powerful as she remembered. Gentle at first, his lips grew more demanding, insisting that hers part in acceptance as he pulled her close, his arms pinning her closer yet, breast to breast, thigh to thigh, soft curve to hard muscle. The heat of victory, the fire of love, the bright sparkle of desire, all woven together into a brilliant mass of sensation, all rushed through her blood when he clenched his fist in her hair and buried his face in its gleaming length, whilst she threaded her fingers through the black waves, as she dreamed of doing.

'Rosamund, I have been hungry for you for so long.'

His breath was warm on her throat. And she sighed and leaned her forehead against his chest, enjoying the familiar scent of him. Until he placed a hand beneath her chin, so that she must look up to meet his silent enquiry. But there were no doubts now.

There was no distance at all to her chamber, to her bed, for a man and a woman of a similar driving inclination.

'Do you want the candle?' he asked, a careful parody of before. But with a different outcome. 'Yes. I am not afraid.'

'Nor should you be.'

And since they were of one mind, there was no difficulty in stripping away garments that might hinder the slide of flesh against flesh. The pleated magnificence of the *bliaut* fell unheeded to the floor, as did his much-admired tunic. There were no more words, only instinct and a desire to touch, to be touched. To own and be owned. It shattered them both, waves of desire flooding them, overwhelming as high waves in the power of a spring tide that would carry all before them. A fast slide of urgent hands, scrape of teeth, relentless assault of lips against shivering skin. Both slick with sweat, driving on to unimaginable pleasure. Her hair, a silken tangle, wrapped around them both. His arousal was hard against her belly, his weight heavy on her slender limbs.

'Let me have you. Let me love you.' The whisper fierce against her breast.

'Take me,' she replied. 'And take my love in return.'

Her thighs parted, inviting, so that his fingers could find and savour the wet heat of her. Impossibly wet, magnificently hot. Then, his control compromised, he was in her, plunging beyond thought, unable to hold back, until he shuddered within her.

Breathtaking. Outrageously so. Limbs entangled, they lay as their breathing settled, until the chill of the chamber touched their skin, forcing them to find shelter under the covers. Gervase pulled the linen over her.

'That's what I wanted. I sat outside your gates and wanted to do that every night.' He nuzzled into her hair. 'You kept me waiting for well nigh two weeks.'

'Was it worth the wait?' She stretched against him, an innocent move that had his blood throbbing again.

'You have no idea.' Gervase eased his weight from her, pushing down the covers so that the soft light highlighted every curve, cast every enticing shadow.

'Gervase…'

'Let me look at you. Let me love you with my body as well as my mind.'

'I thought—' His confession stopped her. Her lips parted so that he had no choice but to claim them again in a kiss. 'What did you say?'

'I love you,' he stated solemnly. 'And we haven't started yet.'

Conscious of the heavy silence at his side, Gervase propped himself on an elbow to look down at her, resisting the impulse to draw his finger across her fine brows, to trace the delectable outline of her top lip. He recalled doing exactly that with his tongue. She was not asleep, but her eyes were closed against him. What was she thinking? She had not found the experience unpleasant, of that he was certain. He had enough skill in bed, enough knowledge of women, to know that her kisses, her responses when her arms tightened round his neck and her thighs parted to allow him access, had been from genuine pleasure. The muscles of his belly tightened again at the thought—he would like nothing better than to do it again. But it touched his mind, bringing a sardonic turn to his mouth, that he had not done his best by her. The first time—well, an initiation of a virgin was not guaranteed to be all joy for her, no matter how careful he had been. He remembered her rigidity, her fear, that first discomfort. And this time he had quite definitely not been in control. Heat and fire had swept them both along, Rosamund as much as himself, but his own need had been pre-eminent, if he were truthful. It had been impossible to withstand the lure of her body. All he had wanted was to own, to possess the woman who had lodged herself in his mind, his heart. So it had been all speed and light and lack of care. Was that the reason for the little groove that had dug itself between her brows?

'You are looking at me!' Rosamund accused, as if she could read his thoughts.

'So I am. And I am thinking…'

'What?' Now she looked at him, uncertain, uneasy.

I am thinking that you deserve better of me. Some finesse, some elegance. I am not the loutish soldier you accused me of being—it's time I proved it, took the time to savour and give pleasure. Instead, because she was still wary, he said, 'I am thinking that you once accused me of looking you over as if you were a cherry pie.'

'You did!'

And so he had with deliberate lascivious intent, in those early days when he had thought to drive her away. How true her words had been. She was just as sweet, just as succulent as that summer fruit, just as rare if they avoided the predations of the blackbirds. Beneath wilfulness, beneath the prickly layer of her candid frankness, she was sweet and soft and entirely seductive. So he would show her and tease the sweetness from her.

'And I am thinking that I am very fond of cherries.'

Slowly, lingering, first with lips, then with fingers, then with tongue and teeth, he stroked and caressed, discovering every inch of her, only to return to where the blood beat heavily beneath her skin. The base of her throat. Her breasts with soft tinted nipples that quickly hardened under his mouth. He splayed his hand over the curve of her hip when she purred and turned her face into his neck. Explored the desperately soft darkness between her thighs whilst desire for her built and tormented him. Satisfied when her grasp tightened on his shoulders, her nails digging in as she gasped at his persistence, his ultimate invasion. Until he groaned.

'What?' She was instantly aware.

'My Rose has thorns. I shall be scarred for life.'

'I shall be scorched for life, I think.' Her eyes wide and wild as emotions rocked her.

'Yes, and I too. Does it please you?'

'Yes. Gervase—I love you.'

'That's as it should be.'

With remorseless skill, with knowing fingers, he pushed her on until her breathing hitched, her whole body shuddered and, skin gleaming with sweat, she hid her face against his shoulder.

'Gervase…'

'Hmm?'

She laughed breathlessly in astonishment as he continued to plant kisses in the soft valley between her breasts. 'I didn't know it could be like that.'

Hearing the serious question in her voice, he halted the kisses and took his weight on to his forearms so that he could look at her. 'It can be.'

'Is it not always?'

'No, not always.' He would be honest with her. If her pleasure was astonishing to her, Rosamund's power over him was a matter of pure amazement. As was her absolute trust in him, allowing him to lead her into a tapestry of new sensations. He cradled her face in his hands, stroking his thumbs over her cheekbones, marvelling at the soft translucence of her skin. 'But I can make it so for you. As you do for me.'

'Then let me.' She spread her hands against his chest and reached up to kiss him. 'Let me give you that pleasure. Because it seems to me there is nothing to compare with it.'

How astonishing that a woman could drive him to madness with soft fingers, even softer lips. She gave no quarter until he was breathless and his command over his responses reached snapping point, balanced on a knife edge. When he could hold back no longer, when his body ached for release, he buried himself in her.

'Look at me,' he insisted, voice harsh with passion, when her lashes fell, lacing his fingers with hers, pinning them on either side of her head. 'Look at the authority you can wield over me, lady.'

Her eyes opened, incomparably green as emeralds, lit as if from within by the reflection of the candle flame. Miraculously depthless, infinitely inviting. And the robber lord found himself falling, drowning in them, until his whole world was encompassed by Rosamund's heart, her soul, her silken body. Yet, deliberately, jaw clenched against the sheer need to give way, he thrust slowly, a careful rhythm that would drive her to madness too, until she shivered uncontrollably beneath him again. Then he was beyond all knowledge, driving on to his own completion as her final shudders died away. Until he could do no more than lie with his head on her breast, his fingers still laced with hers.

'Are you leaving me?' she asked. Her eyes in the candlelight were level and unafraid, but he sensed the uncertainty, the dismay that she would never voice. He would not show her that he had noticed. He would give her that respect.

'No.' He rolled on to his back, and when he suspected that she might withdraw from him to the other side of the bed in a sudden reticence, made sure that he dragged her with him. Sometimes physical strength had its uses. His arms held her firmly until she sighed and gave way, and he tucked her head under his chin. Like a blessing, her hair spread over them both 'My rooms in the west tower have not been made ready for me yet.'

'And you did not order Master Pennard to do so, as soon as you set foot in this place?'

He felt her smile, her lips curve against his chest. 'No. So this is the only bed I can think of where I'll get a good night's sleep.'

She chuckled. 'How convenient.'

'Isn't it? For both of us.'

Her fingers drifted over his belly to his thigh, making contact with the ridge of tissue of the old scar. Lingered there, softly caressing the old wound that had caused him discomfort in the days of their first meeting.

'Did you kill your opponent?' she asked sleepily.

'Hmm?'

'Your leg. You said you were a man of vicious passions, that you killed your enemy.'

'No,' remembering. 'The scar's from a fall from my horse.'

'I'm glad.'

He picked up the concern in her sleepy voice and decided on honesty. 'I have killed men, Rose. You must know that.'

'I know.'

'But only when it was necessary for my own life. Or in battle.'

'Yes. I know you are not the cruel ruffian I thought you.' Her voice slurred as she slid into sleep.

'Glad to hear it, my dearest love.' Gervase eased her closer. He had put her mind at rest and was grateful. 'Go to sleep, Rose. Tomorrow will be a long day.'

He felt warm breath sigh again against his shoulder. 'Will you be here when I awake?'

'Yes.' Her breathing grew deeper, her muscles softened and grew lax within his embrace. He turned his head to kiss her temple and knew that she slept. 'And every day for the rest of your life. And mine.'

* * *

He had promised to be there when she awoke. But he was not. Bright light stroked the contours of the room, one stray shaft of sunlight edging through the window to touch the foot of the bed with gold. It was late. Rosamund awoke slowly, returning to consciousness, turning within the disordered linen coverings that for some reason seemed to be wrapped around her legs, anchoring them. She stretched lazily as if still in the soft wrappings of a dream. Until memory rushed in. She pushed herself up on her elbow, hair falling in a curtain of fire, shivering as the cold air attacked her naked shoulders. The bed stretched emptily beside her. It was cold, she discovered as she ran her hand across it. But the images that captured her mind were hot enough to scorch, to flame her face with colour, and had been no dream. When had he left her? All she remembered was sleeping and wakening, again and again, to the power of his hands, the possessive ownership of his body.

Pressing her hand to lips that were still soft from his kisses, Rosamund sought the one memory she wanted. He had said he loved her. In the heat of desire, yes, he had, when neither of them had been careful enough to consider the words spoken, he had said he loved her. When his body had lured her into total surrender, he had whispered *I love you* against her lips, against her breast.

And had she laid her soul bare, admitting her love for him? She feared that she had. Who knows what she had confessed, as she had melted in his arms, her mind trapped within a space that admitted no other thought than her astonished delight at the feelings he could magic within her at the simple brush of skin against skin? She had slept in his arms, curled into him, something she could never have envisaged, to put her trust, her whole future, into the hands of a man. But she had. Had awoken in the night, or been awoken, to drift again into that magical world of passion and pleasure.

I love you, he had said. And she had answered him.

But what now? Rosamund did not know. He had promised to be there when she awoke, but he was not. Last time, under Henry's uncompromising orders, Gervase had taken her, had kissed her and left her. Had not loved her enough to stay. And last time she had hidden from his departure, too much of a coward to face him. She covered her face with her hands, knowing that this time she could not hide. If they were to have any future together, she must face the day and the Lord of Monmouth.

Why had he not remained with her, to wake with her in the light of morning? Why was he not here with her now, to calm her fears?

This was no good! Rosamund extracted herself from the covers, lacing herself loosely into a chamber robe, wincing at muscles that complained. Taking up her comb, she began to drag it through her hair, grimacing at the snarls and tangles. Then smiled. Had he not held it, pushed his hands through it, wound it around his own wrist to make her his captive?

Rosamund sighed. Then turned her head at the noise at her door, as Edith entered with a tray. Edith, unnaturally silent, with her face as flat as new whey, not a flicker of acknowledgement, when all the castle must have known that Gervase had spent the night in her chamber. Edith stood at her side, hands on hips.

'Well?' Rosamund asked.

'My lord says you must eat. My Lord Fitz Osbern asks that you will join him on the rampart walk, my lady, when you have finished. And to wrap warmly. There's a cold wind from the north.'

Rosamund set her lips in a spirit of mutiny. So he was giving orders even in his absence. Edith left. It did not escape Rosamund's notice that she smirked at the last.

Gervase waited for his love. There were things that needed to be said between them, confessed to if they were to build anything for the future. She had reduced him to glory in a clever little scheme to lure him to her chamber, if he read her right. And he had been well and truly caught. And here she came, her step light, skirts held so that she might run up the steps, her head high. Lust arrowed into his gut as surely as love bound his heart.

'You were gone when I awoke.'

Rosamund tried not to make it an accusation. Her Wild Hawk was waiting for her at the far corner of the battlement walk as he had said he would, the misted outline of the Welsh hills as a backdrop. He must have heard her footsteps on the stone, or sensed her approach, because his body tensed, head turned, as Bryn might scent his quarry in the hunt. Or as a lover would anticipate the nearness of the beloved. Rosamund's heart quickened its beat as he strode toward her his face warming, those predatory eyes softening. Would he repeat his words of love or would he make his fine apologies for imposing his desires on her? It had been her desire too. Whatever the outcome of this meeting, if he did not want her, she would not wallow in regret. If she never wed, she would not go to her grave unaware of the weight of a man's body, of how it could awaken hers. How Gervase's touch could set her on fire. Pride would keep her strong through whatever decision he made. Yet she trembled as he approached. So she would take the initiative.

'I missed you. Why did you wish to meet me here, Gervase?'

With all the impatience she had come to recognise, he seized her hands, pressed his mouth against her fingers. 'So that I am not tempted to strip that very fine gown from your delicious body and tumble you back into your bed again,' he replied in all seriousness. 'Will you hear me, Rose?'

So Rosamund set herself to listen to Gervase, to whatever he felt the need to confess, leaning back against the rough timber so that she might watch his face, keeping her fingers linked with his.

'I have not been as tolerant or as careful of you as I should have been, for which I feel shame. The problem was Matilda, who… No! That's a lie. The problem was mine.' The lines were suddenly deep, lyre-marks between nose and mouth as he struggled for honesty. 'I remembered her here, a young bride, happy enough and content with the match. And then she was killed, and you, a de Longspey, had installed yourself in her place as Lady of Clifford. I resented your presence, an inter-loper, stepping into Matilda's shoes, when your own family had been responsible…even when I felt drawn to you. It was an impossible situation.'

'Oh, Gervase,' she murmured, unable to bear the hurt she could hear in his words. 'I did not realise that you saw me in that light.' But she had suspected it, after his admission before the King. Sorrow filled her for his loss. 'But I was never a true de Longspey…'

'No, you were not, and that is also to my shame, that I did not admit it. You were near enough in my estimation.' His bleak smile was sardonic. 'I was not very logical in my determina-tion to reclaim Clifford, perhaps.'

Rosamund gathered her courage around her. She must know the truth. 'Did you love her? Did you love Matilda? Is that why you resented me here?'

His fingers tightened on hers. 'I did not love her.' He hesi-tated over the blunt admission. 'It was a marriage arranged by my father, between two important local families—and we were very young. No, I did not love her. As for whether she loved me…I think she saw me as some heroic figure. And I let her die.'

'No, never that!' Rosamund brought his hand to her own lips in comfort. 'I thought you did love her.'

'Nursing an unrequited love? I suppose I was nursing a strong dose of guilt. I felt that because I was in Monmouth in my father's name, I had left Matilda here to die.'

'No…!'

'No. I know that. But when I saw you here, I was…drawn to you from that first moment you challenged my right to be in your courtyard. And I hated that you made me feel sentiments I had no wish to feel. If I could not love Matilda, how could I possibly love a de Longspey? Besides, love has no place in a soldier's life where life is cheap and death hovers close. I had vowed not to allow myself the luxury of such sentiments…but chiefly I was driven by guilt that I felt for you what I had failed to feel for my wife. She should have been here, alive and blessed with children, not you.'

'I see.' Understanding the whole, Rosamund's heart bled for him.

'I wanted nothing more than to rid myself of you. It infuriated me that I couldn't and that you defied me at every step.' The tensions in his face eased. 'It infuriated me even more that you should damn me as some border ruffian with no grace or polish.'

She smiled sadly. 'You played the part with great conviction.'

'So I did. If my behaviour would not drive you away, nothing would. Then my eyes were opened when I saw you fall from your horse with the Welsh arrows dealing death. I knew that what I felt for you was not lust, but love. I thought I should explain…'

'Yes…' Rosamund looked away, over the scene where the hills were coming into clearer relief. And since it was a time for wiping away the past… 'I think you know why I was so…difficult.'

'Difficult?' The sombre expression was lit by a smile. 'An underestimation. But, yes, I did, of course. Ralph de Morgan.'

Rosamund nodded, her thoughts still in turmoil. Where did his confession leave her now? Did he still resent her, whatever he said? Dare she ask? She did not think she could support the anguish if he said yes.

'What is it, my lovely Rose?'

'Nothing.' She dared not. 'Just that I'm sorry that my being here gave you pain.'

His arms were warm about her. 'It was my own misjudgement. I was not putting the blame on you. And now…' He stood away from her, a genuine smile dispelling the remembered sadness. 'You refused my gifts before. Will you take them now?' He smiled when Rosamund's brows arched at this abrupt change in direction. 'They were not chosen without thought. Wooing is the devil's own work, especially when the lady proves to be inflexible.' Amused impatience touched the hard planes of his face as from the breast of his tunic he took the jewelled brooch. 'This I went all the way to Monmouth to fetch. It belonged to my grandmother, who defied and ran from her family to wed the man she loved—a true robber lord, as it happened—there are plenty of them in my family—and she had no regret for doing it to my knowledge.' He pinned it to Rosamund's mantle. 'It was a gift to her from the man she ran to and married. Will you have it from me?'

'Yes.' Of course she would.

'The mare is in the stables, eating her head off. She needs exercise. I remembered your grief, how you wept for the loss of your own mare. I wished to heal that wound if I could.'

A warmth began to steal around Rosamund's heart at his words, a delight through her mind. It was indeed a wooing. 'I already love her. You'll never know what it took to send her away!'

'And these to warm your hands.' He kissed every finger before pulling the fine gloves on, first one and then the other, with such care, smoothing the leather.

'They fit perfectly.' She allowed her gloved fingers to curl into his.

'They do. My wooing is complete.' He smiled down at her. 'Do I still see doubt in your eyes, my lovely Rose? When you are my wife, you will know that I rarely say anything I do not mean.'

'Your *wife*…'

'You will wed me, Rosamund. You have refused me on every occasion that I asked. Now I command it.'

This stole her breath. He commanded it, did he? How in character! She ought to refuse him on principle, except she thought it was impossible to do so.

'Do you not know that your hands hold my heart?'

'No.' A throb of wonder shook her.

'You do. I sat outside these damned walls, wishing I could

detest you, and discovering that you are the source of all my happiness. When you were not there, involved in some devious plotting, I found myself wondering what you might be doing. It's too uncomfortable to be away from you. They sing of the glories of love. I have found it nothing but an almighty discomfort! But I love you with all my heart.'

'I didn't know.'

'Did I not tell you last night? For what other reason could a man possibly seek out a woman who questions his every move, disobeys his every order? My authority had never been so undermined as it has since I met you. And you ask me if I love you?'

The laughter in his fierce eyes proved, for Rosamund, a seduction in itself. 'I have never been loved before, you see, and...I did not think that you could love me. You might want me for your wife...but love is far from that. And what you might have said last night...'

His fingers were surprisingly soft against her lips, silencing her. 'You thought I might lust after you, but not love you.'

'Yes. I thought perhaps you merely pitied me.'

'Pitied Rosamund de Longspey? I have never met a woman less worthy of pity. Since we are into honesty, I fought against it. I failed miserably. You'll never know how difficult it was for me to turn my back on you, to leave you, when you were so desirable. But with the King's judgement hanging over my head I had no choice."

'Is that why you came back?'

'I could not lose you. Henry ordered me to take the castle and force you into marriage. I couldn't do it. I adore you. I was about to give up and go home.'

'Eleanor said I should lure you back,' Rosamund admitted. 'And I did.'

Gervase threw back his head and laughed, enough to cause the crows in the trees by the river to stir into flight. 'I thought it smacked of an ambush. But I don't regret it. None of it.'

'Nor I.'

'So, as I was saying, my beautiful wilful Rose, you will wed me.'

'I will wed you,' she repeated.

Gervase pinned her hands flat against his chest, all laughter wiped from his face. She could feel his heart beating into the palm of her hand. With utmost solemnity, as if in the presence of priest and witnesses, he made the declaration. 'I take you for my wife, Rosamund de Longspey.' His kiss on her lips was grave and formal. 'There, it is done. Say the words, Rose, if you would have it so.'

So she did, careful of the exact wording that would stand before the law. 'I take you for my husband, Gervase Fitz Osbern.'

With only the wheeling crows to bear witness, it was done.

'You've given me so much, Gervase,' she whispered, her forehead pressed against his chest as his arms came round her. 'What can I give you?'

'You have already given me everything I could desire.'

'This castle?' A wry smile.

'No. Not the castle. Something much more important. Your love and trust. It is a precious thing, far greater than gold or jewels or cold stone. Tell me you love me, Rose.'

'I love you, Gervase. If I have your heart, you have mine. Until the day I die.'

Standing on her toes, reaching up, she kissed him, and sealed the matter.

Well, that was that. Hugh sucked in a deep breath. Gervase back in control, of both castle and lady, with whom he would no doubt work out his own salvation to their mutual satisfaction. A man and a woman less likely as a compatible match he had never seen, but the spark between them was strong enough to light every torch in the Great Hall. It would be a lively coupling, but a true one. And now he could go home to Hereford. Hugh shivered within the dank walls of his chamber as he pulled on his boots. Every surface seemed to ooze a noxious green slime. Not least the comforts of his town house beckoned. A room without a howling draught, a meal that arrived at the table hot rather than stone cold.

A picture of Nell, chin tilted, stepped neatly into his mind. If he gave her a nudge—a gentle one, of course—she might just step across the line she had drawn, hemming herself in, and for the first time in her life take a decision to please herself. He smiled at the prospect of figuring in Nell's future. The sentiments he had found himself writing in that damned letter had come from the heart. He had no intention of leaving Clifford without discovering the lady's reaction. So it had better be now.

Hugh ordered the saddling of his horse, for his men-at-arms to be ready within the hour, before going in search of Petronilla. To find her stepping into the stable, coming to look for him.

'Hugh…' She seemed breathless. 'You're leaving.'

'Nell.' He bowed, keen-eyed. 'Within the hour.'

'You'll be pleased to be back with your family.'

She would prevaricate, he knew, with no explanation of why she should have found a need to come to the stables at all. She was good at that. But he knew that there was more than a cool, polite response behind the lines of that sleekly fitting robe. If there wasn't, he'd been wrong from the beginning, and he didn't think so. So, because time was of the essence and he was essentially a man of action, he thrust out a hand, grasped the material of her over-sleeve, and pulled her deeper into the stable, into the relative privacy of the stall that housed his stallion.

'Lord Hugh!'

'Some plain speaking here, Nell.' Transferring his hold from cloth to hands, he held tight, even when she struggled for release. 'What do *you* do now? Shall I tell you what I see, if you're not careful?' She stopped struggling. Rather her hands clung to his in momentary panic. 'You'll remain here at Clifford. Ger and your daughter will make their own lives together, as you would wish it, but both are as strong willed as be-damned. And *you* will be caught in the middle. All the decisions will be made around you and over your head, with you as witness to the inevitable clashes of temper and the soft reconciliations of love. You'll find yourself watching the mummer's play from the sidelines, with no role for yourself. Is that what you want?' Petronilla, much struck, blinked. 'Well?'

'No.' Petronilla rallied bravely. 'I'll go to Lower Broadheath, of course.'

'To live alone.'

'Edith will be with me.'

Now, to his satisfaction, a little frown had appeared on his stubborn love's brow. This was going just as Hugh had hoped, and he would not soften his attack. 'Edith will give you company and conversation? That will be enough for you to stave off loneliness?'

'I can travel and visit and—'

'No. *I'll* tell you what you can do, Nell.' Startled, her lips parted, far too invitingly. 'In fact, I'll show you.' And Hugh caught her to him and kissed her soundly, savouring those lips that melted, soft as rose-petals, beneath his.

'Hugh!' she gasped when she could, her hands tight-locked in the folds of his tunic as if she would never let go.

'Petronilla!' he mocked, very gently. 'Tell me you didn't enjoy it.'

'I can't.'

'Well, then.' He kissed her again. Then simply held her close, his cheek against her temple, his arms strong and protective around her. He thought he would like to stay like this for ever, until his stallion abandoned the bag of oats to investigate, and caused them to move aside. But not far. Hugh pulled Petronilla to sit on the low window ledge. In case she should still be in any doubt, he had not finished mapping out the future for his love. He twisted to face her, holding her shoulders firmly.

'Now look at me and listen. This is what you will do. You'll come to Hereford with me. Stay in my home for a day or two, meet my sons and their families. Then I'll escort you to Lower Broadheath. From there you can make your own decision. You can stay there in your own property, and ultimately hate the loneliness of it. Or you can consider me as an alternative.' And he prayed that she would make the decision he found himself yearning for.

Her eyes widened with a positive sparkle. 'Are you offering me a refuge from the dreary increase of years, dear Hugh?' Petronilla smiled at him with such sweetness, such trust, that he had no hesitation.

'I am offering you my heart and my love, lady. As well as a town house in Hereford that will be more to your taste than this place.'

'I always wanted a town house in Hereford.' Smiling, with only the glimmer of tears in her eyes, she sighed as if a weight had been taken from her mind. 'And would you perhaps take my heart in return?'

'Yes,' he replied promptly and crowed with laughter. 'But if I do, you must wed me. Even if I am nought but a plain Marcher lord.' There, he had said it, with great joy.

She looked at him, clear eyed for a long moment, before stating her case. 'I vowed never to wed again.' To his delight she lifted his calloused fingers to brush them with her own lips. 'I have decided to break my vow. Yes, dear Hugh. I have discovered that Marcher lords have much to recommend them. I will wed you.'

So they sat together, hands clasped, the dust motes spiralling round them in a shaft of sunlight, both entirely pleased with each other.

'What about Rosamund? I wonder what she'll say,' Petronilla finally remarked, but not as if she cared greatly at that moment.

'Rosamund is drowning in love and will not notice what you do. Nor will she object. Does my plan please you?'

'Yes.'

The best, the most simple of answers. Hugh made no attempt

to hide his triumph and his face broke into a broad smile. 'Anything else that I can do to ease your mind, dear heart? Can you be ready in an hour?'

'I can. One thing more, Hugh…'

'What's that?'

'Kiss me again.'

Epilogue

Hugh and Petronilla had gone. But still the bustle in the bailey showed no signs of abating. Men-at-arms loaded weapons and equipment into wagons, horses were being led out, harnessed. It was a scene such as Rosamund had seen many times before.

No!

It came to Rosamund, as unexpected and terrifying as a thunderbolt. The Fitz Osbern troops were preparing to go. Gervase was leaving her. Not an hour after he had spoken of his love. After he had commanded that she should be his wife.

Now he was leaving her.

Icily composed, forcing her mind to grasp that one desperate thought, Rosamund watched the organised turmoil around her with the sense of being at the eye of a storm, the still, cool, centre, when all about her was heat and chaos. It was as if she stood divorced from all reality, as if nothing could break through the shattering pain. No one watching her would guess the sheer fright, the utter sense of loss, that compacted her heart in a physical agony.

He had said he loved her. That he would wed her, and she had never doubted him. But his departure from Clifford was well under way. Is this what her future would hold? Had she been so naïve as to believe that if he loved her he would remain with her, always at her side? That she would sit by him, rule the Marcher lands with him, travel with him? As Eleanor did with Henry. Perhaps love, for Gervase, was a *practical* thing above all. Yes, that was it. Gervase would go back to Monmouth or Anjou or wherever business took him, and leave her to rule Clifford under his authority.

At that moment she positively *hated* Clifford.

Well, it was an eminently practical move. Rosamund sought and found Gervase in the general *mêlée,* buckling on his sword as he exchanged a brief word with Watkins. How could she possibly live without him now? It would not be for ever, she admonished herself severely. He would come and visit her when he patrolled his lands. She would be the perfect chatelaine, fulfilling the role he required of her. Why did she feel as if her secure foothold had just been eroded from her world, leaving her struggling helplessly in some bottomless abyss?

He has stolen my heart. How can I bear for him to abandon me now?

Would he really go, only minutes after wooing her all over again, with gifts and kisses? But, of course, he had hardly hidden his intentions, had he? As she now realised, he had been dressed for travel when he had asked her to meet him on the battlements. If she had not been so preoccupied, she would have seen it at once. Now she must accept the pain and make her farewells with pride, showing nothing of her true feelings.

Am I not good at that?

Rosamund walked slowly to his side, dignity heavy on her shoulders. It felt as if her face had frozen into an impenetrable mask. He must never know her loss.

'You are leaving soon.' She was proud of the calmness of her voice.

'Yes. I need to hold court in Monmouth before the end of the month.' Gervase continued to watch the loading of a heavy wagon, raising his voice to attract attention to an animal's loose harness.

Rosamund's heart sank lower, heavier, with every word.

Take me with you. Don't leave me.

How difficult it was not to cry out. Her heart urged her to cling to his sleeve, to plead her case. Her head refused, bleakly fearful of his compassion. She would rather be alone than an object of sympathy. If a love was keen enough, it could exist at a distance. Could thrive on infrequent meetings, intense and passionate, but with long intervals stretching between. Was that truly possible? Rosamund's mind shrieked with the horror of it. Of course she could accept it, if that is what he wanted. It would never stop her loving him.

When shall I see you again?

Nor would she ask that. She stared hard at Owen saddling Gervase's stallion, to prevent the imminent tears.

'Will…will you go back to Anjou this spring?' At least it would give her a pattern to his movements.

'Possibly.' A short answer. Gervase took his mantle from the squire, then, finally, focused on her. 'Now, are you going to stand there all day and exchange idle conversation?'

'I know you must be in a hurry…'

'I am in a hurry. To get to Monmouth before nightfall. Not some time next week.'

'Then you must go.' More harshly than she had intended.

'Well, *I'm* ready, lady. The mare is saddled and bridled, waiting for you.' His hawk's eyes travelled over her, a frown in their depths. Or perhaps it was uncertainty. 'And you're still standing here. Have you changed your mind? As I see it, you can't. The words were spoken between us and can't be undone.'

'Changed my mind?'

He sighed in exasperation. 'Edith has packed your belongings. They're in the wagon. All I don't seem to have is *you*!'

'I'm coming with you?'

'What did you think?'

'That you would leave me there as chatelaine.'

'Rosamund! My love!' His smile softened his face as understanding came. 'Do you want to stay here? Do you want to be rid of me already?'

'No…but I thought…I thought you did not want me with you. You did not say—'

Rosamund got no further. Swooping with startling speed, Gervase clipped her round her waist, drawing her fast against him, one hand beneath her chin to force her to look up and concentrate on his words, regardless of the *mêlée* of horses and men around them all but brushing her skirts. 'I did not think I had to say, lady. But if you wish it spelled out, I am taking you to Monmouth—immediately. Did you think I would abandon you here? You can curtsy to my mother, who will fall on your neck with gratitude if you will wed me and give her grandchildren. You will discuss gowns and veils endlessly with my sister. You will wed me in Monmouth, before a priest, with all due rank as the Lady of Monmouth, and appropriate festivity.' The pressure of his mouth on hers was hard, entirely masterful. Then he sighed and lowered his voice as he lifted his head and caught her quizzical expression. 'If that is your wish, lady.'

'I thought you would come back here eventually—and send for Father Stephen.' Trapped in his brilliant gaze, she was aware only of the melting of the cold lump of ice in her breast.

'And wed you here? With draughts and vermin and cold food to celebrate our marriage? Not to mention the persistent problem of the midden… No. We'll wed at Monmouth. The rats are smaller. Sir Thomas will enjoy ruling the roost here.' The fine lines beside his eyes deepened, his lips curved as he used his cuff, most efficiently, to mop up the suspicion of tears that sparkled on her cheeks. 'I'll not leave you, Rose. Did you think it? You are in my mind and heart. We will live together.'

'At Monmouth?'

He read her unspoken concern. She saw his lips indent at the corners as if he would laugh, but thought better of it. 'I doubt you'll find it comfortable to live with my mother.' Gervase's smile widened to a grin. 'Nor she with you, I dare say. Lady

Maude's of a different cut of cloth from your mother.' With re-markable tact he tucked her hand under his arm and led her across the bailey. 'You can have the pick of any of my castles.'

Rosamund made a little play of considering the offer, but did not need to. Her joy was so great she could barely contain it. His consideration for her was as soft as a velvet mantle, all-en-compassing. She nodded. 'And can I travel with you, when you go to Anjou?'

'Yes. To the ends of the earth, if you wish it.' He settled her fur collar more closely beneath her chin, tucked the fullness of her veiling securely against the wind. Kissed her, the most tender of caresses to her temple, then nudged her forward toward the mare. 'Your belongings are packed. Get on the mare, Rose. You have my word on it. I came back for you because I could not live without you. Now I'll take you with me.' His hands were firm, secure around her waist. 'I'll not lie apart from the woman I love.'

Rosamund stretched up on her toes to brush his cheek with her lips before allowing herself to obey her lord, to be lifted on to the mare without further argument, and with a light heart. The Wild Hawk was hers, and she was his.

* * * * *

Eight years ago Matt Shaffer had vanished out of Natalie Rothchild's life, leaving behind a one-line note tucked under a pillow that had grown cold: *I'm sorry, but this just isn't going to work.*

That was it. No explanation, no real indication of remorse. The note had been as clinical and compassionless as an eviction notice, which, in effect, it had been, Natalie thought as she navigated through the morning traffic. Matt had written the note to evict her from his life.

She'd spent the next two weeks crying, breaking down without warning as she walked down the street, or as she sat staring at a meal she couldn't bring herself to eat.

Candace, she remembered with a bittersweet pang, had tried to get her to go clubbing in order to get her to forget about Matt.

She'd turned her twin down, but she did get her act together. If Matt didn't think enough of their relationship to try to contact her, to try to make her understand why he'd changed so radically from lover to stranger, then to hell with him. He was dead to her, she resolved. And he'd remained that way.

Until twenty minutes ago.

The adrenaline in her veins kept mounting.

Natalie focused on her driving. Vegas in the daylight wasn't nearly as alluring, as magical and glitzy as it was after dark. Like an aging woman best seen in soft lighting, Vegas's imperfections were all visible in the daylight. Natalie supposed that was why people like her sister didn't like to get up until noon. They lived for the night.

Except that Candace could no longer do that.

The thought brought a fresh, sharp ache with it.

"Damn it, Candy, what a waste," Natalie murmured under her breath.

She pulled up before the Janus casino. One of the three valets currently on duty came to life and made a beeline for her vehicle.

"Welcome to the Janus," the young attendant said cheerfully as he opened her door with a flourish.

"We'll see," she replied solemnly.

As he pulled away with her car, Natalie looked up at the casino's logo. Janus was the Roman god with two faces, one pointed toward the past, the other facing the future. It struck her as rather ironic, given what she was doing here, seeking out someone from her past in order to get answers so that the future could be settled.

The moment she entered the casino, the Vegas phenomena took hold. It was like stepping into a world where time did not matter or even make an appearance. There was only a sense of "now."

Because in Natalie's experience she'd discovered that bartenders knew the inner workings of any establishment they worked for better than anyone else, she made her way to the first bar she saw within the casino.

The bartender in attendance was a gregarious man in his early forties. He had a quick, sexy smile, which was probably one of the main reasons he'd been hired. His name tag identified him as Kevin.

Moving to her end of the bar, Kevin asked, "What'll it be, pretty lady?"

"Information." She saw a dubious look cross his brow. To counter that, she took out her badge. Granted she wasn't here in an official capacity, but Kevin didn't need to know that. "Were you on duty last night?"

Kevin began to wipe the gleaming black surface of the bar. "You mean during the gala?"

"Yes."

The smile gracing his lips was a satisfied one. Last night had obviously been profitable for him, she judged. "I caught an extra shift."

She took out Candace's photograph and carefully placed it on the bar. "Did you happen to see this woman there?"

The bartender glanced at the picture. Mild interest turned to recognition. "You mean Candace Rothchild? Yeah, she was here, loud and brassy as always. But not for long," he added, looking rather disappointed. There was always a circus when Candace was around, Natalie thought. "She and the boss had at it and then he had our head of security escort her out."

She latched onto the first part of his statement. "They argued? About what?"

He shook his head. "Couldn't tell you. Too far away for anything but body language," he confessed.

"And the head of security?" she asked.

"He got her to leave."

She leaned in over the bar. "Tell me about him."

"Don't know much," the bartender admitted. "Just that his name's Matt Shaffer. Boss flew him in from L.A., where he was head of security for Montgomery Enterprises."

There was no avoiding it, she thought darkly. She was going to have to talk to Matt. The thought left her cold. "Do you know where I can find him right now?"

Kevin glanced at his watch. "He should be in his office. On the second floor, toward the rear." He gave her the numbers of the rooms where the monitors that kept watch over the casino guests as they tried their luck against the house were located.

Taking out a twenty, she placed it on the bar. "Thanks for your help."

Kevin slipped the bill into his vest pocket. "Any time, lovely lady," he called after her. "Any time."

She debated going up the stairs, then decided on the elevator. The car that took her up to the second floor was empty. Natalie stepped out of the elevator, looked around to get her bearings and then walked toward the rear of the floor.

"Into the Valley of Death rode the six hundred," she silently recited, digging deep for a line from a poem by Tennyson. Wrapping her hand around a brass handle, she opened one of the glass doors and walked in.

The woman whose desk was closest to the door looked up. "You can't come in here. This is a restricted area."

Natalie already had her ID in her hand and held it up. "I'm looking for Matt Shaffer," she told the woman.

God, even saying his name made her mouth go dry. She was supposed to be over him, to have moved on with her life. What happened?

The woman began to answer her. "He's—"

"Right here."

The deep voice came from behind her. Natalie felt every single nerve ending go on tactical alert at the same moment that all the hairs at the back of her neck stood up. Eight years had passed, but she would have recognized his voice anywhere.

* * * * *

Why did Matt Shaffer leave
heiress-turned-cop Natalie Rothchild?
What does he know about the death of Natalie's twin sister?
Come and meet these two reunited lovers and learn the
secrets of the Rothchild family in
THE HEIRESS'S 2-WEEK AFFAIR
by USA TODAY bestselling author
Marie Ferrarella.
The first book in Silhouette® Romantic Suspense's wildly
romantic new continuity,
LOVE IN 60 SECONDS!
Available April 2009.

CELEBRATE
60 YEARS
OF PURE READING PLEASURE
WITH **HARLEQUIN**®!

Look for Silhouette®
Romantic Suspense in April!

Love In 60 Seconds

Bright lights. Big city. Hearts in overdrive.

Silhouette® Romantic Suspense is celebrating
Harlequin's 60th Anniversary with six stories that
promise to bring readers the glitz of Las Vegas,
the danger of revenge, the mystery of a missing
diamond, and family scandals.

**Look for the first title, *The Heiress's 2-Week Affair*
by *USA TODAY* bestselling author
Marie Ferrarella, on sale in April!**

His 7-Day Fiancée by **Gail Barrett**	May
The 9-Month Bodyguard by **Cindy Dees**	June
Prince Charming for 1 Night by **Nina Bruhns**	July
Her 24-Hour Protector by **Loreth Anne White**	August
5 minutes to Marriage by **Carla Cassidy**	September

The Inside Romance newsletter has a NEW look for the new year!

Same great content, brand-new look!

The Inside Romance newsletter is a FREE quarterly newsletter highlighting our upcoming series releases and promotions!

Click on the Inside Romance link on the front page of
www.eHarlequin.com or e-mail us at
insideromance@harlequin.ca to sign up
to receive your FREE newsletter today!

You can also subscribe by writing to us at: HARLEQUIN BOOKS
Attention: Customer Service Department
P.O. Box 9057, Buffalo, NY 14269-9057

Please allow 4-6 weeks for delivery of the first issue by mail.

IRNNEW09

REQUEST YOUR
FREE BOOKS!

HHH Harlequin® Historical
Historical Romantic Adventure!

2 FREE NOVELS PLUS 2 FREE GIFTS!

YES! Please send me 2 FREE Harlequin® Historical novels and my 2 FREE gifts (gifts are worth about $10). After receiving them, if I don't wish to receive any more books, I can return the shipping statement marked "cancel". If I don't cancel, I will receive 6 brand-new novels every month and be billed just $4.94 per book in the U.S. or $5.49 per book in Canada, plus 25¢ shipping and handling per book and applicable taxes, if any*. That's a savings of 20% off the cover price! I understand that accepting the 2 free books and gifts places me under no obligation to buy anything. I can always return a shipment and cancel at any time. Even if I never buy another book, the two free books and gifts are mine to keep forever.

246 HDN ERUM   349 HDN ERUA

Name _____ (PLEASE PRINT) _____

Address _____ Apt. # _____

City _____ State/Prov. _____ Zip/Postal Code _____

Signature (if under 18, a parent or guardian must sign)

Mail to the **Harlequin Reader Service:**
IN U.S.A.: P.O. Box 1867, Buffalo, NY 14240-1867
IN CANADA: P.O. Box 609, Fort Erie, Ontario L2A 5X3

Not valid to current subscribers of Harlequin Historical books.

Want to try two free books from another line?
Call 1-800-873-8635 or visit www.morefreebooks.com.

* Terms and prices subject to change without notice. N.Y. residents add applicable sales tax. Canadian residents will be charged applicable provincial taxes and GST. Offer not valid in Quebec. This offer is limited to one order per household. All orders subject to approval. Credit or debit balances in a customer's account(s) may be offset by any other outstanding balance owed by or to the customer. Please allow 4 to 6 weeks for delivery. Offer available while quantities last.

Your Privacy: Harlequin Books is committed to protecting your privacy. Our Privacy Policy is available online at www.eHarlequin.com or upon request from the Reader Service. From time to time we make our lists of customers available to reputable third parties who may have a product or service of interest to you. If you would prefer we not share your name and address, please check here. ☐

DIAMOND IN THE ROUGH

John Callister is a millionaire rancher, yet when he meets
lovely Sassy Peale and she thinks he's a cowboy, he goes along
with her misconception. He's had enough of gold diggers,
and this is a chance to be valued for himself, not his money.
But when Sassy finds out the truth, she feels John was merely
playing with her. John will have to convince her that he's truly
the man she fell in love with—a diamond in the rough.

THE MEN OF MEDICINE RIDGE—a brand-new miniseries
set in the wilds of Montana!

Available April 2009 wherever you buy books.

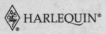

COMING NEXT MONTH FROM
HARLEQUIN®
HISTORICAL

Available March 31, 2009

• **THE SUBSTITUTE BRIDE**
by **Elizabeth Lane**
(Western)
Dashing reporter Quint Seavers, disappointed in love before, is
unaware that independent, practical Annie Gustavson holds a secret
longtime love for him. Living together in close proximity, the
attraction between them is undeniable, and suddenly Quint knows
that Annie is exactly what's been missing in his life—till now....

• **HIS RELUCTANT MISTRESS**
by **Joanna Maitland**
(Regency)
Renowned rake Leo Aikenhead rescues Sophie Pietre, the famous
"Venetian Nightingale," from a bad assault. Resilient and self-
reliant, Sophie has never succumbed to a man's desires before. But
dangerously attractive Leo soon becomes the only man she would risk
all her secrets for!
Second in The Aikenhead Honours *trilogy. Three gentlemen spies;
bound by duty, undone by women!*

• **THE RAKE'S INHERITED COURTESAN**
by **Ann Lethbridge**
(Regency)
Daughter of a Parisian courtesan, Sylvia Boisette thirsts for
respectability. But, charged as her guardian, wealthy, conservative
Christopher Evernden finds himself on the brink of scandal as his body
cannot ignore Sylvia's tempting sensuality....

Unlaced, Undressed, Undone!

• **THE KNIGHT'S RETURN**
by **Joanne Rock**
(Medieval)
Needing a protector and escort, Irish princess Sorcha agrees to allow
a striking mercenary to fulfill this role. But Hugh de Montagne is
unsettled by his immediate attraction to the princess of the realm....

HHCNMBPA0309